CLEOPATRA'S MOON

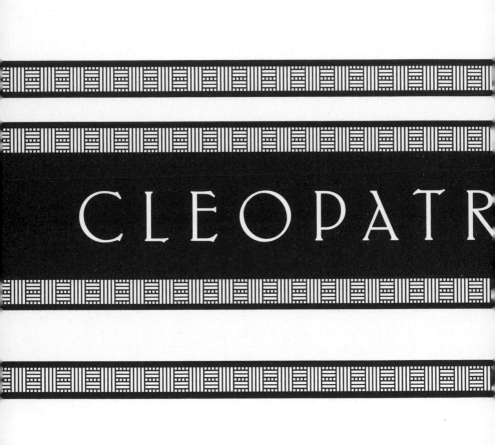

A'S MOON

VICKY ALVEAR SHECTER

ARTHUR A. LEVINE BOOKS
An Imprint of Scholastic Inc.

Library of Congress Cataloging-in-Publication Data

Shecter, Vicky.
  Cleopatra's moon / by Vicky Alvear Shecter. — 1st ed.
    p. cm.
  Summary: Cleopatra Selene, the only surviving daughter of Cleopatra and
Marc Antony, recalls her life of pomp and splendor in Egypt and, after her
parents' deaths, captivity and treachery in Rome.
  ISBN 978-0-545-22130-6 (alk. paper) [1. Princesses — Fiction. 2. Cleopatra,
Queen of Egypt, d. 30 B.C. — Fiction. 3. Antonius, Marcus, 83?-30
B.C. — Fiction. 4. Egypt — History — 332-30 B.C. — Fiction. 5.
Rome — History — Augustus, 30 B.C.-14 A.D. — Fiction.] I. Title.
  PZ7.S53822Cle 2011
  [Fic] — dc22   2010028818

10 9 8 7 6 5 4 3 2 1   11 12 13 14 15

Printed in the U.S.A.   23
First edition, August 2011

The opening of Homer's *Iliad* quoted on p. 36 is from the translation by Ian
Johnston, 2001, at http://records.viu.ca/~johnstoi/homer/johnstoniliad.htm.

The translation of Catullus 85 on pp. 339-340 is by Leonard C. Smithers, 1894,
at http://www.perseus.tufts.edu.

For Bruce, Matthew, and Aliya

TABLE OF CONTENTS

CHARACTER LIST

Egypt
The Royal Family

Cleopatra VIII Selene — The only daughter of Cleopatra VII and Marcus Antonius; twin to Alexandros Helios

Cleopatra VII — The last queen of Egypt. Came to the throne at seventeen; allied with Julius Caesar in the War of Alexandria after siblings tried to overthrow her; married the Roman general Marcus Antonius.

Marcus Antonius — Roman general and politician. Was once married to Octavia, whom he divorced to marry Cleopatra VII. Father of Cleopatra Selene, Alexandros Helios, and Ptolemy Philadelphos, as well as two daughters by Octavia, Antonia-the-Elder and Antonia-the-Younger.

Caesarion (Ptolemy XV Caesar) — Son of Cleopatra VII and Julius Caesar

Alexandros Helios — Twin brother of Cleopatra Selene

Ptolemy XVI Philadelphos, or Ptolly — The youngest son of Cleopatra VII and Marcus Antonius

In Alexandria

Zosima* — Nurse to Cleopatra Selene

Nafre* — Nurse to Ptolly

Iotape — An Armenian princess brought to Egypt as a child and betrothed to Alexandros

Katep* — Cleopatra Selene's royal eunuch and guard

Euphronius — Tutor to the royal children

Charmion — Queen Cleopatra's lady, companion, and handmaiden

Iras — Another lady and handmaiden to Queen Cleopatra

Euginia* — Cleopatra Selene's friend

Olympus — A Greek *iatros*, or healer

Cornelius Dolabella — A Roman soldier left to guard Queen Cleopatra during Octavianus's occupation of Alexandria

Yoseph ben Zakkai* — A rabbi in Alexandria

Amunet* — Priestess of Isis at Pharos

Ma'ani-Djehuti* — Priest of Serapis

Sebi, Tanafriti, Hekate* — Cats of the royal household

Gods

Isis — The Great Goddess, Cleopatra's patron goddess

Osiris — Lord of the Dead

Anubis — The jackal-headed god of the mummification process and the afterlife

Horus — The falcon-headed god of the sun, war, and protection

Amut the Destroyer — A monstrous demon with the head of a crocodile, the belly of a lion, and the legs of a hippo. He eats the hearts of those who didn't live by the rules of *ma'at*, preventing them from entering the afterworld.

Bastet — The cat-headed goddess of protection, especially of women, children, and domestic cats

Rome
The House of Caesar

Octavianus — Nephew of Julius Caesar, who adopted Octavianus as his successor. Later called Augustus, the first emperor of Rome. Father of Julia.

Livia Drusilla — Second wife of Octavianus; mother to Tiberius and Drusus by her first husband

Julia — Daughter and only child of Octavianus by his first wife

Octavia — Octavianus's sister. Married first to Gaius Claudius Marcellus, then for political reasons to Marcus Antonius, who divorced her to wed Cleopatra VII. Mother of Marcellus, Marcella-the-Elder, and Marcella-the-Younger by her first husband, and Antonia-the-Elder and Antonia-the-Younger by Marcus Antonius.

Marcellus — Son of Octavia and her first husband

Tiberius — Livia's elder son from her first marriage

Drusus — Livia's younger son from her first marriage

Marcella-the-Elder and **Marcella-the-Younger** — Daughters of Octavia and her first husband

Antonia-the-Elder and **Antonia-the-Younger** — Daughters of Octavia and Marcus Antonius

Other Romans

Juba II — Born a prince of the African kingdom of Numidia. Captured by Julius Caesar in infancy and raised in Octavia's household.

Marcus Agrippa — A friend and general of Octavianus

Ben Harabim* — A young Jewish man in Rome

Placus Munius Corbulo the Elder* — A Roman statesman with a reputation for marriages that end under suspicious circumstances

Cornelius Gallus — The Roman officer left in charge of Egypt

Isetnofret* — Priestess of Isis at Capua

* Fictional characters

ON A ROMAN SHIP TO AFRICA

In What Would Have Been the Twenty-sixth Year of My Mother's Reign
In My Sixteenth Year (25 BCE)

"Get rid of that body *now*, or my men will mutiny!" the captain yelled from the other side of the door.

A stylus on the floor rolled with the movement of the ship. The flame from the hanging bronze lamp flickered. Still, I did not respond.

"Little Moon," my old nurse, Zosima, whispered. "Please. You must say something."

No one had called me Little Moon in so long. The endearment brought a wave of sorrow and grief crashing up from my center, but I swallowed it down. I had to stay in control.

"Talk to him through the door," I said. "But do not open it."

The captain must have heard our murmurs. "Do you hear me?" he cried. "The longer you hide in the cabin with the body, the more my men think you practice the dark arts. That you are a sorceress like your mother. Do you understand the danger?"

"Tell him we will do what he wants at sunrise," I said to Zosima. "Not a moment sooner."

The captain interrupted her with an explosion of rage. "If we do not act *now*, I will have full-out revolt! Even the slaves are refusing to man their posts!"

I stood up. "Tell your men," I said, calling on the voice Mother used to address crowds, "that in Egypt, the spirit of a body not given the full rites is cursed to roam the place of its death for eternity, bringing misery and destruction. For their own safety, they must let me finish."

No response. Romans in general were superstitious, but Roman sailors were the worst of all. I pinned my hopes on that.

"But sunrise is yet an hour away!" the captain complained.

Despite my best efforts, my irritation bled through. "Surely you can control your men for one hour, Captain?"

Silence. Had I gone too far?

"Do you swear to perform the rites at the first light of the sun and be done with it?" he asked, through what sounded like gritted teeth. "Can I promise my men that?"

"You have my word," I said.

A moment's pause. Then the sound of angry, stomping feet. I breathed out.

I turned to Alexandros. Surely this was all a big mistake. My twin, the sun to my moon, was merely sleeping. We always joked that he slept like the dead.

But I could no longer fool myself that the grayness of his skin, the sunken hollows of his eyes, were just a trick of the light. My brother drank the poison meant for me. And now the only family I had left was gone.

"I need more cloth strips," I said to Zosima. "Get me the softest linen you can find for his head. He must be comfortable."

Zosima handed me a soft, worn shift. It would do. I slashed the fabric with my dagger — the one that had once been Mother's — then took it between my teeth and ripped the rest with my hands.

"Please. Let me . . . let me rend this cloth," Zosima said. "You should not do this."

With the fabric still between my teeth, I shook my head, feeling like a lioness breaking the neck of a small animal. No. I was the only one who could.

There were no Priests of Anubis on the Roman ship. I could not preserve my brother's body in the ancient ways, but I prayed that if I bound him well enough and sacrificed his body to Osiris and Poseidon, the gods would take pity and protect him so that his *ka*, his soul, would be reunited with him in the afterlife. So I would see him again.

I cradled the back of Alexandros's head with one hand and wound the linen strips around it with the other. When I reached his eyes, I began to cry again. But I did not stop working. I kissed his cold forehead before it disappeared under the wrapping.

Muffled arguing above us. Would the men revolt anyway? I looked up and saw Zosima watching me. "Where is Bucephalus?" I asked.

She looked at me blankly.

"His little onyx horse. The one he brought from Alexandria. Please. I do not want him to be alone."

She rummaged through his things and brought it to me. A remnant from Egypt, a present from Father. I placed it on the linen between his folded arms. "To keep you company," I whispered.

Then I reached between my breasts and yanked off the Knot of Isis amulet that had once been Mother's. I tucked it carefully over his heart. "May your heart be light against the Feather of Truth," I prayed.

I covered the amulet and horse with one final layer of linen strips.

The captain commanded several oarsmen to bring the body up on deck. Only two agreed to help. The rest of the crew watched, some grumbling, others placing two fingers from their right hands over their hearts, the sign of protection against evil. I raised my chin as we passed.

In the gray light of predawn, the men balanced my brother's body on the western edge of the boat, for the West was where Osiris, Lord of the Dead, lived. I stood next to the wrapped body of my twin. They waited for my signal. But I could not give it.

"Throw her in too!" someone yelled from behind me.

"Death follows her, just like her mother!"

"She brings bad luck — look what happened to Antonius!"

I stiffened my back and felt Zosima move in closer.

"Quiet! All of you! Let us be done with this," the captain yelled.

I closed my eyes to pray. But I did not know the ancient prayers for the dead. "Forgive me for not knowing the sacred words, O Anubis,

Jackal God of the Dead," I began. "In the name of Osiris, please protect this son of Egypt so that his *ka* may live in happy *Aaru*, with all of those he loved and who loved him. Preserve and lighten his heart so that he may pass your sacred test against the Feather of Truth."

I heard murmuring behind me and felt the first warmth of the sun on my back. I opened my eyes. It was time. But again, I could not give the order. My throat clenched, allowing only a sliver of breath to claw its way in and out.

Muttering behind me. "What is the witch waiting for? The sun rises!"

May our ka*s embrace on the other side, brother. . . .*

I took a deep breath and nodded. The men released Alexandros. I watched my twin's wrapped body disappear into the cold waters of the Mediterranean in a slow swirl of white.

I wanted to jump in after him.

"It is done," shouted the captain. "Every man to his station. We must finish this journey as quickly as possible."

I stared at the sea, trying to breathe, trying to understand how I came to be here. A motherless daughter, and now a brotherless sister. How was it that I went from a princess of Egypt — the daughter of the most powerful queen in the world — to a prisoner of Rome, and now the bride of a petty ruler in the scrubs of Africa?

I closed my eyes, remembering Mother's soft breath on my ear as she whispered, *"You have the heart of a great and powerful queen."* Her last words to me. I spent my whole life trying to live up to them. But I failed. I lost everything, lost every single person I ever loved.

Why? Why have you cursed me? I asked the gods. *Why have you cursed my family?*

But no answer came. I heard only the creaking of ropes, the flapping of sails, the splash of water against the hull.

PART I: EGYPT

CHAPTER ONE

In the Seventeenth Year of My Mother's Reign

In My Seventh Year (34 BCE)

What caused the gods to fall upon my family like starved lions in a Roman arena?

I suspect it began in my seventh year, on a day that I once considered one of the happiest of my life. It was a dazzling, sun-drenched summer morning in Alexandria-by-the-Sea. Outside the Royal Quarter, with the Mediterranean sparkling behind us and rows of date palms swaying before us, my mother and brothers and I sat alongside one another on individual thrones. We waited for my father, the great Roman general Marcus Antonius, to finish parading through the city and join us atop our grand ceremonial dais. The ceremony today would celebrate his victory over Armenia, his eastern enemy. And we — his family and all of Alexandria — would rejoice with him.

Even in the shade of our royal canopy, sweat trickled down my neck and back. The ostrich-feather fans the servants waved over us provided little relief. Strong breezes occasionally gusted from the Royal Harbor, cooling us with the salty bite of the sea.

Despite the discomfort and the glare from the beaten silver platform at our feet, I forced myself to keep still as Mother had instructed, my eyes trained just above the horizon. Zosima, who had carefully painted my face, had forbidden me from squinting in the bright light. I was *not* to ruin the heavy black kohl around my eyes and eyebrows, and under no circumstances to cause the green malachite painted on my lids to flake off. I was not even to turn my head. I would follow all the rules perfectly, I swore to myself. I would make Mother proud.

But excitement and curiosity burbled in my blood as I fought to stay still, stealing side-glances whenever I could. I especially treasured my glimpses of Mother, Queen Cleopatra VII. She sat on a golden throne, looking as resplendent as one of the giant marble statues guarding the tombs of the Old Ones. Diamonds twinkled in a jungle of black braids on her ceremonial wig. She wore a diadem with three rearing snakes and a golden broad collar, shining with lapis lazuli, carnelian, and emeralds, over her golden, form-fitting pleated gown. In one hand, she held a golden ankh of life, while the other clasped the striped crook and flail of her divine rulership. Her stillness radiated power, like a lioness pausing before the pounce. It left me breathless with awe.

I sat up straighter, trying to emulate her, puffing up with pride at the realization that only Mother and I were dressed as true rulers of Egypt — she as the Goddess Isis and I as the moon goddess, Nephthys. After all, was I not named for the moon? My brother may have been called Alexandros Helios, for the sun, but I was Cleopatra Selene, the moon. I wore a flowing dress that reminded me of the liquid metal that the scientists at our Great Library described as "living silver." A silver diadem of the moon sat atop my own thickly braided ceremonial wig. Even my sandals flashed silver.

I had never seen my beloved city so packed. By the tens of thousands, Alexandrians and Egyptians flooded the wide avenues and byways, desperate to catch a glimpse of us or of Father on his parade route. The richest of the noble Greek families sat on tiered benches in the square before us, while tradesmen, merchants, and the poor spilled into the streets, squirming and jostling for position. Some even shimmied up trees, climbed onto the shoulders of the statues of my ancestors, and scrabbled to the tops of pediments and roofs to get a better view of us.

The roar of the crowd as my father approached in his chariot sounded like waves crashing against the rocks on Pharos Island, home of our Great Lighthouse. When Tata climbed onto the dais to join us — his golden armor gleaming, his face soaked with sweat but shining with joy — he looked like a god. The God of War!

In his deep bass, Father began: "I stand before you as *Imperator* to the greatest of all civilizations, made even greater by the loyalty and fealty of its allies. Today, we remind the world that it is far, far wiser to be Rome's Friend rather than her Enemy."

Our people roared in agreement.

"The foolish King Aatavartes of Medea thought to test Rome's strength," he continued, the crowd groaning at the king's stupidity. "He sought to ally with Rome *and* Egypt's enemy in a greedy bid for power and riches. He thought to claim our weapons and weaken us. But he could not, for Rome and Egypt are blessed by the gods, our victory proof of the favor with which the Immortal Ones hold us . . ."

I lost track of Tata's speech then and started counting the golden beads on the fan slave's broad collar. I had gotten up to forty-seven (after having to start over several times) when Father's voice cut through my reverie.

"It is time," he announced, "to make my Dispositions of War, to reward Egypt for her unceasing loyalty."

The crowd whooped and stomped. I perked up. Tata was about to bestow his gifts to us, his family. To *me*! My mind raced with the possibilities. Was I to receive a new crown from his plunderings? A golden chariot? Or perhaps an exotic beast, maybe even one that breathed fire?

Tata turned toward my two-year-old brother, Ptolemy Philadelphos, who sat beside me. Ptolly looked just like our tata, with a head of shining dark curls, mischievous brown eyes, and the barrel-chested body of a bull. The crowds had swooned with adoration at the first sight of him swaggering in his tiny military cloak and boots.

"To my youngest son, Ptolemy XVI Philadelphos," Father bellowed as the crowd hushed in anticipation, "I grant the lands of Phoenicia, Syria, and Cilicia."

The people roared. I drew a breath, stunned. Father was giving us *kingdoms*? I forgot to keep my head facing forward and turned to Ptolly. He scowled furiously, waggling his chubby legs in his toddler-sized throne as the noise reverberated around us. Worried that he might begin to cry or have a tantrum, I took his pudgy hand in mine and bent toward his ear.

"Look at Tata," I instructed. "He is talking to you!"

Ptolly locked eyes with Father. When Tata grinned at him, Ptolly grinned back, showing all his little milk teeth. Then he toddled toward Tata, to the crowd's cooing delight. One of the guards intercepted him and escorted the little general off the dais.

"To my daughter, Princess Cleopatra VIII Selene," Father called, and I felt the attention of thousands land on me like a physical force — an energy that made me sit up straighter and raise my chin, despite my racing heart. "I confer Cyrenaica and Crete, where she will rule as queen. May she rule with as much wisdom as her namesake."

I was queen! Queen of Cyrenaica and Crete! As the people thundered their approval, Tata caught my eye and winked. Forgetting protocol again, I grinned and inclined my head. This sent the crowds roaring even louder, and I heard my name chanted over and over again. I marveled at the power pulsating all around us — power freely laid at our feet, ours for the taking.

I wanted to jump up, to hug my tata, to do *anything* but continue sitting like a block of marble. But, of course, I would not disappoint Mother. I held my breath, pretending to be as solemn and immobile as the giant statues of the Great Ones.

Tata turned his attention to my twin, Alexandros.

"To my son, Alexandros Helios, I bestow the kingdom of Armenia, where he will rule with his betrothed, Princess Iotape of Medea."

The crowds whooped in honor of Father's decisive victory in the region, but I refused to steal even a side-glance in my twin's direction. The Interloper sat between us.

The black-eyed, silken-haired little princess was nothing more than a royal hostage — a guarantee that her father the king would stay loyal to Tata. But I could find no warmth in my heart for her. The way Alexandros acted around Iotape, it was as if Hermes himself had come down from Mount Olympus and hand delivered her to him. Until she showed up, he and I had lived as if we still shared a womb — playing, sleeping, eating, and laughing together. But now it was Iotape my twin sought out at first light and played with until dusk, when Ra's sunboat descended into the Dark Lands. I would not forgive her for taking him from me.

Still, our people continued to cheer at the announcement, celebrating the return of a strong and vital Egypt. Armenia and Cyrenaica had been under our dominion when our Macedonian-Greek ancestor Alexander the Great and our dynasty's founder, his brother Ptolemy the First, took Egypt nearly three hundred years ago. We Greeks had ruled ever since. And now, thanks to Tata, we were stronger than we had been in centuries.

"In addition," Tata bellowed, "I bequeath to Alexandros Helios and his betrothed rule over *all* the lands of Parthia!"

I barely noticed the undercurrent of bewilderment that rippled through the crowds, the whispers of, "How could the General give away lands he has not yet conquered?" After all, my tata was the best general in the world. Of course he would conquer Parthia!

Tata then turned his attention to my older half brother, Caesarion, the only son of Mother's first husband, Julius Caesar. At thirteen, Caesarion was slim and tall, and I thought he looked magnificent in the kilt and pectoral of a pharaoh, combined with his father's bloodred Roman cloak.

"Ptolemy XV Philopator Philometor Caesar," Tata called, "I name you the true heir and only son of Gaius Julius Caesar. And I name you the king of Egypt!"

From the corner of my eye I spied Caesarion lifting his chin, and my heart swelled with love and pride. My brother, the king! The king of Egypt!

But again, murmurs of unease snaked through the crowds, accompanied by whispers of a name I did not then know: *Octavianus*. I blinked, confused. Why should a Roman name be on our people's lips when Caesarion was rightly being named their king? I tried to make sense of the murmurs: "Isn't Octavianus Caesar's heir?" "Is Antonius challenging him?" Some in the crowd even made the sign of protection against evil.

I stole a glance at Mother. She let out a breath that sounded like a hiss. And although her face kept its expression of queenly impassivity, I saw a flicker of concern settle on the tiny space between her brows. But it may have only been a trick of the fierce Egyptian light, for when I looked again, Mother's face appeared as majestic and untroubled as it always had.

Tata glanced at Mother, and his eyes crinkled before he turned back to the crowds. "To my wife, Cleopatra VII Philopator, Queen of Egypt and overlord of all the kingdoms bestowed today . . ." A rumble of cheers, shouts, and joyous exultations interrupted him, almost as if our people were thrilled to move on to what they knew and loved. The cheers swelled until I felt them vibrating in my chest bones. Mother did not move as the entire city chanted, "Isis! Isis! Hail Isis! Isis our queen!"

When the wave of noise crested, Tata began again. "Today," he boomed, "I name my wife Queen of Kings, Ruler of the Two Lands, Overlord of our Children's Territories, and Partner in managing Rome's interests in the East. I have a vision of the future — a vision of cooperation, not destruction. Borne up by the loyalty of client kings and queens, Rome cannot be stopped."

He swept his arm toward the Lighthouse. "And like Pharos that shines into the night, Egypt serves as a beacon to Rome's future. A future of partnership. A future of immeasurable wealth. A future that no man or king can rend asunder!"

The whoops of joy became deafening. Tata grinned and held both arms up in exultation. He bid Mother stand next to him. The bright Egyptian light seemed somehow concentrated on them — I had never seen them look more godlike.

As the priests and priestesses chanted the final prayers, I wanted to jump and cheer and laugh. It was my family's proudest moment! I drank it all in — the masses cheering; the white-robed Priests of Serapis chanting over bowls of smoky incense; the long-haired Priestesses of

Isis extending their thin arms to the sky; the sweet fragrance of flow-ers as countless petals swirled around us, floating through the air like tiny perfumed birds. It was all so beautiful, almost magical. The Triumph of the Ptolemies! The greatest moment of our lives.

But the gods would not stand for us to have such happiness for long. And so began the slow, excruciating process of our undoing.

CHAPTER TWO

At the celebration banquet that evening, I shared a dining couch with my twin, Alexandros; his betrothed, Iotape; and my little brother, Ptolly. We were to the left of Mother and Tata's couch, a position of high honor in acknowledgment of our new titles. My parents, of course, took the center couch, the most honored position of the feast.

We celebrated under the stars in the massive open courtyard of our Great Palace, joined by the glittering nobility of Alexandria. Silken couches seemed to fill every *intsa* of the square. The air vibrated with the sounds of cheering, laughter, and drunken toasts. Nearly naked boys and girls danced to the rhythm of wandering flute and lyre players, twirling and tumbling in and out of the labyrinthine assemblage of couches and low tables. Servants paraded tray after tray of pungent roasted meats, steamed fishes, and ripe cheeses.

My belly was so full, the night so warm — I fought the drowsiness that threatened to overwhelm me, occasionally sitting up to refresh myself. Ptolly had already given in to sleep, despite heroic efforts to keep it at bay. His head lolled on my shoulder.

Nafre, Ptolly's nurse, bent over him to pick him up. "Come, come," she murmured to him, but Ptolly clung to my arm. Nafre smiled in apology.

"Ptolly, you must go with Nafre," I said, putting my mouth near his flushed cheek so that he could hear me. His curly hair was damp with sweat.

"Stay!" he whined, barely opening his eyes. "Stay with Klee-Klee."

I sat up to peel his arms off me and noticed a silver band on his plump wrist. A dull pearl sat in the center of a filigreed Eye of Horus. Nafre took Ptolly, and I turned toward Alexandros.

"Give me your wrist," I commanded. He held out an arm, his eyes following the dancers that tumbled near our couch. "No, the other one!"

He turned to me, and I examined his arm in bewilderment. He too wore a cuff with a large and heavy Eye of Horus in the center. The dullness of the eye's pearl gave it a look of unsettling menace. "Where did you get this?" I asked close to his ear.

"Mother," Alexandros almost shouted so I could hear. "She gave it to me right before the banquet." He turned away to face the dancers, as Iotape on his other side smiled shyly at him.

I looked toward my parents' couch. Mother lay on her left side, holding a golden goblet in her right hand. She took small sips while her eyes raked over the assemblage. I saw no Eye of Horus on her, but only her favorite band, a golden snake with emerald eyes twining around her upper arm. Father did not sip — he *gulped*, signaling for his wine cup to be refilled each time it emptied. I looked at his wrist and saw no band, but on his fingers flashed a conspicuously large Eye of Horus ring.

Why had Tata and my brothers gotten these gifts from Mother and not me? How unfair! I stood to confront her. But before I could march over to my parents' couch, a strong hand covered my left shoulder.

"What are you doing, Little Moon?" Katep, my royal eunuch, asked. "I do not like the look on your face."

He put his ear near my mouth so he could hear me, and I breathed in the spicy-sweet scent of sandalwood and cinnamon that always puffed from his silken robes.

"I want to know why I did not receive a special Eye of Horus!" I said. "Everyone has one but me!"

Katep furrowed his brow. "You were going to ask the queen this? *Now?* You cannot disturb her during the feasting!"

I rose on my toes and looked over his round shoulders to see Mother speaking with the head of one of the noblest families in Alexandria.

"Cleopatra Selene, you must come with me," Katep said, taking me by the shoulders to turn me away from my parents' couch. "You know how the queen feels about the royal children drawing attention to themselves."

I had begun to dig in my heels, but at that I paused. Yes, Mother took our behavior in public very seriously. Mother turned to me in that instant, almost as if she sensed my agitation. She studied my face, and for a strange moment her eyes shone pale like the deadened Eye of Horus amulets she'd given my brothers. Was that a warning? An omen? I let Katep escort me out.

Much later, in the deepest-dark of night, after I no longer heard the sounds of celebration, I sat up, burning to find out why I had been denied such a powerful amulet. I listened for Zosima's heavy breathing, then slid from my silken couch onto the cold marble, inching my way out into the hallway. I expected Katep to rise from his bench across the hall, but it was empty. Good. He would have tried to stop me.

"Ah!" a voice said. "I was warned to expect this." A young Roman soldier emerged from the darkness.

"Expect what?" I asked in my formal Latin, proud of my improvement in the language, as I knew it pleased Tata.

"A roaming princess."

"Oh," I said, walking around him.

"Wait! Princess . . ." The soldier scrambled in front of me, his sword belt slapping against his thigh, the leather straps of his breastplate creaking. "Where are you going?"

"To see my mother the queen. And you shall not enter her wing, for you do not have special permission." I did not know if this was true, but I said it as if it were. Even at that age, I had learned that anything said with uncompromising authority almost always resulted in instant obedience. And, of course, I was full of myself. Had I not just been named queen of Cyrenaica and Crete?

"Fine," the guard grumbled. "I will let the queen's guards deal with you, then. I am not a babysitter for spoiled Egyptian children."

The Roman guard in Mother's wing — where were her Royal Macedonian Guards and eunuchs? — appeared to have helped himself to an extra wineskin or two. He had slid down the painted column in the entranceway, his legs splayed, his helmet covering his eyes.

Soft, flickering light pooled under the door to Mother's chambers. I moved closer, not sure what to do. If there was light and a partially open door, it meant Katep could request permission for me to enter. If there was no light, it meant Mother was sleeping and I was to return to my rooms. But there was light *and* a closed door.

I heard Mother's clear voice on the other side: "Why give him time to prepare? You should attack Octavianus *now*, when he is weak."

That name again. Octavianus. Who was he?

"*De eis me audite!*" came a gruff, familiar voice. Tata! "A victory in Parthia will remind Rome that I fought alongside Julius Caesar and should have been left in charge, not that little *verpa*. Then everybody will acknowledge me as the rightful ruler and see him for what he really is . . ."

". . . a little man with a tiny *verpa*?" Mother asked, and they both laughed.

A bubble of laughter gurgled up my throat too. I did not understand her words, but her tone told me she had said something naughty. I found myself leaning toward the sound of their laughter like a Nile palm curving over the water, my fingers pressing against the dark painted wood, my forehead grazing the cool door.

Silence on the other side. Without warning, the door swung open with a boom, the heavy wood crashing against the marble walls. I yelped in surprise and stumbled backward, barely blinking before I felt the cool tip of a broadsword under my chin.

"Who dares spy on us?" Father roared, his teeth bared like a lion. He looked terrifying, like Zeus-Amun in a rage, ready to strike me down. I stood with my arms out for balance, my chin tipped up under the cold metal, breathing in gasps. I heard the sound of scrambling feet and jingling armor as the soldier who had been sleeping in the hall scurried over to us, the unmistakable sound of another sword being drawn.

The cold metal moved away from my face. Tata looked at me with wide eyes. "Cleopatra Selene?"

Mother made a noise in her throat that I could not decipher. Surprise? Anger? Father grabbed my upper arm and dragged me into the room as if I weighed no more than a linen doll. He released me and slammed the door behind me so hard, the silver wine goblets vibrated on the ivory-topped table.

"Child," he growled. "What were you doing? I could have killed you."

I took in a ragged breath, rubbing my arm where he had grabbed me. For a moment, I wondered if I had wet myself and prayed that I had not. I could not bear humiliating myself in front of Mother like that. *Do not cry, do not cry. Queens do not cry.*

"Here," Mother said to Tata as she handed him a tunic. Tata slipped it over his head, and it was only then that I realized he'd had no clothing on. Mother stood with her hair cascading down her shoulders, wearing only her emerald snake band. She reached for a gauzy robe the blue-green color of our ocean in midsummer, slipped it on, and settled onto the curved anteroom couch in one elegant move, like a cat pouring itself onto a sunny spot.

Father went over to the small table by the wall and picked up a wine goblet with a shaking hand. He took several big gulps.

"Where is Katep?" Mother asked me.

I did not answer for I did not know.

"Who is Katep?" Tata asked.

"Her royal eunuch and guard," Mother said, still looking at me.

"Ah," he said. "I dismissed all your guards."

Mother whipped her head toward Tata. "You what?"

"My men secure the exterior and patrol the halls. I do not need a harem of eunuchs and effeminate, painted men cluttering up my home."

"Marcus, this is *my* palace, my domain. You had no right . . . ," Mother said through clenched teeth.

He smiled his most charming smile, his eyes twinkling. "Relax, darling. I have things under control."

Mother's greenish-gold eyes blazed. I always thought of her face as softer without her ceremonial paint — which one of her ladies, either Charmion or Iras, must have scrubbed off after the feasting — but not in that moment. If Mother had been staring at me that way, I feared I would have burst into flame. I picked at the hem of my sleeping tunic, curling my toes on the cold floor, staring wide-eyed at what felt like the crackling energy between my parents, not knowing what to say or do.

Tata must have taken in a lot of wine at once, because as soon as he put his goblet down, he belched loudly. The sound was so unexpected that I giggled. Mother's eyes turned to me. I hated when she looked at me that way — as if I had both surprised and disappointed her. To my horror, tears filled my eyes.

"Come here," Father said to me as he sat down on a silk-covered bench across from Mother. He picked me up and placed me on his lap. His eyes were red and shadowed, his cheeks bristly. He smelled of wine and of the rosemary coronet he had worn earlier at the banquet.

"No harm done, little one, thank the gods. I would never have hurt you," he said, misunderstanding the reason for my tears. "But never, ever sneak up on me again."

"I did not know you would be here, Tata," I said. "I . . . I sometimes visit Mother when I do not sleep."

He turned to her, his eyebrows up, a crooked smile forming on his lips. "I thought you told me you never had any visitors at night," Tata said.

"I don't," Mother said coldly, which confused me. Did I not regularly visit her in the deep-dark? "Our new young queen of Crete and Cyrenaica is a true daughter of the moon," she continued. "She does not like to sleep."

He chuckled. "Just like someone else I know."

To my surprise, Mother did not smile back at Tata. Most people could not resist his famous sideways grin.

"Now tell me, what did you overhear?" Tata asked me.

"That you do not like that little *verpa* Octavianus," I answered.

Father burst into laughter. "Yes, by the gods, that's exactly right! Henceforth, he shall be dubbed 'that-little-*verpa*-Octavianus' in all our conversations."

Now Mother smiled. Somehow, the tension had broken. I grinned, relishing the idea that I could make my giant of a father laugh and bring a smile to my mother's beautiful mouth. I was not sure what I had said that delighted them so — only that I wanted to do it again. And soon. Father grabbed the sides of my face with his big square hands and kissed me on the forehead.

"Cleopatra Selene," Mother said, and I turned to look at her. She was standing by the door. I had not heard or seen her move. "It is time for you to go back to your rooms."

I did not want to go. I wanted to stay in my tata's lap. So I leaned my head onto his shoulder and wound my arms around his neck.

Father rubbed my back. "Ah, the gods truly have no mercy, giving me *two* Cleopatras I cannot resist." He ruffled my hair. "However, it is very late. It is time for you to go back to your bed."

"No, wait," I cried, remembering why I had come in the first place. "I have a question."

"You may ask it," Mother said.

I pointed to Father's ring and looked up at her. "Why did you give everyone Eye of Horus jewels but me?"

"*That's* the question that has kept you up this night?" Tata asked with a laugh.

I did not like him laughing. This was serious. I slid off his lap and crossed my arms to show my disapproval.

"Well, wife. How will you answer?" Tata asked with a smile in his voice.

Mother was not smiling. I felt pinned to the floor as she looked at me with what I called her Horus stare. Her intensity made it seem as if Sekhmet herself, the lion-headed goddess, growled in warning at me.

"Do not presume to ask the reason for anything I do, daughter," Mother finally said, so quietly I almost wasn't sure she had spoken at first.

My stomach clenched in fear. How had I angered her? What had I asked that I was not supposed to?

Tata reached over me to pour more wine into his goblet. "Did you receive a different amulet?" he asked.

I nodded. I had forgotten that Mother had given me a golden scarab pendant with an emerald in the center. I had not worn it because Zosima had been instructed to dress me in silver, not gold. Also, I had not liked how it felt around my neck. I looked down, slightly ashamed at how greedy I must have seemed. But how could I explain that it wasn't that I wanted more jewels? I just wanted to know that I mattered to Mother as much as my brothers.

Tata took the ring off his finger and held it out to me, as if for examination. The very heft of the hieroglyphic-covered band suggested it had special power. I had never before seen pearls used to depict the center of the eye like that.

"The pearl is dull," I murmured into the tense silence. I knew that Romans considered pearls the most precious of all gemstones.

"That is no pearl." Tata laughed. "It's bone. Human bone from one of Egypt's ancient enemies. From even before Cheops built his Great Pyramid."

A chill tingled up my spine. A human bone meant powerful magic.

"Yes, it's very sacred, according to your mother's strange-smelling priests," Tata continued. "Lots of protection."

"Protection from what?" I asked, confused by Tata's irreverent tone.

"Death at the hands of an evil enemy," Tata said, lounging back against the curved arm of the couch and yawning. He closed his eyes. "But I have no enemies that powerful."

"But . . . do you have an *evil* enemy, Tata?" Did my brothers? Was I in danger too? "Who is it?"

Tata opened one eye to peer at me.

"That-little-*verpa*-Octavianus," he said with an edge. "Your mother seems to fear him more than she has faith in me."

"Marcus . . . ," Mother warned in a low voice.

Tata sat up quickly, as if he had received a jolt of energy. He reached for his cup and drained it. "But you, my little one, like my queen, are protected by different magic."

"Marcus . . . ," Mother repeated, crossing her arms.

"You probably received an emerald amulet. Yes, I am right, I can tell by your face. See, the emerald enhances Venus's gifts. Oh, excuse me, little Greekling — Aphrodite's gifts. Your feminine charms. That's your mother's special magic. And so she shares it with you."

I did not understand what Tata said or meant, but I felt the tension vibrating between them like heat waves in front of the Great Sphinx. The silence continued. I found myself sincerely wishing that I had never noticed the Horus amulets.

"Little Moon," Mother finally said, "call for Katep. You must return to your rooms."

I paused, knowing that Katep was not waiting for me outside. And since she had seemed so upset that Tata had dismissed our guards, I did not want to remind her of this.

"Rufus!" Father suddenly bellowed, and I jumped. "Escort the Princess back to her rooms. And bring more wine on your way back!"

I followed the soldier into the darkened hall, the sound of his hobnailed boots echoing in the tense silence behind me.

By the next morning, Katep and all of Mother's guards were back at their regular posts.

CHAPTER THREE

In the Nineteenth Year of My Mother's Reign
In My Ninth Year (32 BCE)

The dissolution of our world began in earnest with these three words: "I divorce you."

The king of Egypt himself, my brother Caesarion, came to tell us the news. He found us on the grounds connecting the palace and the Great Library, setting up for a game of *trigon*. A girl named Euginia — the daughter of Mother's finance minister — had already taken her position as one of the *pilecripi*, our ball chasers and scorekeepers. Euginia was not bad at the game, and she and I often tossed the *trigon* ball to each other when the boys went off by themselves. I had hoped to convince Alexandros that she should be our third player.

But, as always, Alexandros wanted Iotape. I squinted as I stared at her across the playing area. Strong ocean breezes lifted and then dropped her silken coverings so that she looked like an exotic bird flapping her wings. How could she possibly play draped in so much fabric? I tossed and caught the painted leather ball in my palm as Alexandros *again* went over the rules with his sweet but, I feared, dull-witted "beloved."

"*Salvete,*" Caesarion called to us as he approached. A retinue of advisers and guards flanked the young king. "I will have a word with you both." Caesarion often spoke to us in Latin instead of the court's usual Greek. He had always done so to honor his tata and because, he claimed, the world was Roman now, and the sooner we mastered the finer points of its language, the better.

Caesarion, at almost fifteen, had his father's wiry frame and keen, intelligent eyes. I always thought he looked like a younger version of the statue Mother had erected of her first husband in the Caesarium. Only with more hair.

"Play with us first, brother!" I called.

Caesarion paused. "I believe I will. I cannot remember the last time I played," he said, stepping onto Alexandros's point in the triangle.

"Where am I supposed to play, then?" Alexandros called.

"Tell Iotape to step back," he said. "You will take her position."

Iotape, who was learning Greek and not Latin, did not move at the command from the king of Egypt. Alexandros spoke softly to her in their strange little mix of Persian and Greek. She slid away, blushing.

I grinned at Caesarion and threw the ball as hard as I could. He caught it with his left hand, his painted eyebrows rising at the sting in his palm. He quickly moved the ball to his right hand.

"Well, little sister," he said. "I see now how this is going to go."

He never broke eye contact with me but hurled the ball to Alexandros. "Ha!" my twin muttered, shooting it to me in almost the same movement. "You're going to have to do better than that!"

We kept the ball spinning in a triangle, trying to outwit one another with feints and tricks with our eyes, where one looked to one person but threw it to the other. I had long ago learned the secret to not fall for such tricks: I did not watch my brothers' eyes or even their feet. The only thing that existed was the spinning ball.

I hurled the ball to Caesarion harder than Achilles throwing his spear, and the sphere bounced off his wrist. The ball hit the ground with a heavy thump.

"My point!" I whooped, dancing. "I have beaten the king of Egypt!"

"One point does not an entire game make, sister," Caesarion called.

I pranced and skipped toward him. "You lost, I won! I'm a better *trigon* player!"

To my surprise, Caesarion lowered his head and roared, "There is no teasing the king. You will pay!" My heart stopped in fear until I saw his face split into a grin as he sprinted toward me.

I yelped and took off across the green. But Caesarion caught me quickly. "That is it!" he said as he trapped me in his arms. "Throw her to the snakes!"

I yelled, "No! No!" in mock horror as he spun me. "I surrender! I surrender!" I cried at last. "Let me go."

"Ha! I do not trust you."

"Brother, you insult me."

"There is no insulting She Whose Bite Is Sharper than a Serpent's."

"I promise," I said. "You can trust me."

Caesarion made a snorting noise — quite un-kinglike, I thought — and released me. I stepped back with my hands up. "See?"

"Come, I must speak with you and Alexandros," he said, cocking his head toward my twin and Iotape and moving toward them.

"Only if you give me a ride!" I said, launching myself onto his back with a harpy cackle.

"*Eheu!*" he grunted when I landed on him, but he did not throw me off. I slid down his back when we reached Alexandros and Iotape. "You are getting too big for me to give you a ride," Caesarion complained.

"What was the news you wanted to share with us, brother?" Alexandros asked.

Caesarion's face — which moments ago had been open and light — suddenly closed. "We received word that your father's divorce from his Roman wife is now official."

Alexandros and I looked at each other and then back at Caesarion. We knew Tata had a Roman wife — whom he'd married for political reasons — and that he also hadn't seen her in years. She was meaningless! "That is it? That was what brought you out here?" I asked.

Caesarion shook his head. "Walk with me," he said, heading toward the colonnade of painted lotus columns leading to the Great Library. He signaled for his entourage to stay back as they shooed Euginia and the other children away.

"Isn't Tata's divorce a mere formality at this point?" Alexandros asked. "After all, Tata and Mother have been together many years."

"I'm afraid it is a little more complicated than that," Caesarion said. "You know that Tata married Octavia to cement a peace treaty with her brother Octavianus, yes?"

We nodded.

"Well, by casting her away, he casts away the treaty too."

My stomach clenched. A broken peace treaty was never a good thing.

"But divorce is common in Rome, isn't it?" I asked.

"Yes," Caesarion said. "But in this case, it has deep ramifications. Octavianus is using it as an excuse to declare war."

"But why would Octavianus declare war on Tata for that?" I cried.

"He has not declared war on your father," the young king of Egypt continued, scowling. "He has declared war on *Mother*. On Egypt. On us. Do you understand?"

I froze, my mouth hanging open. Alexandros's head whipped toward him. "But Egypt is a loyal Friend and Ally to Rome," he cried. "How can Rome declare war on Egypt? We supply their grain, we fund their campaigns in the East. . . ."

"And we do not even have a standing army of any strength," I added. "This is outrageous! They cannot declare war on an ally that has no way to protect itself!"

"Octavianus has, in truth, started a civil war with your father — a war between two Romans for sole control of the Roman empire," explained Caesarion. "But he is making it look like it's all Mother's fault, making *us* — making her — the enemy."

"But that makes no sense . . . ," I cried.

"Oh, no. It's quite brilliant, really. Octavianus will have to tax his people to the breaking point to fund the war. Romans would not allow it — indeed, they would throw him from the Tarpeian Rock if he told them it was in the service of fighting their beloved Marcus Antonius. But Romans would not object to taxing themselves into poverty if it meant saving themselves and their favorite general from the clutches of the 'evil' queen of Egypt."

I made an outraged noise, but Caesarion continued. "He is twisting the minds of the Romans at the same time that he dismisses me as the true son of Caesar. Octavianus claims Mother has bewitched your father. That she has him under such a spell, he can't be held responsible for any of his actions or decisions. That she is using your father to take over in Rome."

"And Romans believe these *lies* against a loyal client kingdom?" I cried.

"It is hard for me to understand how they do not see right through him. But we must take the declaration seriously and prepare accordingly."

Dumbfounded, I said nothing more. We stopped under the striped canopy of the royal entrance to the Library. Attendants came running, bowing first to Caesarion, then to us. One bore a golden vessel with warm lotus-perfumed water to rinse our hands and feet; another took our cloaks and anything else we did not wish to carry.

As we entered the light-filled atrium, white-robed, white-sandaled scholars bustled by, bowing absentmindedly in our direction. The march of all our attendants echoed loudly on the worn marble floors.

"Where are we going, brother?" I asked, looking up into Caesarion's serious face.

"*I* am going into the military history section of the Library," he said, stopping in front of the statue of Alexander the Great that graced its entrance. "*You* are going back to your lessons."

"No, I want to stay with you," I said. "I will be quiet, I promise."

Caesarion shook his head. "War is not a game for children," he said. "You must allow the adults to handle it without distractions."

Adults? He had not even had his manhood ceremony yet! I stared openmouthed at my brother. But before I could respond, he added, "Go play, Little Moon. We shall keep Egypt safe for you." And turned away.

CHAPTER FOUR

Our litter slowed as we moved through the Royal Palace's main gates and into the busy streets of Alexandria. Crowds parted before us, but to my surprise, we did not hear the chorus of benedictions and blessings that normally rained down upon us. All of Alexandria, it seemed, had grown tense over Octavianus's absurd declaration of war. I noticed that we had a larger guard than usual, all with drawn swords as they marched in front of, beside, and behind our litter.

Despite the tension that seemed to permeate the city, I was excited. I always loved it when we went out among our people. That day, we were headed toward the Jewish Quarter with our tutor, Euphronius.

"You must understand the lives and hearts of *all* your people," he had lectured before we set off. "And so, today we meet with a rabbi who will explain the tenets of the Hebrew religion."

We had never actually been to this part of Alexandria, and I found the transition into the neighborhood fascinating. In general, even the poorest Alexandrians loved the bright colors of Egypt — saffron, turquoise, red, and blue. But when we entered the Jewish Quarter we saw only tunics and cloaks of dull browns and grays. Also, the Jews did not bow to us, throw flowers, or beg for benedictions like most of our people. Instead, they studiously ignored us. I did not think much about it until Iotape pointed it out.

"They do not honor you," she said in her singsong, accented Greek. "Why is that?"

"The religion of the Hebrews," Euphronius explained, "prohibits them from worshipping idols, which they extend to mean the worship of kings."

I sat up in surprise. "Do you mean to say, they do not acknowledge Mother as their queen and Caesarion as their king?"

"They claim their god forbids it," Euphronius said. "The Jews of Alexandria are a learned bunch, but their faith is a curious one, which involves believing in only a single male god who is often quite jealous and angry."

"But why does Mother allow it?" I asked. "I don't care what they believe. They should bow to her."

"I did not say that they do not honor the queen. They do — in their own way. And so you must learn from the queen's wisdom. She does not force them to act against their faith, thus earning their devotion and allegiance. . . ."

"Not to mention their taxes," quipped Alexandros.

"Yes, which is what makes her such a brilliant administrator," Euphronius added. "The queen is a true philosopher-king in the spirit with which Aristotle tried to imbue your ancestor Alexander the Great."

We arrived at a small brick building that Euphronius called their temple, though I would not have thought it so. In our Temple of Isis we had great brass doors that opened dramatically as if by the unseen hands of the Goddess, thanks to fire-driven machines created by the scientists at our *Museion*. Inside, giant lotus columns, thirty cubits high, soared into the sky. Morning light pouring in from the roof's sun grate made the gold-leaf hieroglyphs on the walls shimmer with an otherworldly beauty. Immense painted statues of the gods reminded us of their power, majesty, and mystery. In contrast, the Hebrew temple, except for the marble columns in the entranceway, felt as if we had entered someone's humble home. No paintings or statues of gods or goddesses adorned the walls; no niches were set off for private communion. Only a ceremonial flame by the altar hinted that it was a house of worship.

A kindly-looking old man with a long, uncurled gray beard greeted us. "Welcome, welcome!" he said, his eyes crinkling with warmth. He led us into a side room away from where a group of men prayed with fervor, their eyes closed, lips moving, and bodies rocking ever so slightly back and forth.

"I am Rabbi Yoseph ben Zakkai," he said. "I met my good friend Euphronius at the Library when he and I debated the nature of the divine many years ago."

Learning that our teacher had a life outside of tutoring us always gave me a jolt. That Euphronius had *friends* was even more shocking.

"Who won the debate?" Alexandros asked.

"He did!" both men said, laughing as they pointed to each other.

As we settled in the rabbi's *tablinum*, the rabbi began, "My friend tells me his young charges need to learn a bit more about the world."

I bristled at the implication we were insulated, spoiled, overprotected little brats.

The rabbi then explained the basics of his faith. "There is only one God who created and rules the world," he said. "He is all knowing, all powerful, and in all places at all times. He is also just and merciful."

"Who is his consort-wife?" I asked, thinking of Isis and her husband, Osiris. "What is she like?"

"Our God has no wife. There is no goddess. *Hashem* created the world and is responsible for its existence. We are here to obey His commandments and laws."

I blinked. No goddess? How could that be? "But the bearing of life is the province of women," I said. "What does a male god know of these things?"

"In my faith, the goddesses Anahit and Astghik are the bringers of life and love," agreed Iotape. "Why would your male god not *want* a consort?" She looked at me and smiled as if for approval.

"Our God supersedes all. There is only one God," the rabbi repeated. "We owe everything to Him, he who has made us His chosen people and revealed His commandments to us."

The rabbi launched into the Hebrew story about their first man and woman. His god placed them in a Garden of Happiness and commanded them not to eat the fruit of a magic tree. But a serpent tempted them and both ate of the forbidden fruit. Their god was very angry and the man blamed the woman.

"But if both the man and the woman ate of the fruit, why does the woman get all the blame?" I interrupted, sitting forward on the wooden bench. I did not look at Euphronius, guessing he was glaring at me.

"Because she is weaker and tempted the man," he said, seemingly surprised at the question. "Therefore, she is more evil."

"But—" Euphronius cleared his throat. I ignored him. "But wasn't she just curious? Isn't curiosity a useful human trait? Why would your god give humans curiosity and then tell them not to use it?"

"Ah, but God was not testing their curiosity or intelligence. He was testing their *obedience*," the rabbi explained. He took a breath to continue, but I jumped in.

"But *why* would a god do this? And why would he test them without telling them he was testing them? Perhaps they might not have eaten from it if they understood what would happen if they disobeyed? And . . . and if he was all knowing, why did he not *know* that his creations would succumb to the temptation of curiosity? After all, didn't he create them that way?"

"Princess," Euphronius interrupted. "I remind you, you are a guest in this holy man's temple. Please do not . . ."

But the old man smiled at me and waved Euphronius off. "No, no, this is excellent. Only through dialogue will we come to understand each other, yes?"

I smiled back at him. Then the rabbi explained a concept I had not heard of before — one that he called "free will." "God created man with the impulse to do good and the impulse to do evil. Free will is the ability to choose to act on either of these impulses. God commands us to follow the Torah and to choose goodness over sin."

"But how is it free will if mankind is *commanded* to choose a certain way?" I asked. "That's like — that is like if I held two hands out for you to choose. In one, I held a pearl, in the other an emerald. If I *commanded* you to choose the pearl, then you are not freely choosing it, yes?"

The rabbi shook his head. "It is the discernment — the knowledge of good and evil — that is at the heart of free will." He unwound an ancient-looking scroll and scanned it, putting one finger up for us to wait. "Ah, yes. Here it is. Genesis. This is what happened after Adam and Eve disobeyed God." He read aloud first in Hebrew and then translated it into Greek for us: "'Behold, Adam has become as one of us, knowing good and evil.'"

"But wait," I interrupted. "Your holy book says your first man became 'as one of us.' I thought you said there was only one god. Why does it say 'us'?"

"A figure of speech," the rabbi said with a quick flick of the wrist. "What is important is the idea that God will bless us if we follow Him, but if our hearts turn astray, we will be destroyed. Each man must choose every day."

"That is not so different than the Weighing of the Heart test Osiris says we must pass," Alexandros pointed out. "If we live by *ma'at*, then we will not be devoured by the evil monster, Amut."

The rabbi paused. "This is different. There are no beast gods, there is only One God."

"And what does our Greek heritage say?" Euphronius asked us, as if he wanted to change the subject.

"That we cannot outrun our fates," I answered. "*Hubris*, the great crime against the gods, was thinking that we could. And hubris took down even the best of men, like Achilles and Oedipus."

My tutor nodded. A slave entered and poured watered wine into clay cups for us. "There are many slaves who live good lives," I said to the rabbi. "But most did not *choose* to be slaves. And they cannot choose *not* to be slaves. Do they not have free will, then? Doesn't this prove that their fates are already decided? Just like our own — that I will rule Egypt and Alexandros will rule Parthia and that the slave will always be a slave?"

"No, see." The rabbi smiled. "Even a slave can choose to obey God. Our only job is to love God and obey His commandments, no matter what the circumstances."

I was more confused than ever. How was it free will if your only job was to obey?

"It is getting late, children, we must return," Euphronius said. So the rabbi finished by explaining that a new age awaited humanity — that the Jews waited for a man they called *Mashiach* — a savior of the people, a man of God who would end all fighting and unite humanity as one.

"Can the *Mashiach* be a woman?" I asked.

Alexandros sniggered. Iotape elbowed him.

"Well, no," answered the rabbi.

"Why not?"

"Because . . . well, because the prophets say the *Mashiach* will be a man."

"But if your god truly wanted to test his people's faith and obedience, then he could very well send a woman, couldn't he?" As always, I thought only of Mother. If Mother could be "queen of kings," then why could not another great woman be their *Mashiach*?

"Theoretically, yes . . ."

"Princess," Euphronius interrupted with a tired edge in his voice. "We do not want to exhaust our most generous host. Let us save those questions for another time."

"But the Jews aren't the only ones saying that a great new age is coming," Alexandros jumped in. "Remember, Virgil says that a *boy* will usher in a golden age and rule a world 'blessed' with peace."

For our Latin studies, we had read the Roman poet Virgil's fourth Eclogue, and Alexandros had great fun claiming *he* was this "Golden Child" the poem referred to. After all, wasn't he named after the sun?

I looked at Iotape, and she had crossed her arms in irritation with my brother too. *That* made me warm to her. But before I could respond, Alexandros said, "I repeat, sister, the poem says 'boy,' not 'girl.'"

I reached over to pinch the soft underside of his upper arm. "You arrogant little —"

"Children!" Euphronius cried. "I do believe it is time to bid our honored host farewell."

Alexandros's baiting and my experience at the Jewish temple opened my eyes to the fact that most men thought women inferior. After all, I had grown up under the shadow of the most powerful woman in the world. I saw great men prostrate themselves at her feet. I worshipped at the altar of the greatest Goddess of All, Isis.

But I began paying more attention, and I grew confused by what I saw. Mother had no women in her court of advisers. Few petitioners were women. Occasionally, we saw a female scholar at the Great Library, but not often. And certainly, no women ambassadors visited the queen. What did it mean? And how had I not noticed it before?

I asked Mother about it some days later when I visited her in the deep-dark. Mother read her correspondence while her servant Iras fought to stay awake and I paced the room, restless. I heard a scratching at the door to Mother's inner chamber and opened it. Mother's little sleek cat, Hekate, shot out. I looked in and spied Tata, unclothed and sprawled on his stomach on Mother's sleeping couch. He snored and I jumped.

"Close the door," Mother said in a hushed tone.

I obeyed. "Why is Tata sleeping in there?" I asked.

"He's not just sleeping, he's sleeping it *off*," muttered Iras.

Mother's head snapped toward her in surprise. Iras colored. "I am sorry, my lady, I meant no disrespect. . . ."

"Leave us," Mother said in a voice so cold, my flesh prickled.

Mother returned to her reading after Iras left, but I could tell by her furious scowl that her mood had shifted. After a minute, she threw the scroll on her desk. "Gods, child, stop that infernal pacing," she said. "What is troubling you?"

"Noth-nothing."

Mother rubbed the spot between her brows, then looked up at me. Her green-gold eyes glimmered in the flickering light of the hanging bronze lamp. "Euphronius reports you engaged in a debate with a holy man of the Jewish Quarter."

My stomach clenched. I'd had no idea that Euphronius reported our behavior to Mother. "I am sorry," I sputtered. "It is just that . . . I only had some questions. . . ."

Mother waved her hand to stop me. "No. Never apologize for asking intelligent questions. Only you must learn how to do so without angering those whom you engage."

"But I did not anger the rabbi, I swear!"

"Well, you angered your tutor." Mother shifted her gaze to Hekate, who washed her paws with great delicacy. She added with a murmur, "I was very much like you when I was young."

I stared, not knowing how to react to this strange admission.

"A curious, restless mind is good in a ruler," she continued. "Perhaps not very conducive to sleep, true, but it does give you the ability to explore angles others have not yet considered."

I sat on a cushion opposite Mother, and Hekate sauntered onto my lap. I touched the little cat's emerald-encrusted collar in embarrassed delight. Mother claimed I was like her! Nothing could have made me prouder. Mother was famous for her quick mind and audacious risk-taking. When her rivals for the Egyptian throne exiled her, she raised an army on foreign land. She escaped assassination by hiding in a rug to align herself with Caesarion's tata, Julius Caesar. And she had, with expert negotiations, regained many of Egypt's lost provinces at a time when Rome took land rather than returned it.

"So tell me," Mother said, snapping me out of my reverie. "What troubled you about the rabbi's stories?"

"Why do men blame everything on women?" I blurted.

Mother's eyebrows rose and she leaned forward. "Do they?"

"Yes! In the rabbi's religion, they blame a woman for a mistake the man made too. And . . . and look how we Greeks blame Pandora for all the ills of the world. And Iotape said that in her faith, the good god created man while the evil god created woman —"

"And what is Isis blamed for?" Mother interrupted.

My mouth hung open as I thought through all of the stories I had ever read or heard about the Great Goddess. I paused. "She . . . she is not 'blamed' for anything. She is honored for resurrecting her husband, Osiris, outwitting the Evil One, and protecting her son Horus so that he could rule Egypt, thus restoring order."

Mother leaned back and smiled. She looked so satisfied I almost expected to hear her purr as loudly as Hekate on my lap. I smiled back, not quite sure why this answer pleased her so much.

"Now you see why Isis is my patron Goddess," Mother said. "And why you must align yourself with the Great Goddess too." She unfastened a chain around her neck and lifted the amulet I had often seen hanging between her breasts. She held it toward me. "The Queen of Heaven, the Lady of the Words of Power, is whom you must follow, not any of the lesser goddesses or gods. For you see, Isis alone is honored as not only an equal to her husband, but the one responsible for his resurrection. She is the true power of Egypt. One day you will become initiated into her Mysteries — as I was — and the Goddess herself will show you how you must live."

The golden amulet, bearing the sacred Knot of Isis, glimmered in the light as it swung from Mother's fingers. "Come, take it," she directed me. "It is even more powerful than the emerald I know you never cared for," she added with a rueful smile.

I scrambled to my feet, upending the cat. Hekate made a sound of irritation at the indignity. "I am sorry, Daughter of Bastet," I murmured out of habit. I turned my back and lifted my hair while Mother fastened the golden chain around my neck. The amulet felt warm from Mother's skin as it hung down almost to my waist. My throat tightened with a strange thrill, as if I had passed some sort of secret test. Mother turned me to face her.

"You are a true Daughter of Isis." Mother closed her eyes and murmured a sacred prayer in the ancient words of Old Egypt — a language I would learn upon my initiation into womanhood. I closed my eyes too, feeling the power of her words pulsating in the air between us.

I will follow you, Mother, as I will follow Isis, unto my death, I swore to her then. *May I live as you live, may I rule as you rule, may I die as you die.*

CHAPTER FIVE

Sing O goddess, sing of the rage of Achilles, son of Peleus —
that murderous anger which condemned Achaeans
to countless agonies and threw many warrior souls
deep into Hades, leaving their dead bodies
carrion for dogs and birds —
all in fulfillment of the will of Zeus.

"Good," Euphronius said, raising a hand to stop my recitation. "But before we move any further, let us discuss this murderous rage of Achilles."

I groaned inwardly and sat back down on my short stool. We had gone through the entire *Iliad* a number of times and were now starting again, this time reciting from memory. I hated it when Euphronius interrupted us to parse out every little line. I preferred it when we just focused on the *story*, the fighting, the great moments of sacrifice, bravery, and passion.

We sat in a small shaded garden outside the reading rooms of the Great Library. I stared up, squinting into the brilliant blue of the sky as waving palm fronds skewered fluffy white clouds. The intermittent calls of shipmen and merchants drifted in from the Royal Harbor.

"Now," Euphronius continued, popping me out of my reverie, "how can Achilles' great rage be the fulfillment of the will of Zeus?"

"Because everything that happens, even bad things, *must* be the will of the gods, otherwise they would not happen," Alexandros said after our tutor called on him.

"Yes, but is there anything people can *do* when the gods have turned on them so viciously?" he pressed.

"No, there is no escaping the fates the gods have set for us," I said, even though Euphronius had looked at one of the other children who accompanied us in our lessons, sons and daughters of the most noble families of Alexandria. I responded out of turn because I was still mulling over what the old rabbi had said about "free will." He was wrong. Fate set our futures.

Euphronius turned to me. "And what happens when humans try to escape their fates? Someone *else*, this time, please," he added.

"They either end up dead like Achilles or blind like Oedipus," said Euginia, my sometimes partner in *trigon*.

"Yes. Now let us look a little closer at what we really mean by *hubris* . . . ," Euphronius continued. But again my attention wandered. I looked over at Euginia, her black ringlets arranged prettily past her shoulders, cascading down her fine yellow linen tunic. How long did she have to sit still, I wondered, while her nurse used heated tongs to create those perfect curls? This detail of her appearance always fascinated me, for she did not seem to me a girl overly concerned with her looks. Especially since she played such a mean game of *trigon*.

Euginia must have felt me staring at her, for she looked at me and gave me a quick smile. I cut my eyes at Euphronius and made a face. Euginia looked down at the wax tablet on her lap, suppressing a grin.

"So, then, if punishment — great suffering and death — is the inevitable result of trying to escape one's fate, why do men continually try?" Euphronius droned on. "What, then, should our role be in relationship to the gods?"

"Excuse me, revered teacher," a voice said.

Euphronius's white scholar's robe whipped around him as he turned to face Mother's lady, Iras.

"The queen calls for her daughter. You must come with me now," she said, turning to me and inclining her head.

My heart soared with excitement, and I jumped up and raced toward her.

Alexandros rose too. Iras put a hand out. "I am sorry, young prince. The call is only for your sister."

Alexandros looked at me, his face flickering surprise, hurt, and then anger in a matter of seconds. I shrugged at him, feeling guilty. I did not know why Mother was not including him.

"The queen instructed me to tell you that she would meet privately with you later, after the evening meal," Iras said quickly.

Alexandros sat back down on his low stool, his back very straight, the tips of his ears red. I turned toward the columned breezeway connecting the Library with the palace, but Iras spoke again, signaling me to pause.

"The queen has one more request," she said. "She asks you to select a female companion."

I blinked. Why on Horus's wing would she want that?

"You may choose one from this group or call for another."

When I did not respond, she looked at me, her painted eyebrows raised as if to say, *"Well? Choose."* I looked back at the girls who had joined us in lessons today. Not all of them came regularly. Except Euginia. She came more than most.

"Euginia," I said quickly, and saw the faces of the other two girls fall.

Euginia smiled at me, rose, bowed to Euphronius, and walked behind me as we made our way to the palace.

Iras led us past the queen's chambers, through short, twisting flights of stairs and small, unfamiliar hallways. When we stepped through what appeared to be a hidden doorway, I found myself almost blinded by the bright sun shining over an enormous rooftop garden.

It was as if we had entered another realm, a floating world of lush green framed by the brilliant aquamarine of the bay behind the palace. Jasmine, delphinium, and rose blooms cascaded over giant, elegantly painted pots. Fan-shaped papyrus plants danced in the sea breezes. Trees, heavy with fruit — yellow citron, bright red pomegranates, gray-green olives, and purple-brown figs — scented the air.

"Ahhh, daughter," Mother said from under a small golden canopy.

"Welcome." Her sheer, pearly blue robe sparkled in the sun like sea foam. A beautiful, long-haired Egyptian girl plucked the strings of a lyre nearby.

I bowed my head as I always did when greeting her in a formal setting, though this was anything but. Still, it seemed the right thing to do. Euginia bowed to the ground beside me.

"You may rise," Mother said distractedly. She smiled, and I felt my middle expand with warmth. I had not seen Mother smile much since Octavianus declared war on her months before. She and Father and all her ministers seemed forever in meetings as they prepared for Octavianus's attack.

"Euginia, daughter of Hypatos. Welcome," she added.

"Thank you, Your Majesty," Euginia replied in a somewhat strangled whisper.

"An interesting choice," Mother said to me.

I did not know what she meant, but I never liked to appear ill-informed around her, so I kept my face expressionless.

"The Lady Iras will escort you out," Mother said to Euginia.

Euginia and I exchanged a look. I knew no more than she did. I was confused, but she seemed terrified.

After Euginia left, Mother said, "Come. Let us bathe."

Bathe? She stood, and I followed her to a more secluded corner of the roof, a deck facing the sea, giving me an astonishing view of Pharos, our Great Lighthouse. Its white marble glinted in the bright sun as immense plumes of black smoke billowed from the fires that burned day and night at its summit. I had never seen our Lighthouse from this height, and the magnificence of its colossal, three-tiered architecture took my breath away. Next to it, the ships moving in and out of our Great Harbor looked like ants crawling past the leg of a giant.

I followed Lady Charmion and Mother toward a pool in the center of the terrace. Mosaics of the goddess of love emerging from the sea glimmered at its bottom. A canopy of white, gauzy linen shaded us from the worst of the sun.

Lady Charmion swept Mother's robe off her shoulders as a servant rubbed Mother's special scent — a heady mixture of lotus, rose, and other mysterious oils — into her shoulders and back. Another servant held a strigil to scrape off the excess oil.

"Your turn," Lady Charmion said in my ear, and I jumped. In silence, she removed my tunic and had a young maid begin rubbing my skin with Mother's oil. I breathed deep, drinking in her unique scent. The muted light streaming through the white canopy, the low female murmurs, and the soft music floating in from the adjacent garden gave the impression of being in a sacred sanctuary.

Mother stepped into the warm, scented water with a sigh. I twitched and fidgeted, wanting to join her. The sparkling water looked so inviting! When the cool metal of the strigil scraped my torso, I burst into a fit of furious giggles. I wriggled away from the woman's ministrations and threw myself into the warm water.

"As impetuous as your father," Mother said. "May the Goddess preserve us."

"I am not!"

"And just as quick to anger too, I see," she added.

"That's not true . . . !" I began in an outraged tone, then realized I was only proving her right. So I lifted my chin and arched my left eyebrow. "I am more like you, Mother. I am a queen."

This made both Mother and Charmion — who had joined us in the water — smile, to my great relief.

I swam toward a blue lotus that had been slapping against the sides of the pool. I turned to show it to Mother. But long, lean Charmion, her wavy dark hair covering her small breasts, was murmuring into her ear. Mother leaned back into her hands while her lady massaged her scalp. I stared at their easy intimacy, resenting how it excluded me.

I brought the bloom over anyway. Mother's green-gold eyes sparkled as she accepted my gift. "Tell me, daughter," she said, after sniffing the flower's blue center, "why did you choose Euginia?"

I blinked, not knowing how to answer, not knowing what, in fact, I had selected her *for.*

"Choosing a lady should not be taken lightly," Mother continued.

My jaw dropped, and I was glad to see that Mother's eyes had closed again as Charmion's nimble fingers worked over her scalp. I had chosen my "lady," my consecrated companion for life? But the selection and ceremony was not to take place for another several years, when I passed from girlhood — and certainly not like this!

Charmion must have read my panic, for she murmured into Mother's ear, "Sometimes, the attendant chooses the master. Is that not right?"

Mother laughed. "Yes. Well, however you came to that decision, you have made an excellent choice," she continued. "She is one I would have chosen for you too."

"Mother," I ventured cautiously, "what does my choice mean?"

"To become your lady, Euginia will move into the palace and be educated alongside you. This great honor raises her family's status. She will likely become your most trusted adviser and friend, someone who devotes her life to you in a sacred oath to the gods."

"It is the process I went through," Charmion added. "Though we started when the queen was a bit older than you are now."

My mind raced with confusion. How was it that I had not been told I would be selecting my lady? Why was Mother breaking with protocol and having me do it years too early and with so little warning or preparation? *Was* there someone else I would have chosen? I barely knew the other girls who floated in and out of our lessons and dinners. No. Euginia was as good as anyone else I could have selected.

"I have moved the selection process up because your father and I leave for Greece — where we will set up our war camp — in a matter of days," Mother added, almost as an afterthought.

It took me a moment to understand what she was saying. "Wait. You are going *with* Father when he goes to war?"

Charmion's hands froze and Mother sat up. With her hair smoothed back and her skin flushed from the warm scented water, she looked like a sleek and mysterious goddess of the sea. An angry one. "And why would I not?" she asked.

"Because . . . because you never went into war with Tata before. Because he is the general, not you."

Mother's face grew very still as her Horus stare pierced me. "Octavianus has declared war against *me*, daughter. It is *my* kingdom that pays for this war; it is *my* fleet that will protect the seas while your father attacks on land. And it is *me* that Octavianus wants to destroy so that he can plunder my beloved Egypt. Why should I *not* join him when there is so much at stake?"

"But . . . but you're . . . you are not a warrior. . . ."

"And if I were a king, would anybody question my presence at the general's side? A good ruler protects her kingdom, no matter the cost."

I nodded, my throat tightening. No matter the cost? Even if it meant her *life*? So many things could go wrong! Her ships could get lost in a storm. She could get a strange sickness and die. She could get run through with a sword!

Worse, I suddenly understood why Mother had pushed up the selection of my lady. She was tying up loose ends, making sure I had the right people around me should she not come back.

Mother must have seen the panic on my face, for she leaned toward me and stroked my cheek. "Do not worry, Little Moon. I have faced enemies far more dangerous than young Octavianus. We shall return victors. And sooner than you think."

CHAPTER SIX

In the Twentieth Year of My Mother's Reign
In My Tenth Year (31 BCE)

Despite the awkwardness of our sudden pairing, I found Euginia's company a comfort in the long months after my parents' departure for war. In the beginning, though, she tended to assent to every request I made. I was used to the push-back I received from my brothers. It took some time for her to develop a backbone.

"Let us climb the Lighthouse again," I said one morning.

Euginia hesitated. "Yes, that would be lovely."

But I knew she disliked the endless airless stairwells, the dizziness as we climbed higher and higher, the roar of the fire at the summit — the very things I loved about our Lighthouse. Why didn't she stand up to me? Her quick capitulation irritated me.

"Euginia, tell me what *you* want to do for a change," I said, trying to goad her into making a decision.

"I will do anything you want," she answered quickly.

I stomped my foot. "By Ares' sword, *you* choose!"

Euginia's face paled. I crossed my arms and stared at her. Zosima saw my expression as she passed by. "Do not give her that Horus look, child! She does not deserve it when she is only being obliging."

Zosima looked back over her shoulder at me and laughed. "Yes, you have a Horus look. It is your mother's in miniature!"

As always, part of me rejoiced in being likened to Mother, while another part of me ached with the reminder of her absence. I watched Zosima as she gathered up the many toys we had left on the floor — the jeweled spinning tops, the alabaster toy chariots, the carved ivory cats on wheels, even Alexandros's favorite onyx horse, Bucephalus.

"And you," Zosima said, straightening and turning to Euginia, "will only survive if you show some mettle. Trust me on this."

Euginia reddened a little. "How about . . . Can we . . . Let us go to the Royal Menagerie instead," she said.

I intended my assent to sound imperious. Hadn't Zosima just said I had a Horus stare like Mother's? But I could not help it. I grinned. "Let's go!"

Euginia indeed learned to "show some mettle," much to Zosima's dismay, for it meant she had to arbitrate our loud, intense arguments about how we would spend our free time. Still, as the months wore on, not even the distractions she provided lessened the blow of Mother's continued absence, which dragged on past the winter and into the spring. When I questioned Caesarion, he always claimed all was well, and I took him at his word. I assumed that Tata's forces were on the march, defeating Octavianus's armies, while Mother waited for him in Actium, in Greece. My brother said nothing to disabuse me of that notion.

But when summer approached, and still my parents did not return from Actium, the palace grew hushed with uncertainty. Fewer servants bustled through the halls, and when they did, they congregated in dark corners and whispered. I held steadfast to my belief that we would win against Octavianus. After all, there were only two generals in all of history better than my tata — Divus Julius, Caesarion's father, and our own ancestor Alexander the Great.

Euginia grew no fonder of visiting Pharos Island and our Lighthouse over time, so I often went without her. The immense statue of the Goddess in front of the Pharos Temple of Isis became a place of comfort. Isis of Pharos, or Isis Pharia as we called her, stared out to sea, her face beautiful, confident, serene. I imagined that she could see over the vast ocean all the way to Actium to watch over Mother. I often brought gifts for the Goddess, especially a fine earth-colored incense powder that I held up as high as I could, watching as the ocean breezes scattered and swirled the sacred scent around her.

Isis Pharia held a giant marble sail filled with the Favorable Winds all sailors prayed for. One blustery day, I stood beside the statue and held the ends of my silk cloak so that the wind filled it and made it billow like the Goddess's marble sail.

"Look, Katep!" I cried, standing like the statue of the Goddess and gazing far out to sea. "I am Isis Pharia! Protectress of All! Keeper of Souls Who Ride Her Seas!"

Katep crossed his right arm over his heart in the sign against evil. "Princess!" he cried. "How dare you mock the Goddess!"

I let go of the ends of my cloak and it whipped out behind me, forcing me to stumble. My stomach dropped. I wasn't mocking her! I was just pretending.

"The Goddess of Life does not take umbrage when her children play at her feet," someone said from behind me.

I turned and looked up into the face of Priestess Amunet, the lady of the Temple of Isis on Pharos. Strands of her long dark hair escaped from her saffron mantle and waved in the whipping wind. Deep crinkles around her eyes and mouth sunk into a complexion that glowed a rich buttery brown.

Katep bowed, and I remembered my manners, inclining my head to acknowledge the powerful head priestess.

"I have watched you approach Isis Pharia many times," Lady Amunet said to me. "The Goddess must be calling you." I blinked, not sure I understood what she meant. "Come, let us get away from this wind and I shall explain."

I followed her under the first massive pylon of the temple, beneath the carving of Isis suckling her beloved son Horus, the first pharaoh of Egypt. We emerged into the shaded forecourt, where shaven-headed priests in long white kilts scurried past.

She took me into the *purgatorium* for purification. A long-haired maiden washed my feet and hands with warm marjoram-scented water, then anointed my forehead with sacred lotus oil. I closed my eyes at the touch of her gentle fingers tracing the Knot of Isis on my skin, breathing in the heavy, sweet smell of Egypt.

After our absolutions, I followed Lady Amunet into a private chamber, a small room with high windows that let in both the fresh sea air and the sounds of sistrums jangling in time to chanted prayers.

"Sit, Princess," Lady Amunet said as she lounged on a bloodred pillow on the floor. "Now tell me," she said once I had settled myself. "How has Isis been calling her daughter?"

I did not know how to answer. So I didn't. A servant came in bearing two faience blue cups. The servant took sips from both to prove they were not poisoned, then passed one to Amunet and one to me.

"Barley beer," Amunet said. "With honey."

I commanded my facial muscles not to wince at the yeasty sharp taste. I knew that this specially brewed beer was from an ancient recipe, as ancient and sacred as the Great Pyramids. My family had been brought up to prefer wine, in the Greek way, but we respected that most Egyptians preferred beer.

"Do you dream of the Goddess?" she asked.

I shook my head. "No. Do you?"

Lady Amunet laughed and shook her long black hair, threaded with silver, behind her. "Indeed I do. And I have dreamt of you wandering alone among rubble and ruins. And so when I saw you standing in the Goddess's shadow . . . well, I could not dismiss it as coincidental."

Ruins? What did that mean? "Are my parents safe in Actium?" I blurted.

The priestess paused. "Why do you ask me this question? The queen's War Council likely has more information than I do." She took another sip.

I did not say that I had hoped that perhaps the Goddess's magic had given her more information than anyone else had.

"However," she said. "My augurs indicate that all is not well. You must know that your parents have been trapped in Actium all winter, yes?"

I nodded even though I had not known. My stomach contracted in fear: Caesarion had never used the word "trapped."

"During their entrapment, a great sickness has swept through the general's camps. . . ."

My head shot up. "Is Mother all right?"

Amunet took another sip of beer. "As far as I know. But I worry that the general may have underestimated Octavianus."

"That is not possible," I cried. "Tata is the better general!"

"Granted," she said. "However, I fear that your father is like the Egyptian who hunts the crocodile but is felled by the small snake he either did not see or ignored."

I opened my mouth to argue, but the Lady of Isis spoke before I could. "Tell me about the amulet that hangs from your neck," she said.

I pulled the Isis knot from under my tunic and held it out to her. "This one?"

"Do you know what this knot means?"

"That I follow the Great Goddess," I said, remembering Mother's words.

Amunet took another sip. "Yes, but this particular amulet means you have been initiated into the Mysteries of Isis. Yet you have not, so I am curious as to how it is that you wear it around your neck."

"Mother gave it to me," I said.

"For safekeeping?"

"No. She gave it to me on the night we talked about Isis and why she is the One I must follow. It was after Euphronius took us to speak with a rabbi and we learned about the Hebrews' religion."

"And what did you learn that day?" she asked.

"That the Jews believe in only one male god and a strange concept he called 'free will.'"

"Why do you call it strange?"

"Because, well . . ." I did not know how to answer at first. It was strange to me because I hadn't completely understood it. I related the story of the Garden of Happiness the rabbi had told us. "He said their god gave his first people a command, but they had free will and disobeyed, bringing evil into the world. . . ." I trailed off.

Amunet stared at me over her shimmering cup of beer. "This idea of 'free will' is neither strange nor new — it is implicit in *ma'at*. What is strange is the belief that a woman making a choice brought evil to the world."

I took another sip of the beer, wondering if I had conveyed the story correctly. But I wondered too why the Priestess of Isis had brought me into this small chamber. Surely it wasn't to discuss what the Jews of Alexandria believed, was it?

"Tell me," she finally said. "Do the Greeks believe in free will?"

"No, we believe in the *Moirae* — the Three Fates who determine our lives at birth. One should not try to escape one's fate because it angers them and the gods. Even Zeus-Amun feared the *Moirae!*"

She nodded. "And what did the *Moirae* set as your fate, do you think?"

I looked at her, confused. Wasn't it obvious? "That I would be queen of Egypt, of course."

But my airway nearly closed as I realized that I would only become queen of Egypt if Mother *died*. I did not want Mother to die. Had my thoughtless rumination called Anubis to fall upon Mother? I quickly touched two fingers over my heart. *I take it back*, I begged Anubis. *O God of Judgment, Preserver of the Dead, Guardian to Hades. I beseech you to keep my mother safe.*

Amunet looked at me for a long moment. "The Seven Hathors and the *Moirae* may claim to set one's fate, but Lady Isis knows that you must still choose right action and live by the rules of *ma'at*. The question I have is whether your mother ignored the rule of *ma'at* by giving you that necklace. The queen knows the meaning of this amulet and who may or may not wear it. Why, then, did she give it to you? And why," she asked in almost a whisper, "would she go into *war* without it?"

Was Amunet going to tell me I had no right to it? Or worse, that my possession of it somehow endangered Mother?

"Isis of Pharia is your safe harbor," Amunet announced after an eternity of scrutiny. "Isis is your savior."

"What is she saving me *from*?" I asked. And more important, shouldn't she be saving *Mother*?

Lady Amunet continued looking at me without speaking, and I struggled not to fidget under her gaze. After a few moments, she rose and brought a white lotus to me. "Spit into it," she commanded.

I paused, but her dark eyes were insistent. I obeyed. She sat back on her heels, closed her eyes, and chanted in the old sacred tongue, plucking the petals my essence touched and casting them into a golden bowl filled with Nile water. The white petals swirled, some barely skimming the surface, others tilting their curved edges just under the water's skin. Amunet examined them and made a little noise in her throat, which alarmed me. What had she seen? What did it mean?

"Come with me," she finally said. I followed her out into the courtyard and into a small, windowless room that reeked of sweat and incense and something else too, sweet and familiar. I stood in front of a cartouche, trying to read the painted hieroglyphic symbols.

"It says, 'Isis Great of Magic,'" Amunet said quietly. "Even Ra was humbled by Isis's magic. It is a powerful force to harness."

"We are in the Room to Call Forth Isis's Magic?" I croaked in surprise. "You are going to do magic?"

"No. I am going to instruct *you* on how to cast the spell the Goddess bids me teach you," she said.

A spell? That *I* was to learn? My pulse quickened in fear and excitement.

Amunet lit a bowl of incense on a low table. The smell was sharp, bitter, and smoky, and I tried not to cough but could not help myself. "Frankincense," the priestess said. After murmuring instructions to a servant, she purified every corner with the incense smoke. The room grew hot and hazy. The servant returned, carrying a large bowl of a dark, viscous liquid and placed it in the center of the room. Amunet picked up an ivory elephant tusk covered in carved symbols, ciphers, and codes.

She stood with me in the center of the room, setting the bowl at my feet. Then she placed the tip of the horn onto the dirt floor and drew a circle of protection around us, chanting a prayer in the old language.

"Now you," she said, bidding me to repeat the secret words as I redrew the circle, which seemed to pulsate as we closed ourselves in. She dipped a brush made of goat hair into the liquid and watched as it dripped. I knew the sweet metallic scent then — blood. A bowl of blood. But from which sacrificed animal?

Amunet began painting with the thick, clotted liquid on the ground at our feet, dipping the goat-hair brush over and over again to make the lines thick and sharp. I could not make sense of the image, thinking at first it was a hieroglyph. But then she gave the brush to me. "Paint over the same lines," she instructed. "You must know the image. You must 'see' it to understand."

I did as she instructed, my eyes tearing from the smoke, my lungs burning with the heat and the clotted smell of fresh blood. Three times I painted over the image, waiting to see whatever I was supposed to see. It was only when my vision grew blurry from the smoke and my arm grew tired of repainting the lines that I understood. I dropped the brush in astonishment.

"Anubis!" I rasped. "This is the face of Anubis. Why are you having me call up the presence of the God of Death?"

CHAPTER SEVEN

"You must not fear the God of the West, He Who Judges Your Heart, Preserver of the Soul for Eternity," Amunet whispered.

My breathing came shallow as I tried to rein in my terror. The jackal-headed god of death and embalming! For what reason would she have me summon *him*? Was Anubis claiming me? But I did not want to die! Not yet!

"Do you feel his presence, child?" Amunet whispered in my ear. "We have called him to us with the blood of a freshly sacrificed black dog — the only way one can ever summon Anubis."

I stared down at the image in blood at my feet, the pointed ears and long snout that I had drawn myself. My throat felt tight, my hands trembled, and my breathing sounded as it did when I finally made it to the highest point in the Lighthouse. What else could this terror be except the god's presence? I nodded.

"Good," she breathed. "The Dark God has a strong presence in your life."

A small whimper escaped my throat, though I had commanded myself to be strong and act like a queen. In shame, I closed my eyes, trying to calm my breathing.

"That means," she continued, "that you may call on him in times of need to curse your enemies and protect the sons of Egypt."

"Protect the sons of Egypt — what does that mean?" I asked. "And how would I do that?"

Amunet stood, eyes closed, as if in a trance, the incense smoke swirling around her like serpents coiling up a tall column. Had she heard me? Should I ask again? I held my tongue, staring into her face. The smoke from the incense made my eyes burn, and I felt tears of both frustration and fear well up in them.

"You need only know how to *call* the Great Jackal God," she said quietly. "You cannot fail if you call him correctly."

But what would I need him for? I wanted to scream. *And him of all the gods! Why?*

Amunet's eyes opened almost with a snap. "Now," she said. "I teach you how to unbind the magic."

"But you must tell me why —"

She gave me a fierce look meant to quiet me. It worked. She sprinkled dirt over the blood-painted image in the reverse direction of our painting, then had me repeat the action. Amunet then redrew the circle with the ivory tusk, again in the reverse direction. When we stepped out of the circle, I took a deep, ragged breath as if something — the god? Fear? — had released me.

The priestess must have sensed my agitation, for she held up a hand. "I cannot answer your questions. I have been led simply to show you the Magic for Calling Forth Anubis. The gods do not explain themselves. Child, do not look so stricken!" she continued. "This is a spell of protection and empowerment. You will use it to save the sons of Egypt. And you will know when to call Him."

"But does . . , does that mean Anubis is my patron god and not the Great Goddess?"

Amunet turned to me with wide eyes. "Absolutely not! Anubis serves Isis, his true Mother, the one who raised him, and not the other way around. It is the Goddess who directs my hand in this. And it will be the Goddess who directs you to call upon her stepson, Anubis. That is all the gods privilege me to know."

I looked down, feeling chastened, but I did not know for what. Amunet clapped her hands, and servants began removing the remnants of her magic. I followed her out the door. "But how will I know the Goddess is directing me? Will I hear her voice?"

"The Goddess speaks to me in dreams and visions. Sometimes she speaks to me with unbidden thoughts. She may well speak to you in the same ways, but we cannot know."

Well, that did not help. "Will you teach me more magic?" I asked, thinking I would feel better if I knew magic beyond just calling up Anubis.

"After your first blood, you will begin training in the old language and the old ways. Then you will learn how to use Isis's magic. It is unusual, but not unheard of, for the Goddess to command a spell be learned before your apprenticeship."

"But what does it *mean*?" I asked again, hurrying after her as she led me toward the temple entrance, where Katep waited for me.

Amunet stopped and turned toward me. "Child, only the gods know what it 'means.' It is not for us to question the gods but to obey."

I followed more slowly after that, wondering where I had heard that phrase before. And then I remembered. Hadn't the rabbi said that very thing about their first man and woman? I shook my head, more confused than ever. How can humans have free will and choose *ma'at* if our only job is to obey?

Euginia normally roused me in the mornings by jumping onto my sleeping couch. Zosima often complained that she could hear our raucous laughter and whoops even down at the latrines. But one morning, I woke on my own, without her tickles or jumps. Had she overslept? I got up and padded into her room.

"Euginia, am I to be *your* lady this morning?" I asked, grinning as I prepared to launch myself onto *her* sleeping couch. But I straightened when I saw she was already out of bed. Her long hair was in disarray, her nostrils red, and her eyes puffy. She was putting all her finest tunics and dresses in one pile on the floor at her feet.

"What is the matter?" I asked, alarmed and confused.

"I must leave to join my father," she said.

"What? You cannot leave! This is where you live! And you . . . you are *mine*!"

She shook her head. "My father says the queen will lose the war. . . ."

I blew out air in surprise, but she continued.

"My tata has left Alexandria. He renounced his position and calls for us, for my family, to join him in exile. He has an estate in Heliopolis and wants to ride out the remainder of the war in safety there."

"He has turned traitor?" I asked in disbelief.

"No, not traitor," Euginia said. "Just . . . just . . . He says he wants to keep his family safe."

"But you have been consecrated to *me*," I cried. "You cannot leave!"

Euginia shook her head. "Our dedication ceremony was never sanctified by the priestesses, remember? We were to wait until after our first bloods. Tata says that I break no sacred law by leaving you now."

My thoughts spun in confusion. Was it true? Were Mother and Father actually *losing*? I knew they had been trapped in Actium for some time, but I never doubted that they would turn things around. Did Euginia's father know something I did not?

"What if . . . what if I commanded you to stay?" I asked, lifting my chin. "I can do that!"

Euginia's large eyes filled with tears.

"You would defy me?" I asked, stung.

"No. It is that I . . . . I cannot defy my father," she said. "If I don't come willingly, he will send guards to drag me away."

"But that is outrageous," I cried. "Our palace guards would protect you! If I gave the order, they would not even let them inside."

"My father has already made arrangements with King Caesarion. Your guards will step back."

I put my hands on my hips. "But why? And why would Caesarion be involved in this?"

"Because Father has told the king that if he does not allow us to slip away from Alexandria without notice, he will spread panic throughout the court and the city about what is really happening in Actium. So you see? We have no choice. I must go."

I could barely breathe as I took in her words. Was it true that my parents might lose the war? Impossible!

"I do not want you to go," I said, my voice dropping almost to a whisper.

"I do not want to leave either," Euginia said. "But . . . but when this is all over, when the queen returns triumphant, I will rejoin you as your lady. Then, by the Laws of Isis and Horus, we will never be parted again. That is a promise."

"I will hold you to it, sister," I said through a tight throat. And so the process of losing everyone I ever loved began.

Mother returned from Actium not long after. She decorated her flag-ship in victory flags and commanded her musicians to blare marches of triumph as she approached the Royal Harbor. All of Alexandria rejoiced that the queen had returned triumphant.

But it did not take long for everyone to learn that it had been all for show. Mother had not "won" at Actium; she had merely broken through the enemy's blockade. Father had broken through with her but then sailed for Libya to prepare his legions there to engage the enemy on land. We — along with all of Alexandria — only learned the truth of Mother's ruse after she executed traitors, those who had secretly and not so secretly supported Octavianus. Later I would learn that Euginia's father had been one of the executed.

But so grateful was I to have Mother safely back, I never questioned her need to eliminate her political enemies — or whether Euginia's father's attempt to keep his family safe actually constituted treason. I prayed only that Euginia would be safe and reminded myself that when every-thing was over, I would find her and bring her back to be my lady.

One night I visited Mother's chambers in what I still called the "deep-dark." She was poring over an untidy pile of scrolls, so I played with Hekate. The green-eyed creature seemed to have gone almost feral in Mother's long absence. She was not interested in the peacock feather I waved in front of her face; she only had eyes for Mother's bare ankles. Hekate crouched behind the shimmering mother-of-pearl screen across from Mother's desk, tensed her back legs — tail swishing — and pounced.

Mother yelped as Hekate bit and scratched her in one lightning strike, then skittered across the gleaming marble and onyx floor in a furious race for the antechamber.

Mother jumped out of her chair in a rage. "You wicked beast," she hissed. "How dare you!" She took one of the still-rolled scrolls on her desk and threw it with all her might into the other room.

I gasped. Never, not once, had I ever seen Mother react with such fury. Charmion and Iras both jumped up in alarm.

"Lady, no!" Iras said. "That is sacrilege! Bastet will surely exact revenge. . . ."

Mother rounded on her. "As if she has not punished me enough? Well, if the good goddess wants to attack me, she will know that I always fight back."

"But . . . ," I started, and Iras shook her head at me in warning. I closed my mouth.

Charmion made the sign for protection against evil and closed the door to the antechamber to keep the cat away. Mother's eyes, ringed by deep, almost purple shadows, seemed huge and feverish. She cursed wildly under her breath as she checked her now-bleeding ankle.

"Get me something," she ordered. Iras brought her a soft linen cloth and began blotting at the deep scratch, but Mother snatched the fabric from her and applied pressure herself. I had never seen her so agitated. She must have felt me watching her because she turned to me, eyes blazing.

"You come in here and rile that creature up with your ridiculous games! This is *your* fault. I need you to leave now!"

"But I did not do anything. I —"

"Go! Take that odious feather with you and GET OUT!"

I looked up at her, frozen in shock, afraid and yet furious that she was blaming me for the cat's attack. Then I threw the feather down and ran out of her room.

Katep, who had been dozing on a bench across the hall, jumped up. "What is wrong?"

"Leave me alone!" I shouted, and ran back to my rooms. I was too agitated to go into my chamber, so I paced outside it, waiting for Katep. To my surprise, Charmion walked beside him.

"Little Moon . . . ," Charmion said.

"I am *not* so little anymore, if you haven't noticed," I spat.

She sighed. "I would like to explain," she said, "about the pressure on the queen right now. Come with me."

Katep handed her a small oil lamp, and my mother's lady and I moved into one of the side gardens ideal for private conversations. Date palms ruffled in the breeze, gray and mysterious in the dark. Occasional gusts of wind, rich with the smells of the sea, teased the scents out of sleeping lotus, jasmine, rose, and honeysuckle blooms. I never again smelled a combination so achingly beautiful — the cool salt of the sea intermingling with the heady perfume of Egyptian blossoms. I filled my lungs with the richness of it, trying to suppress the maddening hiccups that sometimes followed my tears.

"You must understand," Charmion said, her tall, willowy body bending to sit on a marble bench. I sat down next to her. "Your mother has been planning a way to save all our lives, but she only today discovered that one of the kings of Arabia destroyed everything."

I looked at her, not comprehending.

"Let me back up. Octavianus, as you know, is on his way to capture Alexandria." She paused, searching my face. "Did you know?"

I shook my head. This was a surprise, as I had thought that the worst was over. After all, Mother was home safe.

"It appears Octavianus has not come after us right away because he intends on sweeping through all of the kingdoms and provinces of the East to bring them under his sole control first. Then he will attack."

I swallowed, trying to accept the idea that we were in terrible danger. "Why isn't Father stopping him?" I asked.

"He cannot. He went to Libya to marshal his land forces, only to discover his general in command there — indeed, all of his generals and legions — defected to Octavianus. He has no army left except his forces here in Alexandria."

All his men abandoned him? *Gods!* Poor Tata. "Is he all right? Where is he now?"

"He is still in Libya. But although your father cannot fight, your mother has not given up hope. She planned to save us all by sailing to India. King Porus agreed to provide protection."

"You mean we would leave Alexandria and Egypt to Octavianus?" I stood up. Impossible! "Mother would never abandon Egypt. *I* would never do so!"

"Not 'abandon,' no. See, it was all part of the plan. She hoped that with the House of Ptolemy out of Alexandria, Octavianus would be merciful and not destroy the city. Then, with sufficient money and time, she would attempt to negotiate an agreement with him — perhaps to stay in exile and allow Caesarion to rule in her stead."

For Mother, for all of us, to be exiled from our beloved Egypt — unimaginable! To leave it for Rome to pick over like a vulture? I shuddered and sat back down heavily. Until that moment, I had not understood the severity of our situation.

"So why can we not do what she planned?"

"King Malchus of Nabatea burned her entire fleet. We could not sail on the Mediterranean, which Octavianus now controls. So your mother had her fleet pulled overland toward the Red Sea. We would sail to India from there. But the Nabateans of Arabia — hoping to score points with Octavianus — intercepted the fleet and destroyed it all. Your mother only learned today that her escape is burning on the desert sands."

"But Octavianus declared war on Mother, right? So if she abdicates the throne, then he will leave us alone, yes?"

Charmion snorted. "Octavianus wants only two things: the death of your father and Egypt's wealth. Greedy Romans have been waiting for the chance to seize Egypt for decades. And now he has the excuse to do just that. So you see, when Hekate attacked your mother . . . Well, it was as if Bastet herself was smiting her."

I shivered as a sense of dread sunk into my bones. We sat in silence, the little oil lamp's flame sputtering with the occasional sea breeze. I did not know what to say.

As the sky lightened, I turned to see a young gazelle, mouth full of a bright red hibiscus flower, enter our alcove. The tame animal stopped at the sight of us.

"Don't move," whispered Charmion. "Amisi," she called in a soft voice. "Do not be afraid. We will not hurt you."

"Amisi?" The Egyptian word for flower struck me as a strange name for a gazelle.

Charmion pulled another hibiscus from the bush next to her and held it out to the timid creature. "Yes," she murmured, smiling. "We call him that because that is all he eats. Amisi has such an appetite for flowers, he has been known to follow the flower gatherers straight into the palace, munching all the while from their baskets."

I smiled at the image. Amisi, true to his name, came toward Charmion's outstretched hand. I watched as the first light of the sun, streaming through the palm fronds, lit his fur, a beautiful desert-sand color separated from his white belly by a stripe as dark as ebony.

What will happen to you, little creature, when the Romans invade? I wondered, swallowing the tightness in my throat. *What will happen to all of us?*

CHAPTER EIGHT

In the Twenty-first Year of My Mother's Reign

In My Eleventh Year (30 BCE)

After being betrayed by almost every Roman he knew, Father returned to Alexandria a broken man. He seemed brittle, spent, his muscles rangy rather than voluptuous, his curls shot through with gray rather than shining with dark luster. My heartbroken tata was a general without an army, a Roman without Rome.

Tata had little time for or interest in us, his children. I ached for his loud laughter and outrageous game playing, but he took to spending whole days by himself in a small house on Pharos he called the *Timonium*. I worried more about Tata's withdrawal into himself than Octavianus's impending invasion, which seemed somehow unreal. Everybody talked about it, but nothing ever happened. My parents' distress was more immediate and troubling. Would I ever see them smile again?

Months passed, and the seas closed for the winter. Still no sign of Octavianus. My family and all of Alexandria turned inward, like a lotus closing its petals at night. I remember little about that winter except the quiet meals and the distracted, almost helpless look on my parents' faces.

But as spring approached, Mother and Father seemed happy again. I did not know then that it was the happiness of the resigned, of those who had given themselves up to their fates.

In late spring, Caesarion convinced my parents that he was due a manhood ceremony. After all, hadn't he ruled Egypt during their absence? He deserved to be seen as the man he was and not just a boy-king.

My family — and all of Alexandria — embraced our young king's ascension to manhood as a symbol of hope for the future. Caesarion was a good king. And a good king deserved an even better celebration, which Tata held for him in the Roman fashion, with a raucous, wine-soaked feast in the name of the Roman god Liber and his consort, Libera, the gods of inebriation and fertility.

"I propose a toast!" Tata called at the feast that night. The large banquet room erupted in cheers. Father looked less haggard than he had when he first returned from Actium, but a tiredness still emanated from him, even at his most jovial. "A toast!" he repeated, standing a bit unsteadily, his face flushed and sweaty in the flickering torchlight. I looked at his hands and saw no Eye of Horus ring. When had he stopped wearing it? Was that why Octavianus had won?

Father held his wine goblet aloft, waiting for everyone to join him. Ptolly danced to the music of panpipes and lyres, holding his little cup of watered wine over his head. With his mischievous grin, all he needed were horns to look like a baby satyr.

I turned, searching for my cup. Had someone taken it by accident? I did not wish to bring ill luck upon Caesarion by not toasting him. I tried to catch the eye of a servant as Father began his speech. Where was my cup? And where was Zosima?

Father must have finished speaking, for the room erupted in applause and people began to drink in Caesarion's honor. I needed to add my blessing! I was about to take Alexandros's cup from him when a servant shoved a goblet of wine into my hand. Quickly, I brought the cup to my lips.

I heard a crack and felt a stinging pain on my cheek and jaw. I yelped in surprise as dark liquid arced out of my chalice and I fell over. What had happened?

The room grew quiet. Mother stood over me, and the rage and fury on her face made my blood run cold. "You stupid girl," she hissed. "Do you not know better than to take a cup of untasted wine?"

Mother had slapped me — and the wine cup out of my hand — so hard I had crashed to the ground. I held my cheek and scrambled up, straightening my dress. The banquet room hushed as everyone stared at me, and my cheeks burned with shame. Mother signaled her royal guards to find the servant boy who had given me the cup. Apparently, he had raced out of the room as soon as he thrust it into my hands. The room roiled with whispers and murmurs. Within moments, the guards returned, dragging a struggling, barefoot Egyptian youth to face Mother.

"Was it poisoned?" she asked the boy in a slow, dangerous tone.

He shook his head.

Mother stared at him. "Then drink it," she commanded, signaling for the cup to be picked up from the floor. "There is enough there for a sip or two."

The boy's eyes grew wide with fear.

The room became so silent, you could hear the leather of the soldiers' cuirasses creaking as they fought to hold the now-panicked boy.

"Drink it," the queen said again. Somebody placed the cup that had flown out of my hand in front of the boy.

A third royal guard took a dagger and held it at the boy's neck. "You heard the queen," he said. "Either drink this now, or I fill the goblet with your blood when I slit your throat."

The servant's black eyes blazed with resentment as he put his mouth to the cup. The soldier tipped it all the way back, forcing the liquid out the sides of the boy's mouth, like tiny rivulets of blood. When he removed the cup, the boy turned his face in my direction and locked his eyes on mine. He mumbled something at me in old Egyptian, and I shrank back. What awful punishment had he called the gods to rain down on me?

Within minutes, the boy began to sweat and convulse. The poison must have been very strong to work in such a small amount. His muscles tensed and seized, and the guards dragged him out of the banquet room to die in the kitchens. The last I saw of him were his twitching bare feet, the soles caked with grime.

"Danger averted!" Father boomed in a jolly voice. "The queen, as always, the Divine Protector of her children and her people." He turned to her and lifted his cup, his eyes flicking to me for a moment.

The guests lifted their cups to Mother and yelled, "Hail the Savior of Egypt!"

I understood the message from Father. *Act as if nothing happened.* I smiled and waved to show my fortitude in the face of danger, and sat down. But inside, I trembled. After everybody had drained another cup, I snuck a look at Mother and saw her talking into Charmion's ear. I was seized with a sense of unreality. Had someone really just tried to kill me?

Alexandros leaned over Iotape. "Are you all right?" he asked. "You did not drink any of the wine, did you?"

I shook my head, my throat tight. *Isis, please do not let me lose control now,* I begged. I took deep breaths to keep the tears at bay. I looked back at Mother and saw her signaling someone behind me. Then she turned and smiled at a guest who had come to talk to her.

Zosima took me by the arm. "Come," she whispered in my ear. "Let us go back to your chamber."

At the same moment, Father lifted his cup again toward Caesarion, who sat with the sons of Mother's most loyal advisers. "Let us make another toast to Liber, the god of drink and sex!" he said. "Now that you are old enough to enjoy *both*!"

The guests whistled and made catcalls. Caesarion, also flushed, held up his cup and in a boastful voice said, "You're too late on both counts, stepfather. Especially sex!"

Tata threw back his head and laughed. "Gods! Well, I hope not just with your companions!"

The banquet room erupted in loud laughter, cheers, and whistles. *How could they go on as if nothing happened?* I thought. Zosima led me around the crowded dining couches and out of the banquet room.

"Sit," she said, once we were in my chamber. "You are all right now. There is nothing to fear."

Fear? How could I explain that I was not afraid? I was humiliated, confused, angry. But not afraid. Or at least not yet.

Olympus, Mother's royal physician, walked into our chamber. "Did any of the wine touch your lips?" he boomed.

"N-no. I do not think so."

"Well, we must cleanse your system as a precaution anyway."

"Not the leeches!" I gasped. I *hated* that treatment! I shivered at the very idea.

"No, something that works faster. An emetic or purgative. Actually, both." When Olympus saw my face, he added, "This is merely a safeguard. Your mother was very clear about it. She wants to be sure not even an *atomos* of poison entered your system."

I felt slightly relieved that Mother cared enough to drag her beloved physician out of bed, but not much. "I swear. No wine touched my lips!"

Olympus ignored me. "Open your mouth and let me smell your breath," he said. I did as I was told. He furrowed his brow, muttering about humors.

"What was the poison?" Zosima asked.

"I am not sure. I could not tell from smelling the cup. I will check the boy next to see what I can learn from the form of his death."

I shuddered. He turned back to me, patting my knee. "Well, I'm sorry, child. You are going to have a very uncomfortable time of it soon." He looked at Zosima. "Actually, I should be apologizing to you, should I not?"

Not long after taking Olympus's purging potion, I wanted nothing more than to have died of the poisoned wine. At least that would have been over quickly. The potion worked on both my stomach and bowels. Whether it was the royal physician's treatment or the poison or a combination of the two, the violence of my reaction to the medicine put me into the Sleep That Is Not Quite Death.

My *ba*-soul traveled to strange places. Once I found myself alone in the Soma, the sacred Tomb of Alexander. A torch flared, and I saw Amut the Destroyer, the crocodile-headed, lion-bellied, hippo-legged monster, leering at me from across the room, its sharp teeth stained and dripping red. Amut, I knew, devoured the hearts of the damned, keeping them from entering the Endless Afterlife and reuniting with all whom they once loved.

"Is that the poisoned wine?" I asked as red liquid oozed from its mouth in thick, goopy rivulets.

The monster chuckled in an awful, growling way. "No, little queen, it is my mouth watering." Such a stench of putrid decay came from its open mouth that I gagged and retched.

In another journey, I found myself lying on the stone floor of the tombs of all my ancestors. The air smelled of dust and decay, and I shivered in the chill. I looked up to see Anubis, his black fur gleaming, his gold-tipped ears twitching. Had I called him? But I did not remember using Amunet's spell.

I found I had no fear as I stared up at the jackal head of the magnificent shining god. He was so beautiful, in fact, I realized I was smiling at him. My blood ran cold, though, when I saw Amut emerge from the darkness beside him.

Anubis looked down upon me. "Ah, poor little one," he said. "There are many from your line of kings soon to come."

I sat up in a panic. "What do you mean? What are you saying?" I begged, my voice echoing in the dark, cavernous tomb.

Amut grinned. "Oh, tsk, tsk," the monster growled. "Questioning a god. Where is your respect? Surely I shall have your heart now." It smacked its lips.

I put my hands over my heart. "No! You cannot have it! I have done nothing wrong. And I am not dead!" But did I know that? Perhaps my *ba*-soul had indeed flown to the Land of the West.

"I am being called," Anubis muttered, lifting his snout to sniff the air.

"Do not leave me," I cried. I felt safe in the presence of the God of Death. It was Amut who terrified me.

Anubis turned back to me. "Remember," he said. "You must call upon me to save the sons of Egypt."

But who was going to save *me* — the daughter of Egypt? Before I could say anything, he blinked his great dark eyes and began fading into black smoke.

Amut lingered. "I must follow my master," it growled, puffing its hot, putrid breath into my ear. "But not without first leaving you a gift." It gave a gruesome chuckle. "I have awoken the souls of your murderous ancestors whose hearts I have devoured. The poor things could not get into happy *Aaru*. They are here, and it is *you* who will pay for their sins. Do not let them touch you now!"

Amut laughed, the sound fading slowly away. I heard the murmur of voices, men and women — some angry, some moaning. I curled up tighter as terror made breathing difficult. How many of my ancestors had failed Anubis's tests? I thought of the early Ptolemies and the many murders they committed in the name of power, of the rumors that Mother had murdered her own brother and sister in a furious bid to keep her throne. I shook my head. It couldn't be true.

But I could not deny the truth of my history lessons. My royal line teemed with murderers, liars, and backstabbers. According to my Greek upbringing, we, their descendants, would face punishments for their sins. The murmurs and voices grew louder, and I trembled at the unfairness of it. Why would the gods punish *me* for crimes committed generations ago? I pressed my face into the ground in terror, breathing in the powder of my ancestors' bones.

Isis, please keep the restless, devouring spirits away, I begged. Still the avenging spirits continued moving toward me. "Isis, *please*," I pleaded out loud. "Save me!" Hadn't Amunet called her my "savior"?

I felt it before I saw it — a warm, brilliant golden light. The Goddess in all her glory had come. She had come! My heart soared at the sight of her. At first she floated over me, looking like Mother had — gleaming in gold — during so many religious festivals. Then her features melted into the face of the Isis statue on Pharos as she stared out to sea.

"Isis, Mother of All," I whispered, "keep the angry spirits away from me."

She continued staring into the distance. Why was she ignoring me? "Are you punishing me?" I asked.

"Soon it may seem so, but know that I am not." Her voice was as cool and calming as the breeze off the Nile. "My time is short here," she said.

"No, please do not leave me. Stay with me, *please* —"

Her expression was filled with such grief and love and sadness and joy at once that my heart ached. "I will be sent away," she said. "They will desecrate my temples and abandon me to their new gods."

I felt rage burst up my chest. Why was she speaking about herself? Didn't she realize I needed her help? "Please save me from Amut," I prayed. "Tell me what to do!"

The Goddess took her golden shawl and covered her head with it in a gesture of mourning. "Do not forget me, daughter. It is the only way."

"But why are you forgetting *me*?" I sobbed at her abandonment. I was her daughter! Her loyal servant. Didn't she understand that I wanted her — *needed* her — to lift me up out of this dark place and bring me into the light?

I must have spoken those words aloud, for the Goddess turned to me. Head still covered, she laughed quietly, a melodious and sorrowful sound. "Those who destroy me will also claim that they are emerging from the dark into the light. It is how they will justify themselves."

I did not understand. Was the Goddess mocking me? Despair flooded in.

"Poor little daughter," Isis murmured. I looked up in surprise to see her push the shawl of mourning away from her head. She reached down to where I lay, as slow and graceful a movement as a sail unfurling on the Nile. "Cleave to me in your heart," she said. "I will help you, I promise, even as they destroy me."

None of her words made sense to me — not then, anyway. But at the touch of her warm palm on the top of my head, calm entered my heart. Golden light, as thick and slow-moving as honey, poured over me, around me, lifted me, and held me — suspended — in a pool of sweet peace.

"Well, you have had a time of it!" Mother said, smiling down at me.

I looked at her, confused. A time of what? And why was I in her antechamber? Hekate padded over my chest and butted her head against my cheek, purring. I noticed the small cat's swollen belly and smiled.

"Hekate is full with babies!" I announced, surprised to hear my words come out in nothing stronger than a whisper. Mother smiled, and I realized she already knew. She sat down on the sleeping couch next to me.

"Why did that boy try to poison me?" I asked.

Mother sighed. "We uncovered a plot by a group of fanatical followers of the old ways — Egyptians who see the upcoming invasion as an opportunity to overthrow Greek rule and protect themselves from the Roman invasion. 'Egypt for Egyptians' was their motto, I believe."

"Was?"

"Yes. The group has been rooted out, though I am sure another will sprout up in its place. This one began with a young priest from the Temple of Ptah in Memphis. Unfortunately, they saw an opening with you — and you paid the price."

Mother looked down and rubbed my arm. I followed her gaze and saw small red indentations. "Ugh!" I cried. "Leeches! Olympus used leeches on me!"

"It saved your life, daughter. But at least you were not awake to see it."

I shuddered and turned my head to the side. I did not want to look upon the evidence of the treatment. "Mother . . . ," I whispered.

"Yes?"

"What is going to happen to us?"

She stiffened. "I am negotiating with Octavianus for your safety." Her tone had gone cold and official again.

I tried to sit up but found I was weaker than I'd thought. "What does that mean?"

"It means I will abdicate my throne if he will allow Caesarion to rule and allow you and your brothers to live in Egypt."

I stared at my mother, wide-eyed. *Abdicate* her throne? Had it really come to the that? "But where would you go? What would you do?"

She paused. "It does not matter as long as my children live and rule in Egypt."

"What does he answer?"

"Let us just say that he made a counteroffer."

"What was it?"

Mother stood up. "Rest, daughter. I can see how tired you are." She touched my cheek and left the room.

It was only later I learned that the queen of Egypt had offered more than her crown to Octavianus in exchange for our survival — she had offered her very *life* if he would guarantee our safety in Egypt. And the man who would rule the world told her she could keep her throne and her life on one condition: that she murder Father for him.

Of course, Mother did no such thing. Nor did she deliver him to Octavianus as a prisoner, as he also requested. Whether it was love or devotion or a combination of both, Mother never wavered in her loyalty to Tata, despite the vile rumors Romans spread about her later.

The morning I was to return to my own rooms, Father sauntered in from Mother's inner chamber. I did not remember him passing through the antechamber the night before. Tata looked slightly rumpled in his casual brown tunic, his face a bit bristly. He would head for the baths soon, I knew.

"All right, daughter, for your last day in my personal gambling den, we play for high stakes," he said, rolling the crystal Roman dice in his large square hands. Tata had been teaching me a game called *Jactus*.

"I am ready!" I said, sitting up.

He cocked an eyebrow at me. "How many times must I tell you? You must appear reluctant, hesitant, as if your fine sensibility had never even considered sullying your hands with such a base sport!"

I crossed my arms. "Do you tell Alexandros the same thing?"

He laughed. "Of course not! But you are a girl. A smart girl can get away with such an act and catch her opponent off guard. It is all in the attitude!"

"Tata! This is a game of chance! How could catching my opponent off guard help me?"

Father smirked. "You will see when you are older. It is an art your mother has perfected."

I did not know what he meant, and I did not care either. I just wanted to play. Father unfolded a small wooden tray with raised sides and put it on the couch next to me.

"Put your *denarius* in the center, girl. I feel lucky."

"I thought we were playing for higher stakes today," I said as I moved one of my Roman coins next to his on the end table.

"Well, then, put two in!"

I added another coin from my pile and moved an additional coin from his. Father poured the dice in the *turricula* and shook it up. "Gods, I love that sound!" he said.

"Wait, why do you get to go first?" I complained.

"Because I, my good child, *can*." Father dragged a bronze-legged, red leather folding stool closer to me and sat, leaning forward. He shook the dice again and tossed them with a flourish, watching them bounce on the wood with an exaggerated frown of concentration.

I grinned at his playfulness and experienced a sense of unreality, of time stretching and slowing. I saw how Tata's warm brown eyes twinkled, despite his pretense of cutthroat competitiveness. I noticed the close-cropped curls, tousled and grayer than ever; the way the muscles on his bronzed, battle-scarred arms flexed and relaxed as he put his elbows on his knees and leaned forward to see how the die fell. I took in the slow, sideways grin that spread over his face as he calculated the result of his toss.

In that strange, exaggerated moment, I wondered how it was possible to play a friendly game of *Jactus* with Father at the same time that Roman armies swarmed toward us like a vast cloud of locusts, bent on destroying everything we held dear. How could anyone hate my playful tata — or us — that much? I knew Father was flawed, but even the gods had their weaknesses, did they not? I looked down at my hands as my heart swelled with affection and love for my tata.

Time returned to its regular pace as Father reacted to his throw. "Ha! All different — the *Venus*. My take." With a flourish, he swept the four coins in the center toward his pile and indicated with his head that I should replace them with two more.

"Fortuna is with me this morning," he announced. I knew that, ever since all his legions abandoned him, Father felt abandoned by the goddess of luck too. I remember thinking I should tell Fortuna that I would happily lose at *Jactus* forever if it meant she would smile upon Father when it really counted.

I snatched the *turricula* out of Father's hand, poured the dice in, covered the top with my palm, and shook it with all my might. I closed my eyes and breathed on the dice, whispering, "Isis, Isis," then tossed them onto the little tray.

"*Duplex!*" Father roared with a laugh and slapped his thigh. "Two sixes. You have to *add* six coins to the pot. Which I will soon win, I might add."

He rubbed his hands together. I frowned. At this rate, I would lose all my coins too quickly, and I wanted to keep the game going as long as possible. Tata leaned toward me, looking around as if he had a special secret he did not want overheard. His eyes danced.

"Your first mistake was invoking Isis," he whispered with mock seriousness. "Trust me on this, daughter. Dionysus would have been a *much* better choice!"

CHAPTER NINE

As Octavianus approached by land and sea on those last days of late summer, Caesarion, at Mother's urging, fled across the Arabian desert on the way to India. Mother kept us in Alexandria, gambling that Octavianus would not hurt small children. As soon as she got word of Caesarion's safe arrival, she would send us to him in secret.

In the meantime, she took all of her personal treasure — vast mounds of gold, silver, pearls, emeralds, ebony, ivory, and cinnamon — and stacked it over great heaps of kindling wood in her mausoleum. She would set it aflame, leaving Octavianus no way to pay his army if he did not guarantee our safety.

The night before Father and his remaining men would face Octavianus's invading army, my parents seemed especially tender toward each other. I caught Mother tracing the line of Father's jaw and Father running his fingers up and down Mother's arm. When Zosima came to remove us from the *triclinium*, Father signaled us to approach. He grabbed Ptolly and kissed him on the neck, then made blowing noises on his stomach that made my almost-six-year-old brother shriek with joy. When Nafre took Ptolly away — the boy beaming with pride and confidence in his tata — Father watched him for a long time. Then he looked at Alexandros and me.

"I want to remind you of something very important," Father said. "If Octavianus threatens you . . ."

"He will not because he will not win, Tata," Alexandros said, outrage in his voice.

Father sighed. He looked at the floor for a moment, then back up at us. "Just listen. You must remember this. You are the children of Marcus Antonius. By virtue of that and of my bequest, you are full Roman citizens. . . ."

"We know that! Why are you telling us this?" Alexandros said, sounding even more scared and irritated. My heart had begun to race too.

"It is important you know this about Romans. The phrase, 'I am a Roman citizen,' is very powerful — almost sacred. Remember to use it."

I cut my eyes to Mother. She stared off in the distance, her face turned away from us.

"Stop it, Father!" Alexandros whispered. "I want to wish you luck for tomorrow."

Tata smiled. "Yes. Thank you. Come here, my son, the sun." He grabbed my brother in a huge bear hug and pinned him down on his couch in a mock wrestling move. Alexandros grinned and pretended to fight back. Father held him down and kissed him on his forehead. "Boy!" he said playfully. "Why were you not ready for that move? You must always be prepared for the surprise attack!"

"I will be ready next time. You will see," Alexandros said.

My heart lurched. Why these long good nights? Usually, Father roared a farewell by lifting his goblet to us or offered a quick kiss with a pat on the bottom when it was time for us to retire.

"Tata, please don't fight tomorrow," I whispered as my twin left the room. At that, Mother stood up and walked away.

"I must," Tata said. "There is no greater honor for a general than to die with his men."

"Then you think you will be defeated? How can you go into battle thinking that way?" I asked.

"I did not say that. But I would not be a good general if I did not know the odds."

"Tata, please!" I fought the urge to put my hands to my ears. I did not want to hear this. I needed to hear that everything would be all right, that Father would rout Octavianus's army and that the world would continue as I had always known it. I must have covered my ears anyway, for I felt Father's big warm hands move them away from my face. He looked at my palms and gently kissed the center of each one.

"You have your mother's hands," he murmured.

A surge of fear-fueled anger flowed through me. I jerked my hands out of his. "I will *not* say good-bye, Father! You cannot make me! You will come back tomorrow. And if you do not . . . I . . . I will find you wherever you are and . . . and . . ."

To my horror, Father threw back his head and laughed. "Come here," he said, grabbing me in a bear hug and holding me hard against him. "My little Cleopatra."

I hugged him back with all my might. Tata kissed my cheek, pushed me away, and said, "Now go on. Go to bed, my little beloved."

I ran to my chamber. *These are tears of anger*, I told myself. *Queens do not weep like little children. I am my mother's daughter. I will control my emotions.*

I knew Father marched out well before sunrise, for I heard the preparations — the muffled voices of men in the dark, the creaking of leather, the jangling of weapons — when I woke briefly before drifting back to sleep.

Quiet settled on the entire palace like a shroud. For comfort that morning, my brothers and I sought one another out in the main playroom. Iotape and her nurse came too. Ptolly teased his cat, Sebi — one of the kittens that Hekate had birthed — with a braided papyrus rope, cackling every time he pulled it just out of reach.

"Sebi will get angry if you do not let him win sometimes," I warned, wondering where my own kitten, Tanafriti, had gone. Ptolly, as usual, ignored me.

Iotape and Alexandros whispered to each other. I crossed my arms and stared at them until they noticed me.

"What?" Alexandros asked.

"What were you whispering about?"

Alexandros rubbed his eyes. "We are planning on running away," he said in a flat tone.

Before I could respond to this shocking remark, a wail erupted from somewhere deep inside the palace. Our heads snapped up and we looked at one another with wide eyes. "What is happening?" Ptolly whispered. "Was that a ghost?"

Nafre came over to him and picked him up. "Come here, my little prince. It is nothing. I think one of the cooks must have dropped his prized dish, that is all."

Ptolly allowed himself to be taken to the corner, where he snuggled up to a reclining Nafre. I looked at Alexandros.

"What do you think has happened?" he asked.

"We should find out," I whispered. I turned and bid him follow me.

"Come back here!" Zosima yelled once she realized what we were up to. "You must stay here!"

We dashed out into the hall. "Quick, separate," I ordered. "I will take the north wing, you take the south."

I raced off. I turned to see my twin, wide-eyed, still as a statue. He spun as if to go back to Iotape. "Go!" I hissed. "We'll meet up later by the lotus pool."

My footsteps echoed in the empty hallways. Where was everybody? I rounded a corner and saw an old Egyptian servant carrying a linen sack stuffed with palace goods. He stopped when he saw me, his eyes wide with fear.

"May Isis protect you, Daughter of Ra," the old man said, bowing his head.

"What is happening?" I asked in Egyptian.

"All . . . all of the general's men have surrendered to the other Romans. His navy rowed out as if to engage but then put up all their oars in surrender."

Father's men betrayed him *again*?

"And . . . and now," the old man continued, "we hear that his cavalry has surrendered too."

Isis! Poor Tata!

The old man ran away. I stood frozen. What would happen now? Mother would know. I raced to Mother's study, sure she was there.

I burst into the room only to find it empty. Another round of wailing. Gods, why did old women do that! *Think*, I told myself. *Think, think.* Mother would have insisted on seeing for herself how events unfolded, wouldn't she? I thought of King Priam watching Hector battle Achilles from the high walls of Troy. Yes, she would want to watch. But from which observation terrace? My mind raced.

That was when I heard Father's voice, roaring for Mother. He sounded full of rage and despair.

"Cleopatra! Where is everybody? Gods-be-damned, someone answer me! Where is the queen?"

To my horror, I heard his hobnailed military boots marching my way, toward Mother's study. They had forbidden me to come in here without permission. He would be furious that I had disobeyed.

Hide! But where? I dove under Mother's great ebony desk, using the gold-trimmed, backless bench to hide myself from view.

"Cleopatra!" Father roared as he burst into the room. "They betrayed me! To a man, they betrayed me! *Cacat!* Where is she?"

Tata threw his helmet across the room in a rage. I froze at the thunderous, echoing sound of metal crashing against marble, watching his red-crested helmet bounce and wobble on the floor across from me.

"Eros! Where is . . ."

The wailing began again and Father stopped. He muttered a curse when his man came into the room.

"By the gods, Eros. Where is everybody? Where is Cleopatra?"

I could not see Eros's face, but he sounded panicked. "Sire . . . um . . ."

"Spit it out, man!"

"The queen . . ."

Silence. My heart pounded in my ears.

"What? Where is she? I need to see her. They have all betrayed me! All of them!"

"The old women," continued Eros. "They . . . they say a messenger came crying that the queen is dead."

Not possible. Not true. Not true.

"You lie!" It sounded as if Father slapped Eros.

"Sire, please," Eros begged. "They say she was told you had been felled and she could not bear it, so she locked herself in her mausoleum. . . ."

"No! That is not what we planned!" Father seemed to be panting.

"What did you plan, *dominus*?"

"That she would go to the mausoleum only at the signal of my death. And that she would threaten to torch it if that little worm threatened the children. She couldn't have . . ."

I felt my eyes widen. Tata had expected to die? And then I understood. He had intended a warrior's honorable death in battle, but Octavianus took even that from him.

"One of her ladies came weeping into the palace, claiming the queen . . . killed herself over the grief. . . ."

"No! By the gods, this cannot be happening!"

I could not breathe. I could not speak. I wanted to jump out and punch Eros. But the wails of despair around the palace grew. I put my hands over my ears. This was not happening. This was not happening. It was not possible for Mother to die and me not know it.

With my ears covered, Father sounded as if he were underwater. I heard something clang to the floor. Eros: "No, I cannot!"

Father, as if from far away. "Do it, I command you."

A clatter. A fall. A man on the floor. Eros! Blood spurted from his neck and covered the floor in a thick, fast-moving torrent. I recoiled, scrunching even tighter into myself under the desk. Eros's hand clutched Father's sword. Goddess, he cut his own throat! But why? What had Father asked him to do?

I felt weighted down, as if Anubis himself had bound me in his sacred bandages. I saw Father reach down toward Eros's twitching hand and twist his short sword out of it. Eros made gurgling, gasping sounds.

"Eros, you honor me with your faithfulness," Father said.

As if the Goddess herself whispered in my ear, I suddenly understood exactly what Father intended to do. The dreamlike heaviness evaporated, and I shot out from under the desk, tripping over the heavy gilded bench as it skidded out of my way on the slick, bloody marble.

But I was not quick enough. Father, on his knees, had balanced his sword on the floor, the shining tip at his chest. In one sudden movement, he threw his weight onto the weapon.

"Tata, no!" I cried.

He turned to me, slowly as if in a dream, his eyes wide. "Daughter . . . ?" He lifted one hand. "Go, go!" he rasped.

I watched, helpless, as he closed his eyes, groaning in pain. He tried to draw a deep breath, and blood flowed fast and dark over his tunic and leather fighting kilt, running in rivulets down his thighs.

"Tata!"

I ran to the door and yelled for Olympus, for anybody, to come and help. Then I raced back to him. Tata had fallen on his side. I tried not to look, but I saw the tip of the blade just poking out through his tunic in the back.

People rushed in. I heard muttered prayers, in Greek and in Egyptian. Someone else yelled for Olympus.

I knelt by Father. "Do not die, Tata, please! The physician is coming!"

He stared up at me. His usually twinkling brown eyes looked muddy and dark. He blinked slowly. "I missed the heart," he muttered.

I began to cry. His blood pooled at my knees. I held his head and kissed his forehead. He closed his eyes. "Little Cleopatra, go." Then, after a shudder of pain passed: "Why did nobody warn me . . . hurts so much? You would think *someone* . . . mention it."

I could not smile, even though I guessed that was what he was trying to make me do. I rocked and stroked his face and prayed. "Isis, help us. Help us, Isis, please."

Tata closed his eyes, murmuring, "Told you before . . . Dionysus . . . better."

He coughed. Blood filled his mouth. The room crowded with onlookers. Where was Olympus?

One of Mother's Royal Guards appeared. He cursed in Greek at the sight of Eros and Father. He knelt at Tata's side and, to my shock, pulled out the sword that impaled him. I squeezed my eyes shut when I realized what he was doing, but I could not keep from hearing the sucking, scraping sound as the metal left Father's body, or the pitiful groan that escaped Father's lips.

"I order you . . . ," Father said, looking up at the man, panting in agony. "Finish the job."

But the wide-eyed guard did not move. He looked as frozen as I had felt, the sword still dripping in his hands. Olympus ran into the room. "The servants say Antonius has run himself through —"

"As always . . . on top of things," Tata panted. "Finish . . ."

The physician's eyes traveled from Father to the sword and up to the guard's face. "You idiot!" he yelled in Greek. "Now I never will be able to stanch the blood!"

The guard dropped the sword in fear and backed out of the room. Olympus yelled for clean bandages and began pressing the cloths on Father's chest and back. Father tried to use his forearms to push him away, but he was too weak.

"Stop!" he groaned. "You . . . steal my *dignitas!*"

But the physician kept on. The thick, sweet, metallic smell of blood filled the room. I grew dizzy. Visions of sacrificed bulls flashed through my mind, rams spouting blood, rivers of blood, pouring into the glittering sacred bowls the priests held below the animals' wounds, pulsating. . . .

I must have put my hand on the floor at some point, for I saw my smeared, bloody handprint beside Tata's head.

The wailing around the palace grew louder. Alexandros ran in and skidded to a stop, horror-struck. Mother's secretary, Diomedes, followed. "The queen has sent for Antonius. What is happening?"

My father gasped. "What? Cleopatra . . . lives?"

I gasped too, filled with hope. I knew it! It all had been a mistake. Mother would not leave us! And Olympus would fix Father!

Diomedes moved his eyes to the floor and stepped back at the sight of Tata. "Y-yes! She awaits . . . what has happened?"

A servant whispered in his ear. Diomedes placed his hands on his head. "Gods! What will I tell the queen?"

I looked at Father. His face was pale, paler than I had ever seen it.

"My queen lives?" he repeated in almost a whisper.

"Yes, sire! She asks for you. . . ."

At that, he closed his eyes and emitted a low, groanlike chuckle. A more miserable sound I had never heard, before or since.

"The gods . . . so cruel," he muttered. Then more loudly, "Take me . . . see her . . . before I die."

At that, Alexandros fell on his knees beside me. "No, Tata, you will not die! The physician will fix everything!"

"Too late." Father's eyes fluttered for a moment, but then he opened them, trying to focus. "Remember . . . you are Roman . . ." He gasped, searching for air.

"Stop, Tata, please," Alexandros said.

". . . Roman citizen . . ." He looked at Alexandros. "Tell Octavianus . . . he must spare you . . . to save himself. Understand?"

Alexandros nodded as tears coursed down his cheeks.

Tata turned to me, his body a shiver of tiny convulsions. "Philadelphos . . . watch over . . ."

Ptolly! I had forgotten about him. Where was he? I did not want him to see Tata like this.

Litter bearers rushed into the room. Alexandros and I fell back into the warm pool of Father's blood as they pushed us aside to get to him. They lifted up my crimson-soaked father and swept him away in a clatter of stomping feet and urgent shouts. I ran after them. One of Tata's big strong hands hung off the side of the litter, the wrist and fingers loose as if he slept.

Someone grabbed me by the waist and I lost my breath as I flew backward against the arms. "No, Princess," a guard whispered. "You cannot follow."

I fought and kicked and screamed, but the man who held me would not release me. I watched, sobbing, until my dying father disappeared into the blinding glare of an Alexandrian summer day.

CHAPTER TEN

A kitchen servant ran into the playroom to talk to Zosima. "They've got the palace surrounded," she whispered, though I could hear her as plainly as if she'd yelled.

"Where is the queen?" Zosima asked.

"In the mausoleum. They've trapped her with her husband's body. The queen negotiates to save the children. She threatens to burn all the wealth in there with her unless the conqueror guarantees to not kill them."

My stomach tightened. Octavianus threatened to kill us? I looked at Ptolly and breathed out in relief when it appeared he had not heard. *This is all a bad dream,* I told myself. *I will waken and Tata will come roaring in, calling for wine and demanding a game of* Jactus *for high stakes.* I looked down to see if I had my coin purse nearby and noticed dried blood underneath my fingernails.

Hours passed. The sound of Roman soldiers — their thick, guttural accents, their loud laughter — filled the palace. We stayed in our quarters, too afraid even to roam the halls. A servant said that the Romans had taken to spearing the tame animals on the grounds for fun, and I prayed Amisi stayed out of their way. Once, I heard a group of men laughing and grunting, along with the cries and pleas of a young woman begging for mercy. Zosima and Nafre exchanged nervous glances, and I wondered if they knew the young woman under attack.

Ptolly cried himself to sleep in Nafre's arms that night. She had finally delivered the news about Tata.

The palace seemed darker than usual. Torches that had usually lit the paths between the halls and gardens remained unlit. Even the walkways to the Library and the scholars' apartments looked sinister and dangerous. Only Pharos, the Lighthouse, burned as bright as ever.

Standing on our terrace, I stared at the red flames illuminating the night. I felt betrayed even by the Lighthouse. How was it possible for it to keep shining as if nothing had happened? Did the lighthouse keeper not know that my tata was dead? Shouldn't he have withheld the fire in his honor? In defiance of Rome? Yet there it was, glowing as brightly as ever over the gray-black sea, directing Isis knew how many more Roman soldiers to our shore. *Traitor!*

I struggled to manage my rage and grief. Grief over losing Tata and rage against the Romans, who had ambushed Mother and dragged her back to her chambers in the palace. When I went to visit her, the soldier guarding her door announced, "No one sees the queen under Caesar's orders."

"Even her own children?" I asked, incredulous.

"*Especially* her own children." The man smirked.

The unfairness — the cruelty — of keeping us away from our mother on the day of our father's death was beyond understanding.

"Why? Why are they doing this?" I wailed to Katep later.

"They are using your lives to bargain with the queen."

"What?"

"As long as that Roman keeps you away from her, he raises her fear that he has harmed you — or will harm you — in some way. He has made it a punishment of death for anyone who allows you to visit her — or for anyone who allows the queen to visit you."

"But that is so unfair!"

"Look," Katep said. "The Roman knows she tried to follow your father into the Land of *Inmenet*. She turned a dagger on herself when his men burst in, but a guard wrestled it out of her hand. Octavianus holds your lives over her head so she will not try again."

I must have made a sound because Katep turned to look at me. "I am sorry, Little Moon. I should not have spoken so bluntly."

But it was not the threat against our lives that had shocked me. It was the shock of hearing that Mother had tried to . . . had attempted . . .

She would not! How could she have planned to leave us to fend for ourselves? Surely Katep got the story wrong. Mother had intended to use her dagger to *kill* the Roman guard. Yes! That was the only explanation that made sense. Mother would never abandon us like that. She would not!

Tata's sideways grins and growling bear hugs haunted my dreams. I woke searching for *Jactus* dice to play with him or hearing his laughter as he chased us. But Octavianus made my grief even worse by continuing to forbid us from seeing Mother. I worried constantly: Had he imprisoned her? Hurt her? Was she well?

In my despair, I also grew angry *at* Mother. Why wasn't she defying him? She was still queen, was she not?

"She does this for you," Katep continually reminded me. "To keep him from hurting you and your brothers." But I had never before seen Mother in a position of weakness. It frightened me as much as it angered me.

During the long days of waiting, we stayed with our nurses in the children's wing, still too cautious to venture outside. "Roman soldiers are uneducated animals!" Zosima had proclaimed. "We must avoid them completely."

I believed her. I heard the weeping of women they attacked and the agonized cries of loyal servants they tortured. Alexandros cleaved even closer to Iotape during this period, for she and her nurse had moved into our rooms as well. So I turned to Ptolly and he to me. I took to playing long games of make-believe with him to keep him occupied.

Even so, his tantrums grew legendary. He screamed when we told him he could not visit the lions at the Menagerie, or swim in our private bay, or venture out to the Lighthouse. He threw himself on the floor when he couldn't get fresh pomegranate juice or the almond sweet cakes he loved so much. The Romans made us eat what the soldiers ate — mostly bread and beans and sour wine, brought up to us by terrified kitchen servants who, despite threats to their very lives, occasionally snuck in fresh figs or grapes and tiny honey cakes.

We became so desperate for fresh air that we took to sleeping outside on our terrace. The sounds and smells of the sea calmed us all. But it was such a lonely time, especially when I saw how often my twin and Iotape fell asleep clasping hands. I wanted somebody to hold my hand. I wanted my tata. I wanted Caesarion, who, I prayed, was still safely on his way to India. I wanted my mother.

Finally, we got word Octavianus would allow us to see Mother. He had called for a meeting in her chambers. Mother commanded our nurses to bring us early.

Nothing prepared me for her appearance. I knew she had been ill with grief after Tata's death, but I still took a step back at the wraith that met us in her chamber. Her normally glowing skin looked drained of color, as if someone had thrown a sheath of thick linen over the sun. Still, she looked as elegant as she always had in a Tyrrhenian purple gown, the color of royalty. Her favorite golden snake bracelet wound up her arm, its emerald eyes flashing. Golden bands secured her thick dark hair, wound up in the simple Greek way she preferred, and her ladies had painted her eyes with kohl and malachite in a way that usually highlighted their gold-green sparkle. But with a growing heaviness, I saw what had changed. The furious, crackling, intelligent light that shone from Mother's eyes was gone. She looked defeated, empty.

She did not rise from her couch to greet us, but had us come to her one by one. Ptolly went first. She hugged him, and I could see her eyes fill as she looked him over, drinking in the almost uncanny way Ptolly resembled our father — the curly hair, the twinkling eyes, the bull-like body, the way he stood, legs apart, as if ready to jump into action. My stomach contracted as the truth hit me once more — I would never see my beloved tata again.

Ptolly began badgering Mother with questions, which I could see distressed her: *Where was Tata? Why were we not allowed to visit her? Why couldn't we roam the palace anymore?* Ptolly, of course, knew that Father had died, but the sight of Mother seemed to confuse him, and he grew angry and agitated as if Mother were purposely frustrating him. Nafre quickly came to his side and whispered in his ear. She picked him up — even though my brother seemed too big for her to lift — and continued whispering as she took him to the back of the room to show him something, anything, that would distract him from his brewing emotional storm.

Alexandros went up next. Mother hugged him and kissed his forehead. I could not hear what she murmured to him — or what he murmured back — but I could see from the color that rose up my twin's neck that he struggled to maintain his composure.

When it was my turn, I shivered, not wanting to be so close to the dead-seeming eyes, yet longing to lose myself in Mother's embrace. My throat constricted as I stood before her. She opened her arms for a hug. I closed my eyes as I fell into her warmth. Her special scent filled my nose, a fragrance that always soothed, like the Goddess's hand on my brow. As she had with Alexandros, Mother kissed me on the forehead, holding my cheeks between her soft hands.

"You are well?" she murmured when I stepped back. "They have not hurt you?"

I shook my head.

"I have been told you were in the room when your father . . ."

My head shot up and I looked at her. "I am sorry . . . I should have . . . ," I whispered, feeling the weight of everything that had happened. The shame, the grief. I should have stopped him. If only I had moved earlier . . . I could have stopped him!

"Daughter, do not blame yourself. The gods set our fates long ago. I am glad that you were able to say good-bye. It was . . . These things are important. . . ."

My eyes flicked toward Ptolly. Perhaps that was why he sometimes acted as if he had forgotten Tata was dead?

"I am told Octavianus will take you to Rome but that you will be safe," Mother said in a quiet voice, as if she did not want to be overheard.

"Rome! I do not want to go to Rome!" I whispered, following her lead. Despite all the evidence, I had still hoped that Mother would somehow miraculously save us and Egypt.

Mother held my eyes and, for a moment, I felt the power and weight of her Horus-like stare. It lightened my heart even as it scared me. "Listen carefully," she whispered. "Many of my agents are at work here and in Rome; they will look out for your safety. You will know them as followers of Isis. Once we gain contact with Caesarion in India, we will find a way to smuggle you and your brothers to him. Do you understand? We must appear to comply, and when the time is right, unite you."

I nodded. Mother had a plan! Of course she did. Her network of agents would not let us down. I smiled at her, relief flooding every *atomos* of my being. Mother would go with us to India. We would all be together again! It would turn out all right in the end.

Mother smiled back, and I saw the flicker of fire catch in her eyes. Nothing she could have said or done could have given me more courage than that momentary flash.

In that instant, a Roman burst in. "Who dared tell you the children could come before Caesar called for them?" he roared.

CHAPTER ELEVEN

The man — strong, stocky, and with a heavy brow — scowled furiously. He wore an ornate breastplate, and his red cape was of very rich material. Whoever he was, he was very powerful. Was this my father's murderer — Octavianus?

Mother signaled that I should return to stand with my brothers, then she looked at the man. "Why, Marcus Agrippa, surely you would not be so cruel as to keep a mother from having a few private moments with her children — children I have been forbidden to see for weeks, I might add?"

Not Octavianus, but Agrippa, the general who had trapped Father. I thrilled at Mother's sarcastic tone. She wasn't scared of him! She might appear diminished physically, but her spirit had not been crushed.

A short young Roman wearing an even more ornate breastplate and finer cape sauntered in behind Agrippa. "What has caught your ire now, Marcus?" he asked. Three young officers followed him in and took a position behind us against the wall.

"The queen disobeyed our orders and called the children to her before your arrival," Agrippa spat.

"And the guards did not stop them?" he asked mildly.

"Somehow, she convinced them it was *your* wish," Agrippa said.

The young man turned to her. "Tsk, tsk, my queen," he said. Mother bristled at his familiarity. The boy-man continued. "Did we not have an agreement that you would follow my orders precisely . . . or?" He flicked a look at us.

"Yes, Octavianus, we did —"

He slammed his palm on the table, and I jumped. "You will call me CAESAR!"

Mother stared at him. "We did, *sir*, have an agreement with which I complied. The agreement was that you would meet with all of us this morning. There was no specified instruction that the children could not visit with me *first*."

While Octavianus focused on Mother, I took the opportunity to study him. *This* was the man responsible for the death of my father and the destruction of my beloved Alexandria? *This* was the man who had the world on its knees before him? A less imposing person I could not have imagined. He was short — not much taller than Mother — and slight. The muscled breastplate only seemed to accentuate his small frame. He was sunburned, as if the Egyptian sun had tried but been unable to darken his skin in any way. His brown hair, burned at the tips by sun and wind into yellow strands, rested over a triangle-shaped face — wide at the forehead, coming to a delicate point at his chin. There was nothing frightening about this little man.

Until he turned toward me. And then it was as if I stared into the cold, dead eyes of crocodile-headed Amut the Destroyer.

"Well, well, well," he said, and smiled. "The last of the line of the Great House of Ptolemy."

His back was to Mother, and I could see her stiffen as he looked us over. Octavianus strolled back and forth, his hands behind his back. He stopped at Ptolly, seeming struck by his resemblance to Tata.

"Hmmph," he muttered. "No doubt who your father was."

"Who are you?" Ptolly asked, holding Nafre's hand.

"I am Gaius Julius Caesar Octavianus," he said.

Ptolly furrowed his brow. "But that is Caesarion's tata's name. He is the only son of Julius Caesar! And you are not Julius Caesar. I have seen the statues Mother has of him. You do not look anything like him!"

A still, deadly quiet settled in the room as Octavianus watched Ptolly. "I am the true and only son of the Great and Divine Julius Caesar, young man."

Ptolly looked confused. I saw Mother signal Nafre to keep him quiet.

"Any pretenders to that claim are liars and sons of whores," Octavianus continued, with as much emotion as one might say the sun was shining that day.

My heart began to race. My little brother's face was so open and transparent, I could tell the next question out of his mouth was going to be "What's a whore?"

"Ptolly!" I called. He looked at me and I shook my head, praying he would understand my meaning: *Do not say another word.*

"Ah, the Ptolemy tradition continues," Octavianus said. "The cunning female silencing the trusting male." He knelt down at eye level with Ptolly. "Do you miss your big brother Caesarion?"

Mother shifted and I glanced her way. Her expression of dawning horror made me catch my breath. What was happening? What did she see that I did not?

"I miss my tata too!" Ptolly said.

Octavianus stiffened, then rolled his neck ever so slightly. "Ah, yes. My poor, doomed brother-in-law. How I wish it had not ended this way!"

I wanted to scream, *LIAR!* How dare Octavianus try to empathize with Ptolly? Alexandros must have been feeling the same agitation, for he said, through gritted teeth, "And did you know, little brother, that it was *this* man in front of you who declared war on Tata and caused his death?"

Ptolly looked confused. Octavianus swiveled to Alexandros, his face dark and angry. "It appears Egyptian half-breeds are not taught to stay quiet when adults are speaking. That will change when you are in Rome."

"We are going to Rome?" Ptolly asked. "Is that where Tata is?"

Mother kept her face impassive, but I could see the panic in her eyes. Octavianus had seized on the weakest one of us and was playing him like a lyre. Mother stood. "Nafre, I believe Ptolly has had enough for today. Please return him to his quarters."

Octavianus stood up slowly and scowled at Mother. "I am the only person in this room qualified to give orders," he said in a quiet voice.

Nafre paused after turning to lead Ptolly out.

"And I say," Octavianus continued, "that the child stays."

Ptolly's nurse looked at Mother, who mouthed, "Go."

Nafre started walking again.

"Stop!" Octavianus yelled, and she and Ptolly both jumped. He marched over to her and grabbed her wrist so that she released Ptolly's hand. "Soldier!"

One of the guards stepped into the room. "Yes, sir!"

"Take this servant and have her punished for disobeying Caesar's orders."

The man grabbed Nafre by the upper arm. "The punishment, sir?"

Octavianus's gaze traveled up and down her body and he smirked. "Anything the men want."

"No!" Nafre cried, terror in her eyes.

"This is an outrage!" Mother said. "You cannot abuse her in this way! This is the child's *nurse!*"

"Let her go! Let her go!" Ptolly shouted. He began kicking and punching at the soldier, who put an arm out to swat him away.

"Halt!" yelled Mother. She seemed to grow before our eyes, as if the lion-headed goddess, Sekhmet, had entered her body and growled a bone-rattling warning. As in the old days, everyone instantly quieted and turned to her, including out-of-control Ptolly and Octavianus.

"Surely," she said in a cool, dangerous voice, "the great Conqueror of Egypt should not be known as a cruel man. What would that do to his well-deserved reputation — and growing legacy — of clemency?"

I knew from Mother's stories that Caesarion's tata — Octavianus's adopted father, Julius Caesar — was famous for his leniency and mercy to those he had defeated in war. Mother must have guessed that Octavianus desperately wanted to appear as powerful and benevolent as the great Caesar.

Octavianus blinked. "Yes. Quite. Soldier, release her."

I breathed. She had guessed right. The soldier obeyed, saluted, and left when Octavianus gestured at him with a flick of the wrist. "However," he said, turning toward Mother, "let us use this unfortunate incident to be clear as to who gives the orders around here."

Mother had no choice but to acquiesce. She nodded, and I could see how much it had cost her.

Ptolly had buried his face in Nafre's waist, and her hand trembled as she stroked his curls. I looked at Mother, wanting to catch her eye, but she watched Octavianus as if he were a dangerous snake that could strike unexpectedly if she blinked.

Octavianus approached Ptolly again, going down on one knee in front of him. In a soft voice, he said, "Not to worry, little man. Your nurse is safe. Now . . . look at me."

Ptolly refused, shaking his head and pressing his face harder into Nafre's shift.

"Did you know I grew up in Rome with your tata?"

Ptolly sniffed and turned his face slightly toward Octavianus, staring at him with one red eye.

"Yes," Octavianus continued, showing his teeth in a crocodile smile. "He once taught me how to wrestle. Did he ever wrestle with you?"

Ptolly nodded his head, wiping his nose on Nafre's skirt. My stomach dropped. Why was Octavianus doing this? What did he want?

I saw Mother exchange a desperate look with Charmion.

"I bet he taught your brothers to wrestle too, didn't he?"

Again, Ptolly nodded.

"All of your brothers? Including Caesarion?"

Ptolly nodded yet again and moved his face so that he could see Octavianus with both eyes.

"Is Caesarion a good wrestler?" Octavianus asked in an innocent tone.

"Yes," Ptolly said. "Tata said he was quick and smart like his own tata."

"Did Caesarion say good-bye to you when he went away?"

Ptolly smiled. "He gave me his favorite toy chariot to keep until I see him again."

"Where is he? Did he tell you where he was going?"

Mother made a strangled sound in her throat. My heart started thudding in my ears. I understood what he was doing now: He was trying to get Ptolly to tell him where Caesarion had gone so he could hunt him down and murder him. And, for an extra dose of cruelty, he was doing it in front of Mother. In front of us.

Ptolly, too young to pick up the distress of those around him, nodded. "Across the desert," he said. "On a camel."

"Ptolly, stop!" I said. "Do not say any more."

Octavianus turned his head slowly in my direction. "Child, you seem to not be aware of what your mother has already gleaned. I will get this information from your brother one way or another. Perhaps you prefer I remove Ptolemy Philadelphos from his family's protection and question him in private?" He smiled at Ptolly. "Such a sweet little boy. I think I would enjoy that very much."

Dread filled my belly. I looked at Mother. She looked trapped and desperate.

Octavianus breathed out. "Now, Ptolly. Which desert? Which desert was Caesarion riding a camel over?"

"No!" Mother growled. "I will exchange my life for my son's! Caesarion will be loyal to you. He will be Rome's Friend and Ally."

Octavianus stood and crossed his arms, a cold grin on his face. "We have been through this before, my queen. Very noble of you, but I need you for my Triumph. And I cannot let any blood-son of my adopted father live to contest my legacy, can I? Two Caesars are simply one too many."

I thought Mother might faint. She opened her mouth to speak, but only a strangled sound emerged. I had never before seen her without power, without command. But the woman in front of me was helpless to stop the murder of her own beloved firstborn. The horror of the realization took my breath away.

I looked for something — someone — to stop Octavianus. To make this horrible nightmare go away. Agrippa? The young officers behind us? I caught the eye of one of them. He looked about Caesarion's age, also wearing the Roman uniform of a finely tooled leather cuirass and a bloodred cape, though with the cinnamon-brown skin of a North African. Of all of the Romans in the room, he was the only one who seemed disturbed by what Octavianus was doing. I begged him with my eyes to stop Octavianus. But the young African flushed and looked at his feet. Nobody could or would help us.

Octavianus squatted once more, facing Ptolly eye to eye. "Now. Where did Caesarion *go*?"

Do not answer him, Ptolly. Please!

Ptolly jutted his jaw. "I told you already! To the desert!"

Octavianus gritted his teeth. "*Which* desert?"

Tell him you don't know. Tell him you don't know. But I could feel Ptolly's emotional storm gathering like thick black clouds, crackling with vicious bolts of lightning. And I knew it was too late.

"The desert on the other side!" he roared. "The one that goes to *India!*"

CHAPTER TWELVE

Octavianus's men hunted down Caesarion — the king of Egypt, my mother's eldest, the only true son of Julius Caesar — and murdered him in the desert. My kind, quiet, brilliant sixteen-year-old brother, our last hope for escape and survival, was dead.

Before we could even absorb the news, Octavianus took Iotape — ripping her from the arms of my sobbing twin — and sent her back to her homeland. Her family, he announced with a vicious grin, had canceled the betrothal to this "fallen House of Ptolemy."

Our dreams splintered and cracked around us like marble at the strike of a sculptor's chisel.

As before, Octavianus kept us from seeing Mother, so we could not go to her for comfort after learning of Caesarion's murder. Olympus ordered us to drink a tea of poppy before bed, but I refused, forever dubious of any potion or tea the good doctor sent my way. All night, I tossed in bed while my brothers slept. Images of Caesarion skimmed and wheeled in my mind like Nile terns in flight: a shaft of sunlight cutting through the Temple darkness to illuminate his kohl-painted eyes during prayers; his laughter as I jumped on his back for a ride; his furious scowl of concentration when he studied; the clean, grassy smell of his cloak after he had been out riding. . . .

A tapping at the door. Katep stirred. A flash of silver as he pulled out the knife hidden in the belt of his tunic. The air was sucked out of my lungs as, once again, the danger of our situation became clear. The Romans had just murdered my brother. Were they coming for *us* now?

Katep opened the door slowly. Despite my fear, I tiptoed to his side. A young Roman soldier appeared before us, and Katep stepped in front of me.

"I have a message from the queen," the Roman whispered, looking around. "She asks for her children to come to her."

"How do we know you come on the queen's behalf?" Katep whispered back.

"Because she sent me!" he hissed. "I'm here against my better judgment and I'm not asking again."

Katep paused. "The boys . . . have been medicated. Only Cleopatra Selene is awake."

"Well, if she wants to see her mother, she had better come *now!*"

He turned and walked in the direction of Mother's chamber. I shot out to follow him, and Katep grabbed my arm. "Little Moon! What are you doing? This could be some sort of ruse!"

I shook him off. I did not care. It had been weeks since that horrible meeting in her rooms with Octavianus, after which he had again forbidden us to see Mother. Upon learning of Caesarion's death, I guessed she must have decided to defy our tormentor. Katep followed me as I raced up to the soldier's side. "What is your name?" I asked.

"Cornelius Dolabella," came the terse reply.

I looked at Katep. He had earlier told me that a young soldier named Dolabella was Mother's day guard.

"Why are you working at night too?" I asked.

"I . . . I, um . . . asked for night duty too."

"Why?"

He rubbed his red-rimmed eyes. "Because. Your mother needs all the friends she can get right now."

"Mother has no Roman 'friends,'" I said bitterly.

The soldier turned to me, though he did not slow. "That is not true. I have tried to help the queen in every way I could."

"Oh, gods help us," muttered Katep under his breath. "The pup has fallen in love with her."

As we approached Mother's antechamber, fear and dread inched up from my center and stole my breath. "I . . . I changed my mind," I whispered to Katep. "Let us go back."

Katep looked at me questioningly. But before I could explain my sudden panic, Lady Charmion came out of the inner chamber to greet me. Tall, willowy Charmion had always looked meticulously put together, her dark hair arranged so that not even a tendril escaped, her dresses immaculate and elegant. The woman who stood in front of me was a shade of the lady I had known. Her hair hung loose, shot through with gray; her dark dress was stained and wrinkled. Worse, she looked slightly bowed, as if pain had curled her inward like a bloom about to fall off the branch.

The sight of how grief had ravaged her sent a further shock of fear through me. I knew she loved Caesarion. How much worse must the anguish be for Mother? I could not bear seeing Mother's pain, her utter diminishment. I would not survive it. I had made a mistake in coming. I turned to bolt from the room, my breathing ragged, but Katep put a hand on my shoulder to steady me.

"Do not run," he whispered in my ear. "She needs you."

I began to shake. Charmion bid me follow her to Mother's inner chamber, but Katep stayed behind — whether to keep me from running or to act as a second lookout, I did not know. When I glanced back, he urged me on with his head. It felt as if a ball of sticky bread had gotten stuck in my throat.

In Mother's hushed inner chamber, flames from the two small bronze lamps flickered, it seemed to me, in tune with my racing heart. I swept my eyes around the room, looking everywhere — anywhere — but directly at Mother. Her *uraeas* crown gleamed on a small table, the rearing cobra's shadow undulating in the tremulous light. Her golden ceremonial dress, the one that made her look like Isis, lay draped over a side couch, with a turquoise and carnelian broad collar over it. Mother's favorite golden snake armband glittered on a low table. It was almost, I thought, as if she were preparing for a religious ceremony.

Still, I could not look at her. I looked at the floor, at her bare feet, and at the dark, rich fabric that pooled like blood around them. I knew, without asking, that it was Caesarion's old cloak. Mother had wrapped it around her shoulders like a shivering child looking for warmth.

Mother lifted my chin with gentle fingers, and I took in everything at once — her dark hair, loose and unbrushed though not wild like Charmion's; her skin stretched over an almost gaunt face, showing new lines of weariness and grief between the brows and down the sides of her mouth; her eyes huge and shadowed. It was looking into them that almost undid me. Her eyes — the glittering green-gold eyes that used to burn with power and nail me to the floor as if the Eye of Horus itself inspected my soul — looked . . . empty.

"O my daughter, what have they done to us?" she whispered.

I tried to be strong. I really did. But I was not. I shattered into a million pieces. *"Mama"* was all I could say as she took me in her arms.

Her fingers smoothing my hair; her scented linen shift pressing into my cheek; her shoulders curling over me, as if to buffer me from all that had happened to us, to our family. She clung to me as hard as I clung to her. We were not queen and princess anymore. Just mother and daughter.

After a time, Mother asked why my brothers had not come. I explained about the poppy tea. "I must see them," she said, stepping away from me.

I wanted to throw myself back into her warmth. Instead, she took my hand, and I followed her out of her chambers. I relished the feel of her palm on mine, and an odd thought came to me. Had Mother ever taken my hand like this before? As she was the queen and I was the princess, I had always walked behind her in procession.

At the sight of us, Dolabella's eyes grew wide. "What are you doing? You cannot leave, my lady! This goes too far!"

"I thank you for all you have done, Cornelius. But I must see my sons. I will not be long." We continued down the hall, our bare feet moving so quietly I felt as if we floated in a dream.

In our rooms, Mother brushed the sweaty curls off Ptolly's forehead, kissed him, and murmured into his ear. She prayed over him, then wound her way to Alexandros, whispering words of comfort to him about Iotape, as if he were awake and could take them in. I heard her voice catch as she murmured, "My new king." Then she prayed over him as well.

Finally, Mother performed the same ritual on me, placing her soft hands on the crown of my head. She closed her eyes and spoke the sacred words in the old language of the priests. When she finished, she took my face in her hands. "Do you remember your lessons about Egypt's first ancient rulers?"

I nodded. Her hands felt warm on my cheeks, and I looked down, overwhelmed. I had not realized how much I had craved her touch. And how afraid I was of losing it.

"They buried the earliest kings in the sands of the desert, which preserved their bodies for the afterworld. It is from them that the Priests of Anubis learned their sacred art. By leaving Caesarion in the desert . . ." Mother paused and touched the hollow at her throat. "By leaving Caesarion in the desert, your brother's murderers preserved his body for us, for his *ka*. Do you understand? We will see Caesarion — as well as your tata — again in the afterworld."

I could see that this gave Mother comfort. I felt my heart grow lighter at the thought too.

"You must always remember that you are descended from the Great Alexander and from the kings who built the Library, the *Museion*, and the Lighthouse," Mother continued. "Whatever happens, they cannot take that from you."

I nodded, my eyes filling again. Her words made my insides squirm, though I could not say why.

"You are to live in Octavia's house in Rome," she continued. "I have received her sworn oath that she will protect you and keep you safe."

Octavia was Octavianus's sister — Father's Roman ex-wife! I did not want to live anywhere near our enemy or his family. I wanted to stay *here* with her! She must have read my expression, for she shook her head to keep me from arguing. "You *must* live," she said. And then, almost as an afterthought, she added, *"Genestho,"* under her breath. It was the word she used to sign all her royal decrees — "Make it so."

Dolabella made a noise at the door. "My lady, please," he begged. "You must return. The risk is too great!"

Mother kissed my cheek. "You have the heart of a great and powerful queen," she whispered.

She turned and walked out of the room. I followed her, but Katep stopped me in the dark hallway. "No noise," he whispered, holding me fast. "We must let her go."

I peered around him to watch Mother. She glided like a goddess — head held high, Caesarion's cloak swaying behind her — until she disappeared, like a dream, into the dark.

CHAPTER THIRTEEN

The next day, my brothers and I sprinted up the first tier of the Great Lighthouse. I had forgotten how hot the airless stairwells grew in the summer. We crashed out into the open terraces, sighing as the sea breezes cooled the sweat on our faces. I put my arms out. The crackling flames above us pulsed like a heartbeat. How I had missed Pharos!

Mother's visit the night before had, despite everything, filled me with hope. She was taking risks again! After all, she had never before attempted to see us while Octavianus's ban was in effect. And that morning, Dolabella had returned to say that Mother had *ordered* we spend the day with Lady Amunet at the Temple of Isis Pharia. She was finally defying our tormentor.

Once on the island, it was not hard to convince Dolabella that Mother would not mind us climbing up the Lighthouse. It had been so long! I ran to the edge and looked out over the glittering bay, drinking in the invigorating smell of saltwater and sea life. Birds squawked and flew around our heads. Ptolly laughed and chased them.

"The birds are hungry," said a food stall owner from behind us. "Few visit Pharos now that the Romans have come. There are no scraps for them to feed on."

I looked up and down, noticing the mostly empty stalls. Usually, the first tier of the Lighthouse teemed with sightseers, but even the vendors hawking cheap terra-cotta lighthouses and lucky amulets were gone.

"We always had long lines for our treats. Today, you enjoy them right away, yes? Perhaps our famous emmer almond cakes?"

Ptolly's face lit up. "I like almond cakes!"

"One obol each," the man said.

Ptolly looked confused. I could almost read his thoughts: *money?*

"Do you know who we are?" Alexandros asked.

"I do not care if you are the children of the queen of Egypt. You must still pay!" the man said. He wore the plain, rough-hewn tunic of workers from the Rhakotis district.

Ptolly giggled. "But we are! We are the children of the queen of Egypt! I am Ptolemy Philadelphos, that is Alexandros Helios, and," he said, pointing at me, "she is Cleopatra Selene!"

The man laughed. "Gah! You are silly, but charming. I tell you this. I will give you the sweet almond cakes at half price. That is a good deal, no?"

Dolabella muttered under his breath and slapped a handful of coins on the warping wood counter. "Give them what they want. *Now.*"

The vendor frowned.

"Do not worry," I said in Egyptian. "He is a Roman soldier and like all Romans is very grouchy. Perhaps you can give him the sweetest treat? Oh, and we are indeed the Royal Children."

The man smiled. "But of course, *Your Majesty,*" he said in Greek, a twinkle in his eyes. His playful expression reminded me so much of Tata that my stomach dropped with missing him. But like a good royal, I hid my emotion from a subject. I playfully inclined my head in return.

"Give the children their food," Dolabella growled. He turned to me. "This has taken longer than I thought. We must go to the Temple of Isis Pharia now. The priestess awaits us."

"But we have not finished climbing to the top of Pharos," Alexandros said.

Dolabella grabbed the treats wrapped in steamed vine leaves and pushed them into our hands. "I promised the queen I would have you with the head priestess by the *hora octava*. The time approaches."

"No!" Ptolly said, almond paste smearing his upper lip. "We want to go all the way to the top! We *always* go to the top!"

"Maybe after . . . we can finish the climb if you still want to."

We did not move.

"Now! You will do what I command now!" Dolabella shouted, sounding like Father used to when he gave his men orders on the practice fields. But we were not soldiers. We stared at him, our mouths stuffed with sweet cakes.

At that moment, strange cries floated from the interior of the island, muffled but plaintive. The gulls? But then it came again and I froze. The last time I heard that sound . . . an image burst behind my eyes. Tata, dying, soaked in blood. *Gods!*

Ptolly's eyes widened. "Ghosts again," he murmured. "I hate ghosts!"

Alexandros and I glanced at each other. Our nurses, who had finally made it up the winding stairs, knelt by Ptolly to reassure him. More disembodied shouts and cries drifted toward us. Dolabella rubbed his face and groaned.

"What is happening?" I whispered to him. He did not respond. Slowly, the wails and cries gathered like a wave crashing over our heads. I looked out over the island and saw the Priestesses of the Temple of Isis Pharia and the Priests of Poseidon gathering in their courtyards, some crying, some chanting the mourning dirge.

"Come," Dolabella mumbled. "We must go to the Priestess of Isis. It was where your mother wanted you to be."

Wanted?

I could not draw a breath. Time seemed to slow, and all sound disappeared. I saw Alexandros's eyes grow wide with horror. Ptolly dropped his treat as he scrunched his face and covered his ears with both hands, elbows sticking out like broken wings. Dolabella mouthed the words, "I am sorry."

And then all sound rushed back in, and I understood the cries that reverberated off the walls of the Lighthouse — the howls of a people mourning the loss of their beloved queen.

It was as if a tomb door had slammed shut in my soul.

I could not see it then, of course, but Mother had been saying good-bye the night before. Caesarion had been her last hope for our survival and escape. She would have held on for as long as she thought she could help us get to him. But his murder destroyed all that. And when Dolabella warned her that Octavianus planned to ship us to Rome within days — that he was intent on parading her through the streets in chains, then executing her as was required by Roman law — she took the only recourse left to her. The only one that, as Tata would say, preserved her honor.

Still, the shock of her suicide created such a jolt in my being that huge chunks of memory fell away, like the details of a nightmare that fade into mist, leaving only the horror intact.

Some images, though, remained: Alexandros's glazed eyes, staring into nothing for hours. Ptolly putting his thumb in his mouth even though he had long ago stopped the habit. The wind moving through the nearly abandoned palace, echoing like soft moans of grief. Zosima later said that I did not speak for days.

Eventually, I found some comfort amidst Mother's things, curling myself onto her scented couch, wrapping myself in her robe that glittered like sea foam, touching noses with her cat, Hekate. Visiting the little sand-colored *meiu* in Mother's chambers became a sort of special refuge — Hekate's heart still beat, her shiny coat still smelled of Mother, her purr was like an echo of Mother's low laugh.

One day, she was nowhere to be found. I checked under couches and chairs, in small baskets and in dark corners. I called to her, but still she did not appear.

"Looking for something your mother hid from me?" Octavianus asked, sauntering into her inner room. "I would not put it past her to steal what is rightfully mine."

I jumped at the sound of his voice. How dare he accuse Mother of stealing when he was the one taking everything that was hers? I swallowed. "No, I am looking for Hekate, Mother's *meiu*. I . . . I cannot find her anywhere and —"

"Too many cats in this damned palace," Octavianus interrupted, lifting a bronze sculpture of Artemis aiming her bow from a table near Mother's reading desk. "We will have to do something about that."

He sniffed at the statuette. He saw me watching him. "Do you know that you can determine a real Corinthian bronze by its smell? It has a scent like no other." He closed his eyes and breathed the metal again. "Your mother had exquisite taste."

I had another moment of unreality. The small Roman in front of me was responsible for the deaths of my brother and parents, and yet he dared to praise Mother's taste at the same time that he stole from her? Grief and hatred roiled in my center like a slow wave building to shore. I walked toward the door, muttering, "Son of Nyx and Erebus. *Daemon* of death . . ."

"Excuse me," he said, stepping in my path, his gray eyes glittering with malice. "Were you addressing me, *Princess*?"

I did not respond. I did not like being so close to him. I took a step around him, but he blocked me again.

"You see," he said with his crocodile grin, "I could have sworn I heard you call me the son of Night and Darkness. But I must have been mistaken, because surely even you would not be so stupid as to insult me to my face. No?"

He moved closer to me and I could smell his breath, sour like vinegary wine. I forced myself not to step back.

"Because, you see," he said, whispering now, "I am not like the God of Death at all. I am like Apollo, God of Light and Victory. I vanquished the darkness that oozed from the East." He smiled. "Yes, I like that. I will erect statues and altars to my patron god. All will know whom the gods favor."

His smile widened to a grin. Despite my desire to show no weakness, I stepped back. Again, he moved with me. "Yes, and you are Selene, goddess of the moon. The sun and the moon."

He grabbed me by the hair at the nape of my neck and I gasped. He would kill me right here, right now — just as he had Caesarion. He pulled my head back farther, exposing my neck. I narrowed my eyes at him. *I hate you*, I thought, trying to keep from trembling. *May Amut the Destroyer rise from his stinking lair and gobble your heart as it beats in your chest. . . .*

"The daughter of the great whore queen," he said. "Yes, the possibilities are quite interesting. Too bad you are so young. . . ."

I tried wriggling away, but his hold on my hair kept me close. He chuckled. "Just beginning to bud, I see."

I spat in his face. His eyes widened, then turned dark with rage. "You little bitch!" he roared, shaking me like a rag doll. I screamed at the sharp pain in my scalp and kicked out blindly, connecting with something. He threw me off, cursing. I sprinted for the door, but he grabbed my wrist and spun me around. "I could have you whipped for daring to strike Caesar."

"*You* are not Caesar! My brother was the only true son of Julius Caesar." I spoke before thinking. Octavianus pushed me against the wall and pinned me there with his torso, and again I wished that I had held my tongue.

"Maybe the fun of the queen of Egypt was that she was a wildcat," he said. "Maybe that was your mother's magic."

I did not understand his words, but I grasped the threat in them. He pushed his whole body into me, the nipple from his muscled bronze cuirass pressing into my cheek, the brass studs from his thick belt scratching my chest. I stopped squirming, hoping my acquiescence would signal him to step back. It didn't.

Octavianus fumbled with his sword belt. Father once claimed that one well-aimed blow below the belt could fell even Hercules himself. I would have only one try to get Octavianus off of me. But before I could do anything, we both jumped at a man's booming voice.

"Castor and Pollux, Caesar! What are you doing?"

Octavianus stepped back from me but still held me against the wall, his hand around my neck. I flicked my eyes toward the voice. Agrippa. He moved into the room quickly, shutting the door behind him. "You can have any girl or boy in this whole palace, but you cannot touch the Royal Children! We have talked about this!"

"This little Fury had the gall to insult me and spit on me. She should pay!"

"You must listen to me on this," Agrippa said again. "One misstep now and we could have the whole Senate and all of Rome against us. We must appear to treat Antonius's children with extraordinary . . . solicitude."

With a leer, Octavianus squeezed my neck one last time, then removed his hand. I kept my eyes on his, my chin up, but heard Agrippa breathe out as if in relief.

"Tell your brothers," Octavianus said to me, as if the last few minutes had never occurred, "you leave for Rome in three days."

My mouth dropped. "Three days? But we cannot leave yet! We have not had the entombment ceremonies for my family. . . ." It took more than two months — seventy days — for the Priests of Anubis to complete the sacred mummification rites. They hadn't even finished with Father yet! We had to ensure that the rites for both of our parents were performed, or we would never see them again in the afterlife. "You cannot make us leave until we complete our rituals!"

"You Egyptians and your abominable beast gods," Octavianus spat, turning his back to me and inspecting a black marble statue of Sekhmet. "I tire of you. Leave!"

Hot tears gathered behind my eyes and tightened my throat. He could not do this! I looked at the Sekhmet statue, wishing I could make her come roaring to life so she could devour his flesh, tear it from his bones with her fangs as he screamed in agony. . . .

"Did you not hear me?" he asked, moving to test a silk wall hanging between his fingers. "I ordered you to *leave*. After all, you must start packing," he added with a smirk.

Something changed and hardened within me then, as if my spine grew as thick and immovable as one of the giant temple columns in Dendera.

"We are not leaving Alexandria until you allow us to perform the sacred rites for our parents," I said, my voice calm and cold.

Octavianus turned to me, hatred gleaming in his eyes. He opened his mouth to speak, but Agrippa stepped toward him, his arm out in a calming gesture.

The temple column grew wider, taller, blocking out the sky. "If we don't perform the sacred rites with the Priest of Anubis," I said, "Father's and Mother's *kas* will not travel to the Realm of Osiris. Their spirits will haunt you until even Fortuna turns from you in disgust. You do not know the power of the dead in Egypt."

Rage and fear fought for dominance on Octavianus's face. I pressed my advantage. "Without the rites, their restless spirits will call on all of the angry and evil spirits of the dead, deep within the secret burial places of this ancient land, and . . . and . . ."

"Stop!" Agrippa ordered. "Let them have their ceremonies," he whispered to Octavianus. "You cannot start your reign here by angering their gods."

"The ship leaves in three days," Octavianus said through clenched teeth. "And these bastards will be on it."

"Fine, but have them meet with their death priests before they go," Agrippa urged. "We must at least appear to be respectful of their ancient practices. . . ."

The two men stared at each other, almost as if they were holding an entire conversation without words.

"Call for their bestial priests, then," Octavianus snarled. He turned on his heel and stomped out. Agrippa gave me a quick glance before following.

It took me a moment to understand what had just happened. I had won a small victory. He would allow us to talk to the priests about the sacred rites.

But at a huge cost. I had earned the eternal enmity of the man in complete control of my future.

CHAPTER FOURTEEN

The Priests of Anubis created a special ceremony for us, allowing us to complete our ritual duties despite the fact that my parents' bodies were not yet ready for entombment.

We prepared for the rite well before sunrise on the day before our departure. I dressed in my finest white pleated linen gown and golden sandals, and donned a braided ceremonial wig. Zosima applied the moist, thick kohl on my brows and lids. It felt, for a moment, as if she were sealing my eyes shut, like the linen bandages that would forever bind Mother's. Alexandros and Ptolly dressed in royal garb too, wearing ceremonial kilts and tying multicolored broad collars around their bare chests. They slipped on the striped headdresses of royalty.

Katep escorted us out of the dark palace. As we neared Mother's tomb, I swallowed at the sight of the torch-lit *ibw*, the tented temporary Place of Purification where her body was undergoing its ritual cleansing. *Mother is still whole*, I thought as my stomach tightened. A part of me wanted to run into the forbidden tent and see her, touch her, before the priests moved her to *per nefer*, "The House of Beauty," where they would cut her open and pull out her organs for safekeeping in canopic jars. Only her heart would stay in her body. She would need it for the Weighing of the Heart test judged by Anubis.

Was it my fault? I wondered. Had the spell for Calling Forth Anubis made him go after Mother? I had asked Amunet that question many times. "No," she always said. "Anubis shadows you but also protects you. He will help you save the sons of Egypt."

Inside Mother's mausoleum, I stumbled for a moment as I realized Mother took her last breath in that very place. Again, I had to force myself to breathe deeply. To my surprise, the marble-columned room was crowded, not just with priests but with Mother's most loyal associates — Mardian, Apollodorus, her prime minister Protarchus, and favored scholars and philosophers from the *Museion*. Alexandros and I took Ptolly's warm, moist hands as Katep and our nurses left the sacred area.

At the first light, the Priest of Ra intoned, *"Praise to thee, O Ra, when thou risest. Shine thou upon my face. . . ."* The Welcoming of the Sun prayer continued until Ra caressed the high windows, small shafts of light illuminating the gold on the priests' chests, the wall carvings, the gilded horns of the magnificent sacrificial bull.

"You will see this golden light again soon, Mother," I whispered. "I swear it."

The Priest of Osiris raked the ceremonial knife across the bull's throat, and the majestic animal, to my relief, did not fight. This, I knew, was a sign that the gods had smiled on our unusual ceremony. Priests carrying shining silver bowls caught the first blood, and the room grew thick with the sweet metallic scent of it.

As the animal slowly fell to its knees, then flopped to its great side with a half bellow, half sigh, Priestesses of Isis lit small bowls of incense, rattled their sacred sistrums, and chanted the prayers of preparation. Through the haze of billowing incense, I spotted three golden *shabtis*, ceremonial statuettes, on an altar beside the Overseer of the Mysteries. I realized that a different face had been painted on each one — Father, Caesarion, and, finally, Mother.

The Priest of Anubis donned the great gleaming black mask of the Jackal-God. Ptolly whimpered and hid his face in my waist. "We do this so we may we see Tata, Mother, and Caesarion again," I whispered. "We must not fail them." He faced the priest but continued to press against me. I rubbed his back, which was slick with sweat in the late-summer heat of the airless tomb.

Since my family's bodies were not yet prepared, we held the Opening of the Mouth ceremony over their *shabti* statues. The Priest of Anubis bowed his great mask over the golden figures, then the Priest of Ptah stepped forward, touched his own lips with a ceremonial adze, and symbolically cut open Mother's mouth.

"Mother, open your mouth for the breath of life, your *ka*, so you may breathe, eat, see, hear, and feel," I murmured along with the priest as he touched Mother's *shabti*. I repeated the prayer for Tata and Caesarion. When the priests finished, the three of us fell to our knees in the traditional posture of mourning — heads bowed, palms in the air over our heads — and prayed for their safekeeping during their Great Journey.

At the ceremony's end, I almost wept with relief. We had done it. We had ensured that my family's passage to the afterworld was safe. I would see Mother again. I would see them all.

As the Priests of Anubis and Toth removed the *shabtis* and proceeded out of the tomb, the three of us approached Ma'ani-Djehuti, the Priest of Serapis, and Amunet, the Priestess of Isis. I wanted to offer my gratitude but was interrupted before I could begin.

"Now that we have ensured the safe passage of the Great Queen, her son the king, and her husband to the domain of the Lord of the West, we have one more ceremony that we must complete," Amunet announced.

I looked at Alexandros. He gave a slight shrug. Ma'ani-Djehuti nodded to someone behind us, and I heard the door rebolted. Mother's inner circle of advisers and scholars, I noticed, had not exited with the long line of priests and assistants. They formed a wall behind Amunet and Ma'ani-Djehuti. My heart raced. What was happening?

"Egypt must have a pharaoh to maintain *ma'at*, to keep Set, the God of Chaos and Destruction, at bay," Ma'ani-Djehuti explained. "Upon your mother's and brother's deaths, by the laws of *ma'at* and Great Horus, you become king and queen, pharaohs of the Two Lands of Egypt. Only through the sacred crowning ceremony set forth by the Great Goddess and the Great God do we ensure the preservation of *ma'at*."

A young man holding two crowns stepped forward. They were going to crown us? But we were leaving for Rome the next day! Ma'ani-Djehuti must have read our confused expressions, for he smiled at us. "The Roman occupation is a temporary disruption in the Great Destiny that is Egypt. When you are crowned, we tie your fates to Kemet. It will not be long before you are returned to us."

Amunet bid us sit down on thrones that seemed to appear out of nowhere. Ptolly stood beside us. The old priest intoned the prayers of coronation and regeneration. When he raised his arms, I noticed how the excess skin on his bare brown chest looked somehow both soft and parched at the same time. Ma'ani-Djehuti tied a false beard made of goat's hair on Alexandros's chin, identifying him with Osiris. He placed the scepter in the form of a striped shepherd's crook in one of my brother's hands; in the other, a fly whip. Amunet handed me a royal crook and whip as well. Around my neck, she tied a brilliant jeweled broad collar that identified me with Isis.

A young priest passed Ma'ani-Djehuti and Amunet the two crowns, which they held aloft. I kept my head immobile but moved my eyes up to study the flanged blue helmet Amunet held aloft before me, adorned with golden discs bearing the sacred snake and vulture on the brow.

I blinked. I had never seen Mother wear a crown like this. She typically wore either the golden diadem with the three rearing cobras, or the white and red crown of the Ruler of the Two Lands. This was the Blue Crown of War. My stomach tightened at the implication. Pharaohs only wore this special crown, the *Khepresh*, in times of attack. Did this mean we would actually have to *battle* mighty Rome at some point?

Ritual prayers washed over us. Even as I worried, my senses felt overwhelmed by the lingering scent of incense and blood and the rapid Egyptian chanted over our heads. My breathing quickened as I anticipated the moment the crown touched my brow. What would it feel like, this power from the gods that had shone through Mother's eyes?

Amunet and Ma'ani-Djehuti named us King and Queen, Brother-Sister, Husband-Wife, as were the first Great Gods and Rulers of Egypt — Isis and Osiris. I closed my eyes as the crown was lowered. It felt heavy and stiff, as if someone had placed a block of marble on my head. I thought of Mother's last whispered words to me — *"You have the heart of a great and powerful queen."* I mouthed the word *"Genestho,"* just as she had murmured it — *"Make it so."*

Amunet and Ma'ani-Djehuti bowed at our feet as the others chanted the great prayer of Welcoming. Muffled shouts and commands in both Latin and Greek outside the tomb made me jump. I heard the word "Caesar" and knew, with a sinking feeling, that he was outside, demanding entrance. This ceremony would outrage him. But how did he know of it when even we had not?

The scuffling and shouted obscenities outside the tomb drowned out the beauty of the ancient words within. During the chaos, Amunet raised her head and stared at me with such fierceness I almost jumped in my makeshift throne. She leaned closer to me, speaking with a low urgency over the chanting beside us and the arguing outside. "Our agents in Rome are already at work on plans to bring you back to fulfill your destiny," she said. My heart sped up in excitement. Were these the same agents Mother had told me about the night before she died? "Someone will appear with instructions when it is time," she continued. "Do you understand? You must be patient. And trust Isis."

Before I could respond — *Who will contact us? What should we do in the meantime?* — the door burst open with a crash. The chanting stopped as we all looked up, the sudden quiet as disturbing as the harsh sunlight that blinded us in the darkened chamber.

A figure emerged, as dark and as indistinguishable as Anubis in a tomb. As it advanced, for a wild moment I wondered if it was indeed the Lord of the Dead coming to claim us. But it was the Roman deliverer of death — Octavianus.

I caught my breath at the look of pure hatred and rage twisting his face.

"You," he bellowed, pointing at us, "are guilty of treason against Rome."

CHAPTER FIFTEEN

We froze. There was no denying the evidence. Alexandros and I sat on thrones, crowned as Egypt's new rulers, the head priest and priestess on their knees in front of us.

Octavianus took it all in, his slight chest heaving. Marcus Agrippa followed him in, his brow furrowed as usual, along with Octavianus's lictores — the giant Gauls who served as his personal bodyguards. I swallowed as Octavianus walked over to us. "Who is responsible for this?" he growled to Amunet and Ma'ani-Djehuti.

"It was necessary," Ma'ani-Djehuti replied calmly, slowly getting up from his knees. "*Ma'at* must be maintained, or chaos will rule in people's hearts and throughout the land."

"Is that some sort of a threat?" Octavianus asked through clenched teeth.

"Absolutely not," said the old priest. "It is merely a statement of fact."

With a violence that caught me by surprise, Octavianus backhanded the crowns off both our heads. Ptolly ducked behind my makeshift throne as the crowns clattered and rolled away from us. Blood from the sacrificed bull darkened their brilliant blue, the singular color of Egypt.

Octavianus turned to Amunet and Ma'ani-Djehuti. "In case this is not clear, let me explain. *I* am your pharaoh. I am your king. I am your ruler. I am your *God*. I am the ultimate authority here and in all of Rome's empire. Do you understand?" He turned and pointed at us. "Never, *never*, will the spawn of that sorceress bitch you called a queen rule in this land. Do you understand me? I should kill them in front of you so that you barbarians are not tempted to trifle with me again."

I swallowed. Ptolly's breath grew ragged behind me. I wanted to comfort him, but I could not move. If he killed us now, who would conduct the rites for us to join our family in *Aaru?*

Agrippa walked up to Octavianus and put his hand on his friend's back. Octavianus straightened and rolled his shoulders. He took a breath. "But Caesar, you will learn, unlike weak Antonius, never lets emotions rule his intellect. And so I stay my hand."

He turned to Ma'ani-Djehuti. "But I need not be so merciful to you. For the priest who dared defy me, I order death by crucifixion."

"No!" I stood. "You cannot impose Rome's barbaric ways on a sacred Priest of Serapis!"

Alexandros stood up beside me. "The people of Egypt will surely revolt at such a sacrilege," he added.

Octavianus smirked. "Oh, they may complain. But they will stop quickly enough when they face the crossbeams themselves. Besides, they must learn that Caesar bows down to no foreign priest." He lifted his chin in the direction of Ma'ani-Djehuti. "Take him," he ordered. "Take the priestess too. Take them all."

"No!" I cried again, as his lictores grabbed the slight old man and long-haired Amunet by the upper arms.

Ma'ani-Djehuti looked at us, his face relaxing into a reassuring smile. "Do not worry, little king and queen," he said in Egyptian. "He cannot undo what has been done. I die knowing I have fulfilled the Goddess's wishes."

I watched them drag away Mother's lifetime religious advisers. At the door, Amunet turned her face toward Octavianus. She uttered one word: "*Telestai.*" It is done. At first, I wondered why she used a Greek word and not an Egyptian one, and then I realized: She wanted him to understand her.

Then the Lady of Isis spat at his feet.

The next morning, as we prepared for the journey that would take us away from everything we knew and loved, Octavianus came to our rooms. "As you know, I have arranged for my dear sister, Octavia, to take care of you," he said.

He arranged it? Mother had indicated that she had made a secret agreement with Octavia. But, of course, he would take credit for the idea.

"Please send my greetings to my lovely and loyal sister," he continued. "It will be many months before I will be free enough to return to Rome. . . ."

Yes, I thought, *stealing all of Egypt's wealth is quite time-consuming.*

"For reasons I will never fathom," he went on, pacing back and forth, "Octavia truly loved your father. My sister is what every Roman woman should aspire to be." He stopped in front of me. "Kind, virtuous, beautiful, loyal. You will not hurt her by talking about your father's relationship with the Queen, understand?"

I stared straight ahead.

"Understand?"

I nodded.

"Good."

I felt his stare as a beat passed. Then he added, "One more thing: Just as it is unwise to disobey Caesar, it is even more unwise to disobey Caesar's *wife*."

I glanced his way and saw him still watching me. "Yes," he continued. "I give Livia Drusilla full control over all of my property while I am away. And now," he added, "that includes you three."

Was that some sort of warning? I tried to keep my face impassive, but worry crept up my spine.

He seemed to sense my growing fear because he broke into a slow Amut the Destroyer smile. "Enjoy one last look at your lovely Alexandria on your way out," he finally said, turning to leave. "You will never see it again. I have asked the litter bearers to take you past the Caesareum on the way to the Harbor of Good Returns so that you may say good-bye." He gave us a strange smile and sauntered out.

As we passed the Royal Gardens — dry and brown now since the Romans had both trampled and ignored the precious blooms — I thought again about what Amunet had said to me during the crowning.

Was it true? Would Mother's agents in Rome really help us return? But how? She'd said that someone would appear when the time was right. I had to be patient and to trust Isis. I could do that. I would not let her — or Mother — down.

When we were out of the royal complex, our litter bearers closed the heavy linen drapes on each side of the litter. Had someone told them to do that? I looked at Alexandros. He shrugged. We began to swelter. I reached out to open them again when the bearer's hand shot up on the other side of the fabric to stop me.

"We are hot!" I complained.

"It must stay this way," said the bearer. "For . . . for your protection."

Again, I looked at Alexandros. This made no sense. Besides, I wanted to look upon our beloved city one last time. But I would later thank the bearers for their kindness, for on the way to the commercial harbor, we heard an assortment of odd moans and cries.

Ptolly's eyes grew big. He began to rock back and forth. "No, no, no, no . . . ," he murmured. "No more ghosts, no more ghosts."

I touched Ptolly's shoulder, trying to still his rocking. "It is just the servants complaining about carrying our things to the farther harbor," I said. "That is all. Our packs are very heavy, and we have a lot of them." It was true — Octavianus had given us no instructions on packing, so the servants had collected almost everything we owned, including our clothing and jewelry. Zosima had even taken some of Mother's dresses, jewels, and makeup, knowing how much they would mean to me.

Ptolly stopped rocking, looking into my eyes with what seemed like a desperate desire to believe my explanation.

"Truly," I said, smiling. "We have overburdened the servants. That is all."

Ptolly blinked and put his thumb in his mouth. He had resumed some of the habits he'd had as a baby, which confused me. When I had asked Olympus about it, he told me that sometimes young children who had lost much went back to a time when things were better and safer. He told me to be patient and that he would outgrow it.

Still, it disturbed me. I took his hand away from his mouth. "Come, let us play the finger game you love."

"The Little Papyrus Stalk?" he asked with the sideways smile that always reminded me of Tata. I nodded, making sure he wiped his wet thumb on his tunic before I began. I sat forward to block Alexandros as my twin quietly opened the curtain to peek out. I sang a little louder as I heard him gasp.

This little stalk bent in the wind . . .
This little stalk went for a swim . . .
This little stalk opened to the sun . . .
This little stalk said, "Let's have fun!"
And this little stalk cried, "Yes, yes, yes,
I will be the scroll for all your best puns!"

Ptolly giggled as Alexandros closed the curtain and sat back. I stole a look at his pale and bewildered face.

"Again, again," Ptolly commanded.

Alexandros caught my eye, then turned to Ptolly. "Oh, that is a baby's game," he announced with false cheerfulness. "Here, switch with me, sister, and I will show Little Bull a war game that is much more fun."

"Yes, yes, switch! Switch!" Ptolly cried. "Is it a fighting game? Will our fingers battle like Achilles and Hector? Can I be Achilles? Please?"

I slid under while Alexandros climbed over me. We tried to be careful, but we still unbalanced the litter, forcing one of the bearers to stumble, the carriage to sway, and all of the men to grunt in an effort to right us again. My hand trembled as I paused at the opening of the curtain. Twisted shadows on the bright linen looked like the reaching arms of ravenous monsters.

Open it! I commanded myself. Alexandros wouldn't be able to keep Ptolly's full attention for long. I carefully pulled back the curtain. My breath caught.

"Do not look, young princess," one of the bearers whispered. "It is a crime against the gods."

But gods be with me, I could not look away. On each side of the wide avenue as far as the eye could see, crucifixes bore the bodies of the dead and dying — a gruesome colonnade of misery and death. Most were unconscious, but a few moaned and begged for release. Faces swam into my recognition as I fought a wave of nausea: Mardian, Apollodorus, the young man with the brilliant brown eyes who handed our crowns to Ma'ani-Djehuti and Amunet . . . all with the anguished, agonized expressions of the tortured. Octavianus had crucified all the witnesses to our crowning ceremony — not just the head priest and priestess, but every person who had been in the room with us. I swallowed hard and closed my eyes, almost overwhelmed as I pictured the suffering of the frail old priest and the proud Amunet. I prayed that they were not suffering still.

Alexandros forced a loud laugh with Ptolly as a wave of wails rushed our way. I opened my eyes again and poked my head farther out. Another shock: slave traders whipping men, women, and even children as they herded them onto what could only have been slave boats. I clenched my teeth in order not to cry out, my eyes stinging. Our people — Greek Alexandrians, native Egyptians, and Jews — raped, robbed, and now enslaved. *This* was what Mother had been trying to prevent.

I closed the litter curtain, trying to control my breathing. Now I understood why Octavianus sent us along this route — he *wanted* us to see this. I fought another wave of nausea. His message was clear: *The crowning ceremony never happened.* And if we ever spoke the truth, slavery or worse would be our fate.

"Isis protect us, for we are at your mercy," I murmured.

"What did you say, Klee-Klee?" Ptolly asked, using his old nickname for me.

"Nothing," I said, trying to smile. "I am just tired."

I closed my eyes and silently sang Amunet's last words to me, like a prayer: *Agents in Rome . . . bring you back . . . will find you . . . trust Isis.*

Zosima stood behind us on the deck of the Roman transport ship, sniffing back tears as the sailors prepared to set off. Nafre, Ptolly's nurse, had run away before we boarded. She had told Zosima that she would not — could not — live among the Romans she hated and feared so much, even if it meant breaking Ptolly's heart.

Katep, who had begun boarding behind me, had been stopped. "No half men!" a soldier announced. "Orders from Caesar." Katep glared at him and moved to board anyway. Two soldiers grabbed him and pulled him back onto the dock.

"Unhand him!" I cried without thinking. "He is a sacred servant to the crown!"

All went quiet and then, to my dismay, the men burst out laughing. "There is no *crown!*" they hooted.

One soldier bent down to glare into my face. "Let me tell you something, you little half-breed spawn of a whore," he spat at me. "We Romans do not take orders from conquered natives, let alone *little girls.*"

The same soldier straightened and called out to the men dragging Katep away. "Wait," he bellowed. "He might be fun! Some of us might enjoy passing him around!"

More laughter. The men holding Katep began pushing him back and forth roughly. *Gods, I have made things worse! I could not bear it if Katep was hurt on my account!*

"Let him go!" the captain called from above us. "We don't have time for this. I need you two to help my men load that." He pointed to a marble obelisk on rollers pulled by a team of donkeys. The soldiers released Katep with a final shove. Katep stared at me, dazed.

"Go!" I mouthed at him in Egyptian. "Please, go!" His face crumpled — in shame? Defeat? Guilt? — as he turned away from me. It was the last I ever saw of my loyal friend and guard.

We tilted our heads back to stare up at our Great Lighthouse as we sailed out of Alexandria. Our beloved Lighthouse, symbol of our family's legacy, grew smaller and smaller until the whole of it slid under the horizon, leaving just a wisp of black smoke to wave good-bye. Only then did my brothers turn away.

But I stayed, staring into the empty expanse of ocean separating me from everything I had ever known and loved. Mother's dagger — Katep had found it for me — bit into my side as I took a deep breath.

Perhaps I would use the dagger against my enemy someday, as Mother herself had tried.

"I will not give up, Mother," I swore in Egyptian. "I will be like you. I will bide my time and strike, just as you did when your enemies tried to push you off the throne. I will reclaim my destiny and our Egypt.

"*Genestho,*" I added in a whisper, savoring the sound of Mother's own directive on my lips.

PART II: ROME

CHAPTER SIXTEEN
In What Would Have Been the Twenty-first Year of My Mother's Reign
Still in My Eleventh Year (30 BCE)

The almost two-week journey was a blur of Ptolly's tears, seasickness, grief, and worry. When the small brick lighthouse of Ostia, Rome's southwestern port city, came into view, I gasped at the ugliness and chaos of the overwhelmed wharf. I had thought all harbors were as beautiful as Alexandria's, with its swaying palms and white buildings that sparkled like crystals in the sun. But from the sea, Ostia looked like a dung pile crawling with roaches. I grasped both my brothers' hands.

"We . . . we must always remember who we are, no matter what they do to us, no matter where they take us," I whispered, remembering Mother's last instructions to me. "We must swear never to let them part us."

When neither Alexandros nor Ptolly responded, I squeezed their hands. "Vow it, please!" I urged them. "To be together, always!"

"I vow it," each of my brothers said, their voices as low and miserable as the port looked.

Stepping onto the dock in Ostia, I wondered if we had somehow stumbled off Chiron's boat and into Hades' dark domain. It seemed a damned place, dirty and dingy and packed so tightly with sweating, stinking dock men, workers, travelers, and hawkers that Roman guards had had to threaten people with their swords to carve a path for us.

Word must have spread of our arrival, for people began crowding around us. "Is that them? The whore's children?" they cried. "They shoulda drowned them! I spit on them!"

I kept my chin up, pretending I did not hear their insults as soldiers ushered us away. Even so, I had trouble breathing in the hot, fetid air. All wharves smelled fishy, I knew, but Ostia was on a scale altogether new. It was as if we slogged through the gelatinous belly of some enormous, rotting sea monster. When a hot gust of wind blew the stench in our faces, we gagged.

"Ah, the reek of Ostia's *garum* vats," one of the soldiers said from behind us. "*Now* I feel like I am home."

"*Garum?*" I asked. "The cooking sauce?"

The Roman did not answer, but Zosima made a snorting noise beside me. "In Rome, they make it from rotting fish parts," she said under her breath. "They leave fish intestines out in the sun for weeks until they melt."

We walked farther up the quay toward the barge that would take us up the Tiber and into the city. The crowds thinned out as people scurried toward the back of our procession to cheer the Roman soldiers who had begun to disembark. I heard sporadic clapping and cheering for the "heroes of Rome."

Heroes? They think they are heroes? They are nothing more than barbarians whose brawn has made them bullies of the world. . . .

"Shhh," Alexandros said. "Some of them may understand you."

I had not realized I had been muttering out loud. I tried to cover my embarrassment with outrage. "Look at them," I hissed. "Do you really think any one of these uneducated barbarians has learned the language of our ancestors? I bet not a one speaks Greek! There is little risk they will understand me."

"Still," he said. "We are in enemy territory. We must be careful. Our only weapon is silence and the appearance of acquiescence."

*   *   *

Everything about the Roman countryside seemed dark and ominous. The light was not as brilliant as it was in Alexandria. Thick, dark cypresses and pointed pines loomed over us like soldiers at attention. When we reached the city itself, rough cobblestone roads snaked off in a tangle of dark and twisted alleys and byways. I thought back to Alexandria's straight, clean, wide streets, how the Canopic Avenue stretched so wide, multiple teams of charioteers could — and sometimes did — race from end to end. I thought of our rustling palms, of fresh breezes from the sea, and sighed.

From the Tiber River, we trudged to Octavianus's compound on the crest of the Palatine Hill. Ptolly gripped my hand as we looked upon our new home, a seemingly humble house facing the street. "Is *he* going to be here?" he asked for what felt like the millionth time, his face crinkled with worry.

I shook my head, repeating the reassurance. "No. Octavianus is still in Egypt."

We stopped in the front courtyard as a mob of children raced toward us. The sight chilled me, as I was used to formal, ritualized greetings with adults. Why wasn't Octavia meeting us first? I craned my neck, looking for the woman who had given her oath of protection to Mother. We had learned earlier that Livia, Octavianus's wife, was traveling, thank the gods.

"Is he tata to all of them?" Ptolly whispered.

"In a way," our escort said. "Only that pretty blond-haired girl is of his blood. But because his sister does not have a husband, he is in charge of all of her children too."

My heart thudded with anxiety as the children reached us. I looked at their hands to see if they carried rocks or sticks they might throw at us. To my surprise, they were smiling.

"Welcome, welcome," they chanted in Latin. "We have been waiting for you all day!"

The oldest boy, a handsome blue-eyed youth of about fifteen, smiled and said in careful Greek, "As the eldest son of Gaius Claudius Marcellus and Octavia, sister of Caesar, we welcome you to the family. Oh, and please, call me Marcellus!"

His smile was so warm, so genuine, I couldn't help but smile back at him. I had probably not smiled in weeks.

"No fair!" the youngest girl said in Latin. "We do not know what you said! We have not had as many Greek lessons as you!"

Marcellus turned to her. "Tonia, we have gone through this before. They do not speak our language. We must help them —"

"We speak Latin fluently," Alexandros interrupted him. "Our father, you may recall, was the great Roman general Marcus Antonius."

Marcellus raised his eyebrows. "Your Latin is impeccable! This will make it easier for everyone."

"Hey!" the little girl named Tonia said. "My father is the general Marcus Antonius too!"

A pretty golden-haired girl who looked about a year or so younger than me stepped forward — the one the Roman said was Octavianus's daughter. "We already told you they have the same father, Tonia!" she snapped in a bossy voice. She faced us, her bearing proud. "I am Julia, only child of Gaius Julius Caesar Octavianus of the House of the Julii."

She gave me a challenging look, but Marcellus jumped in to present the others. Twelve-year-old Tiberius, dark-haired, somber, and with a handsome face marred by pink acne, nodded at us. His eight-year-old brother, Drusus, smiled more warmly. They were Octavianus's stepsons by his second wife, Livia. There were two pretty girls a bit older than me, Marcellus's sister, Marcella-the-Elder, and her younger sister, Marcella-the-Younger. They both smiled shyly. Finally, Marcellus introduced our half sisters, Octavia and Tata's daughters, Antonia-the-Elder, nine, and Antonia-the-Younger, six.

"Wait!" Ptolly laughed. "How come all you sisters have the same name?"

"We take the name of our father," Antonia-the-Elder explained. "All girls do."

"You can call her Antonia and me Tonia," the younger girl said.

I stared at them, trying to control my sense of disbelief. Did the Romans dismiss girls so absolutely they did not even bother to give them individual *names*? They had to take their father's names — even if there was more than one daughter?

"And you are?" Julia prompted me.

I started. "My apologies," I said. "I am Cleopatra VIII Selene, daughter of Cleopatra VII and Marcus Antonius. This is my twin brother, Alexandros Helios, and our younger brother, Ptolemy XVI Philadelphos. We are of the Royal House of Ptolemy."

An awkward silence followed. I had not meant to be so formal. Ptolly broke the tension with an appeal directly to Tonia. "Call me Ptolly," he said. "Do you want to meet my cat?" The little girl rushed over and they chattered excitedly as Ptolly guided her to the cart where Sebi and our other cats peered out of their wicker cages.

"Come," Marcellus said. "You must be tired from your journey. Oh — here is Mother!"

A woman emerged from the courtyard. Octavia. Our enemy's sister. Father's Roman wife. I had heard she was beautiful, and she was. Golden hair, light eyes, smooth skin, even features. Her hair had been elegantly arranged in a complicated but graceful topknot and decorated with thin lilac ribbons. She wore a tunic under a long sleeveless gown, which the Romans called a *stola*. It seemed like an excessive amount of clothing in the heat, especially since the *stola* was made out of wool. We, like most Egyptians, preferred finely woven linen.

Ptolly and Tonia raced to her. He stopped right in front of her and beamed with Tata's famous sideways grin, and Octavia put a hand on her chest, her eyes wide and her mouth gaping.

"Gods," she said. "You are the very image of my Marcus."

My Marcus?

"Hello!" Ptolly said. "I am Ptolemy XVI Philadelphos, but I am known as Ptolly or Little Bull."

Octavia crouched down to his level and smiled back, her eyes moist.

"Hello, Little Bull. I am Octavia, your new guardian. I was married to your father. And you are the spitting image of him!"

Ptolly grinned wider.

"Mama, he has a cat! They all have cats!" Tonia said.

Octavia nodded, but she seemed to have difficulty pulling her attention away from my brother.

"Mama! Cats!" Tonia repeated petulantly.

"Yes," Octavia finally said, though she did not remove her gaze from Ptolly. "Rome's rats will not stand a chance now, will they?" She straightened and looked at Alexandros, and her face softened again. "Yes, I see Marcus in you as well."

Then she turned to me. Something — surprise? — flickered over her face. But when I blinked, it was gone. "Welcome," she said, smiling, her eyes softening with kindness. I thanked Isis for how different she seemed from her evil brother, and that we were meeting our protectress before facing Octavianus's wife — the woman who would 'manage' us as his property.

Octavia touched Alexandros on the shoulder. "You must be tired and thirsty. Let us get you out of the sun where we can bring you something cool to drink."

I noticed she did not look at me again. I felt hurt and relieved all at once. On the one hand, it did not surprise me that Octavia seemed more interested in my brothers. Some women, I knew, took more to boys and men, and I was glad for Alexandros and Ptolly — especially Ptolly — for it meant they would be on the receiving end of her kindness. But I also felt anew the loss of Mother, her faith in me, her strength and certitude that I was like her and would one day rule like her. A surge of loneliness and longing for her burst so strongly in my chest, I almost stumbled.

Before we could step into the atrium, horses' hooves thundered behind us. Alexandros and I exchanged looks. Roman soldiers? What if they had changed their minds and decided they would execute or enslave us after all?

But only a young man in a finely woven tunic, followed by two attendants, cantered into view. I breathed out in relief. The children wheeled toward him as one. Grinning, the young man dismounted as they crowded around him. He was dark-skinned, with close-cropped, tight black curls, and even from where we stood, I could see he was exceptionally handsome. He carried himself like a nobleman. But he was clearly of African birth, not Roman.

"Juba!" Octavia called as he and his swarm of followers approached. "I was so worried about you! I am glad you are finally home."

Juba? That was the Punic word for *king*. Was he a Moor king? But of what African province? Utica? Zama? Numidia? And what would he be doing here, acting like a long-lost member of the family?

Tiberius peppered him with questions. "Juba, tell me! Did you fight? How many of the dirty Gyptos did you kill? What was Alexandria like?"

Alexandria? He had been a soldier serving with Octavianus? Had he been on the same boat with us? My mouth dropped open in surprise.

The young man looked at us and smiled uncomfortably. He did not answer Tiberius's questions. "I see you have made it to the family in good health, thank the gods," he said, bowing his head slightly at us.

"They call you king," I said in Punic, the primary language of North Africa. "What kingdom do you rule?"

He stared at me blankly. Had my Punic gone rusty? Mother had required that we learn most of the languages of our neighbors. I tried the Numidian Punic, which was slightly different. "I was wondering what African kingdom you rule, since they call you king."

"Stop," Alexandros whispered. "He does not understand you."

"I am sorry," Juba said in excellent Greek, shaking his head.

After I asked my question again in Greek, he laughed, showing brilliant white teeth. "But they did not call me king. They called me by my name, Gaius Julius Caesar Juba. I was from Numidia originally, but I have lived in Rome since I was an infant. The Divine Caesar was my patron, and when he died, the kind Octavia took me in."

Ptolly frowned. "Is everyone in Rome named Gaius Julius Caesar?"

Tonia stomped her foot. "Stop speaking Greek! I cannot understand anybody!"

"Sorry," Ptolly said in Latin. "I asked if —"

Alexandros jumped in, still in Greek. "But *juba* is the Punic word for *king*. Do they not realize they are calling you king every time they address you?"

"No, we did not!" Octavia said in a laugh, clearly fluent in Greek as well. "By all the gods of Olympus, you must *not* tell my brother about this. Romans hate the idea of monarchy. It will infuriate him!"

She embraced Juba and kissed him on the cheek. Juba flushed slightly and looked down. In a flash, I remembered where I had seen him before. He was one of the three young officers in the room the day we first met Octavianus in Mother's chambers. The day Octavianus twisted the truth out of Ptolly so he could hunt down and murder Caesarion. I stepped back, horrified.

"You were there," I gasped. "I recognize you now."

Everybody froze. Juba looked at Alexandros and me. "Yes, I was there," he said in a soft voice. "And I wish I had met the exalted House of Ptolemy under different circumstances."

I struggled against memories — of Caesarion whispering, *"I will see you soon, sister,"* before he left; of Octavianus's evil grin when Ptolly revealed where he had gone; of grief-ravaged Mother wrapping herself in my dead brother's cloak. I swallowed a swell of sorrow.

Alexandros must have sensed my disorientation, for he grabbed my hand. "Cleopatra Selene, not here. We must stay strong," he warned in Egyptian.

"Strong in what?" Ptolly asked, absently falling into Egyptian too.

Tonia threw her arms up in the air. *"Now* what language are they speaking?"

Alexandros looked at Juba. "We are sorry," he said in Latin. "We do not mean to interrupt your homecoming."

Octavia watched me with a concerned look. She patted my shoulder as if to soothe my distress. "Well, let's go in and make an offering to the household gods in gratitude for everyone's safe arrival," she said.

I entered the house of my enemy's sister, clinging to my brother's hand.

That night, I tossed and turned in our crowded sleeping chamber, which the Romans called a *cubiculum*. While boys and girls generally stayed in separate quarters, my brothers and I had refused to be separated, so we were crammed together into the small room, covered by a heavy brown drape for privacy.

When we had first seen the *cubiculum*, Ptolly gasped and asked why they were putting us in the slaves' quarters. Unfortunately, he asked it in Latin. The servant who had showed us to our quarters harrumphed with outrage and scurried away to gossip about us. Yet how else could we have reacted? We were used to wide, open, sunlit rooms with large windows and terraces that faced the sea. This small, dark, windowless cube looked like a storage room for broken amphorae in comparison.

I eventually fell into a dreamless sleep. But then, as I had most nights since we had left Egypt, I startled awake in the deep-dark, gasping for air. A window — why was there no window in this dark oven?

In those first few moments of confusion, I was sure that someone had locked me into an airless, sweltering tomb.

CHAPTER SEVENTEEN

Our enemy's home on the luxurious Palatine Hill — the most prestigious of the seven hills of Rome — looked small from the outside, so that the average Roman walking by could feel pride in the "modest" way the First Man of Rome lived. But on the inside, it exploded with wealth and extravagance. So many buildings and apartments surrounded his home that it was actually more of a series of interconnected estates.

Ptolly charmed everyone in the compound and responded well to the excitement and energy of a household filled with children. He and Tonia grew especially close, laughing and playing as if they had been milk mates. Alexandros spent most of his time with Tiberius and Drusus. After several weeks, Alexandros and Ptolly moved into the boys' wing. I had not been able to talk them out of it. Later I learned that they had been subject to increasingly cruel taunts from the other boys about rooming with girls.

As for me, I was dismayed to find that of all of the girls in the house, it was Octavianus's daughter, Julia, who unceasingly sought me out. Fascinated by my life as princess of Egypt, she pestered me with questions about Alexandria, our life in the palace, or what Mother had been like.

I answered her as patiently as I could, but over time, I began to exaggerate my replies out of annoyance.

"Was your mother very beautiful?" she asked for the thousandth time as we picked figs one late afternoon.

"Yes, my mother was the most beautiful woman in the world," I answered with weariness. "In fact, every man who saw her fell instantly in love." She did not seem to pick up on my sarcasm. I snatched at an overripe fig and it burst in my hand, the moist, pink flesh releasing a scent so pure and sweet I could not keep from licking my fingers.

I picked figs that day out of boredom, confined as I was in Octavianus's compound. In Alexandria, I was used to traipsing off to the Great Library, the *Museion*, the Menagerie, or the Lighthouse anytime I wanted. But here, the girls seemed never to be allowed to step past the compound's perimeter. The boys, on the other hand, often left to attend the chariot races, or they trailed after Juba as he went to the Forum or the public baths, where most of Rome's political business seemed to take place.

"What made your mother so beautiful?" Julia asked. "Did she have fair hair like mine?"

"No, she did not," I answered. "Her hair was as dark as midnight."

"Do you look much like her?"

"Some people say I do."

"But you are not so beautiful! You have a big nose!"

Somehow, our conversations always ended with a vague — or sometimes not so vague — insult aimed at me. I ignored her. I had often overheard people whisper that Octavia was prettier than Mother, and they may have been right. But Octavia's was the aloof, cool beauty of one of Praxiteles' statues, while Mother's beauty was all crackling energy and light. I used to watch people when she entered a room, just to see her effect on them. Everybody — including my brothers and me — turned their faces to her like flowers opening up to the sun. And when she looked upon you and whispered sweet words, it was as if Amun-Ra himself had caressed your cheek.

Despite my best attempts at keeping my expression impassive, Julia must have seen that her "innocent" little insult had hit its mark. With a smirk in my direction, she dropped her basket and sashayed back to the main house. I abandoned my basket too when I spotted an unfamiliar path in the dense collection of fruit trees.

Curious, I followed it, only to realize it led to the slave quarters. I stopped when I spied a man and woman lounging in the shade off the path. Turning quietly back, I paused when I realized they were talking about my brothers and me.

"Those Gypto brats are under *Dominus's* legal control now, yes?" the girl asked. "What is he going to do with them?" I recognized her as one of Livia's new slaves. I snuck closer, crouching behind a warped wooden shed to listen.

"Well," the rust-haired Gaul said, "he can beat 'em, sell 'em, or kill 'em if he wants. Law can't touch him. Really, I don't know why he hasn't done so already."

The young woman, who looked Greek, clucked her tongue. "Well, it would look bad if he hurt them now, wouldn't it?"

The guard grinned. "You know what I think? I think he's waiting for his wife to come home so she can do his dirty work for him and get rid of 'em."

Remembering Octavianus's cryptic comment about Livia "managing" us for him, a familiar pit of dread grew in my belly. The slave girl slapped him on the shoulder playfully. "Do not talk about my *domina* that way!"

"You don't know her well enough yet. The garden slaves claim she grows poisonous plants by moonlight and she's always working on special 'cures.' Ya, she'll 'cure' the house of those Egyptian half-breeds is what she'll do!"

The young woman looked askance at him. I crouched even lower, fearing that somehow my racing heart would give me away.

"It's true. Her body-slave told me she tests her poisons on old slaves. Haven't you wondered how they always seem to die off when she no longer needs 'em? Ah, but you haven't been here long enough to know that."

"Stop it, you're scaring me! And when did you ever talk to her body-slave?" she added in a jealous tone.

He laughed. "All I'm saying is that I'm glad I work for him and not her. Just do not make her angry."

The girl stared off in the direction of Livia's house with a worried expression.

"Ah, relax," the guard said as he nuzzled her neck. "I'll protect you."

I slunk away as their embrace grew more fervent. Could it be true? Was Livia as dangerous as her husband? Part of me wanted to dismiss the conversation as the idle gossip of slaves, but another part of me knew that household slaves always understood the true natures of their masters. Either way, I determined to warn my brothers to never *ever* drink or eat anything Livia Drusilla offered them. It appeared we needed to be on guard from her as much as from him.

As Greek was our first language, my brothers and I were excused from Greek lessons, though we joined the other children for tutoring in mathematics, philosophy, and literature. I was relieved to see that the girls of the household were educated alongside the boys, though sometimes we girls were forced to miss lessons for spinning work.

When I was told that I had to spin thread for cloth, I laughed, thinking it a joke. But I quickly learned that every good Roman woman was expected to know how to spin, weave, and sew clothing for the household. Octavianus often bragged that he wore only what his wife, sister, or daughter made. Nothing was further from the truth, of course. He — or more accurately, Livia — owned hundreds of skilled slaves devoted to that task. But claiming that enhanced his image as an old-fashioned, pious Roman and Livia's as a virtuous Roman matron. So, the girls of the house were forced to learn the art of spinning and weaving for when Octavianus needed to put on a show of upholding traditional Roman values.

When we entered the dark, airless spinning room, the two Marcellas and the two Antonias, as well as Julia, immediately set to work. A slave pushed a basket with a distaff, spindle, and mound of wool into my arms. "You must spin," she instructed. "*Domina*'s orders."

Julia must have seen my expression. "Oh, wait! Let me guess," she said. "Princesses do not sully their hands with such duties, yes?"

"I was never taught such noble work," I said diplomatically, hiding my distaste at the almost overwhelming smell of wool and perspiring

workers hanging heavy in the dark stone room. "In Egypt, we wear linen."
I did not add that most educated Egyptians would never wear anything
made of wool. It was considered unclean and an insult to the gods.

"In Egypt, we wear linen," mocked Julia. "In Egypt, everything is better."
The slave pointed to the elder Marcella. "You. Show her."

Marcella seemed embarrassed, and I could not tell if it was at my
lack of knowledge or at being forced to teach me such elementary work.
She picked up what looked like a hunk of hag's hair — clumped gray
strands — and held it out to me. "Pull this apart until it lengthens. But
not so much that you break it — oh. Well, try again."

As simple as it looked, I ended up accidentally shredding great hand-
fuls of the stinking wool. One of the workers behind me hissed, "Never
mind! Get her on the spindle." But I could not figure out how to hold
the long stick with my left hand while twirling the spindle with my
right. The silent room echoed with the clatters of my wooden imple-
ments on the stone floor.

Finally, Marcella leaned into me. "Ask my mother to be excused
from this work," she whispered. "You should not be expected to take it
up now when we learned it virtually at our nurses' breasts!"

I smiled gratefully at the sweet-natured girl.

"Just be sure to ask her before Livia returns," Marcella warned. "You
do not want to anger my uncle's wife." I must have looked alarmed, for
she added, "It is fine. Aunt Livia typically does not overturn a decision
made by my mother."

I found Octavia practicing her lyre by the *impluvium*, the rain pool in
the courtyard behind her small home. We children had our *cubicula*
attached to the ends of her house like military barracks — the boys on
one side, the girls on another.

"That is lovely," I said when she finished her sad tune. And it was. It
had been surprisingly full of feeling, filled with loss and longing.

Octavia looked up at me with an angry flash. "Oh! You startled me."

"I am sorry. I did not mean to. . . ."

"You are as quiet as a cat." She lowered her eyes as she took a sip from a metal cup beside her. "Would you like some wine? I can have them water it for you."

"No, thank you."

"Well, what can I do for you?" she asked, a perfect smile on her lips.

I suddenly felt shy, though I didn't know why. Octavia was meant to serve as mother to my brothers and me, but the very idea of it left me prickly. Nobody could take my mother's place! Not that Octavia tried much with me. She seemed content to dote on my brothers. Still, Tata had once been married to her, and she had been devoted enough to him to promise Mother that she would protect us.

"Marcella-the-Elder suggested that I . . . well . . ." I hesitated, hating to ask a favor of any Roman.

Octavia brightened at the mention of her daughter. "Sit, Selene, sit." She nodded toward a saffron pillow next to her on the marble rim of the pool. At our feet glimmered a fading mosaic of fish and other creatures of the sea.

I sat. "Marcella recommends that I ask you to release me from spinning duties."

A ripple of irritation moved across her face. "And why would my daughter recommend that?"

"Well, it turns out I have no talent for it, and the slaves were quite put out with the amount of wool I ruined."

"The girls in the house spin under Livia's instructions," Octavia said. "It is no small thing to disobey one of her direct orders."

My stomach clenched. Why did even Octavia seem wary of Livia Drusilla?

"Perhaps I could provide the younger children additional tutoring in Greek," I suggested. "Surely, the *Princeps*'s wife would not take offense if I were making myself useful." When she did not appear convinced,

I added, "Marcella seemed so proud of the fact that your decisions are the only ones Livia Drusilla dares not overturn."

A sly smile curled at the edges of her mouth as she stared at me. Finally, she said, "Indeed. I will tell Livia's overseer that you are officially excused from spinning."

"Thank you!" I cried.

"I wonder," she mused. "Was your mother as skilled at using flattery to get what she wanted?"

I blinked. "But I wasn't trying to flatter you. . . . Marcella is the one who said . . ." It felt as if she were insulting Mother — and me — but I could not pinpoint how. Was I just being oversensitive?

Octavia picked up her instrument and began sweetly strumming the strings. "Please send for the overseer, Selene," she said. "I will take care of everything. You need not worry."

It was a great relief to know I could trust Octavia's word, for from that moment on I was never again asked to join the other girls at spinning or weaving. My mother had chosen well in making an alliance with her. Which only made me wonder about the alliances that would help us return to Egypt. When would we be contacted by Mother's and Amunet's agents? I burned with impatience and curiosity. But then I wondered if the delay was a result of Octavianus still being in Egypt. Perhaps that made it impossible to act on our behalf.

There was no way of knowing what was really happening. And so I waited as Amunet had instructed.

CHAPTER EIGHTEEN

One month after our arrival, the entire household gathered to meet Livia Drusilla, the wife of the most powerful man in the world. She had finally returned from her travels. With her came that all too familiar sense of dread and foreboding. *Would she really try to do to us what Octavianus dared not? How would I ensure our safety around her?*

We stood with Octavia and all the other children with our backs to Livia's wall of death masks, which were designed to show her family's aristocratic lineage. The Romans called the wax masks, molded upon the faces of the dead, *imagines*. At funerals, family members donned them to show respect. (And the Romans thought our death rituals bizarre!) Across from us, the walls were painted top to bottom in blocks of brilliant reds, yellows, and blacks. I had still not gotten used to the way Romans closed themselves off in small spaces painted with elaborate outdoor scenes. Every *intsa* of wall was covered with what seemed to me a jumble of architectural and garden images. Why not just open up the rooms and let true light in as we did in Alexandria?

As the waiting continued, I noticed that I was not the only anxious one in the room. The atrium was heavy with dread. I half expected the death masks themselves to snap their eyes open in terror. Octavia had lined us up in preparation: Livia's sons first, then all of Octavia's children. We came last, of course. Still, everyone twitched and fidgeted like horses before the chariot races.

Juba, the handsome young African who had returned with us from Alexandria, did not make an appearance. I wondered about that since he seemed like such an integral part of the family. Everybody seemed to love him, including my brothers. I often heard the younger children squealing in the gardens, only to find Juba throwing one or more of them in the air or pretending to be the Minotaur and chasing them with horrible roars and grunts. Whenever I saw this, I turned away, my heart heavy with memories of the games we played with Tata.

At the sound of a door opening, Octavia straightened like a soldier called to attention. Livia emerged from her study — the *tablinum* — with an entourage of secretaries fluttering behind her. She wore her dark hair in the Roman style of the day, with the top of the hair pulled up like a crown while the sides flowed over the ears and gathered in a knot in the back. From the high-quality fabric of her long blue *stola* to the golden bobs in her ears, Livia Drusilla dripped gravitas.

I swallowed. She exuded so much confidence, power, and yes, even majesty, that I felt a piercing ache for my own mother. I closed my eyes for a moment, remembering what it felt like to be in her presence, how I fed off her strength. But I did not want this woman to remind me of Mother. She was the wife of my enemy, partner to the man who destroyed my family. The woman who, according to the slaves, might be our executioner.

She approached her sons first, smiling and kissing each boy on the forehead.

"Welcome home, Mother," Tiberius and Drusus said somewhat stiffly. Interesting that even her own sons seemed intimidated by her.

"It is good to be back," she said. She glided over to my brothers and me, her dark brown eyes flicking over us. When her eyes momentarily met mine, I willed myself not to shudder. Hers were not the cold killer's eyes of her husband, but they came close. Very close. "Ah, the new members of the household. A pleasure to finally meet you," she said.

I knew she expected us to respond — to give some sort of formal greeting, at least — but I could think of nothing to say. Alexandros spoke up. "We thank you for having us here. Your hospitality is much appreciated."

She smiled at Alexandros's formality with closed lips. "You must be Alexandros Helios. Yes, I see your father in you, as well as a little bit of your mother."

"You knew our mother?" Ptolly asked, surprised.

"Yes, I met her when she was in Rome years ago with my husband's adopted father. I was only a young girl, but I remember being dazzled by her. And you" — she peered down at Ptolly — "must be Ptolemy Philadelphos."

"Everybody calls me Ptolly! Or Little Bull!" he said.

There was amusement in her eyes, and I concentrated on not curling my hands into fists. She had better not be laughing at him.

"Well. I heard you were the very image of your father. . . ."

"It is true!" Ptolly said, grinning and puffing out his chest.

Livia exchanged a look with Octavia I could not read. Octavia smiled nervously. Why?

"And you," she said, turning to me, "must be Cleopatra Selene. The princess — oh, excuse me — the *former* princess who deems herself too good to follow my household rules."

I had not been prepared for such a casually delivered insult. I wanted to defend myself, to tell her that it was her niece's idea to excuse me from spinning, but there was no way to do so without looking as if she had cowed me. So I said nothing and raised my chin.

Livia narrowed her eyes at me ever so slightly as she waited for me to respond. Alexandros cleared his throat in what I knew was a bid to make me talk. But what could I say — thank you for not killing us this morning? For being married to the man who murdered half my family? For agreeing to do your husband's dirty work and destroy us?

Alexandros shifted his weight in a more urgent appeal. I swallowed the bitterness that was clawing up my throat. "Thank you for opening your home to us," I said, trying not to speak through clenched teeth.

She raised her head slightly, as if in victory at forcing me to speak. As she passed, her stepdaughter, Julia, asked, "When is Father coming home? How come *they* are here but not Tata?"

Livia smiled down at her. "Your tata is busy cleaning up the mess that was left in Egypt and the rest of the East," she said. "And as you know, he cannot enter Rome until after his Triumph." Her eyes darted in our direction at the word.

"Well," Julia said, putting a hand on her hip. "When is he going to have his Triumph?"

"When he is ready," Livia snapped. Julia's pretty mouth tightened into a white line as she slid her hand off her hip.

They despise each other, I realized. And for some reason, this made me happy. Octavianus had ruined my family, so it seemed just that there would be discord in his.

Days after Livia's arrival, I found an abandoned *trigon* ball behind the main fountain in the back gardens and tossed it up and down, relishing the feel of the puckered leather in my palm.

"You have the look of one who misses the game," someone said from behind me.

Juba.

"I played *trigon* with my brothers in Alexandria," I said.

"Were you any good?"

"I believe I was," I said, smiling.

"Let's see about that," he said, backing up and signaling for me to throw it at him.

"But we don't have a third!"

"We can still toss."

I reared back and threw it as hard as I could.

He caught it, grinned, and tossed the ball solidly back. "Who taught you how to play?"

"My brother Caesarion. But I played with my tata sometimes too."

We flung the ball back and forth in silence. I had not meant to put an awkward end to the conversation by bringing up my dead father and brother. Still, the slap of leather on palms, the whoosh of air as the ball soared — I found myself relaxing in a way I had not in a long time.

"Ptolly and the younger ones adore you," I said after a time.

"Ptolly is a wonderful boy. Very resilient."

I didn't mention how he used to rock and suck his thumb not so long ago.

"He looks like your father — is he like him in other ways too?"

"Yes, very much so," I said. "My tata had an irresistible smile and was always entertaining others with his charm. What about your father? Do you take after him?"

A beat of silence passed. "I know very little about my father."

"Oh."

"So tell me," he said, changing the subject. "What about lovely Alexandria-by-the-Sea do you miss the most?"

I was surprised by the question. Nobody ever brought up our home or our past, as if it were bad luck to do so. I told him about the Lighthouse; the tame gazelles that roamed the grounds; and the lions in our Menagerie. But what interested him most was the Library.

"You know, it had always been my dream to study in Alexandria," he said. "To hold in my hands the original scrolls of Aristotle or Euripides . . . It gives me chills even now to think about it." He smiled as if he were slightly embarrassed.

His admission, though, delighted me. "Oh, you would have loved it!" He caught the ball and eased toward me. He did not throw it again. "If you had been a guest in our palace, we would have given you free rein to visit any lecture, class, or debate you wished."

He smiled, his eyes bright. We settled in the shade of a large fig tree.

"Did you know that the world's best scientists and astronomers studied at our *Museion*?"

"I think I heard that, yes," he said, smiling.

"Well, sometimes Sosigenes invited me and my brothers to his private observation deck to watch the night sky."

"Sosigenes? The same Sosigenes who helped my patron, Julius Caesar, fix our calendar?"

I grinned. "The very one. He was my mother's favorite court astronomer. Once, the old man tried to tell me that the brilliant lights falling through the night sky were not the tears of the gods at all but merely rocks bursting into flame as they fell to Earth!"

He looked at me, astonished. "Really?"

I nodded.

"What else did he tell you?"

We spoke of the scientists who made temple doors open via hidden pulleys, of the mathematicians who determined the circumference of the earth by measuring noontime shadows, of the engineers experimenting with heat to make objects move.

Juba sighed. "It sounds like a magical place." We sat in contented silence for a time, Juba looking off into the distance.

"How come you did not have to greet Livia with the rest of us the morning after she arrived?" I eventually asked.

His eyes refocused on me. "What?"

"The rest of the family had to line up as if for military inspection."

He laughed. "You mean, the children."

I nodded.

"As an adult, I was spared that fine custom. I joined her in the *triclinium* later for the evening meal."

So. He'd had his manhood ceremony. I thought of Caesarion's celebration. "Did you have a feast in honor of Liber and Libera too?" I asked.

He smiled. "Just last year. Before I set off to join Caesar in Alexandr —" He stopped.

I looked down at my hands. He had been there! I had almost forgotten.

He cleared his throat. "Would you tell me about your mother? I know very little about her."

My insides melted into warm wax. No Roman had ever asked about Mother besides Julia, who always did so to find some way to insult me or her. The only time Mother seemed to live for me was when my brothers and I whispered remembrances in the dark. I nearly burst at the chance to talk about her. "Mother spoke seven languages!"

He raised his eyebrows.

"She never used translators when she met with diplomats. She had us learn many languages too, which is how we know some of your Numidian Punic."

He looked down for a moment. "Everybody loved her," I rushed on. "Not every Ptolemy king was named pharaoh throughout greater Egypt, because that honor was bestowed only by the sacred Priests of Ra. But Mother was pharaoh as well as queen!"

He smiled.

"And she wrote many books! She wrote volumes on science, mathematics, and Nile farming, among others," I said, aware that I sounded like I was bragging, but not caring.

"Really? Your mother sounds like an exceptional person."

"She was," I agreed, smiling at him. "She was."

CHAPTER NINETEEN

I worried about Alexandros as the months went by, for he seemed more and more withdrawn. One evening, as we all headed to our rooms for the night, I tried to speak with him about it.

"What do you want, sister?" Alexandros said.

The coldness in my twin's voice felt like a punch to the stomach. "I need to talk to you," I said.

"Now? It's late." His eyes flickered to the torch-carrying servant leading Tiberius and the other boys. He seemed nervous, though I could not imagine why.

"I do not care how late it is. I want to talk to you *now!*"

Drusus turned to look at us. Alexandros must have seen it, for he clenched his fists. "Sister, you need to go with the girls. It's not proper for you to follow us like this."

"Why are you two fighting?" Ptolly asked.

I turned to him, straining to smile. "We are not fighting. Come on, Little Bull. Jump on my back. I bet I can still carry you that way!" He grinned and jumped on me. I grabbed his legs and staggered for a moment. "Isis! You are the biggest seven-year-old I know. I'm going to have to start calling you 'Big Bull'!"

Ptolly laughed.

"Put him down!" Alexandros said. "You two are making a scene."

"Ptolly, I miss you," I said. "Why don't you come to my room with me to sleep, just like when we first arrived?"

"Yes, yes!" he nearly shouted. I knew then that he missed me greatly too. Ptolly was too young to be among the boys anyway. He should have stayed with me.

Alexandros frowned. "Ptolly, don't be ridiculous. You cannot go with the girls. . . ."

"And why not?" I cried. "What is so horrible about being with his sister?"

Ptolly kicked his legs to indicate he wanted down. He ran to Alexandros and grabbed his hand. "Yeah, we boys have to stick together," he said. They started walking away, but I followed.

"Ptolly!" I cried. "You have it wrong! It is the three of *us* who need to stick together. Remember your vow? We cannot let them separate us!"

"Go back!" Alexandros hissed at me as we neared his wing. "Go with the girls." He jerked Ptolly's hand, running to catch up with the other boys.

I stood in shock, not moving, long after the flickering torch disappeared into the dark. He could not do this. We had made a vow! And just because the boys in Roman families disparaged their sisters did not mean he had to act that way with me. We were different. I was the moon to his sun!

I wrapped my woolen cloak tighter around me in that dark Roman winter night. *No, I will not wait*, I thought. *I will address it this very instant.* I stomped toward my brother's room, my thick leather soles on the brittle frost sounding like the crunching of broken glass.

I swung aside the heavy drape hanging over the front of my brother's tiny *cubiculum*. "Alexandros," I said. "I do not care what you say . . . Isis! What —"

"Get out of here!" Alexandros ordered me through gritted teeth. "Now!"

I had caught my brother in the act of undressing, and in the flickering light of the small bronze lamp, I saw black-and-blue bruises — some fading into yellow-green, others still red and darkening — splattered all over his torso and arms. "How did you get those?" I nearly squealed. "Who is hurting you?"

He threw a clean tunic over his head. "It is none of your business."

"Tell me," I repeated. "Who is doing this to you?"

"Cleopatra Selene, I warn you. Stay out of my business."

"But you are my brother, my twin, we are bound by the sacred laws. . . ."

"No, we are not!" he almost shouted. I was glad he had fallen into speaking Egyptian. I did not want curious ears overhearing our fight. "Not anymore."

It had to be one of the boys. "It's Tiberius, isn't it?" Livia's eldest. I had thought him cold like his mother — he was usually sullen around adults — but around other children, he seemed to enjoy being cruel. Alexandros did not respond, nor did he look at me. "No? Then gods, it's all of them! Tiberius, Drusus, Marcellus . . ."

"No, not Marcellus."

I was grateful that Octavianus's favorite was not involved. But realizing that Livia's sons had declared war on my brother made my stomach roil in fear. "Are they hurting Ptolly as well?"

"No. I would kill them if they tried," Alexandros said, balling his hands into fists.

"I would as well," I muttered, breathing out with relief. I looked around. "Where is Ptolly? Does he know?"

"He ran to Marcellus to ask him something." He did not answer the second question. "I know what you are thinking," Alexandros continued. "You're thinking, 'How could you be the son of Marcus Antonius when you can't even defend yourself against those snot-nosed idiots?'"

"That is not what I think! It is *because* you are the son of the great warrior Marcus Antonius that they try to hurt you."

Alexandros ignored me, pacing like a cat in a cage. "He is sneaky," he said. "Tiberius. He attacks when there is no one else to see, when I least expect it, when it looks like it is all in jest. If I defend myself, I am pulled off and beaten by any household slave who thinks they have a right to put a hand on me, because *Tiberius* has given them the order to do so." His voice quavered and he stopped talking, trying to regain control. He had been in Rome long enough to know Romans were disgusted by any show of emotion — especially in boys and men.

Even as I felt a stab of sadness at how Rome was changing him, I stared at my twin, aghast. We had grown up as the sacred children of the incarnation of the Goddess. Our persons were off-limits to everyone except our consecrated servants. To have even the lowliest slave manhandle him or beat him at Tiberius's order was beyond conception.

"Then when it is time for military exercises," he continued, "they keep me away from the training grounds."

"What do you mean? They cannot do that!"

"Oh, yes they can," he said with a bitter laugh. "And do you know what they say? 'Caesar has given strict orders that no son of Marcus Antonius will be allowed to train as a warrior.' So Tiberius learns how to fight and practices on me when no one is looking. Or sometimes when everybody is."

"Have you talked to Octavia about this?"

He stopped pacing and looked at me, head tilted in irritation. But before he could speak, a hand shoved the heavy curtain aside.

"I hear a girl's voice. What is going on in here?" Tiberius said, stepping into the small *cubiculum* with us.

Alexandros groaned.

"Oh-ho! Look at this," Tiberius said, eyes glinting. "Brother and sister having a sweet moment. Drusus, come here!"

I stiffened. I used to think he could have been handsome had his face not been covered in angry, inflamed acne, but now I knew it wasn't the skin that was the problem. It was the deep well of cruelty in his eyes. Drusus came running.

"I knew you sick Egyptians couldn't stay away from each other," Tiberius leered. "Just had to get some 'private time' with each other, right?"

"What are you talking about?" I spat.

"You two were going to get married, weren't you? Is that why you can't bear to be apart? Admit it!" he growled. "You were going to *lie* with each other like every other sick Ptolemy that ever lived. You were going to break all the laws of decency. Come on, show us how you would do it!"

I remembered how Amunet and Ma'ani-Djehuti had named us *King and Queen, Brother-Sister, Husband-Wife* during our doomed crowning ceremony. It hadn't seemed at all strange then — hadn't royal brother-sister marriages always been blessed by Isis and Osiris? But after living in Rome, I saw it, for the first time, through their eyes — as an abomination.

I flushed in confusion, anger, and shame. Drusus put a hand to his mouth and giggled. Tiberius grabbed my upper arm and pushed me toward Alexandros's chest. "Come on! Do it, you incestuous Gyptos. We want to see."

"Do not touch me!" I shouted.

"Ha! The girl is the one with all the fight!"

"Leave her alone," Alexandros warned.

Tiberius stepped up to my brother and grinned. "There is not a damn thing you can do to stop me."

Alexandros, red-faced, pushed Tiberius hard. Tiberius must not have been expecting it, for he lost his balance and slammed against the small trunk in the corner.

"Oh, that was a very big mistake, princeling," he said, scrambling up quickly.

"What are you going to do — ask the laundry slave to beat me for you?"

Tiberius advanced. I jumped between them. "Stop it!" I yelled.

Ptolly burst in. "What is happening? Why are you yelling?"

Marcellus came in right behind him. As the oldest and favorite of Octavianus, he commanded great respect among all the boys. "What is going on here?" he asked.

"He pushed me," Tiberius said.

"After you pushed me!" I cried.

Marcellus turned to Tiberius. "Tell me you did not push a girl."

Tiberius shot me a withering look.

"Can someone please tell me what is going on?" Marcellus asked again.

"Tiberius has been beating my brother," I said.

Alexandros groaned behind me. "I can take care of myself, Cleopatra Selene," he said.

Tiberius smirked. Marcellus narrowed his eyes at him ever so slightly. I knew that there was little love between the stepcousins. "Do not bring the wrath of the gods down upon this house by breaking the laws of *xenia*," Marcellus warned.

"The law of caring for guests applies to *guests*," Tiberius growled. "Not hostages captured in war."

"My mother would be outraged to hear how you are acting," Marcellus said.

Tiberius blanched. "Well, then, don't tell her!"

I noticed that Marcellus did not threaten to tell Livia, Tiberius's own mother — probably because she would applaud his actions. Yet the threat of being shamed in front of Octavia made Tiberius step back. With a flicker of satisfaction I realized that Mother had selected just the right person to watch over us. It was as if she protected us even from the other side.

Ptolly grabbed my hand. He looked about to burst out crying. I knelt down. "Everything is fine," I said, trying to force a smile. "Just a misunderstanding."

Tiberius snorted.

"Come back with me," I whispered with a tight throat. "We will play quiet games all night to annoy Zosima, just like the old days."

But Ptolly shook his head. He had made his choice. He would stay with the boys.

"Come on, Selene," Marcellus said. "Let me escort you back to your wing. It is time for all you boys to be in your own rooms."

Tiberius and Drusus scurried out of Alexandros's *cubiculum* right away. I kissed Ptolly on the cheek, but Alexandros would not even look at me.

I walked beside Marcellus, who carried a small bronze oil lamp shaped like a singing bird, the flame emerging from the open beak.

"Will you . . ." I paused, knowing that what I was about to ask would infuriate Alexandros, but pushed on anyway. "Can you make Tiberius stop hurting my brother?"

Marcellus sighed.

"Please?"

"You don't understand," Marcellus said. "Tiberius is not easy to control. And I can't challenge him directly. . . ."

"Why not?"

"Because I have sworn an oath to my mother that I would not. He is Livia's eldest. It is difficult enough for him, knowing that his stepfather chooses me as his favorite, without me appearing to taunt him about it. The best thing for Alexandros to do is stay out of his way."

"Can you at least make him stop commanding slaves to beat Alexandros?"

Marcellus stopped, eyes wide. "What — he orders the *slaves* to beat him? That is outrageous! Yes, I will certainly put a stop to that."

I smiled up at him in relief. Alexandros would still have to deal with Tiberius, but at least the odds were better. Marcellus grinned in return. A warmth spread in my chest as I realized that with Marcellus on my side, I could actually do something. I could truly help my brother. I had made my first alliance.

Marcellus may have ordered the slaves to leave my brother alone, but it was Juba, I discovered weeks later, who gave Alexandros the means to truly protect himself.

I had been looking for a shady spot to read when I came upon them in a remote and secluded clearing. My mouth dropped open when I saw my brother wielding a wooden sword and shield. Juba was teaching Alexandros how to fight! Their weapons thudded rhythmically against each other. When they paused, Juba's low voice floated toward me as he corrected my brother's movements.

I sat down, unnoticed, with my arms wrapped around my legs, my chin on my knees. After a time, they dropped their weapons and practiced hand-to-hand fighting. Juba came up from behind my brother again and again until Alexandros successfully wrestled him to the ground and kept him there. Their laughter hung in the warm spring air.

"I would love to see the look on Tiberius's face when you pull this move on him," Juba said. "He will not sneak up on you again after that!"

They left the clearing without ever seeing me. I wondered if Alexandros asked for his help or if Juba had seen what was happening and offered. Either way, it looked like my brother had made an alliance too.

CHAPTER TWENTY

My enemy's wife dictated in rapid Latin to her lady as they strolled the garden. I usually avoided Livia, but today I needed her approval to leave the compound. Octavia was always gracious if not outright permissive with me — which is why I preferred to ask her — but she was visiting a friend. I had no choice but to approach Livia Drusilla.

Livia stopped talking at the sight of me.

"Excuse me," I said. "I have read most of the scrolls your lady has offered me. I seek permission to go to the public library for additional reading material."

Livia gave some silent signal to her secretary, who snapped closed the wooden wax tablets, lowered her head, and stepped back.

"No."

"But . . ." I had not expected such a terse answer. I cleared my throat. "May I ask why?"

"You cannot go to Rome's 'public library' because Rome does not *have* one," Livia answered.

"I do not understand. How is that possible? Even Pergamum has a fine library. Where do your scholars go when they need to do research?"

Livia frowned and narrowed her eyes at me, a look that could melt a Roman broadsword. It only made me want to raise my chin higher. Her stare of dominance was good, but it did not come anywhere near Mother's Horus stare.

"Scholars go to their *patrons'* libraries," Livia said slowly.

"But what if the patron does not have what they need? What do they do then?"

"They sail to Alexandria to study in your — excuse me, your *former* — library. But not for much longer. Soon most of the scrolls will come here."

"What?"

"Yes. We will build Rome's first public library with the scrolls taken from your family's collection," she said. "Scrolls come with every boat from Alexandria. Until the library is built, most of them are stored in my husband's *tablinum*, which I give you permission to visit."

Our Library, gutted. I could not imagine what a loss this was to our scholars. A surge of anger bubbled up my throat as I realized she was smirking. She *enjoyed* watching me suffer at the news of the destruction of our precious Library! I would not give her the satisfaction. I brightened and smiled at her. "Thank you for the permission to read from this new and most valuable collection," I said, and walked off.

On the way toward my enemy's house, images of the endless colonnade of the dead and dying in Alexandria — so many of them scholars from our Library — burst into memory, and I suppressed a groan. I never knew when these images would descend and take my breath away. Sometimes I saw Tata dying in a pool of blood. Other times I heard the wails of our people at the news of Mother's death.

I shook my head to clear it. Why did the gods send me these visions? Was it so that I would not forget the crimes against my family and my people? So I could keep close my pain in order to mete out a just retribution when I ruled Egypt? And when would Amunet's agents contact us? When would something happen?

I entered Octavianus's *tablinum* and walked straight into a wall — or at least that is what it felt like. I landed on my backside on the bumpy, tessellated floor, which scratched the backs of my thighs. Scroll dowels clattered everywhere and someone cursed in Latin. I looked up.

"Gods!" Juba said. "I did not see you! Are you all right?" His hand reached down to help me up.

"What are you doing here?" I asked, pulling my *tunica* down.

"I needed some additional scrolls for my research," Juba said. "What about you? I would think this is the last place you would want to go."

"Yes, well, I do not have much of a choice, if I want to read anything besides Roman homilies about virtuous Roman women," I answered, referring to the scrolls Livia's lady foisted on us.

Juba chuckled. We bent to pick up the scattered scrolls.

"Livia tells me a lot of these new scrolls are coming from our Library in Alexandria. Is that true?"

"That is the truth, yes," he said, rerolling a scroll.

I looked around the crowded *tablinum* and sighed. I picked up a scroll thrown haphazardly on a table and put it up to my nose, breathing in the faint reedy smell of papyrus. Even the oldest scrolls still carried a hint of green from the marshy papyrus groves on the Nile. The scroll's fastener and tag were made of leather. Papyrus and leather, the smells of the Great Library. I could almost see the sun motes dancing in the beams of light from the high windows . . . hear the low murmurings of scholars deep at work . . . the giggles as Alexandros and I hid from each other among the rows and rows of stacks overflowing with scrolls . . .

"So, you never told me. What scroll are you looking for?"

I cleared my throat. Should I tell him I was hoping to find Manetho's *A History of Egypt* for its analyses of successful dynasties throughout Egypt's long history? Mother had often referred to Manetho's works. I decided to play it safe. "Oh, I am not sure. Anything that catches my fancy. What about you? What are you researching?"

He laughed. "You mean, what am I *not* researching? Everything about our history, I find fascinating."

"Oh! Are there many works on Numidia's history, then?" I asked. Besides knowing that Punic was the dominant language of the land, I knew very little about his homeland. It would not be a bad thing to learn more about Egypt's North African neighbors. "Maybe you can recommend something for me to read about Numidia."

He blinked. "No, I mean *Roman* history. I am doing research on Rome's history."

An awkward beat passed. "I'm sorry. I'm confused. You come from Numidia, yes?"

"I was born there, yes, but I am a Roman citizen," he replied with finality.

I found this attitude surprising but did not know what else to say. So I pointed to his collection of scrolls and said, "How do you carry them all?"

He laughed. "My man has already left with one basketful."

I playfully reached over, snatched a scroll from his arms, and unwound it. "Let's see. Polybius. *The Roman Constitution*. Would that be the document that contains all of the laws Octavianus has broken to take sole control of Rome?"

He took in a hissing breath and looked around. "Gods, Cleopatra Selene! You should not joke about these things in Caesar's own household. Do you not realize the danger?"

"Well, of course I realize the danger!" I snapped, embarrassed by his reaction. I had only meant to make him smile. After a breath, I added, "Thank you for using my full name." Everybody in Rome, except for my brothers, had begun calling me Selene, dropping my mother's name as if it had never existed. It did not matter how many times I insisted they use my correct name. The Romans had taken my parents, my brother, my people, and my home. I would not let them take my name too.

"You are welcome."

I pulled another scroll from his pile and unwound it. "Oh! Caesar's writings on the Wars in Africa. Caesarion used to read some of his tata's books to me. So this is about what happened to you then, right? Isn't that when Caesar killed your father and brought you to Rome?" I knew Juba had also been a prince, taken in defeat when Julius Caesar conquered his homeland, Numidia. He had been barely a year old when he was captured.

Juba pulled both scrolls from my hand and replaced them in his stack. He cleared his throat. "Julius Caesar did not kill my father."

"He didn't?"

"No, he did not. My father and his ally, the Roman general Petreius, committed suicide by battling each other to the death before Caesar's legions arrived. They died honorable deaths as warriors."

I looked down and swallowed. That's what Tata had wanted — an honorable death as a warrior. Octavianus took that from him too.

"What happened to your mother?" I asked.

Juba hesitated. "I do not know."

I could feel my jaw drop. "But how could you not know what happened to your own *mother*, the woman who gave you life, the queen of your rightful kingdom?"

He shrugged. "The destruction of my family was not a popular topic in Rome."

"Was she killed?" I asked. "Did they cut down your brothers and sisters in the desert like they cut down Caesarion? Why did they save you and not anyone else in the royal household? Did your mother live long enough to —"

"I *said*, I do not know." ·

"But why didn't you —"

"Asking 'why' is an exercise in futility," he interrupted. "Do you think I never asked myself why they saved me and killed the rest of my family? Do you think I never wondered what my mother was like? Or regretted never having my father beside me? The important question is not 'Why was I saved?' but 'What will I do with the life that the gods decided to spare?'"

I was taken aback by his intensity, especially since he always seemed so calm and unflappable. "You are a Stoic, then," I muttered, remembering Euphronius's lessons.

"Yes, that's right. I am a Stoic. I do not spend my passions railing against what has already happened or what cannot be changed."

"But where is the line between accepting your fate and just *rolling over*? I am not trying to be rude, but as the rightful king of Numidia, shouldn't you have worked to fight for control of what was yours by birthright?"

He laughed irritably. "When you have discovered a way to stop Rome from doing whatever it wants, please *do* let me know." With that, he grabbed his scrolls and left the room.

Guiltily, I looked down at my hands. Juba was one of the few people in Rome who treated my brothers and me with respect and kindness; I should not have upset him. Worse, I had judged him even though I was no better. What had I done to change *my* situation?

We'd been in Rome ten months and still no agents had contacted us. Remembering the slaughtered priests and priestesses, I had a new and distressing thought. What if there *were* no agents in Rome? What if Octavianus had crucified every single person who might have helped us? What if we really were abandoned to this cruel fate, never to return to Egypt and rule?

I shivered. No. Amunet had instructed me to wait and trust Isis. And I would — I would trust the Goddess of All. I had no other choice.

The painting seemed to cover the sky. A voluptuous woman, fairer and fuller than Mother ever was, lay naked, her head thrown back and eyes closed as if in pain or ecstasy. The artists had added three-dimensional touches — a gold-painted *uraeas* crown on her head; gilded bangles at her wrists; and a giant snake, made out of cloth, bobbing in the wind with its teeth attached to her breast.

Eight men held the image aloft on thick wooden poles. Even with only torches for illumination, I could feel my face redden. Alexandros would not meet my eyes. He was as horrified as I was. Ptolly did not seem to understand.

"Herakles!" he nearly shouted when he saw it. "Look at that snake! Is that how that lady died?"

I could not speak.

"Ptolly," Alexandros said in an undertone as people watched us for our reaction. "That is supposed to represent . . . It is supposed to be Mother."

Ptolly looked up at the painting again. "But that's not what Mother looked like! And this lady has no clothes on!"

The soldiers and servants milling around with torches laughed and made lewd sounds.

"Ptolly, look at me," I said. He turned his kohl-outlined eyes toward me, his golden-striped headdress from Egypt glimmering in the pre-dawn light. Octavianus had ordered that we dress in our official royal garb from home. "Remember what we talked about? We are going to hear people say terrible things about Mother and Tata today. We must be strong and pretend we don't hear them."

Ptolly scrunched his face in an exaggerated scowl. "This is stupid!"

"But there is nothing we can do about it."

Exactly one year after Mother's death, Octavianus was finally celebrating his victory over my parents with a triple Triumph — three days of parades followed by gladiatorial games and feasting. Besides the free wine that flowed, the highlight of each day was heaping abuse on the chained "Enemies of Rome" as they were marched in the parade, ending with their executions and the dumping of their bodies on the Forum steps. Two former allies of Tata — Adiatorix of Pontus and Alexander of Emesa — had been marched and executed the day before.

"But they won't kill *us*," Alexandros had insisted earlier. "Both Juba and Marcellus said that when the Triumph is over, we will be led back to the compound, where we'll be safe."

Octavia had also tried to comfort us. "Soon it will be over," she had said earlier that morning as she held on tightly to Ptolly. "And everything will be all right again."

I shivered now, despite the heat. Sweat already plastered my white pleated linen dress to my back, even though the sun had only just begun to peek over the hills. High summer in Rome was miserable enough without a long trek through the dusty, smoky, overcrowded city. Even from outside the gates, we could tell the streets reeked of urine, vomit, and wine.

Iron chains, painted to look like gold, connected me and my brothers by shackles around our necks. Huge, heavy links dragged on the ground between us. I scratched my scalp under the ceremonial braided wig they had forced me to wear. It was too hot for a wig this heavy, but we were to look as Egyptian as possible. Octavianus did not want people to remember that we were the children of their most beloved general, or that they were really celebrating the triumph of one Roman over another Roman.

Alexandros made a noise and motioned with his head. Octavianus was coming our way. As Roman tradition dictated, his face was covered in red paint, aping the statue of the great god in the Temple of Jupiter

Optimus Maximus. This was the first time we had seen him since those murderous days in Alexandria. He grinned at us as he passed, sending a chill down my spine. The sharp little teeth in that red face made him look like he had just raised his head from gorging on the carcass of a wild beast.

Octavianus walked to his chariot, which had been rolled up behind us. I groaned. That meant we were to be marched directly in front of him, that we were his "prized" captives. Since Mother escaped this humiliation, we would have to endure it for her.

I watched as the Roman senators lined up behind Octavianus. Two white-haired senators in their bordered togas gesticulated angrily at him. I edged closer to hear.

"But the Senate always marches *before* the Conqueror! What kind of message are you sending to make us march behind you?" cried one of the men.

"Ah, but you misunderstand, Lucius," Octavianus said. "It is with great respect that I *allow* you to walk behind me. It is an honor for you."

The senators exchanged a look. "Caesar, this is a break with tradition that smacks of illegal usurpation —"

"Move it! Move it!" cried an officer, gleaming in his bronze armor. "Get it into position now. The Triumph begins!"

At the sight of the man's drawn broadsword, the old senators acquiesced, but not without withering looks at Octavianus. I had just witnessed Octavianus symbolically making himself more powerful than the Senate. And this from the man who claimed he was "restoring the Republic"! What kind of hold did he have on Rome that only two senators dared question him?

Marcellus trotted up on a gleaming white horse. As Octavianus's heir, he would ride on the right side of the Imperator's chariot. I felt a wave of shame that Marcellus would see me like this. I turned my back, knowing that Tiberius, riding on Octavianus's left, would likely be smirking at us. Juba, I guessed, was probably marching with the young officers behind the chariot. Livia, Octavia, and all the rest of the children would watch the procession from a special box in the grandstands.

The lowing of bulls and the roaring of the crowd indicated that the sacrificial animals had passed the gate. All of the fifty bulls would be sacrificed at the end of the Triumph. Soon, Rome would be awash in blood and entrails. We moved in the procession slowly, as carts and stretchers laden with all of the riches stolen from our palace and Egypt glimmered before us in the sun — huge mounds of gold, ivory, onyx, lapis lazuli, emeralds, spices, cinnamon, pearls. A group of men held aloft a painted representation of the billowing Nile, showing its seven sacred mouths. Greek *pedagogi*, dressed in the white tunics and white sandals of our Library scholars, pulled cartloads of scrolls plundered from our Great Library. Nearly naked, sweating slaves groaned under the ropes and pulleys of gigantic obelisks and sphinxes taken from our sacred temples. When they rolled out a giant terra-cotta re-creation of Pharos, our Great Lighthouse, one drunk yelled, "Hey, that lighthouse is not so big!"

I didn't know whether to laugh or cry.

Still, the supposed portrait of my mother in her death throes elicited the most responses. Catcalls, jeers, spitting, hissing, booing, throwing of rotten fruit and rocks — the painting seemed to excite the crowds into convulsions of hatred.

"Whore! Bitch! Slut! Sorceress!" The insults fell on us like hailstones raining down from the sky. We had no way to protect ourselves from the assault. The twisted, hate-filled faces of the Romans lining the streets, I knew, would haunt my nightmares for the rest of my life. The crowds grew even more venomous when they saw us.

"It's the whore's children!"

"The little bastards!"

"Kill 'em!"

I raised my chin at the insults and looked straight ahead. Glancing out of the corner of my eye, I could tell that Alexandros had done the same.

"Where's your great queen now?" voices jeered. Liquid spattered at my feet, and I realized someone had thrown a used chamber pot at us, the strong scent of urine filling the air. Amidst the shouting and insults, I heard Ptolly sniffing, "I hate them! I hate them!" I squeezed his hand.

At the sight of Octavianus, the crowds grew deafening. "Our Savior!"

"Io Caesar!"

"Bringer of peace!"

"Bringer of death," I mumbled.

The procession crawled at an infinitesimal pace. The sun climbed in the sky and bore down upon us, making me pant under its weight of relentless, blinding heat. The reek of human sweat and cheap wine; the cacophony of yells, curses, and roars; the plumes of smoke from sacrificial fires gathering like black storm clouds over the city . . . As the iron chains dragged behind us, I felt as if I moved in a nightmare where my limbs grew heavier and heavier, trapping me in a paralysis of hopeless despair.

But we had no choice. We had to continue on. And I would not give these people the satisfaction of watching me stumble. Over the long, hot parade route, it was Ptolly who worried me the most. I stole a glance at him once and saw that he had been crying, the kohl melting into rivers of black running down his cheeks. He looked up at me with such pain-filled eyes that I could barely breathe. *Oh, sweet Ptolly,* I thought, *how can they make you do this?* Then I remembered that Juba was marched in a Triumph like this when he was little more than a baby. The difference was, he would not have understood the vitriol aimed at him. Almost-eight-year-old Ptolly did.

As if he were still a toddler, I leaned down to pick him up, wanting to ease his physical discomfort if nothing else. Alexandros saw what I was doing and touched my shoulder. "I have him," he mouthed over the deafening noise, lifting Ptolly up into his arms. Ptolly wrapped his limbs around him, buried his face in Alexandros's shoulder, and sobbed.

Some of the comments hurled at us began to change. I heard one woman shout, "By the gods, they are just children!" But the crowd turned on her, yelling "Traitor!" and "Gypto lover!"

That woman is someone's mother, I thought. I wanted to tell her that the painting that almost blotted the sky was not my mother, that my mother would have protected us from this. But then I remembered that we were here without her, and my thoughts grew muddled with despair and confusion. My tongue cleaved to the roof of my mouth in a terrible thirst. Every muscle, straining at the weight of the chains, screamed to rest.

At congested points, the procession stopped and we were forced to stand still in the faces of those cursing us and praising Octavianus. The soldiers, bringing up the rear, bellowed ribald songs about the man who had led them to victory, a tradition Father had told me about. When I focused on the words of their song, though, I flushed in embarrassment. They were not about Octavianus at all.

Poor Antonius,
Trapped in a web!
The queen grabbed his obelisk
And now they're both dead!

I stole a look behind me as the crowds whooped and jeered. Octavianus also looked furious, but probably because he wanted them to sing his *praises,* not remind the people about Father. Any mention of Marcus Antonius could shatter the pretense that this had been anything but his made-up war to take sole control of Rome. My guess was proved right when the officers tried to shut their men up, but most of the soldiers were too drunk to pay much attention. So the commanders chanted a new song that, after a few minutes, hurtled down the line of legions like a wave moving to shore:

Io Caesar!
We give him our hand.

Now we can retire
And work our own land.

This ditty the soldiers belted out with gusto, for that was how Octavianus had gained their loyalty — the promise of land upon retirement. He could never have delivered on that promise without stealing Egypt's wealth. I looked back at Octavianus again. He grinned, chest puffed out, looking like a bloody weasel.

I could not tell how many hours had passed. In front of the viewing stands, I straightened my back, knowing that Julia and all the others watched us. I glanced up at the special box where Livia and Octavia sat, and I spied Tonia weeping on her mother's shoulder. The sight of her tears over her beloved Ptolly filled me with cruel satisfaction. Yet it also made me feel hopeful. Somebody else loved my little brother enough to cry over his mistreatment.

As the crowds pressed even tighter, we neared the last stretch of the procession. It would continue up to the Capitoline Hill and end at the Temple of Jupiter Maximus. Alexandros put Ptolly down. It was almost over.

Then — blackness. I gasped. A blanket had been thrown over us. "Do not fight us, do you understand?" someone growled in guttural Latin, a sword tip pressing into my back.

CHAPTER TWENTY-TWO

"Ptolly! Alexandros!" I cried, but my voice was swallowed up by the blanket and the noise around us. People roared and clapped as someone shuttled us out of the procession.

"Klee-Klee!" Ptolly shouted. Blindly, I reached for him and he grasped my hand. In my moment of panic, I had forgotten the chains that bound us together. I breathed out with relief. We would not be — could not be — separated.

"What's happening?" Alexandros cried.

The sounds of hobnailed boots and jangling metal-link armor meant we'd been taken by soldiers. Were they escorting us back to the compound? But why under a blanket? Then I realized it was probably for our protection in case the mobs worked themselves into a frenzy of hatred and attacked us.

The roughly woven blanket smelled of sweat and old hay. People cursed as we bumped into them. The soldiers pushing us barked orders. An exchange of words. We were brought inside a building and dragged down rough stairs. The smell of wet stone. I shivered as the sweat on my body cooled. The roaring of the crowd above us sounded like rocks tumbling down a hill.

The blanket disappeared, and I blinked into the darkness as someone pushed my head forward to unlock the shackle around my neck.

"Where are we?" Ptolly asked. "I'm thirsty. Can I have some water?"

Our liberator, a sweat-soaked centurion, did not respond. "We will get some water soon," I promised Ptolly, my lips cracking like overbaked clay.

After unchaining us, the soldier ushered us down a hallway and into another dark room. As my eyes adjusted, I saw a filthy man on his knees, naked, bleeding, shivering. He looked up, his eyes huge in dread. In one swift movement, someone threw a garrote around the man's neck and began choking him.

My heart pounded. We were in the *Tullianum?* The pit where they strangled Enemies of Rome? Ptolly hid his face, breathing hard in terror. But . . . but we were supposed to go back to the Palatine! A part of me stepped outside my body. *This is not happening. I am not watching a man get strangled to death in front of me.*

The man's eyes bugged, the cords in his neck strained, and his face turned purple as he thrashed, fighting for air. "Look away!" Alexandros hissed. I jumped and closed my eyes. But the horrible sounds remained — the man's desperate gasps and splutters, the impatient breathing of the soldier behind us. Ptolly crying. The heavy thump of the body as it hit the ground, and then the smell of loosed bowels as his body released.

"Take him up to the Forum and throw him down the steps," the executioner ordered the two men standing beside him when the body stopped twitching. Each man grabbed an ankle and walked toward the wet stone steps. Muffled roars and cheers from the crowds above us echoed at the signal of another successful execution. I could not tell how deeply underground we were, but it seemed as if the sound of the dead man's head thumping on the steps as he was dragged out went on forever. Too soon I realized it was only us, the executioner, and the Roman soldier.

Oh, gods, were we next? Our captor pushed us forward. Ptolly howled. "What are they doing here?" the executioner cried. "I did not get orders that we were to execute the children!"

"But I did," came the rough reply from the soldier who pushed us forward.

"There's been some kind of mistake," I said. "We were told we would be brought back to Octavi — *Caesar's* house on the Palatine after the Triumph."

The soldier ignored me. "Move!" he yelled. "This has to happen quickly!"

"No!" Ptolly wailed.

"Wait!" Alexandros cried. "We are Roman citizens! You cannot execute a Roman citizen without a trial."

I remembered Father, dying, instructing us to use those words. A surge of relief filled my chest at my twin's quick thinking.

"Don't matter," said the man pushing us. "I got orders."

"From who?"

"Caesar's lady. The fancy one."

Livia? This was Livia's doing? The executioner looked dubious. "You will do it!" the soldier yelled, shoving me forward. "I have my orders. Do it now!"

The executioner shook his head. "I don't strangle children!"

"You gonna disobey Caesar, then?" growled my captor.

The man paled. Isis, he was considering it! I looked around wildly. Where had we come in? Could we make a break for it now that the chains were off?

The executioner crossed his arms and raised his chin in my direction. "Either way, I do not kill the girl. It is against Roman law to execute a female virgin," he said.

"*Cacat*, man!" the soldier roared, lunging for me. "I can fix *that* quickly enough."

"No!" I screamed. The soldier grasped my upper arm, but I twisted free. "Run!" I bellowed at Ptolly and Alexandros, but they stood frozen, wide-eyed in shock. The soldier cursed and swiped at me again, grabbing my wig and ripping it off my head. He growled in surprise and disgust. I scrambled for the stairs behind us.

"Run!" I yelled again at my brothers. We took off. The soldier tackled my ankles and I fell down hard on the stone floor, my upper arm and shoulder absorbing most of the impact. I cried out in pain. Ptolly ran back to attack my captor. "No, Ptolly! Run!" I cried. Ptolly kicked out wildly at the man's head, but Alexandros rushed at the downed soldier and booted him in the eye socket. The man howled and released me, covering his eye with both hands.

"Come on," Alexandros commanded, pulling me up by my arm. Pain shot through my shoulder, stealing my breath. I stumbled after my brothers.

"Stop them!" shouted the soldier.

"Let 'em go," the executioner said. "I ain't killing children."

"You idiot!" the soldier snarled. To my horror, I heard his hobnailed boots thundering up the stone steps behind us.

"Leave them be!" shouted the executioner. "The crowds will rip 'em apart anyway."

We burst out into the open and staggered, blinded by the harsh light and a heat so intense it took my breath away. My heart raced as I ran, holding my right shoulder. "Take off your headdresses!" I cried. My brothers ripped them off, their curly hair plastered to their heads with sweat as the gold-striped material floated behind us.

"Blend into the crowd!" Alexandros directed. Holding hands, we pushed our way into the sweating masses. Romans cursed at us and pushed back, but thankfully, they never looked at us, preoccupied as they were with trying to get a glimpse of the tail end of the Triumph — the senators and soldiers who marched behind Octavianus.

An angry-looking soldier, one palm over his left eye, tore past us, retracing the parade route. I breathed out as he disappeared around a tenement building. I tugged at my brothers' hands, moving us away from the throngs looking up the hill to the Temple where the bulls were being sacrificed.

We leaned against the side of a brick building, gasping for breath. I grabbed Ptolly. "You are my hero!" I said, holding him tight to kiss his sweaty head. He broke away, grinning crookedly and acting out the kick with great energy. "Thank you," I mouthed silently at Alexandros, for I knew it was his kick that had disabled my attacker.

"Stupid man!" Ptolly cried.

"Quiet, Ptolly!" Alexandros hissed. "He may still come after us."

That sobered us up.

"What do we do now?" Alexandros asked, looking around. "If the crowds catch sight of us . . ."

"We need to blend in," I said. "And we need to get away from here."

We moved farther away from the parade route, weaving through refuse-strewn winding streets and alleys.

Ptolly spied a public fountain. "Water!" he cried, and raced headlong toward it.

Alexandros cursed under his breath as we both followed. Ptolly fairly threw himself into the fountain's wide basin, taking huge gulps, not even bothering to cup his hands but nearly immersing his face in the pooled water, like a dog. When he raised his dripping head, I smiled.

"Ptolly, you are a genius!" I cried after taking big gulps of the warm, metallic-tasting water myself.

He looked confused. I dunked my hand into the fountain and washed the remaining traces of kohl off his scrunched-up face. Alexandros and I scrubbed our faces too. I unwound my hair, grateful for once for the heavy ceremonial wig that may have saved my life. Both boys ripped off their jeweled broad collars, and Alexandros hid them under some trash in the street.

"We need to look more Roman," he said.

Ptolly pointed to his kilt. "Well, I'm not walking around naked, you know!"

Alexandros smiled. "Trust me, none of us want to see that either. We have to somehow get tunics," he said, looking at my pleated dress. It was covered in sludge and had been ripped in the back, but at least in its sweat and filth, it did not look so Egyptian anymore. I kicked off my gilded sandals. The boys' leather sandals could still pass.

"Wait!" I cried. "Grab the broad collars. We can sell the jewels."

"Good thinking," Alexandros said. He pulled them out from beneath the trash and rolled them up, trying to hide the glimmer of the jewels. We wound our way through the garbage-strewn alleys, avoiding the mangy, bone-thin dogs that stared at us as we passed. Thanks to the broiling heat and the celebrations at the Forum Romanum, we saw few other people.

"I think we're headed toward the Subura," I said a little worriedly. Tata had mentioned this place — a busy, vicious, crowded, filthy area of town that was much like our Rhakotis district in Alexandria. I looked up as we walked in the shade of a crumbling tenement. Roman *insulae*, apartment buildings famous for their height and shoddy workmanship, regularly crashed to the ground. Almost every week, it seemed, we heard of yet another *insulae* tragedy in the Subura. I breathed easier when we were no longer near them.

"I'm hungry," Ptolly announced, grabbing his belly.

"Me too," Alexandros and I said at the same time. We had not eaten since before dawn.

I smelled frying sausages and my mouth watered. "That way." I pointed in the direction of the smell.

Alexandros shook his head. "We do not have any money. We cannot risk drawing attention to ourselves."

"But I'm *hungry!*" whined Ptolly. He turned in the direction of the food stalls anyway.

"Stop!" Alexandros ordered.

"You can't make me!" Ptolly cried, and took off at a run.

We followed Ptolly as he ran, dodging past the occasional staggering drunk. He stopped in front of a vendor squatting over a cooking fire in front of his stall, shaking a pan full of sizzling, popping sausages.

"That smells good!" Ptolly said to the cook, whose face was blackened from the cooking fires of his trade.

The man ignored him.

"Can I have some?"

"You got *denarii*?"

Ptolly shook his head.

"Then be gone," said the man.

Alexandros grabbed Ptolly's arm. "Come on, let's go."

"No!" Ptolly cried. "I am hungry!"

"You don't look starved," the man said.

Alexandros sighed. He pulled out one of the broad collars, snapped off a lapis lazuli jewel in the form of a scarab, and held it out to the man. "We don't have money, but we can trade for this jewel."

The man looked at the twinkling, brilliant blue in Alexandros's hand for a long moment, then up to his face. "Where'd you get that?" he asked.

"Found it."

The man narrowed his eyes.

"Somebody ripped it off the neck of an Egyptian prisoner during the Triumph, and I grabbed it before anyone else could," Alexandros lied.

The man seemed to be considering it.

"Everybody loves Egyptian jewelry now," I added. "You should be able to sell that for a good amount. Way more than what those cost you," I said, pointing to the sausages.

"Fine," the man said. "One for each of you."

Ptolly clapped his hands. But Alexandros acted outraged. "Three sausages? Forget it. We'll go across the road."

"Five," the man said, straightening up.

"Six. And bread for each of us from that basket."

"Fine," the vendor said. "Just give it to me."

The exchange was made. We walked away, devouring the sausages, licking the grease from our fingers and tearing off huge chunks of stale, coarse barley bread with our teeth.

"I'm impressed," I said to Alexandros. "I did not know you knew how to bargain."

"Sometimes I follow Tiberius to the markets. I've learned from the master, as he abuses everyone he comes across."

"This is the best sausage I've ever had in my whole entire life!" Ptolly said with his sideways grin. I could not argue, though I felt a pang of worry. Ptolly's eyes seemed overbright, his pupils dilated. We needed to find safety and shelter, but where? Soon it would grow dark, and I knew that I did not want to be anywhere near the Subura then.

A mild panic overcame me. As royal children we'd always had a cadre of servants taking care of our every need. I had not the slightest inkling of how to do anything for my brothers or myself.

"Cleopatra Selene," Alexandros said under his breath. "We forgot about your armband. Take it off."

I looked at the golden snake coiled around my upper right arm. The light glinted off its emerald eyes, the same eyes that had watched Mother die. Hiding it seemed prudent. But when the soldier tackled me, I had fallen on that arm and shoulder. The skin under the band was already purple and swollen. With a hissing breath, I pulled it off.

"I'll take that," came a voice from behind us, and we jumped. The threat came from a skinny, scruffy man in a dirty brown tunic.

"No you won't," Alexandros told him. "It's ours!"

"I heard what you told the sausage-seller," the man said, casually pointing behind him with a knife. "I want all the jewels."

"Well, you can't have them!" Ptolly cried. "We are tired of you Romans taking everything we have."

"Hand it over," the man said, ignoring Ptolly and showing us the knife again.

I stared at him, trying to decide whether he really would attack us if we refused. I clutched the armband hard between my fingers, but to my surprise, somebody else ripped it from me.

"There you are!" said a bent old man, his head covered in a shawl in the way of augurs. "How did the scam go?"

I gaped at the man.

"I told you he'd fall for it," came the cackling voice. "Now, how many sausages did you save me?"

"N-none," Alexandros said.

"None? You ungrateful little brats!" The old man held a scroll over our heads and threatened to beat us with it. We cowered in confusion.

He turned to the robber. "They were supposed to save me two sausages! Do you believe their selfishness? Do you know how long it takes me to make that paste look like real jewels?"

The robber's knife wavered. "They aren't real?"

The old man snorted. "Gah! Are you as stupid as the sausage-man? What are the chances that filthy children from the Subura would be walking around with real jewels from Egypt? But that is what I count on! People's greed always blinds them to the obvious."

"*Cacat*," the robber said under his breath, lowering his knife. With an irritated growl, he stalked away in search of better prey.

"Come quick," the old man said, straightening up and not sounding so old anymore. We followed him to a dirty brick building. The man looked around before opening a door. I tried to get a clearer look at his face but could not.

"Wait!" I whispered to my brothers. What if this was a trap? Alexandros read my expression and hesitated too, but Ptolly dashed in after the man. I groaned.

"Ptolly," I hissed, following him. "Wait!"

The man took the veil off his head and handed me back the armband. "Stay here," he ordered. "Do not come any farther inside. You must wash first."

Alexandros and I exchanged looks. We tried to make out our surroundings as our eyes adjusted to the dark interior.

"Should we run?" I whispered.

"No!" Ptolly said. "He told us to wait here."

"But we do not know who he is or whether he is bad too," Alexandros said.

"Oh." Ptolly's eyes grew big.

Before we could decide what to do, the man returned with two bowls of water and a couple of towels. "You must wash your hands and your face of the impurities," he said.

"What impurities?" I asked.

"You ate the pork sausages, yes?" We nodded. "Then wash the grease off your hands and faces!" Surprised, we did as we were told. He handed us the clean towels. "Good, good," he said. "Let me get rid of this impure water and then I will take you to the rabbi."

Alexandros and I looked at each other again. We were in a synagogue?

"Who are you?" I asked.

"My name is Ben Harabim," said the man. He had a mass of black curls and a long, uncombed beard, though we could tell now that he was not old at all.

"How did you know we needed help?" asked Ptolly.

He shrugged. "*Hashem* speaks, and I listen."

"Your god *spoke* to you?" Ptolly asked, surprised.

The man laughed good-naturedly. "*Hashem* speaks in many ways. I listen to my heart, for that is often the way *Hashem* speaks."

"And what did your heart tell you?" asked Alexandros.

"That you are lost children in over your heads in a dangerous part of town."

"Well, your god spoke the truth, then!" Ptolly said.

The man chuckled. "Come, follow me." We followed the man through a small airless room into another smaller airless room.

"Rabbi," he said to a middle-aged man bent over a scroll. "These children are lost and need our help. . . ."

"*Hashem* preserve us," said a shaky voice from the side of the room. "I know these children!"

CHAPTER TWENTY-THREE

We looked at the bent old man who had spoken.

"*Aba*, do you recognize these children?" the rabbi asked, putting down his scroll.

"My son, you know I never forget a face!" the old man said. He examined us carefully. "I prayed they spared you and that it was not another bunch of lies," he mumbled. He looked at Ptolly and said more loudly, "You, I do not know."

"I do not know you either!" Ptolly said. "What is this place?"

"You are in a *bet ha-midrash*, the place of learning in a Hebrew temple."

"A synagogue?" Ptolly asked.

"Very good," said the old man. "How did you know?"

"That man who helped us called him 'rabbi,'" Ptolly said, pointing to the bearded man, who seemed a younger, more vibrant version of the old man. "Are you a rabbi too? Many of our people in Alexandria are Jewish."

The man laughed and clapped his hands. "It is true, then? You are the Royal Children of Egypt?"

"Yes," I said, "but who are —"

"Gods!" muttered Alexandros. He turned to me. "Don't you remember when Euphronius took us to the Jewish Quarter to learn from the rabbi there?" He nodded as if to say, *I think that's him.*

"But that was so long ago!" A lifetime. And I could not, for the life of me, remember his name. My heart raced at the improbability of seeing him again. Was this the work of Isis? What if this sweet-looking old man was one of the agents Amunet had told me to watch for? After all, he had been in Alexandria and was now in Rome, just like us. And . . . and it would be a better cover to have us work through a follower of the Hebrew religion than a follower of Isis, wouldn't it?

"Tell me," the old man asked. "How is my old friend Euphronius doing?"

Alexandros and I exchanged looks. In truth, we did not know. We feared he had been crucified with all the others.

"Ah," the old man said wearily. "I am so very sorry."

"But what are you doing in Rome?" I asked.

"I insisted my father leave Alexandria and come to live with me here," said the younger rabbi. "When we heard . . . when Antonius was defeated at Actium, I worried for *Aba*'s safety in such unsettled times."

"I did not want to leave," grumbled the old man. "I do not like this Rome. . . ."

"So you have no message from the Lady Amunet's agents?" I asked. "No instructions for us?"

Alexandros looked at me. We hadn't talked much about what Amunet had said or her plans for us. Whenever I tried, he grew angry, calling me foolish for thinking we could ever survive defying Rome. When plans were underway, I hoped, he would feel differently.

The old rabbi shrugged. "I know no Lady Amunet or her agents, as you put it."

"She was the High Priestess of Isis in Alexandria," I said.

Again he shook his head. "Oh, but how I do miss our lovely city," he sighed. "In Alexandria, there was beauty and learning and tolerance. Here, I see ugly buildings and people who want only to watch the bloody gladiatorial games." He threw up his hands in disgust. "Where are the libraries? Where are the scholars, the poets? This is a place of brutes and beasts, not brains."

The younger rabbi sighed. He had likely heard this complaint many times.

Disappointment tightened my throat. This sweet old man was not one of the priestess's people. He too came here against his will.

"Did you know," the old rabbi said to Ptolly, "it was your ancestor whom we may thank for helping our people survive outside our homeland? For it was upon his insistence that the blessed Torah was translated into Greek."

"The Septuagint," Alexandros and I said at once, remembering our lessons.

"Precisely!" said the elder rabbi.

"'Of the seventy'?" Ptolly asked. "What does that mean? What are you talking about?"

"It means, little Ptolemy," the elder rabbi said, "that your ancestor took seventy-two rabbis, put them in separate rooms, and told them not to come out until they had translated the Torah from Hebrew into Greek. Then they all had to agree on the final translation. Which is, I must tell you, a miracle in itself — that seventy-two rabbis agreed on anything!"

The old man smiled, and I remembered his warmth when we visited the Jewish Quarter so long ago. It seemed as if that day happened to a different person, to a Cleopatra Selene that I did not know and would hardly recognize. "You will see," he continued. "It is because of the wisdom of the Ptolemies our tradition will survive."

It felt so good to hear someone say something positive about my heritage and family that I found myself welling up with tears of gratitude.

"*Aba*, things will get better here in Rome now that Caesar is back. You will see. Caesar brings peace and wealth with him."

"Alexandria's wealth!" the elder rabbi and I snapped in unison. His eyes twinkled as he smiled at me.

"But I am confused," said Ben Harabim, glancing at the younger rabbi, then back at us. "Why . . . How could the Royal Children of Egypt be lost *here* in the Subura?"

"They were going to strangle us!" Ptolly announced.

"What?" the three men cried in surprise.

"They marched us in his Triumph today, then they brought us to the *Tullianum*, to the executioner," I said.

The younger rabbi puffed out his cheeks. "Ben Harabim, have you brought into this House of God, Enemies of Rome?"

"But I was only trying to help these lost children. . . ."

"It was a mistake, a misunderstanding," Alexandros said. "We were supposed to go back to Octavianus's house on the Palatine."

"Some mistake," the younger rabbi said. He sighed. "We cannot harbor Rome's enemies here. We must not anger the Romans or bring any attention to ourselves."

"Pssstah," the old man said. "I will not allow such cowardice." He turned to his son and said in Hebrew, "Is it better to live by the Torah or only read it?"

"You must understand," the younger rabbi said, flushing, "during these years of civil war, the Romans . . . Sometimes people look for someone to blame, someone to take their frustrations out on. So. We will help. We just cannot harbor you here."

"Well, that is good, because I do not want to be here," Ptolly whined. "I want to go home!"

I was so surprised by the word "home" that I must have repeated it without realizing it. Ptolly turned to me, a tantrum brewing on his flushed face. "Yes! Home! With Tonia and Marcellus and Octavia and the rest of my family."

Octavianus's complex on the Palatine was not, and would never be, "home." Nor would anyone in Octavianus's household ever be "family" to me.

"Come here," the old rabbi said to Ptolly. "Do you know the story of Jonah and the whale?"

Ptolly shook his head. "Who is Jonah?"

As his father distracted Ptolly, the younger rabbi turned to us. "Is there someone at the Palatine whom you can trust?"

"Octavia," I said.

"Juba," Alexandros said almost in the same moment. My brother turned to me. "Octavia is probably sitting beside her brother at the celebration feast," he pointed out. "Juba is the better choice to get us out of the Subura right now."

"Good," the rabbi said. "Now, how would I get word to him?"

"Wait," I cried, remembering what the soldier had said in the *Tullianum*. "Maybe we shouldn't go back. The soldier said that Livia gave the orders for our execution."

"No, he did not!" Alexandros said with a shocked expression. "The executioner insisted he had never gotten the orders and that he would not have done it anyway. It was a *mistake*. That is all."

I opened my mouth to speak, but the young rabbi interrupted me, looking directly at Alexandros. "How do we reach this Juba?"

Alexandros and the rabbi continued talking. I looked down, confused. I knew the soldier said it was at "Caesar's lady's" command. What other "lady" would want us dead but the wife of the man who hated us? And if it had worked, it would've been brilliant, as all of Rome would have witnessed that Octavianus was in the Triumph and Livia in the grandstands, neither one personally responsible. Our deaths would have been excused as an unfortunate misunderstanding.

Ben Harabim left to locate Juba. I looked over at Ptolly. He had crumpled against the old rabbi, fast asleep. The old man put his crooked, spotted hand gently on Ptolly's head and recited a Hebrew blessing. I remembered how Mother had prayed over Ptolly the night before she died, and the longing for her touch sank so deep, my bones ached with it.

"Come," the younger rabbi said, lifting Ptolly from his father's lap. "You all must rest."

I turned to the elder rabbi. "Thank you," I said to the old man, feeling my throat tighten again. "Euphronius would have been very grateful for your kindness to us."

"Pssstah," the old rabbi said again with a smile. "It is I who am grateful to Euphronius. *Hashem* works in mysterious ways, for it must have been His will that brought you here to us this day."

I remembered, then, how he had tried to explain the Hebrew concept of "free will" to me so long ago. I understood it no better now, for how could something be both "God's will" and our own "free will" at the same time? And if his was the kind of god that "willed" us to be paraded in humiliation and then almost executed, I could confidently say that I wanted no part of him. Isis would help me. I just needed to be patient.

We were left alone to wait in one of the side rooms of the *bet ha-midrash*. "We should run away now, while we can, before we're taken back to the compound," I whispered to Alexandros. "I swear to you, it was Livia who ordered our deaths. We would be *fools* to go back."

Alexandros flicked his eyes at Ptolly, who was twitching in his sleep on a musty, stained rush mat on the floor. We squatted like slaves next to him. "And do what? How long do you think we would survive out there?" Alexandros asked, gesturing to the Subura. "I'd rather be held in the bosom of my enemy and know what to expect than be murdered or attacked by some filthy, drunken Roman. Worse, slave traders could snatch us and . . . and separate us, selling us to gods-know-where. No. We cannot risk it."

He was right. It was common knowledge that unaccompanied children in Rome — especially in the Subura — were often kidnapped and sold to slave traders. The Romans called the child-stealers *retiarii*, after the gladiators who fought with nets, because they were so skilled at sweeping the streets of unwanted children.

I shuddered at the thought of being separated from my brothers, let alone being sold. Yet I also felt the frustration of our coddled upbringing. We had no talent for surviving the streets of Rome. Alexandros was right. With Octavia and Juba standing between us and Livia and Octavianus, our best chance of survival was amidst our enemy.

Because of the chaos of the revelry all over the city, Juba didn't come for us until nearly sunrise the next day. He was outraged at the "misunderstanding" of our almost-execution and swept us home in a litter surrounded by guards.

Zosima nearly wept with relief when she saw us. An exhausted-looking Octavia looked dazed beside her. Zosima threw her arms around me, and I couldn't help but gasp at the pain in my shoulder.

"What happened, child? Are you injured?" she asked.

I opened my mouth to answer, but all the air left my lungs when I spied someone watching us from inside the atrium. Gods, Livia! How furious she must be that her plan for getting rid of us had failed! What would she do to us now?

"Cleopatra Selene?" Zosima asked.

"I fell," I mumbled.

"The mean man tackled her!" Ptolly cried. "And I kicked him in the head!"

"What?" Zosima and Juba said at the same time. "Who . . ."

"The man that was going to make her not a virgin so they could execute her!" he said. "But I stopped him!" He reenacted the kick with gusto. "I rescued us!"

At everybody's look of horror, I added, "That's right, Ptolly. You and Alexandros stopped him from hurting me, and we escaped."

I looked toward the atrium again. Livia was gone.

"Oh, you were so brave," Octavia said to Ptolly, tears streaming down her face. She knelt. "The gods have spoken. They have saved you for me, my little Marcus."

Little Marcus? I stared openmouthed as Ptolly threw himself into her open arms. She held him tight. "My little Marcus," she kept murmuring. "I am so sorry."

Ptolly snuggled into her embraces like a kitten searching for its mother's teat. "My poor, poor darling." Octavia sniffed. She picked him up and walked toward her rooms, murmuring honey in his ear.

"Come," Zosima whispered to Alexandros and me as she led us back to our quarters. "Let us get you cleaned up."

That night, all I could think about was Ptolly. Would he have nightmares after our horrible experience in the Triumph? Did Alexandros know how to comfort him? In the deep-dark, I rose and snuck into their *cubiculum* to check on him. To my dismay, I found Ptolly's sleeping mat empty.

I pushed Alexandros's shoulder. "Wake up! Where is Ptolly? Where is he?"

Alexandros was always difficult to rouse in the night. "Wha . . . ?"

"Ptolly! Where is he?"

"Oh," he mumbled. ". . . Octavia."

"What?"

"Said he might get scared . . . better for 'Li'l Marcus' . . . stay with her."

"Little Marcus" again? Why was she suddenly calling him by Tata's name? And why would Ptolly sleep in Octavia's room like a baby when he said he was too big to sleep with me in my *cubiculum*?

The thought that took my breath away, though, was this: *She was stealing him from me.* I knew that made no sense — I did not "own" my little brother — but my heart felt otherwise.

I stood frozen in my brothers' dark room for a long time, for when I left to return to my own, the sky was purple in the predawn light. I walked slowly across the grounds, struggling to understand my enormous sense of unease and loss. How many ways did the gods have, I wondered, for taking from me the people I loved?

In the months that followed, it was a relief to learn that Octavianus cared to see us as little as we cared to see him. We went whole days, if not weeks, without running into the man all of Rome called its Savior. I made sure to avoid Livia as much as possible too. Perhaps if we didn't flaunt our presence, I thought, she would not attempt to be rid of us again.

I calmed even more when I overhead one of the slaves gossiping about Octavianus's meetings with client rulers from the eastern provinces.

"Whenever one of them complains about what is happening in their region," the handsome young wine-pourer said, unaware that I had snuck into the kitchens to find a sweet treat for Ptolly, "Caesar reminds them of all the kindnesses he is showing the children of the Egyptian queen. He promises he will accord them the same."

"Do they believe him?" the kitchen slave asked.

The wine-pourer shrugged and snickered. "They don't have much choice now, do they?"

So even after the Triumph, we were still politically useful. That too felt like a shield. Still, as the months wore on, I chafed at our situation. When would Amunet's agents contact us? What was happening in Egypt? Why had I heard nothing?

Senators' sons and daughters often visited the compound to socialize with the children of the household. In the course of these visits, I had earned a reputation as an excellent *trigon* player, despite jeering and teasing from the boys. "*Trigon* is a boys' game!" some of the senators' sons would cry, but not for long.

Like everyone else, I took my turn as *pilecripi*, keeping score and chasing down balls. One day, one of the senators' sons missed a hard throw and the small leather ball rolled almost all the way to the Neptune fountain in the side garden. As I snatched it up, I heard a voice from my nightmares. I froze.

Octavianus rounded the garden path beside a very overweight, very old man. He narrowed his eyes and showed his teeth to me. "Ah, Corbulo! Speak of the little gorgon herself."

Gorgon? I felt my face flush at the insult. Corbulo's wrinkled neck jutted forward from his round, toga-clad middle. He looked like a tortoise stretching its small bald head out of an oversized shell.

"Oh, now, don't insult the child, Octavianus. She appears quite delicious to me," he said with a leer. "I have been curious to know if she favors her mother. I do not see much of Antonius in her, except for maybe the long legs."

I pulled at my *tunica*, trying to cover my calves and ankles, as the old man examined me. Zosima had complained that all my Egyptian *tunicas* were too short, but I always ignored her when she tried to measure me for new Roman ones. Now I regretted it fiercely.

"Oh, yes, I see the resemblance," the old man added. "You forget, I met the fascinating lady when she visited Julius all those years ago. And this one has that certain something her mother had, doesn't she? I can't put my finger on it, but I can't look away either."

Octavianus muttered something under his breath and both men tittered. With as much dignity as I could, I turned away and walked back toward the game.

"Yes, she will do quite nicely," the old man croaked loud enough for me to hear.

I did not feel like playing after that. I tossed the ball back to the group of boys and wandered farther into the garden, confused. What did the old man mean? What was Octavianus planning?

I came upon Julia and one of the senator's sons sitting on a marble bench under a tree. Julia leaned forward and kissed the boy on the cheek. The boy's face burned with what looked like delighted embarrassment before he raced off. Julia smirked at me.

"Sorry," I mumbled, trying to cover my irritation at not finding privacy.

"He's cute, isn't he?" she asked as she watched the boy.

I shrugged and began walking in the other direction. She jumped up from the bench and joined me.

"So, which of the boys have *you* kissed?" she asked.

I made a face. "None."

"Well, why not?"

"Because . . . Because . . ." I looked over my shoulder at the group far on the other side of the garden. They seemed like puppies, barking, yelping, and tumbling over one another in the warm sunlight. "They are just *boys*."

She laughed. "Oh, so it is the men you are after. Which one do you dream about? All the girls love Marcellus, though he hasn't had his manhood ceremony yet."

Again, I did not respond.

"Hmmm. So if not Marcellus, then it must be Juba, yes? He wears the toga of manhood. He is twenty."

A spike of irritation burst up my chest. "Julia, please leave me alone."

"Juba is so very handsome," she continued as if she had not heard me. "Too bad he is like a brother. But what am I saying? You are Ptolemy. You would have no problem with that, would you?"

I stopped. "Julia, what do you want?"

"Nothing. It's just that I have watched you and noticed the way your eyes follow Juba. How you hang on every word he says when you two have your little scroll-fests. I think you like him."

"I don't like Juba in that way," I said, setting off again.

She caught up to me. "Do you ever think about who you will marry?" she asked in an innocent voice. "Tata probably wants you married off soon. Imagine the favors people will owe him!"

The idea of marrying some smug, arrogant Roman made my blood run cold. And the idea that Octavianus might be bargaining favors in exchange for me made bile rise in my throat — especially after that encounter with Corbulo.

"I am never getting married," I said.

Julia laughed. "Of course you will! You are a prize, 'sister.' Although not getting married might be fun too. That way you can take as many lovers as you want. You know. Like your mother."

If I had learned anything in Rome, it was to not respond to Julia's baiting about Mother, so I just stalked off instead. Still, her insinuations rankled. Mother had loved only two men her whole life — Julius Caesar and my tata. Yet Romans continued to spread lies about Mother's supposed wanton nature.

Unfortunately, though, Julia's comments about Juba forced me to admit that she was right about my attraction to him. I had often looked for ways to "accidentally" run into him when he returned from his forays outside the compound. I read books that I thought might impress him; I watched his training sessions with Alexandros, admiring his strength, grace, and power.

Worse, I began comparing him to other boys. I contemplated his kindness every time I witnessed casual Roman cruelty; I remembered his grace every time an awkward boy stumbled. It wasn't long before, to my embarrassment, I began wondering what it would be like to kiss him.

Ever-observant Julia noticed my increasing awkwardness around him — an opportunity she did not let slip past.

"You do know," Julia said one day as we immersed ourselves in the steaming hot water of the baths, "that Juba is the favorite of bored young wives married to decrepit old senators?"

I sighed. Why couldn't Marcella be in the water instead of Julia? It was much more pleasant to talk to her. But both Marcellas and both Antonias stood whispering and giggling as the bath slaves scraped them with strigils.

"I am sure your father loves all those married women having affairs," I replied, trying to move the focus onto her tata, with whom she had a contentious relationship. Octavianus talked incessantly of bringing back Rome's "pious" modesty, especially for women, decrying the freedoms Roman women enjoyed. But, as always, he had to tread carefully, lest people noticed that as he took the freedoms of women away, he stripped *all* Romans of their liberty.

Unfortunately, Julia continued as if I had never even spoken. "Yes, all those bored beauties. They find Juba irresistible. I have heard he's quite shy, and that makes the women even bolder in their pursuit of him."

"I thought *you* had a crush on Tiberius," I countered, knowing it was not true but desperate to take the focus off of Juba.

"Tiberius?" she laughed. "He is my stepbrother!"

"Yes, but I have seen your eyes follow him when you think no one is looking," I lied.

She sat up, only her outraged blue eyes visible through the thick vapor from the hypocaust. "That is not true! I *hate* Tiberius," she hissed. "And, again, he is my *stepbrother*. We are not like you Ptolemies!"

I shrugged and did not say anything else, satisfied that I had rattled her. I leaned back against the marble-tiled lip of the bath edge, watching as beams of sunlight poured through the high windows and danced with the swirling smoke of rising steam.

Despite myself, after Julia's comments, I spent a ridiculous amount of time wondering which Roman beauties had attracted Juba's attention and if he had fallen in love with any of them. This only served to make my discomfort around him even more acute, though that never stopped me from going to my regular spot to watch him train Alexandros.

On one particularly beautiful spring afternoon, I took my place under the sweet citron tree as usual. Juba appeared but my brother did not. After setting out the wooden fighting equipment, Juba looked around. He caught sight of me under the tree. Gods! Did he know that I came here to watch him? My stomach tightened as he approached, and I looked to the side, trying to appear as if I were lost in thought.

"Where is your brother?" he asked.

"I do not know," I said, "but I think I saw Julia chasing him earlier with a question."

"I keep telling him he must work on his speed." Juba chuckled. "I'll give him some time in case he escapes."

An awkward silence stretched. I kept my eyes focused on the scroll on my lap, but I could not read a word. I was intensely aware of his closeness and of the spicy warm scent of his skin. He wore a sleeveless tunic and had his arms around his knees. I sneaked peeks at his arms, wondering what it would feel like to have them around me.

He leaned back on his elbows, squinting into the distance. "What are you reading?" he asked.

I jumped. "Oh. Um. Nothing, really." I could not bear to tell him that I had brought the love poems of Catullus. I had not been able to convince myself to read dry treatises on Egyptian politics and finance that might one day help me rule. But I did not want to reveal I was reading scandalous poems about love either.

When Juba raised his eyebrows, smiling in curiosity, I realized I needed to fend off more questions with a better answer. "Just some writings on the . . . um . . . the Epicureans."

"Really?" he asked, squinting up at me. "I did not picture you as an Epicurean."

"I'm not. I'm just reading about it. But why do you say that?"

"Well, we both know you are not a Stoic." He smiled. "I picture you more as a follower of Socrates."

"Why?"

"Well, for one, you never stop asking questions. And sometimes," he laughed, "those questions are as annoying as a gadfly!"

He thought of me as a *gadfly*? He must have seen the expression on my face because he pushed up from his elbows. "I meant no insult, Cleopatra Selene."

Only Juba and my brothers still used my full name, which I appreciated more than he knew. In the awkward silence that followed, he picked up a wineskin that he'd had draped over his shoulder. "And to prove my goodwill, I will offer you the first sip of our exercise wine."

"Exercise wine?" I laughed.

He smiled, his white teeth gleaming. "Yes, exercise wine. Mostly water with a little bit of wine and honey for energy. Here." He removed the top and indicated he would pour some in my mouth. I tilted my head back and closed my eyes. I felt the sunlight on my face. The smell of leather from the wineskin. Warm liquid pooling in my mouth. The sweet tang of honeyed wine. I swallowed slowly.

He poured some for himself. I watched him close his eyes and open his mouth to receive the liquid, then bring his lips together, throat moving as he swallowed. He opened his eyes and met mine.

"What?" he asked, smiling. "Did I spill some down my chin or something?"

He was so close. The sun so warm, the air so heavy with the sweet scent of citron blossoms. I leaned over without thinking and touched my lips to his, wanting to taste the mixture of sun and wine on them, wanting to taste *him*. I had never kissed anyone before.

I felt him stiffen, then pull away. "Selene," he said, sounding embarrassed. "You cannot . . . You are just a child."

So that was how he saw me — as both an annoying gadfly and a silly child. Mortified, I scrambled to my feet.

"Wait! Cleopatra Selene, I did not mean to . . ."

I didn't hear anything else he said. I ran as fast as I could, past our complex and into the public gardens that Caesarion's tata had built for the people of Rome. I knew it was dangerous for a girl to wander the gardens unattended, but I wanted to get as far as possible from everybody and everything I knew.

When I could run no more, I collapsed under a cypress. Why had I done that? Why had I kissed him? I would never be able to look him in the eye again. I groaned with shame and put my head down on my knees. I had embarrassed myself and embarrassed him.

Worse, I had learned something about myself that cut to the quick. I was not as beautiful, not as compelling, not as enticing as I had secretly hoped I would grow to be. Instead, the daughter of the charismatic, irresistible Cleopatra VII was an awkward, angry "gadfly" who repelled men. I had not only disappointed myself but, I realized with despair, had Mother lived, I probably would have disappointed her too.

CHAPTER TWENTY-FIVE

In the weeks that followed, I avoided all places where I might run into Juba. I could not bear the thought of him looking upon me with pity. To my relief, he must have been trying to avoid me too, for we went a long time without seeing each other.

Sometimes, when reading in the main garden, I would find Marcellus staring at me as he spoke privately to one of Octavianus's endless petitioners. He'd smile and wink over the heads of the invariably balding, portly, toga-swaddled supplicants. Sometimes he even came and sat beside me on the marble bench under the shaded canopy.

"You are always reading, Selene," he commented one day. "You must tell me what you find so fascinating."

I shrugged, feeling both delighted and embarrassed that he had noticed me at all. His kindness was like a balm. Perhaps I was not so hideous, I thought, if handsome Marcellus looked at me without turning into stone.

Still, Juba's rejection forced me to reassess how I might or might not be like Mother. I could accept that I was not as beautiful and compelling as she was as long as I reminded myself that I had her intelligence and drive. Ultimately, that would serve me better as ruler, wouldn't it?

I grew impatient remembering Amunet's orders to wait. Surely, I thought, there had to be *some* movement toward bringing us back to Egypt by now! Then I wondered if I had been too passive. Mother, after all, had always acted boldly and swiftly. Perhaps they awaited some sign from me.

It was time to take action. Unfortunately, I didn't know where to begin. Talking to those who worshipped Isis would have been the natural route, but Octavianus had destroyed all of the Isis temples in the city and banned all worship of the Goddess within city walls. Most of the followers of Isis in Rome traveled to the temple outside Capua to honor the Goddess. I could find no reason to travel to Capua that would not raise eyebrows or suspicions, so I decided to do the next best thing. I would send a message to the Capuan High Priest or Priestess of Isis.

But Zosima would hear none of it when I asked her to convey the message for me.

"Absolutely not!" she hissed, eyes wide with horror at my suggestion. "Octavianus has had every follower of Isis in this household beaten or purged! I will not give him an excuse to kill us, child, and I forbid you from pursuing it as well."

I did not know which made me angrier — that she called me "child" or that she treated me as one. Well, if she wouldn't do it, I would ask someone else!

The Goddess's emphasis on salvation and love attracted large numbers of the poor and enslaved. Despite Octavianus's harsh treatment, surely some of the household slaves still followed the Goddess, even if they kept it a secret. I began taking long walks around the compound, looking for any sign of an Isis worshipper among the bustling slaves. As I had always been known to "wander," nobody thought it odd. Or at least I hoped so.

Once, one of the laundry slaves watched me carefully as I meandered among piles of clothing. The shaded outdoor courtyard reeked of vinegar, stale urine for bleaching, and strange-smelling solvents so harsh they made my eyes water. When I looked at the young laundry slave, she gave a slight bow of the head. Did that mean she knew who I was? Might she help me?

In a casual way, I drifted toward her. Her eyes widened in fear. She looked down, suddenly fascinated by a mud stain on a tunic that she had been scrubbing. She did not look up at me again, even when I stood over her.

"Tell me," I said quietly. "Are you a follower of the Goddess of Egypt?"

She shook her head. "It is forbidden," she whispered. "By Caesar's command."

"So you are not . . ."

"No! I am not!" she said in a hoarse whisper.

I sighed and began turning away when she added, "But I know someone who is. I will send him to you."

My heart thudded in excitement. "Yes? I . . . I thank you," I whispered.

Her lips curled upward slightly. "It is an honor to serve you, Daughter of Ra," she breathed.

For weeks afterward, I searched the faces of every servant or slave who passed my way. But nobody approached me; nobody ever made any kind of contact. Had that girl lied just to get me away from her?

I was wandering on the outer edge of one of the side gardens when I spotted a young, sweat-soaked worker carrying a large basket of blooms from the outer garden.

"Pardon me, young *domina*," he said, holding up what I could now see was a collection of bloodred roses. "Would you like to smell their perfume?"

I paused. Roses were the flowers of the Goddess. Was this an innocent request or did it have some meaning?

The young man took off his floppy, wide-brimmed hat. As I approached, he casually scratched at a grimy circlet of linen around his wrist. He looked at me, then down at his wrist again.

I followed his eyes. There! Underneath the bunched-up fabric was a tiny black tattoo of the Knot of Isis, just like the sacred amulet that Mother had given me. My heart lurched with recognition and excitement. He covered the tiny mark and said, "Flowers fit for a goddess, yes?"

He had the fair, freckled skin and rust-colored hair of a Gaul or Celt. I wondered if he had been born a slave or captured in Gaul or in Britannia. Yet he was a devotee of Isis! Truly the Goddess worked in mysterious ways.

I bent my head toward the blooms and sniffed deeply. As I reached for one, the young man let go of the whole basket. Flowers scattered everywhere.

The freedman in charge of the gardens eyed him with irritation. I dropped to my knees to help gather the blooms as the young man whispered, "The Priestess of Capua has not forgotten you. Plans are underw —"

Suddenly, the young man grunted and toppled over. The freedman had kicked him. "You clumsy oaf!" he yelled. "You do not let a noble help you clean up your mess!" He turned to me. "Forgive this untrained idiot, young mistress," he said.

I stood up quickly, angry at the young man's mistreatment, and opened my mouth to complain, but the young gardener shoved a handful of blooms toward me so quickly, a few petals shot into the air. Small trickles of blood from the thorns he had grasped oozed down the side of his dirt-caked palm.

"Please, take these as an offering to the *Bona Dea*," he pleaded. "May the Great Goddess forgive my trespass."

Smart boy, I thought. Telling me to make an offering to the *Bona Dea* — the good goddess of Rome — sounded innocent enough. But we both knew he meant Isis.

The overseer grunted in approval. I took the flowers gingerly and nodded my thanks. My heart felt like a runaway stallion at the chariot races, but I walked toward our wing with a studied slowness.

Finally, it has begun, I chanted to myself, barely able to contain my excitement. *The Priestess of Capua knows I am ready. It has begun!*

CHAPTER TWENTY-SIX

"There you are," Zosima cried as I returned from the rose garden. "Where have you been?" She sighed. "Between worrying about you and Ptolly, it is a wonder I have any hair left."

I turned. "What do you mean? Why were you worrying about Ptolly?"

"He took sick early this morning with a fever." As a rule, my brothers and I were inordinately healthy, but all fevers were a cause for concern. "They have taken him to the sickroom in Livia's house," she continued. "Livia's doctor is taking care of him."

I dropped the roses and ran, a chill traveling down my spine. Why was Ptolly in Livia's sickroom? Was she up to something? Could poison cause a fever? And even if it couldn't, would she use his fever as an opportunity to hurt him? After her failed execution attempt at her husband's Triumph, I had assumed Livia had decided that the risk of exposure was too great — that hurting us was not worth the effort. Had she just been biding her time, waiting for the right moment to strike, aiming at the youngest and weakest of us?

When I burst into the sickroom, I discovered Ptolly asleep, his face pale and sweating. Octavia sat across from him, staring into his closed eyes. She looked up when I entered.

"How is he?" I asked.

Octavia looked haunted, tormented even. "What is wrong?" I asked more urgently, trying but failing to keep the panic out of my voice.

Her face cleared as she rearranged her expression into one of mild concern. She even tried to smile. "Some sort of fever that came on suddenly," she whispered. "I brought him some medicine." She held up a clay drinking cup as if she were toasting me.

"Should we wake him to administer it?" I asked. If the medicine might help, why had she not given it to him yet?

She smiled apologetically. "I cannot wake a sleeping child," she whispered. "Isn't Marcus so beautiful, so peaceful when he sleeps? He always did sleep deeply."

I realized I was not sure whether she was talking about Ptolly or Tata. The hairs on the back of my neck prickled. Did she think Ptolly *was* Father?

"Should I . . . do you want me to wake him and give him his medicine?"

She hesitated. "Yes, maybe you should do it." But she did not move.

The odd look on her face and the fact that we were near Livia's rooms added to my unease. I remembered how very soon after arriving, I overheard one of the slaves claim that Livia grew poisonous plants by moonlight and that she would likely use one of her potions against us.

"Who . . . who made up the medicine?" I asked, trying to sound casual. "Did Livia mix the tincture?"

Never taking her eyes off Ptolly, Octavia answered, "No, I . . . yes. Livia mixed it by her own hand. She is quite an adept healer, did you know that?"

I felt cold, then hot with fear. Could it be possible that Livia had ordered Ptolly moved near her *medicus* just for appearances, so it would look like she was taking special care of him when she was doing the opposite? Would she take advantage of his fever as an excuse to kill him so there would be fewer questions?

"I will sit with him now," I said. "Give me the medicine. I will make him drink it soon."

I held my hand out, willing her to give me the cup. She stood, still staring at him, then sighed. "Yes, I think it would be better if you administered it." She ignored my hand and placed the cup on a low table as she walked out of the room. I waited for her footsteps to disappear down the hall, then rushed to the cup and sniffed it. I detected only the sweetness of honey over an earthy, rain-on-mud smell. But how could I tell if it was poisoned? What did poison smell like? Bitter or sweet? How would I know?

Zosima stepped in after Octavia left. "How is . . . What are you doing?"

I straightened. "Livia mixed this medicine," I whispered.

Her eyes grew wide. She understood my meaning — I had warned Zosima and my brothers well about Livia. Without saying a word, she took the cup and walked out of the room to dispose of it.

Ptolly's fever clung to him like a choking vine. I tried to get him moved to my *cubiculum* so I could watch him there, but word came from Livia that he was to stay in her quarters.

"She does not want his illness spreading to the other children," her lady announced. This, of course, only made me more suspicious. Did Livia want him under her roof so that she could harm him without witnesses?

So I virtually lived by his side, taking breaks only when Zosima or Alexandros sat in my place. We surrounded him like multiheaded Cerberus guarding the gates of the underworld, making sure no potion or tincture mixed by Livia's hands crossed his lips.

Livia's physician seemed competent enough. He referred to himself as an *iatros*, healer, instead of *medicus*, so we knew he was Greek. The Romans turned to the Greeks for everything of importance.

"Look who I have brought!" I announced on the fifth day of Ptolly's illness.

"Sebi!" he cried when he saw his cat in my arms. My cat, not about to be left behind, followed. I did not know how Livia felt about our cats settling into her house, but I did not care. Sebi curled up at Ptolly's side immediately, and I said a prayer to Bastet that, through our cats, the goddess would keep him safe from Livia too.

The *iatros* came in soon after, holding a shallow wooden bowl filled with bloodsucking leeches, which he would use on Ptolly to balance his humors. I put my head down between my knees so I would not get sick when he placed the slimy creatures on Ptolly's bare back. Ptolly laughed, despite his growing weakness.

"You had better watch out, sister. Now that I know how much you hate these little bloodsuckers, I may sneak in your room at night and put some on you while you sleep!" he teased.

"Don't you dare!" I said, raising my head. "That is not funny and I will . . ." But I had to lower my head again at the sight of the glistening dark creatures leaving trails of slime on my little brother's back.

When I wasn't with Ptolly, I took long walks through the various gardens and courtyards of the compound, hoping to find the young gardener with the Isis knot tattoo. I had heard nothing more from him or anybody else, and I found this odd — so odd that I began to wonder whether I had dreamt the entire encounter.

One afternoon, I forced myself to stroll around Octavianus's *peristylum*, the open garden attached to his house, hoping I might find the mysterious young Celt there. Usually, I avoided any place where I might run into Octavianus, but I had tried every other garden in the network of estates.

In the small marble *impluvium*, a white lotus floated in sparkling water. In a flash, I remembered the shimmering turquoise water in Mother's secret rooftop pool, the joy of presenting her with a blue lotus. How Mother had smiled and taken an exaggerated sniff to please me. How she had reassured me — days before leaving for Actium — that all would be well . . .

I shook my head at the memory, puzzled as to why my enemy would have a flower so closely associated with Egypt in his personal garden. I looked around at the proliferation of pots crowding the small space, many of which were filled with strange and exotic blooms and leaves.

"Admiring our work, mistress?" the head gardener, the one who had kicked the Celt boy, asked.

"Beautiful," I answered stiffly.

"This one comes from Spain." He pointed to a bright pink flower, multilayered with white-ridged edges. "And that one comes from Gaul." He indicated a thick stalk bearing yellow blooms in a tower formation.

I understood then. Octavianus, through flowers, was showing off all the areas of the world he controlled, including Egypt. I sighed with irritation. But then I realized the head gardener might know something useful to me.

"Where is the boy I saw picking roses last week?"

The man laughed. "I have many boys who pick roses for me! Which one do you mean?"

"He . . ." I was about to say he bore the Knot of Isis mark but quickly caught myself. "The Celt boy, the young man with freckles," I began.

"Now, why would you want to know that?" a voice boomed behind me, and I jumped.

Marcellus. He grinned at my surprised expression. "I thought I saw a nymph gliding among the flowers and I was right!"

"*Dominus.*" The man lowered his eyes and turned to go.

"Wait! Do you know which boy I mean? Do you know where I might find him?"

The gardener's face closed in wariness. "I am sorry, young mistress. The boy I think you mean was flogged and sold days ago."

"What? Why?"

"I do not know. I do not question *Domina*'s orders." He turned and scuttled away.

"Oh, don't tell me you have a crush on a mere garden boy, Selene!" Marcellus said, smiling down at me. "You must set your sights higher! Although," he laughed, "almost everybody falls for a slave at least once, even the best of us."

"I didn't . . . I don't have a crush . . ." I did not know what to say. Livia had the boy whipped and sold. What did this mean? Was it because I had talked to him about Isis? Because he made contact with the priestess for me? But how would she know? And how would I learn the priestess's plans if my messenger was gone?

"Gods, Selene, you look like you have seen a *daemon*! Are you all right?"

"Yes. I . . . er," I stammered.

"Ah, poor thing. You really did fancy yourself in love with this boy, didn't you?"

"No, I . . ."

"Come. I was about to visit your little brother. Would you like to escort me there?"

I nodded dumbly. We turned toward Livia's house, Marcellus's warm hand on my back.

The leeches, it appeared, did nothing to reduce Ptolly's fever. "Little Bull, you have to hurry up and get well so we can leave this house and go back to Octavia's!" I told him one morning.

"I don't wanna go back to Octavia's house," Ptolly whined. His words surprised me, but I shrugged it off to the peevishness that came with feeling miserable.

Octavia's gentle voice echoed down the hallway. "How is my sweet boy doing?" she asked, and then winced as she entered the room. "Oh, I didn't realize he was asleep," she added in a softer voice.

I whipped my head around back to Ptolly, only to see him pretending slumber. But why would he do that?

Octavia turned to me. "How is he today?" she asked in a whisper, coming to his side. She stroked his head and frowned. "He is still much too warm!"

"He is," I agreed.

She adjusted a small pillow on a three-legged stool and sat. "Why don't you go? I'll sit with him now."

"I have nowhere else I want to be," I said softly. "We can sit together, if you like." In avoiding Livia, I had found I ended up avoiding Octavia too, which I did not like. Her presence calmed me, and I even hoped Livia would come by and see her with Ptolly and me as a reminder that she dared not hurt us while Octavia was nearby.

"How is Tonia holding up without Ptolly to play with every day?" I asked in a low voice.

Octavia smiled. "She is furious that I won't allow her to visit him. But we cannot risk any of the other children getting sick. By the gods, but she does have a temper!"

"Ptolly and Tonia are so much alike," I agreed, smiling. "They are both just like their tata."

She stood up. "Yes, well. I just remembered that I need to talk to both Antonia and Tonia about their studies. I will come back to see my little Marcus later."

She left the room so quickly, I could only stare after her, wondering if I'd said something wrong.

When we could no longer hear her footsteps, Ptolly opened his eyes. "You were faking!" I whispered. "Are you mad at Octavia?"

Ptolly shrugged. "A little."

"Why?"

"I told her she should call me by my real name. She keeps trying to treat me like a baby. But I am nine now, and I do not want to sleep in her room anymore or be called 'little Marcus.'"

Was that why Octavia seemed so sad and haunted that first day of his illness? His assertion of independence pleased me, but I guessed that it also hurt Octavia. I hated the idea of one of us hurting the person responsible for our safety, but there was nothing I could do. Ptolly was growing up.

I spent most of my time with him reading his favorite battle scenes from *The Iliad*. His enthusiasm for the blood and gore of the poem never waned. "Read the part where Menelaos hits Peisandros so hard on the head with his sword, his eyeballs pop out!" Ptolly demanded.

I smiled, as it always amazed me how — when it came to the violent scenes — Ptolly had impeccable recall. But then I grew concerned, noticing that he had closed his eyes with fatigue after making the request. Just then Juba walked in. "Good morning, young Achilles!" he said.

Ptolly opened his eyes and smiled at him. This was the first time I had crossed paths with Juba since I tried to kiss him. Distracted as I was by my fears for Ptolly, I had almost forgotten the entire humiliating event. Almost.

"Good morning to you too, Cleopatra Selene," Juba said, smiling.

"Good morning," I mumbled, pretending that I had lost my place in the scroll and I was trying to find it.

"Juba, you usually come when Alexandros is here," Ptolly said. "You are early."

Shame swelled in my chest at this confirmation that Juba had indeed been trying to avoid me. I continued searching the scroll so I wouldn't have to look at him.

"Read!" Ptolly commanded me, closing his eyes again.

I read aloud until he slept, which wasn't long, all the time aware that Juba was watching me. When I stopped reading, the only sound in the room was Ptolly's breathing.

"Cleopatra Selene," Juba said quietly, "I wanted to apologize . . ."

"No," I said. "Please don't. It is forgotten." I smiled brightly at him. "Truly, that was ages ago. We need not revisit it."

Juba looked down. "It is just that . . ."

Gods, I could not bear to rehash it! "So, why have you come in the morning when you usually visit later?" I interrupted, desperate to change the subject.

He stopped and took a breath. "I am going to a banquet at Varro's tonight."

"The scholar Varro?"

"Yes, he is one of my patrons. We are celebrating the publication of my first book."

"I did not know you were working on a book! What is it called?"

He smiled sheepishly. "Oh, I thought I had told you about it. It's called *Roman Antiquities*."

Again, I felt that strange surge of anger that I usually tried to suppress around Juba. "And yet you do not write about Numidian antiquities or the great battles of your grandfather, Hemipshall the Second?" I asked.

He raised his eyebrows, staring at me.

"I am sorry," I said, looking down. Why could I not keep my mouth shut? "Publishing a book is an impressive accomplishment. Please, tell me about it."

He pulled up a wooden stool and talked excitedly about the project and the positive reviews it had garnered. His eyes lit up as he spoke, and I understood, more deeply, that Juba was a scholar at heart. *How he would have loved our Great Library*, I thought once again. How *I* would have loved to show it to him and introduce him to our famous philosophers!

But that life seemed like a dream now. So I focused on the present — the warmth of his smile, the light in his eyes. We discussed the long and expensive process of getting his scrolls copied for distribution and his plans for future books. Ptolly never awoke, despite our enthusiasm. And we both pretended my clumsy attempt at kissing him never happened.

CHAPTER TWENTY-SEVEN

"Do not give him that water!" commanded the doctor.

I jumped at his sharp tone. "But he is so thirsty!" I cried.

"Please," Ptolly said, licking his cracked lips. "Just a little."

The *iatros* scowled. "I have just given him a tincture of feverfew, and I do not want it diluted before it takes effect."

"Just a little?" I repeated, hating to see Ptolly suffer.

The *iatros* sighed as if greatly put upon. "Fine, but not too much."

I held the honeyed water to my brother's lips, supporting his head as he closed his eyes. Ptolly had continued to deteriorate, his fever lingering, his strength gone. I tried not to notice how even the act of drinking exhausted him.

"That's enough!" the doctor said.

Reluctantly, I pulled the cup away.

"More?" Ptolly whispered.

The doctor narrowed his eyes at me. But how could I not slake my little brother's thirst? I could not bear the sight of the dry, sunken hollows of his eyes or the parched, peeling skin around his lips. For the thousandth time, I wished that Olympus, our royal physician in Alexandria, were here to help me.

When I let Ptolly drink his fill, the *iatros* turned on his heel and left, muttering in Greek, "How can I do my job if this meddlesome child is constantly interfering!"

He must have forgotten Greek was our first language. I knew he was going to complain to Livia, especially since I had refused to let him bleed Ptolly again. I could not bear to see my brother grow even weaker at the doctor's ministrations.

"Thanks, sister," Ptolly murmured as I put the cup down.

Zosima had made a salve of beeswax and chamomile oil. I dipped my finger into the small clay cup and spread the ointment on Ptolly's mouth, tracing the pale and peeling contours over and over again, as if by sheer repetition I could bring back the sweet pink plumpness of his little-boy lips.

"Tell me another story?" he mumbled.

The weaker Ptolly got, the more he wanted to hear about our lives in Alexandria. It was as if my stories of Egypt were calling to him, like snatches of a beautiful song he could almost, but not quite, remember.

"Which one?"

Ptolly shivered and turned on his side, bringing his knees up to his chest. "I am so cold," he muttered.

I looked behind me at the doorway from which the doctor had just left. He would probably tell me not to add blankets to the thin wool covering already spread over him because his chill was likely the result of the tincture taking effect. Ptolly shivered again, and I felt a surge of defiance. How could he expect me to sit back and watch my baby brother suffer? After kicking off my sandals, I climbed onto his sleeping couch behind him, curling around his body and rubbing my hands over his goose-pimpled arms. I willed my body to heat him and, within a few minutes, his teeth stopped chattering.

I raked my fingers on the scratchy wool. Our cats, Sebi and Tanafriti, responded to my summons by jumping onto the couch, one curling into his chest, the other around his head. I could feel his muscles relax as our combined warmth entered his body.

"'Nother story," Ptolly prompted again, and my heart lurched at how young he sounded, younger than even his nine years.

I sighed. "Which one?" I repeated.

"When they tricked you."

I chuckled. I knew which story he meant. It had become his favorite. "It all started because I hated you with all my heart when you were born. I wanted to send you back to wherever you came from!"

He made a gurgling, giggling sound in his throat.

"Alexandros and I were four. I had complained bitterly about hearing your wails echoing down the empty halls when I awoke in the deep-dark," I said. "Everybody tried to get me to like you, especially soft-hearted Katep. Do you remember him?"

He shook his head and I swallowed, recalling Katep's kindness, the pretty roundness of his face, the soothing scent of sandalwood and cinnamon of his skin.

"One night, I was especially ill-tempered about your loud screaming. . . ."

"You? Ill-tempered?"

I smiled, pleased he could muster the energy to tease me.

"So Katep turned to me and said, 'The baby misses his *mother.*' See, he knew I missed Mother terribly during the long period she traveled to help Tata recover from his war in Parthia. But I refused to have empathy for you. . . ."

"Typical."

"Shush. Anyway, one night, your cries seemed particularly loud and miserable. So Katep said, 'Come, let us see if we can help the milk nurse.'"

"Nafre."

I paused. Not since leaving Alexandria had he uttered the name of the nurse he had adored — the nurse who had left him on the dock because she could not bear to live among Romans. "Yes. Poor Nafre looked exhausted as she paced with you on her shoulder.

"'I order you to make that baby stop crying!' I told her. But Katep said, 'She cannot, because he misses his *mother,*' trying yet again to get me to feel for you."

"Could have told him . . . never work," he whispered.

"I told her to feed you and she said she already had. See, you were a little pig even then! All of a sudden, you belched like one of the burly dockworkers from the Harbor of Good Return!"

I paused, thinking how happy I would be to hear him burp now, for that would mean he would have eaten something.

"Well, as soon as you burped, Nafre shoved you into my arms and scurried off, claiming she had to wipe off her shoulder. I looked into your face, you looked up at me, and then . . . you smiled! I gasped. Your grin looked so much like Tata's — though toothless. I turned to Katep in surprise.

"'See,' Katep said. 'Ptolemy Philadelphos loves his sister — She Who Shines like the Moon, She Who Soothes like Hathor.'"

Ptolly made a noise in his throat. In previous tellings, he had giggled at Katep's overly formal Egyptian words.

I continued. "When I looked down and saw that you were still smiling at me, I had a total change of heart."

"And then?"

"And then you grew up to torture me."

"No, Klee-Klee," he muttered. "Tell it real."

He was using his baby nickname for me, as if his soul — and his memories — were growing younger. Traveling backward. It terrified me. My throat tightened, and I had to take a deep breath before I could speak again. "Fine. Zosima later confessed that she, Katep, and Nafre had planned the whole thing. See, you always smiled after burping. So the three of them waited for just the right time to strike. By throwing me in your line of vision as soon as you burped, it looked like you reserved your most charming, most loving smile just for me."

"G' trick," Ptolly said sleepily.

"It was a good trick." And it had worked. From that moment on, I had loved my little brother with as much ferocity as I had once hated him for his loud crying.

Ptolly did not say anything else, and I thought him asleep. I pushed myself up to check. His eyes were closed. I could see the tiny blue veins in his eyelids.

"Don't go," he whispered, barely moving his pale lips.

I lay back down.

"Klee-Klee?"

"Hmm?"

"I miss Nafre."

I closed my eyes, hearing the grief in his small voice. "I know."

"Do not leave me," he whispered. "Like . . . Mother and Nafre."

My heart lurched. I cuddled up to him, surrounding him with my body, pouring my affection and love into him as if I could comfort him from the outside in. "I will never leave you, little brother," I whispered into his ear. *"Never."*

I must have fallen sleep. The light was strange, as if a spring storm had come and gone. I wondered if the rain had cooled the air. Is that why I was so cold? I cuddled closer to Ptolly.

My heart began to beat faster. Someone was watching me. I lifted my head toward the center of the room. The cats' eyes — glittering, focused, intense — regarded me with a seriousness that stilled my breath. Sebi and Tanafriti, sitting like two statues in a tomb. Sentinels. Brother and sister cat, guardians to the realm of Osiris.

I sat up. My stomach tightened, pulling the air from my lungs. Our cats waited for me to realize what they already knew. But I refused to believe them.

I shook Ptolly, begged him to wake, tried to warm his cold skin with my hands, pretended that the blue around his mouth was a trick of the disappearing light. The silent cats stood as witnesses to my horror, as if guarding the portal for the *ka* that had already left my little brother's body.

My sweet Ptolly, I promised never to leave *you*, but why, WHY, had I not made you promise never to leave *me*?

CHAPTER TWENTY-EIGHT

I stayed with Ptolly, refusing to remove my arms from around his cold body. Hands, voices tried to pry me from him, but I would not budge.

Zosima finally broke through the horror. Talking to me in a low, soft voice, as if I were a toddler on the edge of a cliff, she said, "Let us prepare him for the Priests of Anubis. We will dress your brother like a true prince of Egypt."

She brought me water scented with lotus oil and I washed his body. I straightened his limbs, combed through his curls, and dressed him in Alexandros's old Egyptian kilt, pectoral, and linen cloak. I cradled his small, cold head and set a coronet of rosemary and laurel in place of the golden diadem that Octavianus had long ago melted down to pay the soldiers he'd used to destroy my family.

Zosima and Alexandros helped me surround his funeral couch with fragrant blooms and small pots of burning incense. Someone hung pine and cypress branches around the door frame, a Roman tradition, I later learned, to signify that death had polluted the room.

Although I did not remember her entering, Octavia also refused to leave Ptolly's side. Grief seemed to have torn her apart as well. She had crumpled at his feet, sobbing. I felt an even deeper kinship with her then. She had understood how special Ptolly was. She had loved him deeply too.

Ptolly's *ka*, I sensed, hovered nearby. It would have no peace until we completed the full rites of Anubis as we had done for our parents and Caesarion. It was the only way Ptolly would be reunited with them in the afterworld.

"I will not fail you," I promised. "I will find a way to entomb you in the sacred traditions."

Octavianus had a different plan. He commanded that Ptolly's body be burned in the Roman manner. He had banned the worship of

Isis and other Egyptian gods from inside the walls of Rome; he said he could hardly allow such practices in his own household. I overheard him arguing with Livia outside Ptolly's death room while I pretended sleep.

"We are in Rome, and we do things our way," Octavianus said in an angry whisper. "We burn him on the pyres outside the city walls on the fifth day and that is it!"

Livia, to my surprise, argued for my wishes. "Husband, if the boy's body disappears, it could be made to look suspicious. But if we allow them to have their Egyptian rites, then you appear kind and magnanimous. You need people to see you that way right now."

"I see no advantage in honoring their barbaric death rituals," he said before stomping off. "The boy burns!"

After they left, I sat up and rearranged the flowers surrounding Ptolly's body. Kissing his cold forehead, I vowed again to honor him in the ancient ways. Or die trying.

That afternoon, I asked for an audience with Octavianus and was refused. Thyrsus, Octavianus's man, shook his head after blocking me from his *tablinum* door. "The *Princeps* is busy now."

"But I must see him!"

Thyrsus took me by the elbow. "I am sorry about your brother," he said in a low tone. "But Caesar is not to be disturbed."

I snatched my arm out of his grip. "I MUST see him," I cried loudly. "It will anger the Gods of Death if he ignores me!"

Thyrsus paused. Seeing the opening, I pressed on. "When a son of Egypt dies, all the gods of the underworld surround his body, demanding they be honored in the ancient ways," I announced even louder as I saw wide-eyed servants, slaves, and associates drifting toward me. "Don't you know they are gathering still? Don't you *feel* them?"

Thyrsus grabbed me. "You must go!"

"No!" I screamed. "I must see him!"

The most powerful man in the world burst out of his room. "What is the meaning of this? Thyrsus, remove her!"

"I have been trying to!" Octavianus's man said with exasperation as he grabbed my arms behind my back.

"I will speak with you!" I yelled as I writhed like a slippery octopus in Thyrsus's grip. "You must honor the newly grieved!"

Octavianus turned to look at the growing crowd of witnesses to our exchange. He would not dare abuse me or banish me in the face of associates and clients who might spread gossip about his behavior. His image was too important. I had counted on that.

Octavianus glared at me. But then he smiled. "Of course, of course, my dear girl," he said, playing to the crowd. "One must indeed always honor the newly grieved."

He drew me in to his study, gripping my elbow with unnecessary firmness. When the door closed behind me, he sniffed and pushed me away from him.

"You smell like death," he said. "I will have to purify this room after you leave."

"You must allow us to perform the ancient rites for my brother," I said.

He smirked. "You don't seriously expect me to listen to the demands of a barbarian *girl*, bastard spawn of a witch, do you?"

"The gods punish those who act with hubris," I said. "Would you risk having them turn on you?" I had prepared this argument, knowing that Octavianus was just as superstitious as most Romans, if not more so. He feared lightning, the dark, and angry gods. I prayed I could use that to turn him to my view.

But Octavianus shook off my words. "I honor *my* gods. I am under no obligation to honor yours. And I will not have this conversation again. The boy burns. And when you leave this room, you will leave calmly. Do you understand?"

"You would dare anger Anubis?"

To my surprise, he threw his head back and laughed. "A dog god? You and your beasts. They have no power in Rome."

"If the gods of Egypt have no power here, then why did you ban the Goddess from Rome? Anubis is a true son of Isis. He is not a god who angers easily, but when he does —"

Octavianus put his hand up in my face. "Stop! Your little attempt to frighten me won't work. My patron god is Apollo, the God of Light and Wisdom. He banishes the evil surrounding your dark gods. He —"

I grinned at him. Something in my expression gave him pause. Like a sorceress speaking an incantation, with my wild and unkempt hair covering most of my face, I muttered, "'O God of the Silver Bow, who protectest Chryse and holy Cilla and rulest Tenedos with thy might, hear me, O thou of Sminthe. . . .'"

Octavianus looked confused, as if the words sounded familiar but he could not place where he had heard them.

"'Hear me, O thou of Sminthe,'" I repeated. "'I am calling Apollo your god, he of Sminthe, the *mouse* god himself.'"

I could see fear mingling with his confusion. "Before you insult my so-called beast gods," I said, "remember that it is Apollo's priest, Chryse, who calls him 'mouse god' in *The Iliad*. The mouse cowers in fear of the jackal. The jackal *devours* the mouse whole."

His palm slapped my face so hard, I reeled backward. I put my hand to my stinging cheek.

"You dare insult Apollo in my own home?" he hissed.

"I do not insult. I merely speak the truth."

He grabbed my wrist and twisted it hard. I gasped. "Do not say another word, or I swear by Apollo's chariot that I will burn you *alive* alongside your brother," Octavianus said in a low, dangerous tone. "Do not ever dishonor me or my patron god again, do you understand?"

He brought me closer, twisting harder. I tried to breathe normally, but with the pain and the rank smell of *garum* on his breath, I could not. I nodded.

He let me go with a push, and I skidded into his desk. Something rolled off it. Without thinking, I reached for it, but his hand slapped me away. He swept up what clattered to the ground and slammed it back down on his desk.

He saw me staring. "My signet ring," he gloated. "Made from your mother's golden armbands. I do take such pleasure knowing that what once graced her body now touches mine."

He grinned at my look of disgust. "Now. Get out."

I rushed out of his *tablinum* and back to Ptolly's body. "Help me, O Goddess," I begged as I curled into myself at his feet. "Help me save my brother."

Exhausted from weeping, I dozed as images floated in and out of my awareness. Ptolly called for me: "Klee-Klee, where are you?"

Amunet emerged from smoky shadows. "Isis is your savior!" the priestess said.

"Well, who was Ptolly's savior?" I cried.

"You are," Amunet whispered. "Anubis demands it."

I woke with a start. The room was dark. Someone had put a blanket over me. I looked around. Alexandros slept on a pallet on the other side of Ptolly. I heard a slight snore and saw Juba behind me on a low stool, his back against the wall, chin on chest.

I swallowed as my dream came back to me. "Anubis demands it," Amunet had said. I lay down on the hard floor, remembering the strange day she taught me to Call Forth Anubis. The day she told me I would need that power to curse my enemies and protect the sons of Egypt.

I gasped, sitting up to stare into the closed, waxy eyelids of my baby brother. My heart raced with a new understanding and hope.

Juba stirred and sat up, rubbing the back of his neck. "Cleopatra Selene? Are you all right?" he whispered. "Do you want me to pull a pallet for you too? That floor cannot be comfortable."

I shook my head, rubbing my cheek where the stone floor had left little marks. I moved closer to Juba. "Will you help me?"

"Of course," he said. "Anything."

I looked at him in the flickering glow from the almost spent torch in the hallway. Exhaustion and pain were etched on his face — a reminder that other people grieved for my baby brother too. "I cannot let them burn him," I said. "We must perform the sacred rites."

"I agree. But nobody has been able to convince Caesar of that."

"You have tried?" I asked, surprised.

He nodded. How loyal Juba was to my brothers and me! It took me a moment before I could speak again.

"I need your help in getting . . ." I paused, wondering how I could make this request without shocking or disgusting him. "Would you help me get . . ."

Juba leaned forward. "Whatever you need, Cleopatra Selene. Just tell me."

I took a breath.

"I need the blood of a black dog."

CHAPTER TWENTY-NINE

Juba startled. "What?"

"Fresh blood from a newly slaughtered black dog," I repeated.

He shook his head, eyes wide. "Cleopatra Selene," he whispered. "I am afraid you are going mad."

"I am not, I swear!"

With one hand, he rubbed the wild locks off of my face, leaving his palm cupping my cheek. I closed my eyes and leaned into his hand, melting into his touch. "Oh, child," he whispered. "You cannot . . ."

I reared back as if I'd been slapped. *Child* — again? I was no child, I knew that now. My soul felt as old and dried up as the Red Lands of Egypt's deserts.

"There is no other way," I said, my voice hard. "I cannot do it myself. I need you to do this for me."

"But why would you need such a thing?"

"To convince Octavianus to let us take care of Ptolly the proper way."

"How in Hades' name would dog blood help you do that?"

"For a ritual," I explained. "One that the Priestess of Isis in Egypt herself taught me."

When Juba did not speak, I tried again. "I have jewels from my mother that Zosima hid for me before we left Egypt," I said. "I could give you those in exchange for what I need."

Juba shook his head. "Money is not the issue. I just do not understand why —"

"Please, Juba," I begged. "I am not mad now, but I fear I will become so unless I succeed. The Lady of Isis told me I would need it to save the sons of Egypt. Ptolly is a son of Egypt. Do you not see? The Goddess knew I would need this! She is my savior, my protectress. I *must* honor her wishes."

Juba flicked his gaze to Alexandros, who had stirred. "You will not harm anyone with this? It is for Ptolly?"

"No, I will not harm anyone. And yes, it is for Ptolly!"

"Gods, where will I find the blood of a black dog?" Juba said, then put up his hand. "Never mind. One can find anything in Rome for the right price. What else?"

I closed my eyes, remembering. "An ivory tusk, carved with images of my gods destroying their enemies. And a goat-hair brush."

Juba exhaled loudly. "You are not making this simple, are you? But I have friends who are secret worshippers of the Goddess. They will help me."

"We do not have much time. I must perform the ritual right away, before Octavianus throws my brother on the pyre."

Juba nodded, and I closed my eyes in relief.

At first light, Juba left to gather the things I needed, still looking none too happy about it. I paced in front of Ptolly's body, thinking, thinking. I had to be able to get near Octavianus's sleeping room in the hours just before sunrise to perform the ritual. But how could I do that without being detected by him or Thyrsus?

I looked at the low wooden table next to my brother where two full cups of poppy tea lay untouched. Livia had ordered her *iatros* to make them for us after Ptolly's death, but I had set mine aside and convinced Alexandros not to touch his either. And because no servant dared enter this "Room of Death," nobody knew that we had the sleeping potion at our fingertips.

I smiled.

*   *   *

As the day wore on, Alexandros watched my manic pacing with a question in his eyes, but he never said anything. Most of the time, he seemed lost to himself anyway, staring at nothing, saying nothing, but like me, never leaving Ptolly's side.

When darkness fell that evening, Zosima nodded to me and took away the cups of poppy tea. She was to sneak into the servants' quarters and add the sleeping potion to Octavianus's and Thyrsus's goblets of night wine.

I waited for Juba. He came into the room as he had the night before but this time carrying two additional pallets — one for himself, one for me.

"You will sleep here again tonight?" I asked, surprised.

"I feel compelled to," he said grimly. "Something tells me you may need my protection."

When Alexandros finally dropped off to sleep, Juba whispered in my ear, "My man has procured what you asked for. You will find the things hidden behind the oleander bush by the small fountain in the old garden."

Ptolly's *ka* came to me when I dozed. He reached his arms up to me, but when I went to pick him up, he disappeared. I must have cried in my sleep, for I woke myself up, gasping for breath. But his *ka's* visit only strengthened my resolve.

In the deepest dark of night, I snuck out of the room, watery moonlight lighting my way to the baths, where the hypocaust workers would soon begin stoking the great fires that would provide us with heated water. With shaking hands, I crept into the cavernous marble room, stripped, and immersed myself in the chilly water. I was not able to purify myself as Amunet and I had done at the Isis Temple, but this would have to do.

I shivered as I climbed out and donned the white linen tunic Zosima had left for me. It stuck to my still-wet body. Gods, why had I not thought to plant a towel too! The fabric clung to my newly rounded breasts and hips. When had this shift grown too small?

Blindly, I felt around the floor until I found the sharp edge of the dagger I had instructed Zosima to leave for me. It was Mother's dagger, the one Katep claimed Mother had tried to use on herself before getting captured, but I knew better. She had intended to use it on her attacker. I would do the same if I were caught. When my fingers brushed the cool lapis lazuli handle, I released a long breath, unaware that I had been holding it tight within my chest. I hid the dagger in the folds of my belt, checking multiple times that I could draw it out quickly.

I found the clay amphora filled with a black liquid under the oleander bush. I put my nose to the clay jar. Yes, blood. But where were the ivory tusk and goat-hair brush?

I felt around in the dark and found two bundles. The small one contained the ivory and brush. The other one felt wet and heavy. When I opened it up to peer in by the light of the moon and stars, I almost cried out.

The head of the black dog! Gods, I hadn't asked for this. Why did Juba's man leave the head here? My heart raced from fear, fatigue, lack of food. Would the god be angry? Did he see it as defilement?

But what if — what if it was Anubis himself who spurred Juba's man to leave the head for me? What if it was a gift from the great Dark God? I would have to take it with me. I closed my eyes and lifted my face to the darkness in prayer:

O you, Opener of the Ways, Dark Pupil of the Sun,
Guide me safely through the terrors of my own unseeing;
Walk with me in my journey of Peril.

I slid without notice into the colonnaded garden outside Octavianus's room. Thyrsus lay in front of his master's *cubiculum* on a rumpled rush mat, a tray with wine and two cups by his head. I hid in the shadows of the corner columns and cleared my throat. Nothing. Thyrsus was a notoriously light sleeper. It appeared the poppy wine had done its job.

Too afraid to step into the center of the *peristylum*, where the moonlight might make me obvious, I put down my bundles and set to work in the shadows. With the ivory tusk covered in hieroglyphs and magic symbols, I drew a circle of protection on the sand around myself. I could not remember the ancient words Amunet had used, but I thought the god would forgive me for that.

I closed the circle with a trembling hand. Fear gripped my lungs and I fought for breath. I remembered then the terror I felt with Amunet on the day she showed me the spell. This intense fear meant the god was near.

I dipped the goat-hair brush into the amphora of blood. With a shaking hand, I drew the god's profile on the sand at my bare feet — the long snout, the tall ears, the fierce eyes. "O Great Son of Osiris, Jackal Ruler of the Bows, God of the Necropolis. I ask your protection for a son of Egypt," I prayed as I painted. "May you guide my hand in delivering him intact to you, so that his *ka* lives on according to your judgment. . . ."

Fear traveled up my shaking hands all the way to my chattering teeth. I dropped the brush in the amphora and removed the dog head from its soaked woolen wrapping. I stared into one blank, dark eye.

The god's fear held me. "What do I do with this symbol of your greatness, O God?" I asked.

I stood, swaying, waiting for an answer. Nothing came. I thought about my original plan. To have Octavianus see the spell in blood and fear that he had angered the Dark God. To have that sight fill him with such terror that he would change his mind about caring for Ptolly's body in the Egyptian manner.

But a new thought stopped my breath. What if he never saw the blood-soaked image? What if I had made a mistake in putting it in the corner? I groaned inwardly. Octavianus had to know that Anubis had been called and that Anubis would demand the sacred rites for a prince of Egypt. He *had* to!

Then, as if the god himself spoke to me, I knew what I must do. I thanked the god and asked that the circle of protection I had drawn follow me into my enemy's sleeping chamber.

I stepped over Thyrsus and waited for my eyes to adjust to the dark of the *cubiculum*. Octavianus lay as if dead, one arm over his eyes. The room stank of stale air and sweat.

Such a surge of hatred roiled in my blood at the destroyer of my family, I grew dizzy for a moment. An ugly whisper of a thought — *kill him* — entered my awareness. Goddess help me, but I considered it. Drugged as he was, he was completely at my mercy. My fingers traced the dagger hidden in my belt. I could cut his throat, I could watch as his vile blood poured forth, ending the nightmare of pain and death he had caused.

Mother would do it, I prompted myself. *She wouldn't even hesitate.* With a shaking hand, I withdrew the dagger and held it over his skinny neck.

Mother would want me to do this, to avenge her! I repeated. But still, I could not make my hand move. Was Anubis staying me? I remembered an image in Amunet's temple of Anubis weighing a heart against the Feather of Truth. Anubis, Judge of Truth, wanted me to live by *ma'at* and pass the test. I would not dishonor the god or risk Ptolly's *ka* with an act that would do nothing to get us back to Egypt. I slid the dagger back into my belt.

Still, I wanted Octavianus to *suffer*. I pulled his blanket aside ever so slowly. He did not move. I slipped the heavy, blood-soaked head of Anubis's representative on earth into the bed beside my enemy, as if it were about to take a bite of his torso. Before releasing my hands, I prayed over it. "May your power frighten our enemy. May it be enough to save Ptolly's *ka*."

I stretched the blanket over them both, wiping my bloodstained hands over the ends of his coverlet. Before bolting from the room, I looked into Octavianus's face. "Just so we are clear," I whispered. "Do not dishonor *my* gods!"

CHAPTER THIRTY

I almost tripped over Thyrsus on my way out of Octavianus's *cubiculum*. Stepping back into the circle of protection I had drawn earlier, I unbound the magic by redrawing it in the opposite direction. Then I scooped up all the evidence of my work and raced away, holding it all against my waist.

I thought I had made it when a giant Gaul with long blond braids stepped out of the shadows.

"Halt!" the man cried in his Gaulish-accented Latin. "Announce yourself!"

I groaned inwardly, but Zosima had coached me carefully on what to do if I came across one of his guards.

"It is just me," I said. Zosima told me I must make my voice sound sultry or seductive, but the best I could do was to keep it from trembling. "*Dominus* called for a girl earlier."

The man narrowed his eyes at me. "At this time of night?"

I shrugged, allowing the linen dress to slide over my shoulder. His eyes followed it. "You know what he is like when he cannot sleep."

"I've never seen you before," he said. "And slaves don't wear white."

Gods! I could not panic. *Think, think.* Again, I shrugged, allowing the material to fall farther down my shoulder. "I am a new girl. And . . . and my specialty is pretending to be a Vestal Virgin," I said in a conspiratorial voice.

"What's that on your dress?"

I looked down. Some of the blood from the woolen cloth had seeped onto the white fabric at my hip. The guard moved toward me suspiciously.

Please help me, Anubis, son of Isis. "Oh! This is embarrassing! See, I . . ." I looked down again at the stain. "I began my monthly bleeding and the

Great One grew angry. He made me leave and he went to Liv . . . *Domina's* house because he said I had polluted his room."

Who knew what kind of strange superstitions his people had about menstruating women? I only prayed that they included getting far from me.

They did. The giant Gaul took a step back. "Well, do not contaminate me either! Go. Get out of here."

I raced away, my breathing sounding to my own ears like the wheezes of a dying monster. I snuck back into the baths and stripped. I did not have time for a full immersion, so I dipped my arms up to my elbows to clean off any traces of blood. As fast as I could, I dressed in my old clothing, wrapped up the bundle — including my bloodstained white dress — and went around back to the slaves' entrance to the underground hypocaust.

I ran down the stairs, startling the nearly naked slave stoking the flames. Smoke, red fire, unbearable heat. How did the poor man stand it? The sweat-soaked Iberian looked at me with wide, frightened eyes.

"Throw all of this into the flames," I commanded, slipping a golden coin into his hand. "Everything. And do not unwrap it or look into it or you and all your descendants will be cursed forever, for it contains powerful magic that must be destroyed."

The slave nodded fearfully and disappeared into his glowing red world with my bundle. I paused, listening for the sound of the clay amphora breaking and the hiss of blood on fire.

As soon as I heard it, I flew back to Livia's house, the grass cold and slippery with predawn dew. The sky, although still dark, was turning purple. Sounds of a stirring household echoed around me — the hushed, sleepy voices of slaves, the hiss of torches as their oily tips caught fire, the shuffling of bare feet on stone floors.

I tiptoed back into the sickroom. Again, my heart lurched at the sight of my little brother's body. I whispered into his ear exactly what I had done, hoping his *ka* would be pleased. With shaking fingers, I touched his waxy, cold cheek and returned to my pallet.

My body vibrated with tension and fear, my teeth chattering even though I clenched my jaw to still the noise. I threw the blanket over my head, curling into myself.

A rustling behind me. "Cleopatra Selene, are you all right?" Juba whispered.

I could not unclench my jaw or stop shivering.

Juba moved beside me. "What happened?" he asked.

I wanted to thank him for his help, to let him know that I had completed the magic for Calling Forth Anubis. But when I opened my mouth, no sound emerged. Instead, to my horror, I began to cry — great racking sobs that I had tried to hold in, as Alexandros still slept. I could barely breathe for the grief that swelled up in my center like a giant wave blotting out the sun. When the wave crashed, I could do nothing but let it carry me away. I remember only the warmth of Juba's hand as he rubbed my back.

The hiss of whispers. Juba speaking softly to someone right outside my door. Where was I? I remembered with a pang so deep I almost winced: I was in the room with Ptolly's dead body. I heard Alexandros sit up.

"What is going on?" he called.

"Check that one," a voice said. My blood chilled. Octavianus. Stomping feet. Someone pulled the blanket off of me. Octavianus himself jerked me up by my upper arm.

"Caesar, please!" Juba said. "There is no need for roughness! I have been here all night, and so have they."

Octavianus pushed me toward someone: the guard from the night before with his long blond braids. My heart sank.

"Well?" Octavianus demanded. "Is this the girl you saw last night?"

I kept my eyes down but could feel the man inspecting every inch of me. I prayed that with my rumpled, dirty tunic — much wider and looser than the tight white *tunica* I had worn last night — my wild, slept-on hair covering most of my face, and my red eyes, puffy from crying, I would look nothing like the clean girl with slick wet hair that he had seen last night.

"Answer me, you idiot!" Octavianus demanded.

"The one I saw last night was prettier," he said. "And . . . and taller. Her hair was darker and not as wild."

I breathed out, grateful that the big oaf had never really looked at my face but kept his gaze at chest level.

"No. No. This is not the girl."

Octavianus spat at my feet and growled.

Juba stepped between me and the guard. "Caesar, what has happened?" he asked. "You are alarming me."

But before Octavianus could respond, the guard offered in his rough Latin: "Sire, the whore said she had . . . well . . . that she had started her monthly bleeding, so perhaps we should ask after all the young women who are, you know . . . having their regular blood. . . ."

Octavianus stared up at the guard. Another beat passed, and the man swallowed. Octavianus turned to Juba and said in Greek, "Please tell me my guard is not this stupid, Juba. I really need to hear that right now. Even if it is a complete lie."

Juba chuckled nervously.

Octavianus looked back at the wide-eyed giant, moving his neck as if he had a crick in it. "The story about her monthly bleeding was a *ruse*," he said in Latin through clenched teeth. "That is how she tricked you into not stopping her as she left my room stained with *blood*, you stupid ox!"

He spoke to Juba again in Greek. "Take him away from me and have my captain of the guard punish him. Lashing, crucifixion, hanging, I don't care. Just get him away from me."

Juba hesitated, glancing toward me in concern. But he had no choice. "Come," he said in Latin to the guard. "Caesar bids you follow me." Not understanding his death sentence, the man happily followed Juba out of the room.

Octavianus narrowed his eyes at me. "You had something to do with it, I know it."

"To do with what?" Alexandros asked.

"I have no idea what he is talking about," I said to Alexandros, thankful my voice sounded thick and raw from crying myself to sleep. With Juba gone, I felt more vulnerable; even the room seemed darker, like heavy clouds had just blocked the sun.

"We . . . we have not left Ptolly's side since . . . since he died," my twin said. "What has happened?"

Octavianus glanced over at Ptolly's body, then back to the pallet by the door where Juba had lain. I could see the doubt working through his thoughts. Juba said he had been there all night watching us, and the young Numidian's honesty and integrity had never been questioned. His word was stronger than anything either one of us could have said.

Which left, I hoped he saw, only one last possibility — that the god Anubis really had sent him a message. A low rumbling of thunder vibrated overhead, as if the god himself spoke. Perhaps the sudden darkness had been clouds gathering after all. If so, I prayed for lightning. Ever since Octavianus had nearly gotten struck by lightning years ago, he had an unnatural fear of storms. I thanked the Goddess for sending one now, even though storms were common that time of the year.

Fear seemed to radiate from Octavianus's skinny chest like sweat steaming from a horse run hard in the cold. Another far-off rumble sent the knob in his throat bobbing. "I will not waste another moment on this nonsense. I do not care what you do. Summon your dog priests if you want. But none of your barbaric practices take place anywhere near my grounds or within the city limits of Rome, do you hear me? None."

With that, the leader of the world turned on his heels and hurried away.

*   *   *

With its colonnade of Doric columns and sculpted pediment, the Isis Temple outside Capua looked more like a temple to Athena. But when we crossed the threshold, it was as if we entered Egypt. Brightly colored lotus columns soared to the sky; robed priests and priestesses chanted over bowls of smoky incense, jangling sistrums in time to their song; lotus blossoms floated in golden bowls; painted images in the Egyptian style told the story of Isis's grief and Osiris's resurrection.

A woman dressed in Egyptian blue linen — the color of life and rebirth — emerged from the billowing smoke of incense as if by magic. "Welcome, Children of Ra," she said in a low and musical voice, bowing. "I am Isetnofret, the Lady of Isis at Capua."

Isetnofret. Isis is Beautiful. My throat clenched at the sound of her name. I had longed to meet the lady for years, but I had never dreamt it would happen under these circumstances. Although she looked more Greek than Egyptian with her olive skin and long, curly hair, it was as if Amunet's voice spoke through her. I wanted to throw myself into her arms, to never leave this place that was so reminiscent of home.

But, of course, I did nothing of the sort. After our formal introductions — in which she invoked Isis and bid us cleave to the Goddess of Love and Hope during our grief — she directed us to follow her into the temple's inner sanctuary. Juba, who had accompanied us on the journey, carried Ptolly's shrouded body behind us.

After ritually cleansing our hands with Nile water poured from a golden *hydria*, she brought us to the entrance of the *ibw* — the Place of Purification — where the mummification of Ptolly's body would begin, a process that would take more than two months. The Head Priest of Isis stepped forward and bowed, his shaved and oiled head gleaming in the torch-lit passageway, eyes rimmed in kohl. He wore robes of black, the color of death. Two Priests of Anubis, bare-chested and in giant jackal masks, flanked him. An acolyte took Ptolly's shrouded body from Juba and placed it on the large table inside the chamber.

The masked Priests of Anubis stepped in front of us and crossed their arms in a symbolic gesture to remind us that we were still of the living. We could not follow our brother into the sacred chamber. The fierceness of their masks reminded me of Ptolly's reaction when he saw them during the ceremony for Mother — how he had pressed against me in terror.

The priestess bid us away. I felt Alexandros move, but I could not. Panic surged up my middle. Ptolly looked so tiny and lost on the large metal table. The Anubis masks *scared* him! Didn't they know that? Who would comfort him? I could not leave him there alone with strangers.

Isetnofret put her arm around me, but still I did not move. "Come," she whispered, and I caught the sweet, spicy scents of lotus oil and myrrh, the smells of Egypt. "You have saved a prince of Egypt by giving his *ka* a place to dwell for all eternity," she murmured.

"But I promised him I'd never leave," I whispered.

"And you have kept your promise. I have heard from our followers in Caesar's own compound how you battled him to ensure your brother's *ka* survives."

Was that what it was — a battle? She took me by both shoulders and turned me to her, so that my back was to Ptolly and the masked priests. "Do you see how the Power of Isis worked through you? You opposed Caesar and *won*. The Goddess has not abandoned you. She will bring *ma'at* to Egypt and return you to the throne as the gods have destined.

"But you must be patient," she added. "The Goddess's timetable is not ours."

I allowed her to lead me away. And through the grief and confusion that lingered through the months that followed, one phrase echoed in my mind as if the priestess had yelled it into a bottomless well: *You opposed Caesar and won.*

. . . opposed Caesar . . .

. . . and won.

CHAPTER THIRTY-ONE
In What Would Have Been the Twenty-fifth Year of My Mother's Reign
In My Fifteenth Year (26 BCE)

No matter how many times I visited his tomb, I never got used to the sight of Ptolly's heartbreakingly small mummy. It seemed impossible that his loud, vibrant, intense physicalness could ever have inhabited the tiny shell that was all of what was left of him.

Ptolly's mummy faced east to welcome the sun, which was reborn every morning in the same way he was reborn in the afterlife. Colorful hieroglyphic spells on the sides of his wooden sarcophagus ensured his safe journey. His image had been painted on shiny, varnished cedarwood and placed atop the body in the sarcophagus. The artist had not captured the mischievous glint of his eyes or the energy that had seemed to vibrate off his compact body. But the likeness — the curly dark hair, the big brown eyes, the hint of a slightly sideways smile — was true enough.

I sprinkled incense and sacred Nile water — brought to the Temple with every boat from Alexandria — around his body. I also arranged fragrant blooms on the offerings tray. And then . . .

"In honor of the first visit of my fifteenth year," I announced to Ptolly, unwrapping a linen bundle with a flourish, "I bring you your favorite treats!" Ptolly had always had a weakness for sweets, especially for almond cakes. I smiled, remembering how his cheeks bulged as he stuffed as much of the cake as he could into a single bite.

Even though it had only been a matter of days since I last visited, I began — as I always did — by telling Ptolly about happenings at the compound.

"Octavianus has recovered from his latest sickness," I started. The leader of the world constantly complained of stomach trouble and of weakness of breath. "Livia is forever brewing new concoctions for him to try. I am hoping," I added in a whisper, "that she gets her recipes mixed up and accidentally poisons him!

"Sometimes I feel Livia watching me, and I am sure she is wishing me ill. Why she has not tried again to remove Alexandros and me is a mystery. I am convinced that something — or someone — is staying her hand." I sniffed a lotus bloom. "I suspect, Little Brother, that it is Octavia. Although I know you grew tired of her smothering, she is still the only other person in the household that Livia respects." I did not add that Octavia continued to refer to him as her "little Marcus," for I knew his *ka* would find that displeasing.

"Alexandros spends a lot of time writing, but he never shares his works with me. I wonder if he is composing love poems, though he gives no hint of who has caught his eye." Alexandros, since Ptolly's death, had withdrawn even further into himself, an ongoing concern for me. Sometimes, as on that day, I could not even inspire him to accompany me to Ptolly's tomb. But it did no good to remind *ka*s of the pain their passing caused, so I said nothing.

I also did not mention that Alexandros continued scoffing at my plans for returning to Egypt. Once, he wheeled on me in an uncharacteristic rage.

"Stop it!" he had hissed. "It will never happen. The gods have abandoned us. I never, *ever* want to hear any more of your foolishness again, do you understand?"

He had stalked off while I stared after him, feeling as if he had punched me in the chest.

I shook the memory off. "Marcellus spends more and more time shadowing Octavianus, which only makes Tiberius nastier than ever," I continued. "I am sure it galls Livia that everyone — not just her husband — dislikes her firstborn. . . . And Tonia is so big now you wouldn't recognize her," I said of Antonia-the-Younger, his favorite playmate.

"She sends this for you." I slipped a small letter she wrote to him in between the blooms.

"Juba is forever researching obscure facts that he hopes to use in future books," I added. I didn't dare admit even to Ptolly's *ka* that my attraction to Juba had never waned. Indeed, it had only grown stronger, though I hid it well. Or, at least, I hoped I did.

Juba often escorted Alexandros and me to Capua. If Juba could not personally escort us, he sent one of his men. He never explained why, but I guessed that he worried about our safety. Traveling was dangerous in and outside of Rome — there was always the chance that we might be set upon by bandits. I often wondered if Livia hoped to take advantage of the travel risks to somehow make us "disappear." After all, she usually authorized only two spindly stable boys to escort us for protection. Together the boys could not have fought off a one-armed, one-eyed cripple. Juba's intercession was yet one more way he surreptitiously protected us from the wife of my enemy.

"Zosima is always trying to get me to dress differently. She wants me to cover up with a *palla* all the time, which I do when I travel, but I don't see why I need to within the compound." I mimicked her lecturing tone: "*You have the body of a woman now. It is indecent for you to show your arms or to wear dresses of such thin fabric!* Really, I think she has forgotten how we dressed in Egypt. The Romans and all their old-fashioned ways!"

I placed a small pebble on Ptolly's offering tray. "This is from Sebi," I whispered, listening to its hollow clink against metal. Even though I had brought his cat into my *cubiculum*, Sebi never seemed the same after Ptolly's death. A heavy listlessness seemed to cling about him. When he occasionally played like a kitten — in this case, batting a smooth pebble around in my room — I took it as a blessing and brought Ptolly a likeness as a gift.

Gazing into his painted face, I wondered what Ptolly would have thought of the Capuan Lady of Isis. Would she have reminded him of Egypt and brought back good memories? Or would she have only confused him? I recalled how soon after his entombment — in a tomb that the Lady of Isis had paid for with donations from local believers — I had found myself increasingly furious with her.

I had confronted Isetnofret one afternoon as she exited the Room of Supplications. "We've been in Rome for years, yet you have done nothing," I had accused. "Ptolly might still be alive today if only you had taken some action! If only you had contacted me! Amunet promised me her agents would work on our behalf, but you —"

Isetnofret had grabbed my upper arm and whisked me toward her private rose garden. "You must not speak openly about these matters," she had ordered in a low voice. "You do not know who is listening!"

It had never occurred to me that there might have been spies even in the House of the Goddess. But once inside her small garden, she had allowed me to pour out my rage and grief in a torrent of hot tears and furious whispers.

When I'd finally finished, the Lady of Isis nodded her head sadly. "I do not like the delays either," she'd said, "but these things take time. Rome's plundering has weakened Egypt's infrastructure to a greater degree than anybody could have predicted. Once things stabilize, we will move forward with our plans to reinstate you. You must have patience."

"But what *are* the plans? And why can't you —"

She put a hand up to silence me. "I will not risk anything by speaking too early. And I remind you that Rome is like a snarling beast," she said. "We must wait until the brute gets distracted or weakens before we act."

Her assurances soothed my impatience somewhat, but not my guilt. I could not move past the idea that Ptolly would have survived his fever if only I had figured out a way to get us back to Egypt.

I sighed as I gathered my things in Ptolly's tomb. "I'm sorry, little brother," I murmured to him, as I always did before I left his side. "I'm sorry I failed you."

*   *   *

I headed for the priestess's private garden, where she and I continued to meet. Whenever I visited, the priestess pushed books on me that I could not get in Rome — books on trade practices in Egypt, on the history of my family and its twisted relationship with Rome, on the Nile and its inundations, on anything, really, that might help me understand the politics, trade, and challenges of my kingdom. When my destiny was fulfilled, she swore, I would be ready.

She was waiting for me on a bench under a shade trellis overflowing with pink climbing roses. "Sit," the Lady of Isis ordered. "I have a question for you."

I sat on the edge of the cool marble and looked at her expectantly. Sometimes she tested me on my readings. I was ready to show her that I had indeed gained a greater understanding of the complexity of the Nile's network of irrigation canals.

"Tell me," she said. "Do you dream about the Goddess?"

I blinked, remembering how Lady Amunet had long ago asked me that question. I had told her the truth, that I had not; in Egypt, I still had the dreams of a child. But lately, I had indeed been dreaming of the Great Goddess. Isis came to me in my sleep, wearing the golden disk diadem on her head, her voice like the murmurs of the waves behind our palace in Alexandria. At the end of every dream, she beckoned to me. "Follow," she said, before she turned her back to me and disappeared into the blackness, her mantle of stars widening to become the night sky. I always woke before I *could* follow her, and then felt nearly mad with disappointment. So strongly did I want to be with her, I would have gone to my death if she'd asked.

"The Goddess has called you," the priestess said with satisfaction after I described the dream. "It is time for you to be initiated in the Mysteries of Isis."

My heart raced with excitement. Hadn't Mother said I would one day be initiated into her Mysteries? For a moment it was as if Mother were there with us, smiling at me, as if I had pleased her immensely. I suppressed a shiver of pleasure.

"What does being initiated mean?" I asked.

"It means you will consecrate yourself to the Goddess, that you have proven your loyalty and been blessed by her love. It also means that we are moving closer to the time of action."

I must have looked confused, for she added, "We must take Egypt back from those who oppose the Great Goddess, namely Caesar and Rome. Traditionally, only an initiate of the Mysteries of Isis or Serapis could rule in the Two Lands. Fulfilling this sacred obligation is the first step toward reclaiming your destiny,"

She stood, her face shining with determination. "The full moon approaches. You must return within three days to begin the purification process. Twice you have defeated Caesar over the rites of the dead. Now it is time to claim victory over the rites of the living."

CHAPTER THIRTY-TWO

As soon as I returned from Capua, I raced to find Alexandros, hoping that he would want to be initiated into the Mysteries with me. I planned on then going to Juba and asking him to escort us. I did not want to rely on Livia's stable boys, for they would certainly report my doings in Capua to their *domina*. The less Livia knew about my connection to the Goddess and the temple, the better.

I found Zosima washing fruit in basins behind the kitchen. "Have you seen Alexandros?" I asked.

"No," she said, though her eyes flicked in the direction of the back gardens. I grinned at her. "Wait!" she cried as I raced away.

The private gardens were lush and thick with myrtle, cypress, and boxwood. "Alexandros?" I called.

Rustling, in the direction of the grove of trees behind the flower-beds. I headed that way, calling his name again, then stopped, sure I had heard murmurings. Ptolly's cat burst out of the bushes with a small green snake wriggling in his mouth.

I jumped. "Gods, Sebi! You scared me half to death," I said to his retreating backside, his tail high in the air with victory. "Alexandros?" I called.

I heard more murmuring and a sharp breath, so I quietly followed the sound around a copse of tall cypresses.

"Sister!"

I jumped. Alexandros had stepped out from behind a thicket.

"What are you doing here?" he asked, his face flushed, his tunic wrinkled and covered in leaves and brush.

"I was looking for you."

"That I can see. Why don't you head back and I will catch up with you later, yes?" He seemed nervous, distracted.

"Is everything all right?" I asked.

"Fine. Just go, please."

More rustling in the bushes behind him. Alexandros looked alarmed. Then I understood. My cheeks flushed.

"Yes, um. Just . . . find me soon. I have an important question to ask you."

He nodded, his attention already shifting to the person he was trying to hide from my view. My chest swelled with curiosity, but I knew now was not the time. As I walked away, I was aware of the look of great relief on Alexandros's face at my departure.

I knew I should have kept walking, but I could not resist. I turned, trying to catch a glimpse of my brother's fancy. One of the new servant girls? The nubile young performer who sometimes danced for Octavianus's banquets? I could barely see through the thick foliage, but I spied a thatch of blond curls, accompanied by a distinctively male whisper and a low-trebled masculine laugh.

I gasped, covering my mouth. Marcellus? My brother's lover was *Marcellus*? I shook my head in surprise. *Oh, wouldn't Octavianus love that*, I thought. His Golden Boy with the son of his enemy. Pretty Marcellus! I ran back to Zosima, giggling the entire way.

I caught up with Alexandros on the way to the *triclinium* for dinner, but he was in no mood to talk. When I asked if he would come with me to the Temple of Isis for the Mysteries, he looked aghast.

"The Goddess hasn't called you?" I whispered, surprised.

He shook his head and continued walking.

"Brother, wait," I said. "Please don't be embarrassed about this afternoon."

He groaned.

"If you want to keep it a secret, I will do so too, though I do not understand it."

"You do not understand why it would be necessary to keep it a secret?" he hissed. "Then you surprise me, sister, for I thought you would see what a disaster this is!"

He stomped away, the color high on his neck. Gods, perhaps this was more serious than I'd thought. It seemed as if Alexandros had fallen hard!

At dinner that night, Alexandros shared a couch with Marcellus and Juba as he often did, though he seemed to be pointedly ignoring his lover. I reclined with Antonia-the-Elder and Julia. Livia and Octavianus, thankfully, dined alone that evening, leaving us to our-selves. Alexandros's discomfort and intensity surprised me. I thought it was sweet, though, and I stifled a chuckle.

"What is so amusing?" Julia asked.

"Nothing," I answered, picturing Octavianus's face upon learning of Marcellus's predilections. I suppressed another giggle but not very successfully.

Both Marcellus and Juba looked in my direction. Marcellus grinned. "Well, Selene, you look like Jason when he first set eyes upon the Golden Fleece. What tickles you so?"

I widened my eyes innocently. Juba and Marcellus smiled back at my light mood, but Alexandros seemed mortified.

Julia, who never could stand being excluded, sat up angrily. "What is so funny, Selene?" she repeated. "You must tell us."

I shook my head. "Not my business to tell."

"Why not?" she asked with an edge. "What would be so awful if the rest of the world knew? Unless," she continued, her voice dropping, "you have something to hide yourself. Who is the lover that brings such a flush to *your* cheeks?"

"*My* lover?" I said, confused. But she was not staring at me — she was staring at Alexandros. I bristled at the insinuation. Tiberius and Julia usually found some way to imply that Alexandros and I had an incestuous relationship, simply because of our Ptolemaic ancestry and Egyptian legacy.

"Yes, yes! Do tell us," Marcellus said, grinning, seeming to miss Julia's intimation. "We want to know what man is brave enough to dare!"

Julia cackled, and this time, I really did flush at the insult. Gods, one would think he would be extra solicitous to me, the sister of his *lover*! But then my stomach dropped. Maybe it was not a joke. Maybe, like Juba, he saw me as an unattractive gadfly.

Marcellus looked at my face and sat up. "Selene, I jest!"

Julia continued laughing. I looked at Alexandros, but his eyes were on Julia with an expression I could not read. I guessed my expression was easy enough to decipher. I signaled for my shoes and sat up. A slave scurried over and began tying my sandals.

"Wait," Marcellus said. "I meant no insult."

"I was not hungry anyway," I said brightly. "Besides, I feel like taking a walk. Perhaps I'll flush out and frighten away any poor unfortunate male who happens to cross my path." I walked out.

I heard footsteps behind me. Figuring it was Alexandros, I kept going. How *dare* he sit back and let his lover insult me like that!

"Selene, wait!" To my surprise, it was Marcellus. I kept walking. He quickly caught up. "Selene . . ."

"My name is Cleopatra Selene. . . ."

"Cleopatra Selene. Let me apologize. Please. I meant no insult."

I stole a glance at him as we walked. I could see why my brother would fall for him. He really was beautiful, with his mop of curly blond hair and gray-blue eyes. He looked so sincere and sorry, I wavered, but I did not slow down, heading toward the small fountain at the corner of the gardens.

"Thank you for the apology," I said coolly, "but I am still surprised you would insult the sister of your lover. Just so it is known, it is not a good strategy for ingratiating yourself with me."

"What?"

"Unless you are just using him," I said, narrowing my eyes at him. "Then it would not matter that you insulted his twin. Do I need to worry about that?" I felt a surge of protectiveness for Alexandros.

Marcellus shook his head and laughed. "What in the name of Hades are you talking about?"

We had reached the little fountain and I turned to him, hands on hips. "Marcellus, truly, you can drop the pretense. I saw you together in the gardens this afternoon. There is no sense in my pretending I don't know. Rest assured I will keep it a secret as long as Alexandros wants me to."

He ran his hand through his curls, a bewildered look on his face. I crossed my arms, surprised that he seemed at such a loss for words.

"How long have you and my brother been together?" I asked.

To my surprise, Marcellus burst out laughing. "You thought . . . you think that Alexandros and I . . . that we are *lovers*?"

"Well, yes," I said, a little confused. "I . . . I saw you."

He stopped laughing when he saw my expression. "All right. I am sorry. I will stop laughing. But truly, the irony . . ." He began chuckling again.

"I *saw* you!" I repeated.

"When? Where? What did you see?"

"This afternoon! Your blond hair . . ."

"Julia and both Marcellas have blond hair," he said. "What made you think it was me?"

I made a face. Julia was always so hateful, I could not imagine Alexandros spending any time with her, and the Marcella sisters were as bland as sheep. If my brother had any taste, it could only have been Marcellus!

"I heard masculine whispering and a masculine laugh. . . ."

"That's it? You jumped to the conclusion that it was me based on a thatch of blond hair and a masculine laugh?"

I nodded, uncertain now. He sighed and sat down on the scalloped edge of the clam-shaped fountain. "Selene, you have noticed that your brother is . . . well . . . to be blunt, masculine himself?"

"But his voice . . . Alexandros's laugh is higher than the one I heard."

"You seem not to have noticed that your brother is nearly a grown man. His voice changed long ago! And I spent my afternoon assisting

Caesar with the governance of Rome and not with Alexandros in the woods."

I flushed. "Well then, who did I see? Who was with him in the woods?"

"I do not know, nor do I care. What troubles me is how quickly you assumed that it was me."

"Why? Is Alexandros not good enough for you?" I asked defensively.

"That is not what I meant," he said. He stood, moving closer to me. "It is that you would think me his lover when you hardly notice . . ."

I looked up. "Hardly notice what?"

He bent down and whispered against my lips, "How much I want to be yours."

I stiffened in surprise. He pressed his mouth to mine, and I panicked. I did not know what to do, how to breathe, where to put my hands. But I did not want to reveal how much I did not know, so I tightened my lips and kissed back.

Marcellus pulled away, chuckling. "You have not done this before, have you?"

I could feel my face burn.

"No, no, don't be embarrassed," he whispered. "Let me show you." He took my face in his hands and said, "Close your eyes." I did. "Now, just focus all your attention on the sensations. Don't do or think about anything else."

His hands were warm on the sides of my face. He kissed the corner of one side of my mouth, then the other. I shivered, finding to my surprise that I was having difficulty breathing normally. He ran his tongue over my closed lips.

"Open your mouth," he whispered. I did. After a time — I could not tell how long — he murmured, "You are a quick learner."

I was flooded with warmth, my skin tingling, a heaviness in my lower abdomen. He had wrapped my hands around his neck and pressed himself against me. I was drowning in sensation. I had lived so long wrapped in my own grief that the feel of his skin, his scent, the taste of his mouth, overwhelmed me.

Marcellus moved his mouth to my neck, kissing it slowly. I shivered again. It was dusk, and the light was almost purple, adding to the sense of unreality. Small circles of brightness burst around us as servants lit torches and lamps in the great house and courtyard.

"Marcellus!" someone hissed.

We jumped apart. Juba was staring at us with a shocked expression. "What in the name of all that is sacred do you think you are doing?"

"What does it look like? Why have you followed us out here?"

"I came to talk to Cleopatra Selene," Juba said. "I was worried about her."

"I think I have it covered, friend," Marcellus said.

The awkward moment lengthened, and I realized they were both waiting for a reaction from me. Only I did not know what to say. I felt like I had stood up too quickly after drinking a great deal of undiluted wine.

Juba cleared his throat and looked at me. "I also came to tell you that I am able to escort you after all. I have made the proper arrangements so that I can be away for several days."

I smiled in relief. When I had asked Juba earlier to escort me to Capua, he had said he was not sure he could get away on such short notice.

"Leaving? With him?" Marcellus turned to me. "What is he talking about? Where are you going?"

I cleared my throat. "The Temple of Isis on the way to Capua," I said.

"But why is Juba escorting you? I'll take you instead!"

"I have already made arrangements," Juba said. "And I think Caesar would not be too happy to hear that you had ducked away from your duties at the Rostra to attend the rites of the banned Goddess."

Marcellus looked at me, then back at Juba. "Can we have a moment alone, please?"

Juba hesitated. "Fine." He looked at me. "We leave at sunrise." He turned and walked stiffly away.

"Selene — Cleopatra Selene, why do you have to leave right away? Couldn't you postpone it a bit? You can visit Ptolly's tomb anytime, right?"

I nodded. But this time I wasn't just going to visit Ptolly. "Yes, but I *want* to go tomorrow."

A look of hurt flitted across his face, but he replaced it quickly with his typical charming smile. "Well, I shall wait for you then!"

Looking up at Marcellus, another strange feeling of unreality seized me. Had I just been kissing Marcellus? Pretty Marcellus, the Golden Boy? My enemy's favorite?

"I . . . need to get back," I said. "My nurse will be looking for me. . . ."

"Your nurse? You do not need to account to her. You are not a child!" .

I smiled up at him, pleased. "Nevertheless, she will be wondering."

"Come, I'll walk you back," he said.

As we neared the girls' wing, Marcellus whispered, "You know that we will have to act as if this never happened, yes?"

Was he brushing me off? I flushed with shame.

"That does not mean, however," he said, "that you and I have to act that way when we are *alone*." He touched my wrist.

Marcellus, nearly twenty, never lacked for attention from fawning women — or from fawning men, for that matter. Everybody, it seemed, desired the beautiful, charismatic successor to the ruler of the world. But what if this was all a big joke to him — the seduction of the whore-queen's daughter, as Octavianus would put it? What if Marcellus was dallying with *both* my brother and me in some kind of sick game? I shook my head slightly to clear my thinking.

"Selene," he said, bending to look into my eyes, which I had averted.

"Cleopatra Selene," I mumbled.

He smiled. "Cleopatra Selene. You are not saying anything."

"I think," I said, "considering that we have to act as if nothing happened between us, around others, perhaps it would be better if we acted that way when we are alone too."

"But —"

"Thank you for walking me back," I said stiffly. And then I turned and hurried toward my *cubiculum*, trying to hold on to as much of my tattered dignity as possible.

CHAPTER THIRTY-THREE

I met Juba before dawn in the torch-lit gloominess of the stables. Sleepy grooms walked our horses out to help us saddle them and tie up our belongings. I jumped when a nearby rooster shattered the purple-gray stillness with its shrill crowing. Juba laughed softly. I smiled back, a little embarrassed.

"Selene! I'm glad I caught you before you left!"

Marcellus approached us in the dark. Juba looked at me and then back at Marcellus, who hurried up the slope to us in his beautifully draped white toga and gleaming leather sandals.

As Marcellus came near, Juba asked him, "Aren't you worried about what everyone will say about you coming to say good-bye to Cleopatra Selene?"

"Ah, but I have made it clear that I have come up here to say good-bye to my good friend Juba," he said, winking at me. "And if Cleopatra Selene happened to be here too, well . . ."

"Marcellus, this is a bad idea, and I do not wish to be used as your cover," Juba said tightly.

"I am not asking you to," Marcellus said.

Juba turned and walked back into the stables.

"Here, let me help you with that," Marcellus said, patting my horse's rump as he came over to help me tighten the straps. My mouth went dry and I suddenly felt very small standing next to him. In my sleepiness of the morning, I had almost forgotten my strange evening with him. Almost. But when his forearm brushed against mine, everything came flooding back: the scent of him, the memory of his mouth on mine.

"I wanted to ask if you if I offended you last night," he said softly, so no errant horse boy or stable slave could overhear. "I suspect I did, only I do not know how."

When I did not respond, he added, "Will you at least tell me so that I can make amends? Perhaps I moved too fast? For that, I am sorry. Well, not sorry, but . . ." He smiled down at me, and my stomach contracted. I continued tying and retying the leather straps on my pannier. My silence seemed to agitate him, which only made me more self-conscious and unable to formulate a thought, let alone a sentence.

"I . . . I must return to the atrium to start greeting our early clients. Will you come see me when you return, Selene? I mean, Cleopatra Selene. Yes?"

"Well, that about does it!" said Juba in a loud voice, rejoining us. "Thanks for stopping by to wish me well on my journey, friend!" he said, clapping Marcellus on the back. And then to me: "It is time to go."

Marcellus paused. "Yes, well. May Mercury protect you and keep you safe from danger and dark magic on your journey," he said loudly, with a false cheerfulness. He smiled at me, and again I marveled that such a beautiful young man would take even the slightest interest in me. I tried to smile back but I felt frozen, like a rabbit under the shadow of a swooping hawk. He turned and walked back toward the house.

Juba and I mounted and rode our horses out of the stable yard. At the crest of the Palatine Hill, we paused to take in the stirrings of the beast that was Rome. Already the city teemed with people, slaves pouring out of homes like ants on the march. Citizens and freedmen flooded the streets too — seeking escape from their horrible *cubicula*, I surmised — in search of fresh bread and morning wine.

What did Juba see when he looked out over the city, I wondered. I suspected it was not what I saw, for when I gazed across Rome, I saw the fumes and vapors of Hades' netherworld. Smoke curled from countless household kitchens, bakers' ovens, hypocausts, blacksmiths' furnaces, and funeral pyres, joining over the valleys to form a dark cloud of lung-searing ugliness below us. From this height, we could still breathe fresh air, but it wouldn't be long before we would find ourselves coughing at the stink of black smoke, sweating bodies, illegally dumped chamber pots, rotting refuse, gutted fish at fish stalls, and the sweet scent of blood from early morning sacrifices.

Once out the Porta Capena, the gate that led to the Appian Way, we rode past the parade of tombs. Burials and cremations were outlawed inside the city, so as wealth poured in from Egypt and other conquered lands, the rich of Rome built massive houses of the dead along this road. I sighed, noticing how many of the recently built tombs evoked the grandeur of Egypt in the form of obelisks and even pyramids. It was the Roman way — destroy the originating culture, then steal its art and beauty.

After a time, I fell into a trance as I bobbed with the rhythm of the horse, closing my eyes to feel the morning sun. I jumped when Juba spoke.

"The way you are handling Marcellus is really quite masterful," he said.

"Sorry?"

"If you wanted to make him obsessed with you, ignoring him ensures it."

"I do not know what you mean," I said, feeling criticized but not understanding how or why.

"Marcellus has been blessed by the gods with many gifts. Everything comes to him easily, including women. As a result, he has grown only to be interested in those who show no interest in *him*. It becomes a challenge, you see."

"No, I don't 'see,' Juba. What are you trying to say?"

"I am not trying to say anything. I am just admiring how you seem to know exactly how to manipulate Marcellus to your favor."

I flared with irritation. "Manipulate? But I am not doing anything!"

"Precisely! Excellent work."

My mouth dropped open in surprise. He thought my tongue-tied confusion and reticence around Marcellus was an act?

My expression gave Juba pause. "You have noticed how he has been slowly turning on the charm around you, yes? And that the more you ignore his attempts, the harder he tries?"

"No, I had not. And I . . . I do not say anything to him because in truth, I do not know what to say," I admitted.

Juba looked at me and smiled. "I keep forgetting how young you are."

"By the gods, Juba!" I growled. "I am in my fifteenth year! Girls my age are getting married and having children *all the time*."

"Not for much longer, if Caesar has his way," he said.

"What do you mean?" I asked.

"Caesar wants to move up the minimum age of marriage for girls from twelve to eighteen and for boys from sixteen to twenty," Juba said. "He believes we need to shore up Rome's lax morality, to go back to the purer days of Roman *pietas* and *virtus*."

"How would that help restore this so-called Roman piety?"

"Well, it's not only that," Juba continued. "He wants to change the laws to discourage cheating between spouses."

I stiffened. He would, I knew, find some way to insult my parents with this campaign.

"If the husband catches the wife with a lover, he is allowed to murder the lover without question or consequence," continued Juba. "And he is allowed to divorce the wife without having to return her dowry."

"And if the wife catches the husband with a lover?" I asked.

He looked blankly at me.

"There is no consequence for the husband cheating?"

"Well, no," Juba said, seeming nonplussed by the very question.

I sighed. Of course not.

"Caesar also wants to encourage the educated classes to have more children. Especially since the number of slaves — not to mention immigrants — already far outstrips the number of citizens."

I frowned, trying to remember how Mother had managed the prickly populations of Greeks, Egyptians, Jews, slaves, and immigrant traders in Alexandria. My heart sank as I realized I did not know, and I would never be able to ask. I made a mental note to ask Isetnofret if any of Mother's ministers had left records I could study.

"I think he may wait awhile to introduce the legislation," Juba continued. "Still, he's a genius. He has convinced Virgil, Horace, Ovid, and Livy to write about Rome's 'pious' history. That will soften the Senate in preparation for the morality laws to come. It's a brilliant strategy, really," he added with a sour face.

I smiled. "Friend, I do believe I detect a note of cynicism about your hero!"

"It is just that I am not so sure — as a writer — how I feel about him using poets and historians of their caliber to push —"

"Lies?" I asked. Hadn't Octavianus used a masterful campaign of besmirching my mother to turn all of Rome against my father?

"Public policy," he said flatly.

"Aren't you doing the same thing, though?"

"What do you mean?" he asked, indignation sparking in his eyes.

I paused as my horse shook his head. Was that a warning to keep my tongue? We'd had this argument so many times before. . . . "Well," I said slowly, overriding the warning. "*You* only write about Roman history, Roman geography, Roman language, Roman painting — all to the glory of Octavianus's idealized Roman world."

"Not at all," he said. "I write about what I'm *interested* in. And he is not commissioning the works from me as he does with Virgil. I write what I want."

I laughed. "You are like Odysseus, only you don't know you are lost at sea."

"What are you talking about?" he asked, tightening his grip on his reins.

"Why don't you write about Numidian heroes like your ancestor Massinissa or your great-great-uncle Jugurtha? What about the bravery of your own father? You have forgotten your homeland, your destiny, and even the kingship that Rome stole from you," I said. "You've even lost your name! And you use your scholarship to stay distracted from what the gods originally planned for you."

His face darkened. "How would you know what the gods planned for me? Perhaps they planned that I should die in Numidia, but by the grace of Julius Caesar, I was spared. Have you ever thought of that? I am a scholar because those are the gifts the gods endowed me with, and living in Rome as a *Roman* citizen is how *that* destiny is fulfilled. . . ."

"But you were a prince of your people! Julius Caesar stole your future as king as surely as Octavianus stole mine. Shouldn't you fight to reclaim your —"

Juba's jaw worked. "No!"

I persisted. "I think you get angry because you know I am right."

He looked at me with a fierceness that made me break eye contact. "You, right?" he said with more malice than I had ever heard from him. "Every time I talk to you, it reinforces for me that *I* have made the right decision, not you. I do not want to spend my life bemoaning my fate or wondering what could have been!"

Now it was my turn to tighten my hold on the reins. "Yes, of course," I said, my voice dripping ice. "I can see how much better — excuse me, *safer* — it is to lose yourself in intellectual pursuits rather than fight to claim what is rightfully yours."

Juba set his mouth. "I do not fight battles I know I can never win."

"Ah, but that is the difference between you and me. I carry the blood of Alexander the Great. And he never fought a battle he ever considered he might *lose*!"

"And how do you propose you could win any kind of battle against the most powerful man in the world, eh? You are like an ant throwing crumbs at the giant Cyclops!"

"Just because I do not have a plan formulated *yet* doesn't mean I will never have one."

Juba made a scoffing sound in his throat, and I urged my horse to trot ahead of his. Which one of us was right? Was it better to stoically accept what the Fates handed you? Or to push back, to use the emotional energy that the Stoics strived so hard to control, to *shape* your own fate, like Alexander? When did acceptance become acquiescence to an intolerable situation? Should I follow Mother's lead and fight until the end, controlling even my own death? Or should I be more like Juba, creating a safe little life in the shadow of that which ultimately sought to oppress or destroy me?

A surge of defiance straightened my back. I was the daughter of the greatest queen of Egypt who ever lived. Even if it meant my death, I would fight to reclaim what had been stolen from me. It would be a dishonor to her memory to do anything else.

Juba and I did not speak again until we arrived in Capua.

CHAPTER THIRTY-FOUR

As they did every full moon, devotees of Isis had gathered to sing her praises and honor her beauty. The air nearly vibrated with anticipation as her followers gathered to take her Great Journey. By sunrise, the induction into the Mysteries would be over. Some, it was whispered, never made it back from the Goddess's side. Others, touched by the Goddess, spoke of prophetic visions. My heart raced with excitement. What would it be for me?

At dusk, two young priests — heads shaven and eyes rimmed in kohl — escorted me into the courtyard. I walked out barefoot, clean from my purification bath and wearing a pure white shift of tightly woven linen, taking careful steps over the uneven grassy grounds of the clearing beside the Temple.

Prayers and chants vibrated through the evening air. Bursts of scent from the early blooming roses wafted in the balmy breeze. Two other initiates joined me in the center of the small circle: a woman bent like a grandmother, her long gray hair unwound, and a young man whose newly shaved head gleamed in the darkening light.

After what seemed like hours of chanting and prayer, someone put small clay bowls in our hands. "Drink," one of my priestly escorts ordered. "For your journey begins now."

I drank. Wine with something else, something unfamiliar, bitter yet not unpleasant. I tilted my head back and took the liquid into me as if the Goddess herself poured it into my mouth. More chanting. Shadows flickered as priests and priestesses held torches for us in the night air.

The strange drink filled me with warmth, bringing a tingle into my toes and out my palms. I wanted to dance, to weave myself in and around the hypnotic chants. I put my hands over my head and swayed. Suddenly, an image of Ptolly flitted past me — of his little body dancing to the pan flutes at Caesarion's manhood ceremony. My eyes filled. Ptolly's *ba*-soul was here, watching, grinning, blessing me, I was sure.

I could hear my heart beating in my chest. A feeling of great love swelled inside me for all of us — all those who hurt and yet so earnestly and purely loved the Goddess. Everything vibrated and pulsed with light and power. The world shimmered, and I gasped at its beauty.

A woman's voice — the priestess's? — urged me to lean on her as she guided me inside the Temple. A dark room. Small bronze lamps on tripods in the corners. Priests and priestesses chanting, the smoke from pungent incense weaving in and around their swaying faces. "Lie down," someone ordered.

I did. I lay in the sun under a blooming sweet citron tree. The sky a brilliant blue. Juba smiled at me and leaned over to kiss me. I closed my eyes. His skin was so warm. So smooth. I pressed myself against his bare chest, shocked to discover that my chest was bare too. I surrendered to the sensations — the feel of his warm lips, the pounding of his heart as I caressed his skin, his soft kisses along my neck. How much I had longed for this!

"My queen," he murmured, and I froze. Despite how much I desired him, I did not want to be "his" queen. I wanted my rightful legacy in Egypt.

The Goddess laughed, a light, breathy laugh. I pushed Juba away. He looked surprised and hurt. "I am sorry," I said. "My destiny has always been to be the queen of Egypt."

I wore a gown of gold as I glided away from him. "A queen must sacrifice her personal desires for the good of her people," I said to no one in particular. I had heard Mother say so many times.

I was in the woods. Marcellus called to me. He was sitting on a tree stump, wearing the bright white toga I had seen him in the morning I'd left for the Temple. "Come here," he called. I looked down and found a shining bronze mirror in my hand. I held it out to his face. His reflection blinded us both. I dropped the mirror, though I never heard it hit the ground.

"I desire you," he said, standing so close I could feel his breath on my hair. "What do you desire?"

"Sovereignty," I murmured.

"No," he said, surprised. "You must desire *me*!"

I looked up at him. "I desire power over the house of Octavianus."

"I will give you anything you want," Marcellus said. "Beginning with me."

"I want Egypt," I said.

The Goddess's laughter wound around me like a gentle breeze, low and knowing. I turned around, confused. Where was the Goddess? I could hear her, but I could not see her.

"I want what my mother wanted!" I announced to her, to Marcellus, to the air. Mother wanted independence for Egypt. She knew we could not fight Rome — who could? — and sought to ally herself instead. Why couldn't I do the same?

"You must choose," the Goddess whispered.

Choose what?

"Selene!" Marcellus whispered, smiling. I had forgotten he was there. "Come with me."

"Cleopatra Selene," someone else whispered — Juba.

"You must make a choice," the Goddess said.

"Is that my only choice — to choose between *men*?" I asked. "I want what Mother had!"

"Your mother chose two men," she said with light laughter.

"No! She chose independence for her country. She chose power and freedom," I yelled.

Almost as if in response, a pulsating energy moved up from the ground into my bare feet. It thrummed up my body and radiated out in a bright light, first from my toes, then my fingertips, then the top of my head.

"I choose power," I said. "I choose freedom."

"Yesssssss," the Goddess answered in the breeze. "That is all one can ever choose."

My eyes snapped open. A cold floor. A blurry vision of swaying chanters. Flickering flames. The smell of sharp, cloying incense and human sweat. A priest stood over me and read from the Book of the Dead, beseeching the gods on my behalf:

Let no evil come to me from you.
Declare me right and true in the presence of Osiris,
Because I have done what is right and true in Egypt.

"Anubis calls," someone whispered. Arms grabbed me. Others wrapped me in thick red cloth, blinding me, binding me. I could not breathe. Bodies held me down.

"You must die before you can be reborn," the priestess breathed into my ear. Someone covered my nose and mouth. Were the embalmers, the Priests of Anubis, mummifying me alive? I bucked and arched. Rage, terror, as my body fought. *Air, give me air!* Why were they killing me? I thrashed, every inch of my being screaming for air. Whirring spots of light exploded behind my eyes.

I floated. Stillness, in between Time. No breath, no life, no sound. A sea of nothing.

"Welcome, Little Moon," a woman said.

"Mother!" I rejoiced, trying to turn toward her but moving as if trapped in liquid amber. Mother!

She was in the golden dress of Isis, the one she wore on the day of her death. "I am the Mother of All," she said, and she transformed into the True Goddess, Isis, with her raiment of glittering stars and a golden disk on her head. I threw myself at her feet, a movement that took a lifetime.

"Let me stay with you, please," I begged. "Do not send me back."

"But I am with you always," the Goddess of All said.

"No, you left me!" I cried.

"Stand, child!"

I stood, quivering with fear. Had I angered her? I could feel her moving away from me like a toy boat on the Nile floating out of my reach. "Wait! I will do whatever you want. Just stay with me," I begged.

"I am always with you," she whispered into the nothingness. "You chose power. Where does it live?"

Was she testing me? I wanted to get my answer right. I thought back to my choice in the earlier vision. Marcellus and Juba were there. Was I supposed to choose the power represented by either of them? Was I supposed to do what Mother did and align with Rome through its leaders?

"Where, child, does your power reside?" the Great Mother prompted again.

"With Marcellus?" I asked. Is that why she put him in my vision?

"Where . . . ," she whispered again.

And then I understood. "In you!" I cried, desperate to give her the answer she sought. "The power is in you! In my True Mother. In the Goddess. I surrender it all to you!"

But she was already gone, the echo of her sigh falling around me like mist.

CHAPTER THIRTY-FIVE

When I awoke, I lay on my side, curled and naked like a newborn, wrapped in a blanket of the softest linen. My eyes fluttered open. I was in the sanctuary of the Great Goddess, at the foot of her immense painted marble statue. I stared up into her open arms, her head slightly bent with a smile of welcoming. Someone had placed a brilliant blue mantle over the statue's head, covering her hair. Roses covered her feet, rich, sweet, mysterious.

Isetnofret, the Lady of Isis, stood in front of the statue and drew her arms up toward the Goddess. "Take to your bosom these Initiates who now devote their lives to you, O Great Mother. You allowed them a sip from the cup of death and blessed their return. They are reborn in the light, born again into their new lives under your care."

I belong to the Goddess now, I thought. Then I smiled. I always had.

After prayers of gratitude for surviving our journey and donning the saffron tunics of the newly initiated, we feasted and celebrated with the other devotees of the Goddess in a banquet room overflowing with food. I lounged with the other initiates, the three of us smiling shyly at one another.

"Come with us," Isetnofret said into my ear. I followed her into a room curtained off from the banqueting hall, where a small group of shaven-headed priests and long-haired priestesses waited. She posted a guard to ensure our privacy.

The head priestess turned to me. "Tell me what vision the Goddess sent you, what she said to you."

"She asked me to choose," I said hesitatingly.

"And what did you choose?" Isetnofret asked.

"Power," I said. "I chose power."

A slow smile broke across the priestess's face. "Very good." She exchanged looks with the others.

"Why?" I asked. "What does it mean?"

"It means the Goddess has blessed our plans," she said. "The people of Isis suffer in the Land of Kemet, for *ma'at* has been disrupted. We finally have a plan to reinstate you on the throne. And now we know the Goddess approves."

"How? How will we get Egypt back?"

"Cornelius Gallus," she said.

I shook my head, not understanding. Isetnofret began to pace. "He is the low-ranking officer Caesar left in charge of Egypt. He has been showing a certain restlessness for more control over what Caesar bids him manage. The priests of Egypt have approached him about returning *ma'at* to the land. He is open to our plans."

"What plans?"

"To marry you. You would rule beside him as the great queen you were destined to be."

I sucked in a breath. "But . . . but the Goddess did not show me Cornelius Gallus. . . ." She showed me Juba and Marcellus, but no one else. And she did not show me Egypt, I realized suddenly.

"The Goddess is not always literal, but she makes her intentions clear. She wants you to have power. We needed confirmation, and we got it."

A thrill surged up my spine. "But marrying Gallus — how would that balance *ma'at* if Rome still rules?"

"Rome rules because of its mighty military. But it does not know how to rule the Ancient Lands."

"Octavianus would never allow it," I said. "He would declare another war on me and our people!"

"Octavianus is preparing to go to Spain within the next three months," Isetnofret said, "where rebelling tribes are destabilizing Rome's control again. A well-timed rebellion in Alexandria would leave him too stretched, too weak, to do anything about it. And since Egypt controls the grain that feeds Rome, we have only to remind him of his dependence on the bounty of the Mother Goddess."

"But if I rule as queen, then Cornelius Gallus would be considered king. And no Roman would ever allow another Roman to take that title."

"True, but Gallus is prepared to claim that he marries you merely to satisfy the priests and the religious classes. As long as he doesn't name himself king, he breaks no Roman law." Isetnofret smiled. "And as soon as it is clear that our plans are stable and there will be no war, we would eliminate Gallus."

Murder him? My shock must have shown on my face, for Isetnofret touched my shoulder and said, "Do not worry. It would not be by your hand."

Gods, but the murder would be in my *name*, on my behalf! I thought of the rumors and accusations I had heard about Mother in Rome — that she'd had my aunt Arsinoe killed, that she had killed her younger brother too. I always dismissed them out of hand, but suddenly it did not seem so unimaginable. If someone dared take Egypt away from Mother, she would not have hesitated to act in defense of her crown.

Yet Mother never betrayed her Roman husbands. She understood that alliance was the answer. Perhaps Isetnofret did not realize how impossible it would be to do anything without a Roman consort. Besides, murdering a Roman citizen would create a backlash big enough to threaten my rule. No, there would be no murder in my name. When the time came, I would stay their hand. They would see the wisdom of it. I would make them.

I set my jaw and nodded at the priestess.

"The Goddess has spoken," Isetnofret said. "In my visions, she calls you 'Queen.' Do you see? And now your journey with her confirms it."

The prospect of going home, of stepping into the legacy and the life destined for me . . . A calm peace settled over me. This was the will of the Goddess. I smiled up at Isetnofret.

She grinned back. "We prepare for revolution."

*   *   *

When I returned to Octavianus's complex, I rushed to find Alexandros. The priestess had warned me not to talk to him in detail about our plans — indeed she warned me not talk to him about them at all — but I did not like keeping something so big from my twin. Besides, he might become inspired enough to undergo the rites himself at the next full moon.

Alexandros was in the main garden on a bench under one of the shade trees. At my approach he slammed shut a wax tablet he had been writing on.

"By the Eye of Ra, brother!" I exclaimed, grinning. "One would think you were writing to a secret beloved, the way you closed that!"

"I am doing nothing of the sort," he replied testily. But the flush that crept up his neck reminded me of his mysterious lover in the woods.

"So who were you kissing in the woods last week?"

He scowled. "You said you knew!"

"Well, I had thought it was Marcellus, but Marcellus denies it."

"Marcellus!" he nearly barked. "Why would you think that?"

"I saw blond curls and I thought I heard a male voice . . . never mind. Just tell me who it was!"

He stood up. "Oh, gods! You told him about seeing us? Now he will wonder too. Julia will kill me!"

"Julia?" I squeaked. "You were with Julia?"

"Not so loud," Alexandros said as he sat back down.

"But why Julia of all people? Are you looking to get us killed?"

"She has pursued me," he said defiantly.

"Well, of course she has! Nothing would make her father angrier than to see his daughter with the son of the queen of Egypt! She lives to spite him. Are you mad?"

Alexandros shrugged. "Maybe so. But you are mad for bringing it up to Marcellus. He is too close to Octavianus to trust. For anything." He rubbed his hand over his face. "I will tell her we need to stop. She will see the sense in it."

I was going to berate him for his poor judgment, but a new thought gave me pause. "Brother, do you — do you love her?"

A look of bewildered horror moved over his face. "You do not know me at all if you think I could," he said in a low tone as he got up to leave.

"Wait!" I grabbed his arm. "Don't you want to know about the Mysteries? Don't you want to know about the Goddess's plan to return us to our rightful throne?" I whispered.

He pulled his arm away from me. "I want nothing the Goddess pretends to offer. She has failed us too many times."

Once again, he stalked away from me in a rage over the Goddess. I touched two fingers to my heart in the sign of protection against evil as I watched him go.

Later that afternoon, I went to Livia's *tablinum*. Although I had plenty to read from Isetnofret, my restlessness after talking to Alexandros made it hard to concentrate, and scanning scrolls always calmed me. Even so, my stomach flip-flopped with worry. What would Octavianus do if he found out about my brother and Julia? Why had the Goddess not called him?

"There you are!"

"Marcellus!" I said. "You scared me."

"Why did you not come see me the minute you came home?" he asked teasingly.

"What did you do to your hair?" I cried. His blond curls were gone, shorn close to his head in the Roman military fashion.

He rubbed his hands over his scalp, more brown than blond now. "Well, I cannot have someone I care about confusing my curls with those of a girl's, now can I?"

I reddened.

"You don't like it?" he asked.

"But your beautiful curls!"

He laughed. "Yes, Mother is furious with me too. But I have sacrificed them at the altar of the household gods, which has appeased her."

The haircut made him look older and more serious, but at the same time, even more handsome. I stared at the strong planes of his face, the blue eyes that seemed even bluer now, the full, sumptuous mouth. He must have noticed me looking at his lips, for he smiled slowly.

"What are you doing here?" I said, quickly turning my attention back to the pigeonhole stacks of scrolls.

"Looking for you," he said. "I saw Juba, so I knew you were back."

"I thought you said it would be better if we acted as if what took place between us never happened," I said.

"Ah! So *that's* what has upset you."

I shook my head. Now that my focus was on getting Egypt back through Gallus, I could not afford to risk anything with Marcellus. Better to stop it now. "I am not upset," I said, crouching to look at the scrolls on the lower shelves.

"What are you looking for? Maybe I can help." He came closer. Despite myself, I could feel my heart rate quicken. Why did I respond to him this way?

I stood. "Nothing in particular."

"Come here," he said, taking my hand lightly by the fingertips. I followed him to a corner of the small study where a row of shelves blocked us from view of the doorway. He turned to me with half-lidded eyes and his signature sensuous smile.

"This is a bad idea," I said.

"No it isn't," he whispered, moving closer. "I have missed you."

He wound an arm around my waist and pulled me into a kiss. I shivered at the feel of his lips, confused by the disparity between what my thoughts said — *Do not do this; cannot risk plans for Egypt* — and how my body responded to his touch.

I put my hands on his chest. "Marcellus, please."

He chuckled in my ear after kissing my throat. "I can feel your heartbeat. Your body does not lie."

"My heart races because I am scared," I said, trying to convince myself that it was true.

He pulled back. "Scared?" His tone sounded surprised. "Why would I scare you? I will not force you to do anything you do not desire."

"Do you know what Octavianus would do if he knew his Golden Boy and the daughter of his enemy were together? He would *kill* me! He's wanted to all these years, and this would be the perfect excuse. . . ." I closed my eyes, thinking of what he would do to Alexandros too if he found out about him and Julia.

"Caesar doesn't have to know."

I held my hands firm on his chest. "No."

"Is it someone else? Did Juba steal you away on your trip?"

I laughed. "Gods, no!" Why would he think that? I remembered then what Juba had said about Marcellus — that it was my reticence he found so compelling. I had become a challenge, a sort of test of his irresistibility. I moved away. I did not want to be a casualty of his narcissism.

He touched my arm. "You have the loveliest skin," he murmured. "Like honey in sunlight."

"I really must get back to my reading," I said, turning my back to him in dismissal.

But instead of leaving, he put his hands on my waist and pressed his body against me from behind. The contact so surprised me, I gasped. He chuckled low against my ear, and I closed my eyes.

"Why do you fight me?" he whispered.

I pulled away again. "Juba said you only found me interesting because you have not yet conquered me — and that you will forget me as soon as you do."

"Sounds like someone is jealous."

"He is not jealous! He still thinks of me as a child."

Marcellus watched my mouth. "Then he is a fool," he murmured.

I turned toward the door, but he reached for my wrist. "Wait. Need I remind you that Caesar is grooming me as his heir?"

I laughed. "Oh, and is that supposed to make me fall into your arms?"

He shrugged and grinned. "Only if you find power seductive."

Power. I had none. Not yet, anyway. And he was going to have it all. He would rule the empire one day. I remembered my initiation vision. Was he to play a role in helping me regain Egypt?

I blinked, looking at Marcellus with new eyes. Perhaps marrying Gallus was only a small step. Perhaps I needed a powerful ally in Rome for protection once I was back in Egypt. Suddenly it seemed clear. I could do what Mother had done. I would ally myself with a leader of Rome.

I smiled up at him. This time when he bent to kiss me, I arched up to kiss him back.

Although I had decided to ally myself with Marcellus, I had to be careful. If Juba was right, he would tire of me as soon as he "conquered" me. So I would not let him fully seduce me. My reluctance seemed to add to his fervor, which both excited and frightened me.

I wondered about telling the Priestess of Isis about my connection with Marcellus. Would she approve? Or would she think I was taking an unnecessary risk? I could not ask her, because she had warned me not to discuss our plans, even when I visited Ptolly's tomb. She would contact me, she had instructed, never the other way around. But the waiting for word from her was agonizing.

Which is why, when I received a tiny note in demotic, a form of Egyptian writing, hidden in the folds of a freshly laundered *tunica*, I could barely keep my hands from shaking. The note was brief:

IMPRINT OF CAESAR'S SEAL. NEED FOR GALLUS. STATIM.

I groaned. The priestess wanted me to steal Octavianus's seal? But that was impossible! Outrageous! Did she think I could just interrupt him at dinner and ask for his ring? Why did the Lady of Capua think I could do something like this?

I paced inside my *cubiculum,* trying to regulate my breathing. After a time, I saw the sense of creating a counterfeit seal. Gallus — as well as our agents here in Rome — would likely need to forge documents to keep suspicion at bay as plans moved forward. But knowing that did little to reduce my sense of dread over the difficulty of the task.

For several nights, before bed, I lit a small fire in a clay bowl in front of a statuette of Isis Pharia I'd taken from Egypt. I pinched a bit of incense and sprinkled it over the flames in an offering to the Goddess. I prayed for her help:

> You who showed us the path to the stars,
> You who nourish all the fruit of the world.
> I pray you, end my great travail and misery.
> Fill me with your Wisdom,
> Guide my hand in the Work I do for you and Egypt.

On the third night, as I drifted off to sleep, the room still thick with smoke, I dreamt of the day I begged Octavianus to allow us to give Ptolly the Egyptian rites. Over and over again, I saw myself in his *tablinum* as he twisted my arm and pushed me into his desk. How the force made something clatter to the floor. How he swatted my hand away before I could touch it, slamming it back down on his desk. How he had grinned when he told me he'd had his signet ring made from Mother's gold. . . .

I sat up. The Goddess had shown me. I understood. "Thank you, Great Lady of Light," I whispered. "Thank you."

Days after receiving my instructions, I worked a small ball of wax in the palm of my hand as I sauntered toward Octavianus's *tablinum*. I was in search of a scroll I could not find in Livia's collection — that was my excuse for being there, if anyone asked.

Octavianus often signed documents between the sixth and seventh *horas*, after the last of his clients completed their morning ritual of kissing his ring and asking for favors. He demanded silence then. So I had paid a young slave boy to release a large snake in Octavianus's atrium just as a large group of female slaves came by. The uproar, I hoped, would draw the *Princeps* out of his study.

The screams were louder and more frantic than I had imagined. I rushed into the house through the back servant's entrance, peering around the hallway just in time to see Octavianus and Thyrsus stalk over to the screaming women. "By the gods, what is the matter?" shouted Octavianus in a fury.

"It is an omen! A bad omen!" one of the women wailed.

I massaged the wax ball more furiously, softening it with the heat of my fear. I snuck into his study. There. His heavy seal ring lay beside the red Samian inkwell, just as it had been in the memory-vision the Goddess had sent me. My heart beat in my ears so loudly, I was sure the sound would call him screaming back into the room.

With shaking hands, I pressed the seal cleanly into the warmed wax. The ring clattered as I put it down, and I winced at the noise. But nobody came. As I rushed to the doorway, I placed the imprinted wax into a small box to protect its design.

Peeking out, I saw that one of the guards was trying to cut off the snake's head. I bolted out the back of the house, listening to Octavianus call for an Etruscan haruspex to divine the meaning of the snake that appeared below the death masks of his ancestors.

When I finally looked at the wax imprint of the seal, I had to fight the temptation to smash it against the wall. A sphinx. Octavianus had adopted the Egyptian sphinx as his symbol. My stomach roiled with disgust. He had found yet another way to gloat over the destruction of my beloved Egypt. But I did not destroy the mold. I replaced the lid and planned my next excursion to the Temple of Isis in Capua.

Weeks after delivering the wax base of my enemy's seal, I received another message from the priestess. I was to meet her agents by the central fountain in the heart of the Subura. COME IN DISGUISE, the note instructed, AND WAIT. OUR AGENTS WILL APPROACH YOU.

On the assigned morning, I shrugged into a slave's cheap brown wool tunic that Zosima had filched for me and slipped my feet into rough rope sandals. I grabbed a dark mantle to put over my head. Just before I stepped out of my *cubiculum*, Zosima hissed, "Wait!" She handed me a small bronze plaque hanging from a rope chain. "You must wear this."

I groaned. The plaque read PROPERTY OF CAESAR. I shook my head, handing it back to her.

Zosima was adamant. "Girl slaves are preyed upon," she said, the furrow between her eyebrows deepening. "But nobody dares hurt any of Octavianus's slaves. Even criminals are afraid of him."

She slipped the rope over my head. Zosima had seemed hurt that I had not confided the reason for my subterfuge, but I had to keep her safe too. I made my way out of the compound through a little-used path by the stable.

As I passed, a horse reared and whinnied. "Whoa, boy, whoa," said a familiar voice trying to calm the beast down. Octavianus. I stiffened into stone as if I had looked into the face of Medusa herself.

Footsteps. I moved the mantle to cover my entire face. "You, girl!" he called. "Run back and tell my man to bring me the scrolls I left in my *tablinum*. Now!"

My stomach contracted. What would he do to me if he found me out? I kept my eyes down as I turned in the pretense of obeying.

"Did I not tell you to *run*, stupid girl? Or do I need to take a whip to you?" he roared, incensed at my hesitation.

Footsteps. An intake of breath. "Caesar," another familiar voice said — Juba? "This is one of your wife's slaves. Her loyalty is commendable — she defies even you to serve Livia."

Octavianus growled. "She had better be thankful you recognized her, for I would have beaten her within an inch of her life for not obeying me. Be gone, miserable girl!"

I scurried away as he repeated the order to one of the stable boys, holding the mantle tightly under my chin. I stopped at the far side of the stable and leaned against the wood, shaking with fear. Romans regularly beat their slaves, sometimes even killing them, which was their legal right. Discovering my ruse would have given Octavianus just the excuse he wanted to beat the daughter of the queen of Egypt.

Running footsteps. *"Princeps!* The co-consul just sent a messenger. He wishes to speak with you immediately."

"Gods!" Octavianus groused. "I leave for Spain in a matter of days! Can I have no peace even for a short ride?"

"His messenger said it was critical, sire."

The sound of a whip petulantly thrown on the ground. "Fine! Tell my boy to unsaddle my horse," he commanded as he stomped off.

I closed my eyes in relief. When I opened them again, I cried out in surprise. Juba was standing before me with a thunderous look on his face.

"What in the name of Jupiter do you think you are doing, Cleopatra Selene?" he demanded.

CHAPTER THIRTY-SEVEN

"How did you know it was me?" I asked. I had been so proud of my slave-girl disguise!

"I need to know why you would do something so dangerous," Juba said between clenched teeth.

I shrugged, not answering. He stepped closer. "Do you not have any idea the risks you take leaving the Palatine? A young girl on her own, without a male escort?"

"I am not so young," I shot back. "Besides, I have this." I released the mantle to show him the bronze placard announcing me as a slave in Caesar's house.

Juba rubbed his left ear. "I am glad to see you taking some precautions, but Cleopatra Selene! You must trust me on this. It is not safe for you."

When I did not respond, he asked, "Where are you going in this ridiculous disguise?"

"To the Subura."

"What? This cannot be so! Why would you go to the dirtiest, poorest, most dangerous district in all Rome?"

"Are you done now?" I asked. "I wish to go on."

Juba sighed. "I am going with you, then."

"No, you are not! I do not need your so-called protection!"

He chuckled while shaking his head, as if trying to cover his anger. "Nonetheless, I cannot in good conscience let you roam by yourself."

"You may do whatever you wish," I replied, starting to walk. It would likely be easy enough to lose him in the crowds.

I walked behind him through the tree-filled valley between the Palatine and Caelian Hills, on our way to the teeming center of the city. I watched as people nodded to Juba or greeted him, and I bristled at my invisibility. It was one thing to be invisible by choice; it was quite another to be invisible because people thought I was his slave.

The streets of Rome were busier than ever. Thanks to the flood of wealth from Rome's conquered lands, the city roared with the sounds of new construction and foreign slaves. Scaffolds teetered precariously along half-built walls as workmen scurried up and down the wooden beams like ants on a feeding frenzy. Carpenters banged, sawed, and called out to one another in hoarse voices. Loose tiles, hammers, and crumbling bricks rained down on hapless crowds, so those who dared step outside rushed past building sites with arms overhead for protection. The air was thick with wood and plaster dust. A tumult of voices — in Latin, Greek, Celt, Iberian, Persian, and others — clamored to be heard over the din.

"Why don't we cut through the Argiletum?" Juba asked, turning and bending to speak into my ear so that I could hear him. I willed myself not to shiver at the feel of his warm breath. I had thought that my dalliance with Marcellus would have burned away the attraction I felt for him. It had not.

I nodded, though I thought I should still go straight to the Subura. I did not want to be late for the priestess's agents. But, if I were honest, I did not want to leave Juba's company either. We turned toward the street of booksellers and cobblers. I would just accompany him for a few minutes.

Juba smiled sheepishly as he pointed to a small, dusty bookshop at the end of the crowded lane. "Let us stop in there. Just for a minute. I want to see if they have my new book."

"You wrote another one?"

He nodded. "It is called *Omoioteles*."

"*Equivalences?* Equivalences of what?" I asked, puzzled by the book's Greek title.

"Language," he replied. "In it I prove the Greek origin of the Latin language."

Again I thought how much Juba would have loved our Library in Alexandria. Even in the Argiletum — which was less hectic than the main throughways — the noise discouraged conversation. People called out greetings, sellers hawked cheaply copied scrolls, cobblers banged mallets on leather.

Like most Roman shops, the dusty bookshop had little light, so it took a moment for our eyes to adjust. He sought out the bookseller, a portly man in a threadbare toga, while I wound my way around the pigeonhole stacks of scrolls, breathing in the familiar, reedy scent of old papyrus.

A flash of sunlight from the front, and then a voice. "Juba, darling, I thought I saw you come in here!"

"Vistillia," he said, smiling. "How nice to see you."

Curious, I inspected the woman, whose richly dressed attendant followed meekly behind. The woman was draped in an elegant *tunica* and *stola* of the finest, thinnest aquamarine linen, a new favorite import from my beloved, ransacked Egypt. She wore pearls in her ears and on her wrists. Even though she was clearly not a young woman, the force of her beauty, confidence, and sensuality was undeniable. I felt a surge of jealousy. Was this one of the older married women Juba dallied with?

"How silly to look for your own book in a store such as this when it is well known that the best houses in Rome already have a copy," she said, smiling up at him. "I myself have three!"

Juba smiled back, looking slightly embarrassed.

"I heard that you visited Cecelia Metella's villa recently," she said with an exaggerated pout. "And yet you have not visited me in some time! You will have to make this up to me!"

Juba murmured an answer that I could not hear. The woman moved closer and placed her hand on his arm in a very intimate way. The sight of her pressing her breasts "innocently" against him incensed me.

Without thinking, I blurted, "Oh, master," in a singsong voice. "I believe I have found the other scroll you were looking for."

Juba looked at me, confused. The woman turned her painted face in my direction. "Master?" she cried. "You did not tell me you purchased your own slave girl!"

"I . . . I . . . ," Juba stammered.

"Yes, here it is," I interrupted, grabbing the nearest scroll. "Cato the Elder's speech on Roman piety. You know the one — where he rails against unfaithful *wives*, blaming them for the undoing of Roman morality."

The woman stared at me, then laughed. "Oh, how funny. But Cato wrote no such thing! That sour old coot just wrote about farming, didn't he?" she said, turning to Juba.

Juba glared at me. "Cleopatra Sel —"

"Cleopatra!" the woman squealed. "You named your slave girl *Cleopatra*? In Caesar's own compound! That is just hysterical, darling. But what a fitting name for your little pleasure slave."

My mouth dropped open in dismay. She thought I was . . . that I was his . . . ?

The woman came over to me and removed the covering from my head. "Ah. Now I understand why you named her thus. She really does look like the statue of that wicked queen."

She must have been referring to the statue of Mother that Julius Caesar had erected in the Temple of Venus Genetrix in the Forum of Caesar. Octavianus, mysteriously, had not seen fit to topple it, perhaps because he dared not destroy anything related to his adopted father. Whenever I was able to slip away to the small temple, I spent many hours staring into the marble face that Caesar and my father loved and all Rome feared.

"Tell me," she continued. "Does she perform as well as one might think with a whore's name like that?"

I felt my cheeks grow red. Glancing at Juba, I saw that he was trying to suppress a smile. He was enjoying my humiliation! How dare he? The woman turned her back to me and faced Juba again. But I could not let the insult pass.

I tapped the woman on the shoulder. "I should clarify, *Domina*," I said with exaggerated innocence and respect. "I am not his 'little pleasure slave,' as you so eloquently put it." I leaned forward as if we were exchanging important secret information. "For *that* kind of work, my master prefers the boys in the baths."

With one final smirk in Juba's direction, I tossed the scroll back into a basket and stomped out of the little bookshop.

CHAPTER THIRTY-EIGHT

I watched my rope-sandaled feet as I hopped from raised stone to raised stone so that I could cross the road without sinking into the nauseating stew that sluiced down the lane. A man yelled, "Move it! Move it!" forcing us to make way for a mule team hauling a massive slab of marble on a metal sledge.

The crowd grumbled and cursed. According to Roman law, no delivery carts were allowed within the city during daylight hours because of the way they tied up the already overcrowded roads. But if you were rich enough, you could get away with anything. My stomach dropped when I saw the hieroglyphs running alongside the top of the marble as it passed me. I wondered which sacred temple in Egypt the Romans had ransacked so that a rich senator on the Esquiline could redecorate his mansion.

Once in the Subura, I headed for the central courtyard fountain across from the clothes cleaners, where I had been instructed to wait for the priestess's agents. I sat on the rim of the fountain while women and slaves of all ages and nationalities gathered water from the fountain's greenish spouts. The smell of urine was so overpowering, I wondered for a moment whether the fountain spewed waste instead of water.

Then I remembered how the cleaners bleached their fabric. A pair of Roman men reached under their tunics and relieved themselves into the oversized terra-cotta *pythoi* right outside the cleaners' stall. Two slaves dragged one of the urine-filled vessels inside. I shivered with distaste, knowing what was next. They would pour the fresh urine into a low vat, where they stomped and worked the fabric with their feet, using the liquid to bleach the cloth a pristine white. I looked at the weeping, ulcerated sores on the slaves' feet and ankles and shuddered.

"It's enough to make you never want to wear white again, isn't it?" a voice said in my ear.

I jumped. Juba! "How did you find me here?" I asked.

He shrugged. "Wasn't too hard. I knew you were headed to the Subura."

"I'm surprised your lady friend let you leave her side so quickly."

He grinned. "It was easy enough. I told her that my slave could not get away with such insolence and that I needed to catch you so that I could beat you." I must have looked surprised, for his expression changed. "A joke," he said. "I do not beat slaves. Oh, and very nicely done," he added with a smirk. "I was looking for a way to avoid her not-so-subtle invitations. Though now I fear I shall be dodging invitations from her *husband* too!"

I tried not to laugh. "I would say I'm sorry, but I'm not. So why did you follow me?"

"I told you, it is unsafe. Somebody must watch over you."

"Gods, Juba! I have been taking care of myself for a long time. I do not need your protection."

"But why come here of all places?"

"I am meeting someone."

"*Here?* Who in the world would you meet here?" he asked, stepping around me to rinse his hands in the trickle of one of the fountain's grimy, algae-covered spouts.

Somebody touched my shoulder — a man, smelling of wine and grease. His tattered brown tunic sported rings of sweat stains under his arms and fleshy chin.

"How much?" he asked, grinning and showing brown teeth.

"Excuse me?" Could this be the contact I was supposed to meet? How would I know?

He pointed with his head to a tavern and its adjoining row of abandoned stalls covered in dirty draping. "How much? One of them stalls is free. I could pay you two *sesterci*."

I stared at the man, still uncomprehending.

"A bargainer, eh? Well, you're young and clean." He reached for his tattered coin bag under his belt. "I'll go up to one *denarius*, but not an *as* more!"

"She's not for sale," Juba said irritably.

The man looked from Juba to me. "You sure about that? I likes 'em young."

I stood up, my face burning, my fists clenching. "How dare you, you ignorant, unwashed, uneducated, poor excuse of a man!"

"*Pax, pax*," Juba said, grabbing my arm and walking me away to the other side of the fountain. "Remember where we are — you don't want to incite the man to violence."

I looked back. The man had disappeared into the crowds. Another man pushed his way out of one of the curtained stalls he had pointed to, adjusting the belt of his tunic.

"Gods!" I muttered. "Why would that man think that I was a prostitute?"

"Because you weren't doing anything but sitting pretty," Juba said.

"What?"

"The women at the fountain are collecting water or washing things. They are busy, preoccupied, working. But you sat facing out, appearing to all the world as if you were on display."

"But that is outrageous!" I cried. "I was just waiting. . . ."

"That is life in the Subura. Come on, let's go someplace else. I've heard one of the stalls around here has the best stuffed chickpea pancakes around."

"No," I said. "I have to wait."

"Who are you waiting for?" he asked. "You never told me."

I looked around without answering.

"Why can't you tell me?" Juba asked.

Suddenly, I thought, *What if the person would not or could not approach me while Juba stood near?* "I really wish you would leave," I said.

"Gods, Cleopatra Selene. Please do not be subtle on my account," he said with a laugh. "But I cannot leave now because I am curious. Who is this mystery person you have come to meet?" He grinned and crossed his arms.

When I again did not respond, his expression changed. "Wait, you are not meeting a *lover* here, are you? Is that why you want me to leave so badly?" He stepped closer. "It's not Marcellus, is it? But why would you meet him here? But if not him, then who is it?"

I continued ignoring him. Let him think I had a lover. Better that than discovering the truth.

"Are you mad?" Juba said. "You cannot . . ."

"Of course I can. Why do you continue to see me as a child?"

His face registered shock and surprise and something else I could not read. "But . . . I thought . . . I wanted to . . ." He paused. "How serious is it?"

Whatever I was going to say was drowned out by the shouts of a group of soldiers who had rumbled into the fountain square.

"There!" an officer said, and the men — thundering in their hobnailed boots — spread out and encircled a group of people. Women screamed. Chickens squawked and ruffled their feathers in outrage. Men cursed in Latin, Persian, Gallic, and other unfamiliar tongues.

"What's happening?" I whispered.

"I don't know," Juba said.

"Got 'em!" one of the soldiers announced.

The crowd parted as people scurried away in a panic. The soldiers held a struggling old woman and a young man with a shaved head in their grip. I gasped. My two fellow initiates from the Temple! They must have been the ones I was sent to meet.

"Did you get the one from Caesar's house?" yelled the officer.

"It's this one!" answered the soldier, holding on to the struggling young man.

"No, you idiot!" the officer hissed. "They were meeting someone from the *inside*! That's who Caesar wants us to bring back — the traitor from his *house*!"

CHAPTER THIRTY-NINE

My heart raced. This was a trap? To catch *me*? How ... how could Octavianus have discovered the plot? Thankfully, it sounded as if they did not know it was me — only that it was someone from the compound. Had he found out about the stolen seal? My breath constricted in my throat.

I looked at the old woman, who'd tied her long gray hair back under a mantle. She seemed serene, unlike the young man, whose face contorted with frustration as he tried to twist out of the soldier's hold.

"Who were you going to meet here, you witch?" the officer spat at the old woman. When she did not answer, he slapped her.

"Gods, we have to help them!" I hissed. A crowd surrounded the soldiers, murmuring angrily at the officer's treatment of the old woman.

"Looks like they set up a trap but missed their quarry," Juba agreed. "I'm going to find out more."

He walked up to the officer. They seemed to know each other. As they talked, the old woman caught my eye and signaled with her eyes that I should get away. But I could not. How could I leave them to this? What would they do to them? My heart thudded in my ears as I realized they would torture them for information. They would reveal my identity — the priestess's too. Goddess help us! What would Octavianus do to me? To Alexandros?

The soldier holding the young man must have loosened his grip. In an instant, the young man twisted away and ran off.

"Get him, you idiot!" the officer bellowed when he saw what had happened. But the boy had already melted into the multitudes. Even denser crowds surrounded the soldiers then, deliberately blocking their ability to go after him. The helmeted officer screamed into his cadet's face, the cords of his neck bulging, spittle bursting like sea spray.

Someone laughed. The furious officer looked at the growing mob of angry Suburanites, his eyes wild with rage.

"Let go of the grandmother!" someone cried.

"Yeah, what'd she do, dilute your wine too much this morning?"

Angry murmurs rippled through the press of people. The soldiers looked at one another. There were only a handful of them against countless bitter locals just looking for any reason to erupt at perceived injustices, including a senseless attack on a sweet old woman. I realized then that even soldiers were scared in the Subura.

"Release her," the officer said to the man holding the woman. "She is too old to run away." He turned to the crowd. "We will not hurt her!" he bellowed. "We only want to question her!"

More grumblings. A glint caught my eye as the old woman pulled a dagger from her belt. Was she going to attack the officer?

No. She wrenched the dagger across her throat in one rapid movement, slicing deeply through the soft wrinkled flesh of her neck. Dark, almost black blood spurted forth like the first gushes of a pump being primed. People screamed. I moved forward to help the old woman, but Juba, whom I hadn't even realized had returned to my side, held me back. The crowds surged toward the soldiers in a rage. The men pulled their swords, standing next to one another as if about to fall into testudo formation. The old woman fell to her knees in front of them.

I moaned in horror, and not just for the old woman. Flashes of Alexandria. Father's man, Eros. Blood pumping from his slashed throat. Blood, everywhere blood. The heavy metallic-sweet smell of it as it poured out of my father in front of me . . .

"Selene," Juba hissed. "Look at me." But I could not tear my eyes from the woman, now drowning in her own blood as people yelled threats and insults at the soldiers. He grabbed my chin, forcing my face toward his. "*Look* at me."

I blinked, dizzy, trying to catch my breath, trying to focus on his eyes. I heard the officer barking out orders, the people grumbling.

"Bring the old woman to the Palatine," the officer barked. "Caesar will want to see the body."

I shivered. The body. Were they talking about Father?

"Keep looking at me," Juba said.

His brown eyes locked on mine.

"Gaius, you still around?" the officer asked.

"Right here," Juba said. I did not want him to turn from me. I gripped his arm, desperate. He lifted the mantle to cover my head as the officer came up to him.

"For the love of Mars, what was all that?" the officer asked. "I hate coming in here — these people are animals!" Sweat poured from his brow. He narrowed his eyes at Juba. "Did Caesar send you here to report on me?"

"What? No," said Juba, blocking me from the officer's view.

"You're not going to tell him we lost the boy, are you?" asked the officer. "I don't think he was important. He was probably just trying to steal the old woman's bag of coins. It's *her* we wanted," he said, sounding as if he were trying to convince himself.

"You said they were meeting someone from Caesar's household?"

The officer nodded, his eyes shifting continuously for signs of trouble from the crowd. "Yeah. Caesar's people in Egypt discovered a counterfeit seal, and he's convinced someone from the inside made the imprint because the workmanship was so good. But my men jumped too early and we missed 'em. Gods, where do they get these kids? No discipline at all!" He turned back to Juba. "The traitor probably slid away at the first sign of trouble," he said. "So, what brings you to this pit of slime anyway?"

Juba must have made some gesture.

"Oh-ho!" the officer said. "I see now. Nothing like a hot tryst in the Subura for a little change of pace, eh?" I stiffened. "I'm going to need a drink before we head back and face Caesar. How's about a quick nip in that tavern right there? She can join us if you want."

Juba shifted. "No, Lucius. I really just want to . . ."

"All right, all right. I know what you want. Never mind. I have to report to Caesar anyway." The officer finally clomped off in the direction of his men.

Juba turned toward me. "Follow me," he ordered under his breath, taking me by the wrist.

We moved in the opposite direction from the soldiers carrying the old woman's body. I looked back at the pool of blood glimmering a thick, dark red. A filthy barefoot boy dipped one hand into the bloody puddle and pulled out the dripping dagger, holding it up to the sun and grinning as if he had found some momentous treasure. A woman waved the boy away, pouring a bucket of water over the blood. Rivulets of red streamed down and around the uneven cobblestones.

Juba gave me a slight yank to keep me moving. I did not recognize any of the streets we followed but caught sight of the Forum of Julius Caesar rising to my left. I tried to twist my wrist away.

"I don't want to go there!" I said, feeling desperate. The Forum was the heart of Rome's business and political world. It swarmed with senators and military men — the same men who had betrayed my father.

Juba shook his head. "That is not where we are going."

I breathed easier when he turned toward the slope of the Quirinal Hill. "Here," Juba said. He pushed me into a small tavern near the Gardens of Sallust. I stumbled in the sudden darkness; he pulled me to a little table in the corner.

"Whatchu want, sire?" the tavern lady asked.

"Wine," said Juba. "Your best."

A man sitting by himself near the door chuckled. "That means don't spit in it, Tullia!" he yelled a little drunkenly.

I pulled up a short wooden stool, still shivering from confusion. Juba poured wine from a beaker into rough clay cups.

"Drink," he ordered.

I held the cup to my lips. I had the strange sensation of not being certain where I was. If I walked out that door, would I be back in the palace in Alexandria? Where was Ptolly — who would tell him about Tata?

"Cleopatra Selene," Juba said. "Your eyes . . . you need to stop looking everywhere. Focus on one thing. Look at me." I stared into his eyes again. "That's right," he said. "Breathe deeply. No, no, don't look away."

He put his hand on my cheek to keep me focused. His touch was so warm. I closed my eyes, wanting to go away, to sleep forever.

"Shhhhh," he whispered into my ear. "It is over."

He wiped my cheek. I had not realized I'd been crying. I nestled into his shoulder, and he wrapped his arms around me, pulling me close. Slowly, so slowly, my racing heart began to beat in a more regular rhythm. I came back into myself.

"Better?" he murmured.

I nodded, not wanting to leave his warm embrace, but he pulled back and instructed me to take another sip of wine.

"What happened, Cleopatra Selene? Did the gods send you visions? What did you see?"

"My father. And his man, Eros. Eros slashed his throat like that . . . and then Tata . . . He took his sword and he . . ."

"You were there when your father fell on his sword?" he asked.

I nodded again.

"Gods," he whispered. "I did not know. . . ."

But why would the Goddess send me such a vision? What was she trying to tell me? Was cutting my own throat to be my fate too? I said another silent prayer for the old woman who took her own life rather than risk mine. I worried for our plans too, as well as for the safety of the Priestess of Isis. Had Gallus betrayed us to Octavianus?

"Now," Juba said, more quietly, leaning into me. "This is important. Tell me the truth. Are you the traitor from the inside they sought?"

CHAPTER FORTY

"Traitor to whom?" I asked.

Juba paused. "To Rome, of course."

I did not answer, but he scanned my face. Then he groaned and cursed under his breath. "Gods! How can you be so . . . so stupid?"

I stood up, sending my wooden stool clattering. The men in the tavern swiveled in my direction. "I should ask you the same thing. How can you be so *stupidly* loyal to those who took everything from you?"

I turned and headed for the door of the dark little tavern.

"Cleop —" Juba stopped himself from saying my full name. "Wait. Please," he said, catching up with me as we stepped out into the bright light of the street. "I am sorry. I am just worried for you. Do you realize how close you've come to being executed as an Enemy of Rome?"

"What do you know of any of this?" I asked.

"I don't. But I have put the pieces together. Are you aware of what has happened to Gallus?"

I stopped and shook my head cautiously, my pulse speeding up. Pedestrians jostled us as they wound their way to the taverns and eateries around us.

"We can't talk here," he said, grabbing my hand. "Follow me."

Juba led me down the Via Salaria, weaving in and around the crowded lanes toward the entrance of the Gardens of Sallust. Shaded with porticoes and dotted with small fountains, pools, and temples, the Gardens were one of the more beautiful, peaceful places in Rome. Lush cypress, pine, sycamore, and boxwood absorbed most of the cacophony of the city, dulling it to a muffled roar.

The Gardens were largely unoccupied at this time of day, though judging from the affectionate embraces of the couples in the shaded porticoes, it was a favorite assignation for young lovers. Juba led me to an immense willow tree. We parted the thick, drooping boughs that surrounded a marble bench like a curtain and sat down. The long silvery green foliage stirred ever so slightly in the breeze.

"What happened to Gallus?" I asked.

"What were you *planning* with Gallus?" he returned, almost at the same time.

"You first," I said.

He sighed. "He has committed suicide."

"What?"

"Caesar discovered a plot. Gallus was aiming to wrest control of Egypt from him. Caesar exiled him, and he fell on his sword at the dishonor."

Gallus dead. I could not think. Our plans gone. How much did Gallus reveal?

"Now, tell me," Juba continued. "What does this have to do with you?"

I hesitated. Could I trust Juba? Or would he reveal what he knew to Octavianus? He had been so good to my brothers and me. But who could say whether Octavianus had put him up to it in order to spy on us?

I shook my head. No. Juba was likely the only reason — besides Octavia — that Alexandros and I still lived. Alexandros! What if they jumped to the wrong conclusion and thought he was the traitor? Gods, had I put my brother in danger?

I stood. "We have to go back. I am worried about my brother."

"Wait," he said, grabbing my wrist.

His sudden grip caused a surge of panic, as if I were trapped, cornered. I could not lose Alexandros! I could not — must not — allow anything to happen to him.

"Just listen to me," Juba said, releasing my wrist and speaking in a soft voice as if he were gentling a horse. "We both want to make sure Alexandros is safe. I have an idea that may help both of you. But first, tell me what you were planning with Gallus."

"The priestess and her people had word that Gallus was restless in Egypt. They engineered a plan where I would marry him and take control of Egypt. . . ."

"What? And how would you do this? By murdering him? You would have done this?"

"No, though it makes sense to forge a union with a Roman." *Like Mother,* I thought. "Thanks to you, I have come to accept that nothing can be accomplished without Rome," I added.

Juba frowned. "But the plan was discovered."

"I do not know what was discovered or when. Clearly they knew there was a plot and suspected someone from Octavianus's compound."

He sighed and rubbed his eyes. "I'm sure Caesar suspects *you.* Gods. I'm going to have to wait. He will probably be too angry right now to listen to my proposal."

"Your proposal for what?"

Juba cleared his throat a couple of times, almost as if he were nervous. This surprised me. What could he possibly be nervous about?

"Cleopatra Selene, from the moment I first saw you — even in Alexandria — you have compelled me to question things I had never before questioned. Which, I admit, I did not always appreciate. I would have been happy to live as a Roman scholar for the rest of my life, but . . . but your challenges haunted me. And your gadfly questions dogged me."

I looked down, remembering how insulted I felt when he had called me a gadfly that disastrous afternoon under the citron tree.

"So, telling no one, I have been exploring my options for reclaiming my legacy in Numidia."

My mouth dropped open.

He smiled ruefully. "I have been learning Numidian Punic. And . . . and I have been exploring what kind of case I can make to Caesar to convince him to let me rule there." He took a breath. "I was going to propose . . . I was thinking of asking him about . . . of asking you . . . to marry me."

"What?"

He flushed. "You are a princess of Egypt. The people of Numidia would welcome you as a co-ruler. I need your strength, your determination to rule beside me . . . and it would be a way to get Alexandros out of Rome and away from Julia too."

I stared, still shocked. He stepped closer. "But . . . but that's not the only reason. I . . . well, I care for you very deeply. I want you beside me. I want you to be my queen."

I took a step back. The vision from the Goddess. Juba had called me his queen! But in the vision, I walked away from him — and toward Marcellus. What did it mean? I had wondered why the Goddess hadn't showed me Gallus. Had she known what would happen to him? Was Marcellus my future? But then why was this happening now?

When I did not say anything, Juba cleared his throat again. "That is why I was with Caesar in the stables this morning," he continued. "I told him we needed to ride privately. I wanted to present my case to him before he left for Spain."

"And then I walked by and he spotted me."

"Yes."

A bird chirped and sang in the limbs above us before flying off. Light dappled the ground at our feet; the willow's limbs swayed in the warm breeze.

"Why did you not tell me this earlier?" I asked. "Or include me in the planning?" Was this just another example of a Roman man making decisions and plans that affected my life, my future, without ever consulting me? Even so, I could see the wisdom in protecting me in case Octavianus didn't take the offer well.

"I . . . I did not want to say anything in case I did not succeed," he confirmed. "I have to make a strong case for this. So, I have been doing the research first. I've been studying my country's history, what is happening there now, how Caesar is likely to react to my request, how strongly the governor of the province would fight the change in government, whether the people of Numidia would revolt. There is much to learn and consider."

"A scholar to the very end," I muttered.

"Cleopatra Selene . . ."

I shook my head, trying to understand how we got to this point. There was a time when I would have melted at his offer, and part of me still rejoiced at the idea that he cared for me. But was he really asking me to forget my own legacy to help him pursue *his*?

"I did not want to spring this on you this way," he said. "I wanted to wait until I had a chance to talk to Caesar, to feel him out about sending me back to my homeland."

"What about *my* homeland? What about Egypt?" I asked.

"What do you mean?"

"Am I simply to abandon my dreams of my homeland to help you recover yours?"

Juba scowled. "You must see that Caesar is going to put an even greater stranglehold on Egypt after this fiasco with Gallus. But in Numidia we can create a new Alexandria. . . ."

"Juba, I cannot turn my back on Egypt."

"Cleopatra Selene, you must let go of this fantasy that you will ever rule in Egypt. Egypt's wealth is too important, too valuable to Rome for Octavianus to risk allowing you even to go near it again. But you were meant to rule. Together we will create a kingdom worthy to be Egypt's successor."

I sat down on the marble bench, confused. Juba sat next to me. I felt him looking at me. He brushed a strand of hair off my face.

He turned my face toward his. How I had ached for this for so long! He touched his lips to mine, softly, gently. I closed my eyes as a wave of longing and desire for him washed through me. But I pulled away.

"I am no longer a lovesick little girl," I said.

"I am no longer an idiot denying my feelings for you."

I stood up, more confused than ever. I remembered the vision of our skin-to-skin embrace under the sweet citron tree, of how right it felt to be loving him. He stood behind me, moved my hair off my neck, and kissed me lightly up to my earlobe. I shivered at the feel of his hands on my waist, his warm mouth on my neck.

"We were meant to be together," he whispered.

Without thinking, I turned and kissed him back, winding my arms around his neck. Despite what I had told myself, I had never really stopped wanting him. The feel of his warm skin, his hands on my back, the taste of him . . . This was different than what I felt when I kissed Marcellus. With Juba it felt as if all my souls — my *ka*, my *ba*, and all my true selves — fused together into a single desire. For him.

"Be my queen," he murmured against my neck, and I froze, remembering the vision again. I had walked away from Juba. I had told myself, *A queen must sacrifice her personal desires for the good of her people.* Did the Goddess want me to sacrifice my desire for Juba? Is that what this all meant?

"What?" he whispered.

I pulled away. "This . . . cannot happen."

He looked baffled. "Why?"

How could I explain?

His expression changed. "Is it Marcellus?"

I did not answer. I did not say anything. I could not ignore the possibility that the Goddess intended me to regain my throne through Marcellus, especially now that Gallus was dead. Didn't Mother ally with Julius Caesar when her brother tried to overthrow her?

"Cleopatra Selene, you must see that this is a game Marcellus plays. I've told you before . . . You intrigue him because you haven't fallen at his feet. I have seen it happen too many times. As soon as the girl falls in love with him, he loses interest. Worse, if Caesar finds out . . ."

"Marcellus is Octavianus's chosen successor," I said quietly. "He . . . he may help me return to Egypt."

I realized then that I had made my choice. My personal feelings — Juba's feelings — were irrelevant in the face of a chance to reclaim my legacy. But if that were true, why did it feel as if my insides were being torn from my bones?

"You believe that he pursues you to *help* you?" Juba said, sounding hurt and angry. "It is all a game to him!"

"I cannot walk away from a future in Egypt. If I forge a strong alliance with him, he could reinstate me. . . ."

"He would do no such thing! Are you mad?"

"Maybe I am," I whispered as my throat clogged. I kissed his lips very lightly before turning away and stepping out from the shade of the willow tree. I did not want him to see my tears. I did not want him to know that despite my bravado, my chest ached with what I'd always known but never admitted, even to myself. I loved Juba. I always had.

But none of that mattered. Egypt came first.

CHAPTER FORTY-ONE

Octavianus's freedman Thyrsus found me by the rain pool in Octavia's *peristylum*, where I had gone to try to make sense of the day's events. "Caesar has been looking for you. He awaits you in his study," he said. "You must come now — I will escort you."

"I know where his *tablinum* is," I said as we reached Octavianus's house.

"He is not in the downstairs *tablinum*. He is in Syracuse."

"Excuse me?"

"That is what he calls his private study upstairs," he explained. "Come. It will be easier if I announce you."

I followed him up the airless, dark stairwell, forcing myself to keep my breathing steady. I would not show fear, no matter what Octavianus said or claimed he knew.

"Selene is here to see you, sire," Thyrsus said after knocking on the small wooden door.

"Bring her in."

I entered a small, sweltering room covered in frescoes featuring theater actors in exaggerated grotesque masks. The heavy black and red paint of the mural's background made the room seem even smaller. The room reeked of stale sweat and sour wine and the slightly oily, charred scent of writing ink made from lampblack.

"You may leave," Octavianus said to Thyrsus, but his man hesitated, looking anxiously at me.

"Bring some wine," Octavianus ordered. After Thyrsus left, he turned to me and inspected me slowly. "Tell me, have you spoken with your brother today?"

"No." I had looked for him after I had returned from the Subura, but he was nowhere to be found. Neither was Julia.

He grunted. His unsettling gray eyes bore into mine as if he could read my thoughts. I kept my face impassive, remembering Mother's skill at this game.

"What do you know about Cornelius Gallus?" he asked.

"Who?"

He smiled dangerously. "You are too smart to play dumb, Selene. Tell me what you know."

"I know that you left him in charge of Egypt," I said.

"Anything else?"

"My nurse has heard some gossip."

"And what would that gossip be?"

"That he has died."

"Ah. Do you know *how* he died?" he asked, putting the tips of his fingers together to create a triangle with his hands.

"Suicide."

He stared at me and let the silence drag on. Sweat trickled down my spine.

"Not quite. It seems my good friend Cornelius decided that he deserved more power and recognition than I had allotted him," he said in a quiet tone. "The fool.

"So," he continued, "I had him executed."

I drew in a breath. He smirked. "Of course, the official version is that he 'fell on his sword.' Either way, thanks to his inept stupidity, I now claim all his holdings too. Worked out quite nicely for me, don't you think?"

I suppressed a shudder. Octavianus stood up and circled me. Too close. Why was he so close? Every inch of me wanted to recoil in disgust, but I concentrated on steadying my breathing. The man lived on others' fear. I would not feed him.

"My agents tell me someone from my household may have been involved in this grab for Egypt," he said softly as he walked behind me. "Your brother says he knew nothing about it. I believe him."

He circled back to stand just inches from my face. "And do you know why I believe your bastard brother? Because of the two, *you're* the one foolish enough to try to defy me."

I carefully arranged my expression into a look of innocent confusion. "I do not understand what you mean. . . ."

He chuckled, and it was as if low-growling Amut the Destroyer had entered the room. He moved closer still to me, so that I had to use every ounce of self-control not to wince away from him.

"Your wine, sire," Thyrsus announced, stepping in.

Octavianus stepped back. "Thank you. You may leave now."

Thyrsus hesitated. "Sire, *Domina* asks for your presence in her —"

He snorted. "Go."

Thyrsus left, looking back at me. Octavianus grasped the neck of the wine decanter and poured himself a cup. "Would you like some?" he asked with exaggerated politeness.

"No. Thank you."

He came close again, and I could smell the sharp tang of wine on his breath. "I will discover the truth," he said. "But in the meantime, I have decided to marry you off and remove you from my premises."

"What?" My heart thudded. Like every paterfamilias, Octavianus had complete power over me in this regard. "But . . . but you changed the law to move up the age of marriage for girls to eighteen! I am only —"

"Oh, I know what I've been saying. But those laws don't apply to you, as you are not a true daughter of Rome." He took a sip of wine, then licked his lips. "There are some senators' sons who have indicated interest, but I would not subject them to you. You would eat them alive. So I will marry you to someone who would eat *you* alive first — Placus Munius Corbulo. The Elder."

I gasped. Corbulo was the wrinkled, bald, tottering man I had seen in the garden with him so long ago. He had to be almost sixty!

"A despicable old leech, but he is filthy rich and he has expressed an interest in tasting Egypt," he said with a narrowed-eye smile. "Honestly,

I don't know how his other wives stood him, but they all died mysteriously after marrying him anyway."

I struggled to keep my face blank. I would not give him the outraged reaction he sought. I concentrated on the twisted face of the tragedy mask painted on the wall — the open mouth, frozen in silent horror.

"I leave for Spain in two days," he said. "But rest assured I shall pursue the matter while I am gone. I am sure Corbulo will be more than amenable to the arrangement, and I, for one, will enjoy watching you live the life of a miserable Roman matron. For as long as you survive, anyway." He smiled at me. "Seems somehow fitting, doesn't it? Your mother destroyed a good Roman marriage, so we will arrange a good Roman marriage that will destroy *you*."

He took a gulp of wine and brushed his wet lips with the back of his hand. "You may leave now."

My feet skittered on the wooden steps leading down from his private study. I wanted to run, to get away from Rome and Octavianus as far and as fast as possible. I thought about stealing away to the Temple in Capua, but I knew he would find me there, and I could not risk hurting any more innocent devotees of the Goddess. What would he do to the priestess if he knew of her involvement? Gods! I would have to avoid her to keep her safe!

But I had to do something, go somewhere. Could I somehow make it to Ostia and onto a ship to Egypt? Or Africa? Anywhere but Rome! I could not bear the idea of being first used, then killed, by some arrogant Roman! Old feelings of despair and rage circled up my throat as I faced the utter powerlessness of my situation.

I went in search of Alexandros. If Octavianus was going to marry me off, what would he do with him? I stopped at the courtyard fountain, trying to calm myself. Octavianus's people would be watching me carefully now. I did not want anyone reporting how seriously he had disturbed me.

Julia emerged from the direction of the gardens. "Oh, hello, sister," she called, a flushed smile on her face, but she did not stop. She merely grinned at me and sauntered away. I put my hands under one of the fountain's dolphin spouts, trying to rinse away the memory of Octavianus's threat.

"Did you know Octavianus was looking for you earlier?" Alexandros asked.

I jumped. "Gods, you scared me!"

A small leaf hung by the stem on the dark curls at the base of his neck. He had emerged from the same thicket Julia had just walked out of. I groaned. "Brother, shouldn't you and Julia be more careful? Or are you *trying* to get caught and then killed?"

Alexandros shrugged. "Julia enjoys taking risks. What can I say? And it is not as if I am going to refuse her."

"Oh, Isis! Please tell me you aren't actually sleeping together!"

Alexandros did not respond.

I closed my eyes. "He will kill us both now."

"He doesn't know," Alexandros said. "And he's leaving for Spain, so we are safe."

"Are you . . . are you *mad*? The slaves and servants must know. They know everything! It is a matter of time before word gets to him. And what if she gets pregnant?"

"We are careful." Alexandros dipped his hands in the fountain's basin. "Besides, I don't care anymore," he muttered, sounding despondent.

"Why? Have you finally fallen in love with her?"

He laughed bitterly. I stared at him, confused. I had been so wrapped up with my plans for Egypt and Gallus, I had barely paid attention to my twin. My stomach clenched. What was going on?

"Tell me," I said.

"Surely you heard the news too," he said.

"What news?"

"Iotape."

I looked at him blankly. Then I remembered the beautiful little girl my brother had been betrothed to in Alexandria, she of the shining black eyes and silken hair.

"What about her?"

"She has married King Mithridates of Commagene," he said. "My betrothed married someone else."

"But . . . but . . ." I did not know what to say. Had he held on to the hope that they would somehow marry, even after all these years?

Alexandros swallowed hard, and he kept his eyes on his fingers under the water. "One of the slaves here is from Medea. He helped me get letters to her and delivered letters from her to me. We have never forgotten each other. We were going to find a way to be reunited. We were going to disappear and live a simple life together. . . ." He trailed off, his voice thick with suppressed emotion.

I'd had no idea that my brother held on to the hope that one day, he and his childhood love would be reunited. While I had been pining for Egypt, he had been pining for Iotape. Alexandros cupped his hands and brought the cool water to his lips.

"So what happened?" I asked.

"My letters must have been discovered. I had not heard from her in some time. The slave from Medea told me today that her family forced an early marriage." Alexandros rubbed his wet palms over his closed eyes. "So you see," he added wearily, "I don't care what happens now. Let him discover us and kill me. I will just wait for Iotape on the other side."

"Alexandros, please don't talk like that."

He sat on the side of the fountain. "What is left for us, sister? Why are the gods torturing us like this? Perhaps they really did want the end of all the Ptolemies and we are just postponing the inevitable."

"You can't give up!"

"And do what? We have outlasted the goodwill Octavianus needed by keeping us alive. He can marry you off to someone, but not me. No Roman girl would have me. So what am I going to do, trail after you when he marries you to some fat old Roman? Live with you as a hanger-on, without *dignitas*, without independence?"

I had never thought how all of this was for him. Nor considered how his future was even more limited than mine.

"Alexandros, please don't give up. I . . . I have a plan!"

He gave me a rueful look.

"With Marcellus," I said.

"What can *he* do?"

"He is interested in me."

"Cleopatra Selene, he is interested in anything that moves."

"Still. Perhaps I can convince him to —"

"To do what, sister? Haven't you learned not to trust anybody from the House of Octavii yet?"

"But if there's a chance . . . if there is something I can do to convince him to support us in going back to Egypt . . ."

"So you are going to seduce the successor to the most powerful man in Rome on the *offhand* chance that he *might* help us return to Egypt?"

I crossed my arms. When he put it that way, it sounded both tawdry and hopeless.

"Mother tried that already. And look where it got her," Alexandros sneered, walking away from me. Then, over his shoulder: "And us."

CHAPTER FORTY-TWO

The golden fabric sluiced down my body like water, smooth and shiny, settling into Egyptian pleats under my breasts. *This touched her body once,* I thought as I slid my hand down Mother's dress, which Zosima had saved for me in secret so long ago.

Zosima combed out my hair and I closed my eyes, thinking of Alexandros. It seemed preposterous to me that he could have thought he would one day reunite with Iotape. And yet, he reacted to my plans with Marcellus with the same sense of disbelief. Was he right? Was I fooling myself?

I shook my head, causing Zosima to make an irritated noise as the comb lost its grip on my hair. This was different. Unlike Mother, I would be creating a base of support from *within* Rome, not just from the outside in Egypt. With Marcellus, I had a real opportunity to change the course of our future, of Egypt's future. I would be a fool if I didn't seize it.

And if I wanted others to think of me as a potential queen of Egypt, I needed to start looking and acting like one, which was why I was taking such care with my appearance. Octavianus's farewell banquet seemed as good a time as any to begin. After all, even if my Egyptian dress irritated him, he could do nothing about it. He would leave for Spain before sunrise.

Zosima arranged my curls on the top of my head, leaving only a tendril or two at my neck. She wound golden ribbons in my hair and hung a small pair of Mother's emeralds in my ears.

"Paint me with kohl," I directed.

She paused. "Are you sure?"

I looked at her. She did not ask again.

After the kohl dried, Zosima rummaged through our old chest and lifted a small alabaster vial. "Ah," she said. "Here it is."

"What is that?" I asked.

She took a small brush and dipped it into the jar. "Powder of gold."

"What?"

"The priests saved it for the most sacred ceremonies honoring Ra. It gives the god's own protection, as if the light of the sun glowed from your skin."

I closed my eyes as she brushed the powder across my cheeks, between my breasts, in the hollow of my neck, on my shoulders. I shivered, imagining the soft kisses of Juba's mouth in those places. . . . My eyes flew open. No. *Marcellus's* mouth. Marcellus.

Marcellus was my future, not Juba, I reminded myself. As much as it pained me to refuse his offer, I *had* to follow through with my plans for Egypt. Mother, I knew, would have done the same.

I waited until the very last moment to enter the *triclinium*, after everyone had been seated and the lamps lit. I walked in with my head held high. I did not say anything. I did not have to. All conversation hushed as I took my seat, joining my twin on the outer end of the circle. I glanced at the center couch. Octavianus scanned me from head to toe. Livia had one eyebrow up. Octavia paled.

Despite the fact that I had wanted to draw attention to myself as a princess of Egypt, I wavered in the face of Octavia's discomfort. She did not like discord. I gave her a small smile of apology.

On the ends of the most important couch sat Octavianus's close friends — Agrippa, Maecenas, Virgil, and Horace. Agrippa scowled as usual, but Maecenas's eyes glittered when he looked at me. Virgil seemed more interested in Octavianus's response and watched him instead. Horace grinned and winked at me.

I reclined slowly, then smiled. "Please accept my apologies for my tardiness," I said.

"You look like a . . . like a queen!" Tonia said with excitement. I smiled at her even as I felt the pang I usually did when I looked into her rounded, pretty face. Ptolly would have been close to twelve years old too.

Julia, sitting with Marcellus and Juba, narrowed her eyes at me but then smirked. She liked being the center of attention, but she liked disturbing her father even more. And she could see that I had done just that. Juba's expression was unreadable. But then I let my gaze wander to Marcellus and saw that he was devouring me with his eyes. When they met mine, he treated me to one of his slow, sensuous smiles.

"To what do we owe this magnificent apparition?" he asked.

I shrugged, allowing the silky fabric to slide down my shoulder ever so slightly.

"Perhaps she is celebrating that you are leaving for Spain too," Julia said to him.

I tried to swallow my surprise. "You are?"

Marcellus nodded and sipped his wine. "I was going to go next month, but Caesar wants me to join him now." He looked at Juba. "Juba is going as well."

"Why such short notice?" Alexandros asked. "What has happened?"

"Caesar wants to test my mettle on the battlefield a bit, I think," Marcellus said, grinning at Octavianus. "A good officer must always be ready to act on a moment's notice. And Juba, you requested to join us on this leg too, did you not?"

Juba nodded.

"I fear someone has broken his heart," Marcellus continued. "Why else would our resident scholar actively pursue military engagement?"

Juba worked his jaw, ignoring Marcellus. I concentrated on keeping my face impassive.

Julia couldn't resist. "Who, Juba? Who broke your heart?"

"He won't say," Marcellus said, "but Lucius Clovius saw him meeting his mysterious lady-love a few days ago in the Subura!" Clovius was the officer sent to catch the "traitor" from the complex.

"The Subura!" Octavia gasped. "Juba!"

Juba stared daggers at Marcellus.

"Our friend seems to have lost his sense of humor," Marcellus said. "And he will not divulge the identity of his mystery girl. Clovius said that she seemed vaguely familiar and guessed that she was a noble-woman in disguise so she could sneak away from her husband."

Octavianus groaned. "Why is it every time I try to pass laws to improve the morality of our great Republic, someone from my own family does something to undermine me? Juba, please remember that under my proposed laws, if the husband catches you, the paterfamilias will have the right to kill you and pay no penalty!"

It's a good thing Rome didn't have those laws when you had an affair with Livia, I thought. He stole Livia away from her first husband while she was pregnant with Drusus. But I kept my mouth shut. Given his threat to marry me to Corbulo, I did not need to antagonize Octavianus any more than necessary.

"The lady in question is not married," Juba said.

"Then what is the problem?" Octavia asked with genuine concern. "And why were you meeting her in the Subura, of all places?" She paused, her eyes growing wider. "Oh, please do not tell me that Marcellus's friend is wrong and she really is a plebian, Juba! You *cannot* mix with the lower classes!"

"I really don't wish to discuss this right now," Juba said.

"Well, nothing like fighting barbarians to shake you out of your lovesickness," Marcellus said. "We should see plenty of action, should we not?"

The conversation turned to the war. During dinner, I tried to assess how Marcellus's quick departure affected my plans. I had hoped to continue the slow seduction to tie him to me. But he was going to Iberia! And now so was Juba.

Octavianus focused on the poet Virgil. "So, *amicus,*" he said. "How goes the epic poem I have commissioned?"

"What epic poem?" Julia asked, sounding pouty as she plucked a fla-mingo tongue steamed in vine leaves from a plate held by a slave. "I did not know anything about this."

"Well, little empress," Maecenas said, "our gifted poet is writing an epic of Rome's history to rival Homer himself."

I tried not to snort. No Roman could ever match the genius of our Homer.

"Tell me how it goes, Virgil," Octavianus repeated, turning back to the poet.

Virgil, a quiet, slim man in his early forties, shook his head.

"Oh, do not be shy," Maecenas said, popping a tiny roasted dormouse whole into his mouth and crunching the tiny bones with relish. "It will be brilliant like all your works." He gave me a sly look as he licked the honey off his fingers. "In fact, he has been editing the section in which the hero Aeneas chooses duty to Rome over the love of a beautiful queen."

Octavianus smirked. "Yes, the story of Dido. A reminder that bedding a foreign queen brings nothing but destruction to good Romans, and that our Aeneas made the choice Antonius should have made — to honor his duty to Rome and leave his whore queen to her own devices."

Was he so obsessed with maligning Mother that he would commission an epic poem as a thinly disguised insult to her?

I felt someone looking at me. Marcellus. I lowered my eyes and smiled coyly, glancing away so as not to draw attention to our flirtation. I caught Octavia's eye, and for a moment her face was twisted with such venomous hatred I blinked in surprise. But when I looked again, she had composed herself. What offensive thing had Maecenas said this time? Neither Livia nor Octavia, I knew, held the rich, effeminate Etruscan in high regard.

I turned back to Marcellus to see if he had caught the small drama between his mother and his uncle's closest associate. But it appeared as if he had never taken his eyes off me. Looking through my lashes, I smiled again.

"I am not very hungry," Juba said, standing abruptly. "Please forgive my rudeness, but I must prepare for my sudden departure."

With that, he left the *triclinium*.

"Poor Juba," Marcellus said, smiling. "He really does have it bad."

CHAPTER FORTY-THREE

After dinner, I walked to the fountain, gambling that Marcellus would seek me out there. Instead, I found Juba.

This was the first time I had seen him privately since our conversation in the Gardens days ago, and I froze in surprise. "Juba, wh-what are you doing here?"

"Sorry to disappoint you."

"I am not disappointed. It is just that —"

"I wanted to say good-bye," Juba interrupted. "I leave tomorrow for Spain, as you know. With Fortuna's help, I may not come back."

My stomach clenched in fear. "No, that's not possible! You will come back from the war, I know you will!"

Juba looked down and chuckled. "No, you misunderstand me. Leaving now gives me traveling time with Caesar to do what we discussed before — convince him to let me rule in Numidia as my legacy."

He was pursuing his plans without me. Part of me felt proud of him. It would not be easy, I knew, and I respected the courage it would take to try to convince Octavianus of anything. But another part of me felt confused. Was I making a mistake? Was I really willing to lose him forever?

"What will you do if Octavianus denies you?" I asked. "Numidia has been run by a Roman governor for some time, has it not?"

"Yes, but the Romans do not understand Numidians. There has been some unrest. I think my people will embrace me as the bridge between the two cultures. He will see the wisdom of it."

"How do you know that?"

"I cannot be sure. But what I do know," he said, looking into my eyes, "is that I'm not coming back here to see you with . . . with Marcellus."

I looked down. Why was the Goddess testing me like this?

Juba let out a breath. "I had to see you one last time. . . ."

I felt my eyes fill. I closed them. Felt him move closer. He took my chin in his hands. "Cleopatra Selene," he whispered close to my lips, and I felt a shiver move down my chest to my abdomen. "I . . ."

Heavy footsteps on the gravel walkway to the fountain. I jumped back from Juba and I saw a look of surprise and hurt flit across his face, just as I had seen it in my initiation vision.

"Cleopatra Selene," someone hissed. "Are you there? It's me."

Marcellus.

"Gods, I should have brought a lamp. This is ridicu —" He stopped when he saw us. "Juba! What are you doing here?"

"I did not realize I would be interrupting a romantic assignation," Juba answered coolly. "I will leave so you can be alone."

"Yes, why don't you," Marcellus said with an edge.

Juba turned and strode away, his back tense. Why were we always walking away from each other?

"What was that about?" Marcellus asked. "Is he . . . is he trying to woo you from me?"

I laughed nervously. "No, no. I think he wanted some advice for, um . . . wooing the girl from the Subura."

Marcellus breathed out. "Oh, that's right. Poor fellow." He turned to me and smiled. "You look like a goddess tonight. Like the glittering Goddess of Love."

Yet I felt as cold and remote as Nephthys/Artemis, the Goddess of the Moon. He ran his fingers down my neck, but I pulled away. "You are leaving," I said.

"I can think of nothing else but you, Cleopatra Selene. You have bewitched me."

I swallowed. Those were dangerous words. Octavianus had convinced all Rome to turn against my father with the claim that Mother had "bewitched" him. "I have done nothing of the kind!"

He laughed low in his throat. "It is a poetic phrase. Come here. I want to kiss a goddess." He leaned into me and kissed me softly on the mouth.

I reminded myself of my plan . . . to ally with Marcellus . . . to regain Egypt. I could do this. I kissed him back, and after a time, Marcellus pressed his whole body against mine, running his hands down my back and hips. He made a small groaning noise in his throat, which frightened me. Was I really ready to consummate our affair? What if, in doing so, he lost interest in me as Juba predicted? I could not risk it.

I tried wriggling away, but Marcellus kept me tight against him. He began pulling my dress up around my hips.

"No!" I said, finally disentangling myself. "I cannot."

"Selene," he whispered. "I am leaving to fight in battle. I may not come back."

"Of course you will come back," I said a bit harshly. That was the second time I'd heard that phrase tonight — only this time, instead of fear, I felt irritated.

Marcellus seemed to interpret my reaction as nervousness. "My young little virgin," he said with a sigh. "I keep forgetting. I won't push you. I will just have to bear the exquisite agony of waiting for you.

"The question is," he continued, "will you wait for *me*?"

Gods, his leaving changed everything. Would I lose my only chance at extracting some kind of future in Egypt?

"*Is* there someone else vying for your affection, Cleopatra Selene?" he asked with suspicion.

"N-no!"

"Then why do you hesitate?"

"Your uncle told me he plans on marrying me off to Corbulo. The Elder," I said.

"What? To that murderous old lecher? Why in the world would he do that?"

"I do not know, but I fear it will happen soon."

"It can't. Corbulo is in Stabiae. And we leave for Spain tomorrow. He has no time to negotiate with Corbulo — and believe me, Corbulo will turn it into a negotiation. Besides, I will not allow it! I . . . I will marry you first!"

I did not say anything. We both knew he could not stop Octavianus. And Marcellus may have been a legal adult, but he had no right to rule his own life as long as the paterfamilias lived. That would be true even if he were forty! Still, my heart raced with hope, for the offer was proof of Marcellus's growing attachment to me.

Marcellus began to pace. "We . . . we cannot have a descendant of Alexander the Great treated this way. Corbulo is a murderer! I will convince Caesar that our union could serve as a symbol of the unification of the Roman West with the Egyptian East. He would have to see what a powerful tool that would be in our management of the eastern provinces."

I closed my eyes with relief. Yes. That was exactly right. The irony, of course, was that my parents had tried to do that very thing — unite Rome and the East through marriage. But because Marcellus voiced it, rather than a foreign queen, it might sound reasonable to Octavianus rather than power hungry.

"Marcellus, you can't tell Octavianus about us yet. He would —"

"Do not worry." He put his arms around me again. "I will explore our options carefully without letting on that I have fallen under your spell."

I groaned inwardly, hating how men blamed their own lusts on women's "magic." But I did not say anything. Instead, I pressed against him harder as we kissed.

"Wait for me, yes?" he breathed. "You will see. I will convince Caesar. He will not deny me anything I want. And I want you."

CHAPTER FORTY-FOUR
In What Would Have Been the Twenty-sixth Year of My Mother's Reign
In My Sixteenth Year (25 BCE)

I spent the months after Marcellus's departure generating endless alternate plans should he fail to convince Octavianus that a union between us made good political sense.

At the first sign of Octavianus's rage or rejection, I told myself, I would steal away to Ostia with Alexandros. Through the network of Isis worshipers in the harbor city, we were sure to find secret passage back to Egypt. But I would not go to Alexandria. Instead, I would travel to Heliopolis. There I would convince the Priests and Priestesses of Ra — who had, according to Isetnofret, promised to financially support our efforts to retake the throne — to melt their hidden caches of gold so I could raise a mercenary army.

This plan, of course, was weak for many reasons. I knew nobody in Ostia; I was gambling that the Isis devotees in Ostia would help us rather than turn us in; and there was no way of knowing if the priests of Heliopolis would trust me enough to fund my efforts. But it was all I had.

After much research, I settled on Nubia as the most viable source for raising a mercenary army. Long known for their skill in warfare, Nubians in general had little love for or interest in the doings of Rome. I wondered if perhaps I could do without having to purchase an army at all. What if I could convince the Nubians that Rome was planning to invade them? Surely then they would see the sense of joining with me in kicking Rome out of Egypt in a preemptive move for self-preservation.

The downside was that Nubia might then demand ownership of Egypt as a price for her help. The Nubians had ruled in Egypt hundreds of years ago. Who could say whether they would not want to do so again?

I even considered contacting King Phraates of Parthia, Rome's biggest enemy, and offering myself as wife to one of his sons in return for his protection in securing my throne. But Parthian involvement would surely end in war with Rome. It did not help that Phraates was dangerous and unpredictable. He had killed his father as well as thirty brothers to hold his kingdom. Without an army of my own, how could I hope to keep him from taking over Egypt just as Rome had?

And so I went, around and around. As the months flew by, my heart grew heavy with doubt that my alliance with Marcellus would come to anything, especially since I had not heard from him. What did it mean that he did not write to me? Had he found someone new? Tired of me already?

Worse, I noticed that Alexandros occasionally received letters from Juba, who also never wrote to me. I felt his rejection like a slap, even as I understood it. Pondering the meaning of their silence during my regular afternoon stroll around the garden, I stopped when I saw Livia's lady bustling toward me.

"*Domina* requires you in her *tablinum*," she called. "Now."

My stomach dropped. I had managed to turn avoiding Livia into a high art. A direct summons could not be a good thing. I swallowed my fear and followed the lady to the house of my enemy's wife.

"Ah, Selene. Come. Sit," Livia said after her lady announced me. She leaned back in her thronelike chair inlaid with mother of pearl; a chair, I knew, that had come from our palace at Alexandria.

I sat stiffly on the low backless bench across from her desk, wondering what she wanted. Livia stared at me as if trying to read my thoughts. She wore a rose-colored gown, pearl earrings, and a golden torque her husband had brought back from his last trip to Gaul. Quite understated, really, for the richest woman in the world.

"Is there something going on between Alexandros and Julia?" Livia asked.

I blinked. One of the house slaves must have talked. I widened my eyes in innocence and shook my head.

Livia arched an eyebrow. "You know, it would be just like my step-daughter to pick the one person who would anger her father the most. Caesar often complains that he has two spoiled daughters — Rome and Julia. But I disagree. It is only Julia who is spoiled. He has much better control over Rome."

She seemed to be waiting for a reaction from me. I lifted my chin and held her gaze, even as my pulse pounded. Had she told Octavianus? What would he do to Alexandros?

Livia smiled, looking away for a moment. "I have not brought you here to discuss your brother, though I urge you to ask him to be more discreet," she said. "I brought you here because I want to show you something." She pulled out a small basket of letters, some rolled, others folded. "These came for you."

"Then why do you have them?" I asked, fear and outrage swirling together like smoke from two torches.

"I have your letters because they endanger your life."

"What?"

"These are letters from Marcellus to you," she said. "Love letters, I believe." Then she smirked. "Perhaps it would be more accurate to call them *lust* letters."

Anger surged up my spine. "You read my private correspondence?"

She wrinkled her nose. "Let's just say that I hope Marcellus is a better politician than he is a poet."

How dare she? I put my hand out. "Give them to me!"

"Not yet." She leaned back and put the tips of her fingers together, studying me. I suppressed a shiver, remembering how Octavianus had placed his hands the very same way before announcing that he was going to marry me off to a wife murderer.

"What are you up to, Selene?" she asked in almost a whisper. "I would think you would have been smart enough to take Juba's offer. He is, after all, soon to be named king of Numidia."

I swallowed. How did she know about his offer? Then the full impli-cation of her words hit me. "Octavianus has made him king?"

She tipped her head ever so slightly. "I intercepted his letters too, though I thought you might have heard nonetheless. Yes, Caesar is naming Juba client-king of Numidia, though it is as yet unannounced. A brilliant move, really."

I stared at her, unable to breathe — not just in outrage at her meddling but in shock that Juba had succeeded. A part of me had always worried he did not have the internal strength to push Octavianus to his own ends. Yet he had done it. He had done it!

"Juba too mentions Marcellus, which is why I kept his letters as well. Really, Selene, you have been a very busy girl. But I am trying to protect Juba. If Caesar learns that he knew about you and Marcellus and did not report the information, I fear he will lose his newly earned command. I have always had great affection for our new Numidian king."

When I did not respond, she leaned forward in her chair, arms gripping the armrests carved in the shape of papyrus plants. "So I ask you again, Selene. What are you up to with Marcellus?"

"Marcellus has pursued me," I said, trying to find my footing again.

"Marcellus pursues anything in a *tunica*," she muttered. "However, he seems to have plans for you. For your future. I find that very curious. Who gave him that idea?"

I said nothing. After a long moment, she said, "You do realize that if Caesar finds out about this, he will —"

"Kill me." *And we both know it would be by your hand*, I thought. But I did not say anything. There was no sense in further antagonizing her. Finally, I asked, "Does he know?"

"No. But I am concerned about Marcellus's lack of caution in writing to you about his plans. It shows a certain weakness of character, a naïveté, if you will."

"Unlike Tiberius, who we both know is much more devious."

She paused. "I wouldn't use the word 'devious' for my eldest son. The word I would select is 'cunning.' A type of intelligence that would serve the Roman empire better than innocent stupidity, don't you think?"

I felt the force of her ambition and power vibrating in the air around me like an unheard growl. Livia hated that her husband had named Marcellus his successor over her own firstborn, Tiberius. That was clear. But to what ends would she go to achieve her aims? And how would she use what she knew to manipulate this situation in her son's favor? She now had two pieces of information that could cause our deaths — Alexandros's relationship with Julia and my hopes for a union with Marcellus.

Livia ran her buffed fingernails over the basket of letters. "I have wondered whether I should warn Octavianus about Marcellus's attachment to you, or let him discover it for himself."

I felt my heart skitter unevenly. "Why *haven't* you told him?" I asked. "Then you would finally be rid of us."

Livia blinked. "I have no desire to get rid of you," she said. "Indeed, I've done everything I could to protect you! Despite what you may think, Selene, I admired your mother. In fact, I always suspected that she and I would have gotten along famously."

Anger clawed up my chest. How dare she pretend she had not at least once tried to get us murdered? And how dare she imply that she and my mother were alike! Mother would have crushed her with one look.

"To answer your question, I have not told my husband about Marcellus's passion for you because it appears your lover is doing plenty to incriminate himself. Once my husband discovers it, he will finally see what a foolish choice he has made in naming Marcellus his heir. Tiberius will then be the only rational choice."

"Why are you telling me this?" I asked.

"Because I need to warn you against one thing."

"Which is?"

"Octavia."

"Octavia?" I laughed.

"Yes. Marcellus is her only son. If she were to discover that her beloved boy has fallen for the daughter of the woman who stole her husband . . ."

Livia was so transparent, I almost laughed in her face. If she thought she could turn me against Octavia — the woman who had given my mother her sacred oath to keep us safe — she was sadly mistaken.

I said, "I do not understand your meaning."

She sighed. "Perhaps it is better that way. I believe we are finished here."

My spine stiffened in irritation. I was not leaving without what was rightfully mine. "The letters, please."

"Oh, no. They are headed for the fires of the hypocaust."

"Give them to me," I demanded, standing.

She arched an eyebrow and sat back.

"Then I will take them!" I reached over and snatched at the scrolls. I unrolled one, almost ripping the papyrus in my haste. Blank. I opened another. And another.

"You underestimate me if you think I would keep them for just anyone to find," Livia sneered. "No. I burned everything as it came in, except for one or two that I can use to incriminate Marcellus." She stood up. "I hope I do not have to use them, but I am prepared to do so if necessary. Again, you may leave."

As I turned and left, I felt her stare of hatred piercing my back like an archer-battalion's worth of arrows.

Livia continued intercepting my mail — or at least I assumed so, since I never received anything from either Juba or Marcellus. But it was Juba's letters I wanted to read the most.

I was brimming with curiosity. Numidia had been a Roman province run by a Roman governor for decades. How did that governor feel about being replaced by a client-king? What about the Numidians? Did they consider Juba a Romanized traitor or welcome him as a true son of Numidia? Clearly, naming Juba king ran the risk of destabilizing the region. And yet somehow — some way — Juba had convinced Octavianus to take the risk anyway. How?

But whenever I asked Alexandros about it, he shrugged. "He doesn't give me details," he said. "Mostly he writes about how the battles are going."

I knew I should have been proud and happy for Juba, but instead I felt a stinging sense of loss. He had wanted me as a partner in his new adventure. Did I make a mistake in rejecting him? My heart said yes, but my mind always veered back to my initiation vision. I had walked away from Juba and toward Marcellus. How much clearer could the Goddess have been? My destiny was Egypt, not Numidia.

Still, I could not stop thinking about him. Once I dreamt we lay naked under a canopy of white on a terrace facing the sea. The sounds of the ocean, the faint cries of seabirds, the flapping of silk window coverings — it was as if I had returned to Alexandria with him. But it wasn't Alexandria, because my beloved Lighthouse was not there.

Sleepily, he turned to face me, a smile on his full lips. "My queen," he whispered. I smiled back, leaning down to press my mouth on his, whispering, "My king."

I never knew how to interpret these dreams. Were they merely a reflection of my wishes, or was the Goddess reprimanding me for not accepting his offer? How was I to know? Again, I wished that I could have spoken to the Priestess of Isis, but I had continued avoiding her after the Gallus fiasco in order to keep her safe.

But if I did speak to her, I would demand an answer to a question that plagued me night and day: Why would the gods return Juba's kingdom to him, but not Egypt to me?

As the months wore on, I found it impossible to break the stranglehold Livia had on letters coming from Spain. Most were hand delivered to her by soldiers — whom I dared not approach — but occasionally messenger boys carrying stacks of correspondence arrived at the compound. Those I tried to bribe, but they ran from me with terror in their eyes. What punishment had Livia threatened them with?

Worse, after a time, letters stopped coming altogether. Did it mean the fighting in Spain was not going well? Even though it was not unusual for correspondence throughout the empire to get lost, damaged, or stolen, the lack of any news at all coming from Spain set my teeth on edge.

The only good news I received was that the elder Corbulo — the man Octavianus was planning to marry me to — had died. Word was that his boat sank while he was sailing between his villas in Stabiae and Herculaneum. His body washed ashore near Pompeii. When I took a deep breath after hearing the news, I found that, for the first time since Octavianus's threat, I could fill my lungs all the way.

Marcellus returned home almost six months after Livia had announced she was intercepting all my letters. We greeted him as a family the morning of his return, but by that evening, I still had not seen him alone, which worried me. Had he changed his mind about me? Had something gone wrong?

I turned over on my sleeping pallet and sighed. Tanafriti, curled at my feet, and Sebi, purring at my side, brought their heads up. Their ears twitched and their tails jerked, their eyes gleaming in the dark. "What?" I murmured.

"Cleopatra Selene, are you up?" A male voice. My heart thudded. "It is me, Marcellus."

I breathed out and ran to the privacy drape. "Marcellus, what are you doing?"

He looked around the dark hallway, then slipped into my *cubiculum*, closing the drape behind him. "I could not get away earlier," he whispered. "But I had to see you." He held me tight against him. "Gods, it was torture not seeing you when I knew you were so close," he whispered.

He kissed me softly at first, barely grazing my lips, then with more intensity. I was surprised to find that I felt nothing. I no longer responded to his touch the way I had when his attraction to me was a novelty.

We kissed some more, and he led me to my sleeping couch. I hesitated. He gave my arm a little tug, and I sat next to him.

But Sebi did not like the intrusion. He hissed at Marcellus.

Marcellus jumped. "You have a snake in your bed?"

"It's just the cat," I said. "Shhhh," I murmured to Sebi. "It is okay, *Meiu*-man."

"It sounded like a snake!" Marcellus grumbled. Like many Romans, he was deeply discomfited by cats and their mysterious ways. "Why did you not write me back? I was afraid you had stopped caring for me or found someone else."

"I never got your letters," I whispered.

"What do you mean? Somebody intercepted them? What fool would dare open one of my letters!"

"Shhhh. Keep your voice down. A 'fool' named Livia, by the way."

He gaped at me. "She knows?"

I nodded.

"Has she told Caesar?"

"No. She says she wants him to discover it on his own so he sees for himself what a foolish choice he made in naming you heir."

"That witch!" he said with a growl. "I suppose she wants to convince Caesar her little dark-haired demon should be heir. I shudder to think of Tiberius in charge!"

"Did you talk to Octavianus about us?"

"Not exactly," he said.

"What do you mean?"

"I could barely mention your name without him getting angry. Furious, more like it. Then, after a while, he said he had a special plan for you."

I groaned.

"Do not despair. We just need to give him more time. You'll see." He brushed my hair off my forehead. "Did you miss me?"

I did not respond right away.

"Cleopatra Selene, you did not answer me."

"Of course I missed you," I said quickly. "You were all I could think of." I tried not to wince at how false I sounded, hoping he did not notice.

"Come here," he whispered. We kissed, and after a time he lay down on the rumpled linen blanket of my sleeping couch and brought me down beside him. He smelled of sun and leather and even a metallic hint of blood, as if his time in the baths could not fully remove the scent of soldiering from his skin.

"Marcellus, I don't think this is such a good idea. . . ."

"I will go slowly, I promise," he murmured. When I still did not respond, he whispered, "Imagine, Selene, if we had a child. A son of my blood mixed with the blood of a descendant of Alexander the Great!"

He wanted a son from me. And I wanted Egypt in return. A business relationship. I wondered what alliance Juba would be making in his homeland. What beautiful Numidian woman would he marry now to secure his throne and establish an heir? I sighed. Now was not the time to be thinking of Juba.

Marcellus misunderstood my sigh. He kissed me with more urgency, reaching under my tunic and running his hands up my body and down my hips. Despite my distraction, his warm hands felt good, and I moved like Tanafriti did when I petted her and she purred.

Marcellus sat up and shrugged his tunic over his head, then lay back down with me. I ran my hands over his warm skin. With the heavy drape drawn, it was impossible to see him well, but I could feel the contours of the muscles in his arms and chest as he pulled me to him.

Sebi hopped off in a huff. Marcellus froze. "What was that?"

"One of the cats," I said.

"*One?* How many are there in here?"

"Well, Tanafr —"

But in that moment, Marcellus jumped and nearly roared out a curse as he grabbed his shoulder. He scrambled off the sleeping couch in a fury. "Your cat . . . your *vae* cat just attacked me!"

"Marcellus, please! You'll wake the whole wing!"

"Look at this!" he cried. "There's blood on my shoulder! Where is that cat? I will kill it!"

"Marcellus, you cannot threaten the goddess Bastet's sacred animal!"

"Well, it attacked me!"

That stopped me. What did it mean? Why had she done so?

Someone whipped open my drapes, carrying a small lamp. "What in Hades is going on in . . . Oh, gods be merciful!" It was Zosima, her face like a theater mask of horror.

"Bring the lamp here!" Marcellus ordered, wanting to inspect the bloody bite. But my nurse could only stare at him, as naked and beautiful as a young god in the flickering light.

"Bring it here *now*!" he ordered again in a hoarse whisper. Zosima walked toward him while looking at me with wide, disbelieving eyes. I pulled my tunic down over my hips and looked at Tanafriti in the corner, her chin high, her tail twitching as it usually did after a successful hunt.

Marcellus picked up his discarded tunic and blotted the bite. "Does a cat's bite have venom?" he asked. "Like a snake's?"

"No," I assured him, getting up. "She must have thought you were hurting me, for I've never seen her attack anybody before."

Zosima's mouth dropped open even farther. In Egyptian, she muttered, "Are . . . are you mad? With *him*? You will get us all killed!"

"What's all the commotion?" a new voice asked outside my *cubiculum*.

And I groaned, realizing that yes, there was yet one more way to make the evening worse. The voice belonged to Julia.

CHAPTER FORTY-FIVE

Julia poked her head inside the drape to my *cubiculum*. Her eyes grew wide at the sight of Marcellus. She looked at me and put her hand to her grinning mouth. "Gods! I cannot believe it!"

"Shut the drape," Marcellus ordered. "We do not need the entire household overhearing us."

"What's all the commotion?" she asked again, stepping in as he ordered.

"Her cat *attacked* me!" He turned to me. "Are you sure I don't need to see a *medicus* about this?"

"I'm sure," I answered, wondering if he fussed like this on the battlefield. I took the tunic out of his hands. "Can you please put this on?"

He realized my nurse and Julia were staring at him, and he flushed, smiling. He threw the tunic over his head.

The four of us looked at one another awkwardly.

"Everything is fine," I said to Zosima. "Return to your room."

She narrowed her eyes at me, and I knew I was in for a long lecture later.

"Please," I whispered.

She put the little terra-cotta oil lamp down on the chest near my bed with an exaggerated bow. Then she left. I could hear her muttering angrily down the hall.

Julia stood with her weight on one hip and her arms crossed, a smirk on her face.

"I guess we all have our secrets now, don't we?" I said to her.

"What's your secret?" Marcellus asked Julia.

She gave me a warning look.

"I can keep yours if you keep mine," I said to her.

"Cleopatra Selene, soon we won't have to sneak around. You'll see," Marcellus said.

Julia's mouth dropped open. "Marcellus, did you get hit in the head in Spain? Your mother will *never* accept this!"

"Mother has no say in this."

"But Tata does, and he hates her even more than Octavia does!" She turned to me. "Sorry."

Octavia hated me? Yes, she had always been warmer to my brothers, but *hate* took it too far.

Marcellus turned his head to look at his shoulder again, frowning as he inspected the bite mark under his tunic. "I think I will have the *medicus* look at it anyway," he mumbled. He kissed me distractedly on the mouth, moved the drape out of his way, and left.

I felt such a sense of unreality, I almost laughed. Had all this really happened? Did I really have a naked Marcellus in here, interrupted from making love by my cat? I shook my head. And then to end up in the dead of night with Julia, of all people, in my *cubiculum*!

"Does your brother know about you two?" Julia asked.

I shrugged, remembering his disapproval of my attempts to ally with Marcellus.

"You know, as I think about it, this could be a very good thing for us," she said.

"What do you mean?"

"It's very tidy and neat, don't you think? Perhaps they'll see this was the work of the gods, that we were meant to pair off this way."

It was my turn to stare. "Julia, your father will never . . ."

"Stop! Don't say that!" she said, stamping her foot. "Over time, he will come to accept it. He *will* let us be happy. He has never denied me anything. When he sees how much I love Alexandros, he will relent. I am sure of it!"

Livia's lady came for me soon after sunrise, just as Zosima had begun admonishing me. "*Domina* wants to see you in her *tablinum* now," she said.

"I'll come as soon as we are finished —"

"*Now!*" She cut me off.

I met up with Alexandros on the way to Livia's house. "She called you too?"

He nodded. "I hear you had an interesting night last night."

"Gods, so much for Julia showing any kind of restraint!"

He smirked. "She thinks it is wonderful — she thinks it will bolster our chances for being together."

"What do you think?" I asked.

"I do not care. The gods will do with us what they will anyway. Nothing matters anymore."

"Brother, I *hate* it when you talk that way! Besides, I think she really loves you," I added, lowering my voice. "That could be useful. Do you love her?"

He looked at me dubiously. "Love? I already told you. I'll never love anyone but Iotape."

"But you were just children when you were betrothed!" I blurted out. Had he gone mad? For how could he seriously think he would ever have seen her again?

And then it occurred to me that perhaps the fantasy had *kept* him from going mad.

Alexandros turned to me, his brows furrowed, his eyes furious. "I would have given up Egypt — I would have given up *everything* for her. But the gods took her *and* Egypt from me. I made countless sacrifices to them, begging them to return her to me, begging them . . ." He stopped, his voice thick. "But the gods have forsaken me," he said in a low voice.

There was nothing I could say.

When we entered Livia's *tablinum,* I was surprised to see Marcellus and Julia already there. Julia had her chin set in the air as if she and Livia had already exchanged words. Livia had an inscrutable expression on her face. I looked at Marcellus, but he would not look at me. A silent tension hung in the room, which immediately set me on my guard. I breathed out, however, when I saw Octavia in the corner. She was our last remaining buffer between Alexandros and me and her brother and his wife.

"Ah, good," Livia said. "We have been waiting. You may know that Caesar has been quite ill in Spain. . . ."

Alexandros and I smirked at each other. I hadn't known, but I found it funny that Octavianus always managed to fall ill when battle loomed, leaving his men to do the fighting but taking credit for their victories. My tata always fought alongside his men like a true hero.

"My husband's latest sickness has convinced him to tie up loose ends," Livia continued. "He has sent Agrippa with special instructions. In order to secure the line of succession, my husband has decreed that a wedding be held today."

Marcellus's head shot up in surprise, then he looked at me, hopeful. Had Octavianus understood what Marcellus was trying to tell him? Could all my dreams and plans for Egypt finally be coming true?

"Marcellus, before the end of this day, you will marry Julia."

Julia?

"What? No!" Julia cried. "I do not want to marry Marcellus! Is this some sort of joke?"

"No, it is not a joke, Julia," Livia said calmly. "Agrippa will preside at the ceremony in your father's absence."

Marcellus blanched. My stomach twisted. Octavia seemed pleased. Julia burst into sobs. "But I love Alexandros! Why can't I marry Alexandros?" she wailed.

My twin looked at the floor. Did he not realize how much she loved him?

Livia smiled sadly. "I am sorry, stepdaughter. Love has little to do with it. You will do as instructed; the ceremony will be concluded before sundown."

Marcellus gaped at Livia. "But . . . but surely Caesar will give us time to adjust to the idea. . . ."

"No. This ceremony must happen right away for the safety of Rome. The line of succession must be clear."

"I won't do it!" Julia shouted. "We are *first* cousins! Roman piety forbids it, doesn't it? And I am not even fifteen! I thought that wasn't allowed — that Tata changed the laws! So how could he command this?"

"I am afraid you have no say in the matter," Livia continued. "Or Caesar will disinherit you." She looked at Marcellus. "Disinherit *both* of you. We must act on this immediately, for if my husband found out about your attachment to Antonius's son, Julia . . . Well, there is no telling what he would do."

Livia turned to look at me, her face as impassive as a queen's. I held her gaze. She shifted to Marcellus, and he looked away. I felt a flash of anger at him. *Do not let her intimidate you. Fight!*

"Caesar had a suspicion, based on conversations with his 'chosen heir,' that there might be something between you two as well," Livia added. I heard Octavia draw in her breath with a hiss. "He is pretending, though, that this serious lack of judgment on your part, Marcellus, was just an anomaly. In his weakened state, he must have faith that he has made the right choice."

Marcellus nodded. He had yet to meet my eyes.

"What will happen to us?" Alexandros asked.

"You leave for Africa right away." Livia paused. "Selene, you are to marry the king of Mauretania."

"What?" I squeaked. I knew little about Mauretania — only that it was west of Numidia and run by nomadic chieftains. "You must be mistaken. Mauretania isn't even a Roman province! Numidia . . . Numidia is Roman. I am to marry the king of *Numidia*, yes?" Gods, surely he meant to unite me with Juba!

Livia shook her head. "No, I am sorry. Agrippa came back with specific instructions. You are to sail for the Mauretanian coast tomorrow."

I looked at Octavia for help. She could put a stop to this! But she was whispering to Marcellus, who had joined her in the corner. Her son hung his head as she spoke quickly. When she caught my eye, she scowled and turned back to Marcellus, continuing to whisper at him in hissing undertones. She either could not or would not help me.

"Slaves are already packing your things," Livia continued. "You and Alexandros will head for Ostia this afternoon."

My throat squeezed so tight, air barely made it to my lungs. Once, when I was very young, I played in the sand near the Great Pyramid of Khufu. I grabbed whole fistfuls of the sparkling sand, but it kept slipping through my fingers. I had wept with rage: I wanted to *hold* Egypt in my pudgy toddler hands. But I could not then. And now I never would.

"You can't send Alexandros away!" Julia cried. "You can't!"

"Julia," Livia said. "You will see over time how impossible this situation is. It really is the best for everyone. . . ."

"No!" she sobbed, and ran out of the study. "I hate you! I hate you all!" Her sobs echoed down the columned portico.

"You may leave, Selene and Alexandros," Livia finally said with a sigh. "Marcellus, you stay here."

But I could not move. I felt someone tug my arm. "Come on, sister," Alexandros murmured. "We are done here."

We found Zosima, agitated and confused, standing in the courtyard between our wings. "Strange servants are packing all of our things. What is happening?" she cried.

"We are being sent away," Alexandros said.

Zosima grabbed me by the upper arm and shook me. "I *told* you it would end badly! What a foolish girl . . ."

"Zosima!" Alexandros called sharply. "There is nothing any of us can do. But at least we leave Rome alive. At least we leave Rome." She released me. "I must talk to Julia," Alexandros said. He looked at our nurse. "Go and supervise the packing of our things."

Zosima stomped away, muttering, "The cats! We must gather the cats. Do we still have their wicker carriers . . . ?"

I sat down heavily on a marble bench in the shade, staring at the rain pool of the *peristylum*. Despite the warmth, I shivered. I had grasped at the only tool I thought available to me to take us back to our homeland — and I had failed. I would carry the weight of all our deaths, for just as surely as I would die in the dusty Berber lands, so would my brother and our nurse. Despair weighed my stomach down like stone. Why was I being punished like this? Why had the Goddess misled me?

"Sister," Alexandros said, and I jumped. "You have been sitting here this whole time? Come, look on the bright side."

I grunted. "What bright side would that be? The one where we die at sea or the one where we die in the desert?"

"The one that says we never have to see this accursed place again."

I sighed. "Did you talk to Julia?"

"No, they wouldn't let me. They have forbidden us from seeing Julia or Marcellus, even to say good-bye."

I closed my eyes. It really was over.

"I am sorry, sister. Did you love Marcellus, then?"

I shook my head. It wasn't about Marcellus at all. "I do not understand," I said. "If you cared at all about Julia, how you can be so pleased?"

"Because we are *leaving*. We are finally getting out of Rome. And we still have each other. That has to count for something, no?"

I opened my mouth to argue, but he spotted a servant carrying an empty platter of food. "We have not had our morning meal," he called out. "Have someone bring something out for us."

The servant nodded and scurried away.

"How can you think of eating at a time like this?" I asked.

"Nothing ever dampens my appetite, you know that. Plus," he said, smirking, "we should fill up on the extraordinary cuisine of the Romans while we can."

"Yes, *garum* cooked in *garum*," I muttered of the foul-tasting fish sauce Romans used on everything.

He chuckled. "I should have told the servant to hold the *garum*. Goddess knows what they will bring me."

"Cheese in *garum*. Fruit in sweetened *garum*. Olives in *garum* . . ."

"Stop!" he laughed. "Or I really will lose my appetite."

"Alexandros," I asked. "Do you not feel any remorse about never seeing Julia again? She is heartbroken at losing you."

He sighed. "I do care for her. It is not that I don't. But the prospect of leaving Rome once and for all . . . I feel like Persephone being led out of Hades for the first time." Alexandros lifted his face to the sun.

"I do not understand you," I said, chuckling despite myself. But I had to admit, seeing my brother hopeful took the sting out of everything that was happening. And, as he said, we were not being separated. Maybe Alexandros — finally out from the shadow of Octavianus and Tiberius — could come into his own.

A servant came, bearing a small table and a platter filled with nuts, olives, soft cheeses, pear slices, barley bread, and two clay cups of honeyed water.

"No *garum*, I see," I noted. "Perhaps Fortuna really has taken pity on us and is showering us with blessings."

Alexandros grinned, missing my sarcasm. He looked over the plate with such anticipation and relish I couldn't help but think of Ptolly, and I felt my heart contract even as I smiled at my twin. Gods, what I would have given to have him here with us now — now that we were finally leaving! I reminded myself to have the Isis Temple near Capua send Ptolly's body to us. I would not be separated from him again.

Another servant approached with a goblet of wine. He brought it to me and bowed.

"I did not call for this," I said, my mouth full, pointing with a hunk of bread to my water cup.

"Yes, but *Domina* sends this in celebration of your upcoming nuptials in Africa. Her best Falernian."

I scowled. Livia was gloating. That witch! I bet she thought this was all quite humorous. Grand entertainment she could rehash at her dinner parties for the amusement of all — how her husband sent the daughter of the queen of Egypt to live in a tent with a toothless nomadic chieftain. "I do not want it!" I said. "Take it back."

"But *Domina* insists —"

"No!"

Alexandros laughed. "Don't be stupid. When do you think we will have such a fine wine again? I'll take it," he said to the servant, grabbing it out of his hand.

The servant recoiled, eyes wide. Everything slowed. I saw a grinning Alexandros bring the goblet to his lips. Remembered the sting of Mother's slap when she had knocked a poisoned cup of wine out of my hands . . . And I knew.

"No!" I yelled, grabbing at the goblet and upending it. But I was too late. He had taken a big gulp.

Alexandros's eyes widened in surprise. "*Pax*, sister! I would have shared some with you."

I looked up, but the servant had run off. I turned to Alexandros, trying to contain my panic.

"What?" he asked.

Perhaps I had been mistaken. But then Alexandros began to cough and clear his throat. "Falernian never burns like that," he muttered, his voice sounding raw.

I jumped up in alarm. Alexandros continued coughing, his face turning red. I must have screamed. Zosima came running. Alexandros was having a hard time catching his breath between coughs.

"Get the *medicus*!" I yelled at Zosima. But somebody had already sent for him. The *medicus* yelled at a servant to bring salted water, then grabbed my brother's chin and tried to get the concoction into him. In his agitation and panic for breath, Alexandros pushed the *medicus* away with his forearm. "You must!" the physician commanded, drenching the front of Alexandros's tunic. My twin's face was red, the cords straining in his throat as he struggled. The *medicus*'s assistant held his arms behind him as the doctor forced a cup of the briny water into his mouth.

I found myself alternately trying to breathe for my brother and holding my own breath in fear. The physician reached for another cupful, but Alexandros turned to the side of the bench and began to vomit.

"Good," the doctor said. "Good."

He tried to steady Alexandros, but my brother was bigger than he was. Alexandros ended up on the ground on his knees, still retching. Zosima brought a cool cloth. I knelt next to him and dabbed his sweating neck and face.

"More!" the *medicus* yelled, and his servant sprinted away with the empty clay jar.

When Alexandros's spasms stopped, the *medicus* forced him to take more of the salted water. This time it didn't take half as much to make my brother sick again.

A crowd surrounded us. I heard Julia's voice. "Alexandros!" she wailed as she ran past everyone and almost knocked me over to get to him. "What has happened?"

The *medicus* murmured something to her.

"Poison? Somebody poisoned him?" she cried.

The word made it too real. My hands trembled. "How do you know?" I hissed to the doctor. "And how did you know to come out here so quickly?"

"A servant," he said. "Ran to tell me that there had been an accident with the wine."

"An accident?"

"Yes," he said, not meeting my eyes. "That the wrong person drank it."

The servant said *Domina* sent *me* the wine to celebrate my good news. A cold fury grew in my stomach. Why? Why would Livia do this? And why *now* when we were leaving her accursed home anyway?

My limbs began to shake, but I stayed near Alexandros. The doctor purged him another time and instructed the servants to carry him to Livia's sickroom. I could barely breathe. Gods, not the room Ptolly had died in!

A weeping Julia was led away by one of Livia's freedmen. I trailed after the doctor. "Will he recover?" I asked. "He only took one swallow. . . ."

"I need to see the cup he drank from."

I ran and picked it up from the dirt where it had fallen. The *medicus* sniffed it and made a face.

"Is he going to be all right?" I asked again.

"Well, we purged him fairly quickly, which will help. But . . ."

"But what?"

He looked at my horrified face, then said, "He didn't get very much in him and he expelled it pretty quickly. And the fact that he is young and strong . . ." He trailed off, following Alexandros to the sickroom.

Fear turned into rage, and I trembled with fury. I would kill Livia with my bare hands, I swore as I marched toward her *tablinum*. Bursting through the door, I came at Livia, and she jumped back.

"You!" I growled through gritted teeth. "You *dare* try something like this *now*?"

Livia looked at me, her eyes wide. "Selene, what —"

"You meant that poison for me, but now Alexandros lies convulsed —"

Somebody behind me took in a gasping breath. "Alexandros?"

"Yes!" I cried, glancing at Octavia's horrified face. I turned back to Livia. I would reach for her neck. I would squeeze the life out of it. "What is the poison? Tell me now, or I swear I will tear your heart out with my teeth."

Livia looked confused and angry. "What have you done?" she asked.

"What have *I* done? You are the one . . ." But then I realized she was not looking at me. Her narrowed eyes were on Octavia.

CHAPTER FORTY-SIX

"Tell me, Octavia!" Livia yelled. "What have you done?"

"She . . . she *seduced* my Marcellus!" Octavia spat. "The whore's daughter thought to bewitch my son just as her mother bewitched my husband! She would destroy him like her mother destroyed Antonius. I would not have it! Not again!"

I stared at her, uncomprehending. Livia's face was red with fury. "So you tried to *poison* the girl? In my own home? They are leaving! Marcellus is marrying Julia *this afternoon*! Isn't that enough for you?"

Still unbelieving, I turned to Octavia. "You . . . *you* poisoned my brother?"

"It was meant for *you*! The spawn of a whore who seduced my Marcellus. You deserve to die, you slut, you evil child of a she-monster!"

Livia sat, her face ashen.

"It is your turn to suffer now like I suffered at the hands of your mother," Octavia continued, her face twisted with hatred. "All of Rome, feeling sorry for me, witnesses to my humiliation, discarded and overthrown for a whore queen. She stole my Marcus!"

A chill ran down my spine. She used to refer to Ptolly as "my little Marcus" because of his uncanny resemblance to Tata. And he got sick soon after he told her he wanted her to stop. . . .

The room grew hot as I struggled to breathe. "By the gods, please tell me you did not poison Ptolly. Did you?"

"I was going to, but you stopped me," she answered, her normally graceful features contorted in a grimace.

"What?"

"I had the poison in my hands, ready to give it to him, when you came in. I was watching him sleep, do you remember? He looked so much like Marcus when he slept."

My heart hammered in my chest.

"But you said you would give it to him when he awoke. What a gift from the gods!"

"No!" I cried. "I . . . I never gave it to him!" I remembered then — I had Zosima get rid of it because I thought Livia had made it from her secret nursery of poisons.

"Yes, but the gods took him anyway, proving they favored me."

"You would have *killed* Ptolly simply because your husband chose my mother?" I shook my head, turning toward the door. I needed to be with Alexandros.

"My brother should have killed all of you in Egypt," Octavia said, moving to block me. "Instead I had to be reminded of your mother every time I looked at your face! Even the guards in the *Tullianum* couldn't free me of the burden."

"That was you?" A flash of memory: the soldier saying it was "Caesar's lady" who ordered our execution. I had thought he could only have meant Livia. "But you swore to my mother that you would keep us safe!"

She cackled. "Never! I wanted you destroyed."

"That was me, Selene," Livia said. "I am the one who gave my oath to protect you."

I looked at her. "But Mother said she had received a sworn oath from Octavia. . . ."

Livia looked flustered, her color high. "I did not think your mother would believe *me*, the wife of her conqueror. She knew of Octavia's reputation for kindness. It seemed like the best choice at the time."

So we lived thanks to Livia, believing all the while that the "loving," lovely Octavia had spared us.

"You have the blackened heart of Set, the Evil One," I growled to Octavia in Egyptian, making the sign against evil. Her eyes flickered with fear. I turned away from her, facing Livia. "Alexandros . . . Please, you have to help him."

"I have some knowledge of herbs. I will consult with the *medicus*," she said, sweeping by me and leading me out of her *tablinum*.

I took one last look behind me, into the twisted, triumphant eyes of the woman all Rome worshipped as the model of piety, goodness, and virtue.

Despite the poisoning, Livia insisted we leave for Ostia that afternoon as planned.

"You cannot expect us to move Alexandros in this condition!" I argued when she came to see me in the sickroom. My twin's breathing was labored, his lips almost white, his body covered in a thin film of clammy sweat.

Livia looked pale and drawn. "I cannot guarantee your safety here, do you understand?"

"But —"

"I will send the healer's best medical slave to attend to Alexandros. The *medicus* has already purged the poison and given him the herbs he thinks will help. There is only the waiting now. . . ."

I did not know what to say. We were being hustled out of Rome like meat gone rancid. Sitting beside Alexandros's sickbed, I pressed my forehead to his shoulder, closing my eyes in despair. Why was this happening?

"I am sorry, Selene," Livia said. And to my surprise, I believed her. I believed that this was not how she had wanted things to end.

The journey to Ostia was slow and painful. I refused to leave my brother's side, so I rode next to him on the back of an ox-driven cart normally used to transport lettuce. Alexandros, in and out of awareness, did not seem to notice his surroundings even when he was carried onto the Tiber barge. I stood guard over him, clutching my dagger — Mother's — hidden in the folds of my belt, as if somehow I could cut the poison out of him.

At the Ostian harbor, the captain of the transport ship stopped us when he saw servants carrying Alexandros on a medical litter. "No!

Absolutely not," he cried. "We cannot board someone this sick. It is a bad omen!"

I was too tired to respond. The medical slave handed him a scroll bearing Livia's seal. The captain's sun-leathered face paled as he read the note. Nobody dared disobey Octavianus's wife. He allowed us to board, grumbling and cursing the whole time.

I descended into the belly of the boat with Alexandros, to a small, dark room normally used for storage. The captain did not want us on deck, where all the sailors and passengers lived and slept, because he feared Alexandros's condition would spook his sailors. Despite the heat and darkness, I was grateful for the privacy.

I sent Zosima and the healer-slave above deck. I wanted to be alone as I prayed for my brother's life.

The ship rolled and creaked as sailors barked orders and threw thick ropes on deck. The rowing drum began as slow and low as the thudding of a dying beast's heart. Other sounds drifted in: the pounding of feet as sailors raced to their positions. The rhythmic slaps of large banks of oars in unison. The sharp cries of seabirds looking for scraps.

When I could no longer hear the cacophony of the Ostian harbor, I relaxed.

"We succeeded, brother," I whispered. "We have finally left Rome behind us!"

But he had slipped away from me, his *ka* already on its journey to reunite with Ptolly and the rest of our family.

I could do nothing but hold him as I wept, lost, once again, in an ocean of grief.

CHAPTER FORTY-SEVEN
ON A ROMAN SHIP TO AFRICA
In What Would Have Been the Twenty-sixth Year of My Mother's Reign
Still in My Sixteenth Year (25 BCE)

I stared into the swirling waters that took my brother's body.

"Come," Zosima said. "Let us go back down to the compartment, where it is safer."

But I would not, could not leave. My hands gripped the sides of the ship. I beseeched Poseidon, in the name of Anubis, to preserve his wrapped body so Osiris would recognize him in the afterworld. So Alexandros's *ka* would know where to settle. So I would see him again. I prayed for hours that Anubis would save this son of Egypt.

As the time passed, Zosima created a makeshift tent over my head to protect me from the harsh sun. The Roman sailors continued to avoid me in fear.

"The witch has bewitched herself!" someone whispered as he passed. "That is why she does not move!"

The glare and glitter of the sun blinded me — but I wanted to be blinded. I wanted not to see, not to hear, and not to feel. Zosima tried to get me to drink water or wine, to eat, to return below. Anything. Something. I heard her murmurs and pleas and attempts to distract me as if she were a mosquito droning in and out of range.

What if Juba had been right all along? Should I have stopped fighting and become a Stoic like him — calmly accepting the misery that the gods pushed my way? If I had not tried to align with Marcellus, would Alexandros still be here with me? But then I grew confused. Juba *had* taken action — and now he ruled Numidia. The irony! He got Numidia back when he had never yearned for it. And I would die alone in the deserts of Mauretania.

All that day I stood, keeping vigil for my lost twin. The sky turned indigo, then black with the night. I struggled to breathe as I imagined Alexandros all alone on the ocean floor. The dark waves looked like the quivering coat of some giant restless beast, a monster that swallowed my brother, that devoured all my dreams.

A gust of wind whipped past me like a slap, droplets of sea spray stinging my skin. I looked at the rising moon, only three-quarters full but laying a blanket of silver on the undulating black. *Isis, I ask you, why? Why have you spared me?* Living with all this grief was a worse punishment than death. What "wisdom" was I to glean from the horror of my lost family?

But I got no answer. I stared into the moon's face, examining its marks, lines, and crags like an augur inspecting a sacrificed lamb's liver. I closed my eyes and smelled the scent of roses, the Goddess's sacred flower. I felt her presence. My soul reached out to her like a babe raising its arms to be picked up. *Help me,* I beseeched.

You are not your mother, Isis whispered.

The world grew silent — a strange sensation, for only moments ago the air was thick with the sounds of waves splashing against the ship's hull and the wind snapping the thick linen sails. I focused on the words the Goddess had whispered in my ears. Then I grew enraged.

That was the great wisdom — the great comfort — the Goddess had to offer me? I laughed even as tears coursed down my cheeks. *I did not need a reminder of my failures, O Great Mother of All!* If I had been my mother, I would have saved my brothers. I would have known what to do to reclaim Egypt.

No, the Goddess said then. *Your mother did not save your brothers. Your mother lost Egypt.*

I looked up into the brilliant face of the moon, confused.

You are not your mother, Isis murmured again in the wind.

I shook my head. Of course I was not my mother! Mother had been brilliant and effective. She had allied with two of the most powerful men in Rome to save her crown and her kingdom's independence. She had succeeded for decades. I tried aligning with Marcellus and failed miserably, and my attempt to come to rule in Egypt ended with Gallus's murder and the senseless death of an initiate of the Mysteries.

Mother had power and control over her life, even as a young girl. I had neither. And when she lost her power and her kingdom, she took control over the only thing left to her — her death.

My heart quickened at the thought. Control over her own death. Power to choose death on one's own terms. In my initiation vision, the Goddess asked me to make a choice. Was that the choice she had meant? I paused, holding my breath at the thought. I could do what Mother did.

I could end my life.

Yes, that made sense! I could end my life on my own terms, leave with dignity, just as she had. I could slip into the cold water, fill my lungs with wet blackness, and rob Octavianus of his last triumph over me, just like Mother.

The ship roiled as I grasped the rail more tightly, Mother's knife pinching into my waist as I bumped into the wooden sides. I heard frightened murmurs, feet running. The wind whipped the sails so hard, it sounded like a slap.

You are not your mother. . . .

"I know that!" I yelled as I fought to keep my balance on the deck. Why did she keep *saying* that? There were more startled murmurs from the night crew of men on deck who heard my outburst. But I did not care. I felt rage crawling up my center like a vine choking a tree at the Goddess's inanely obvious words.

Where is your power?

Gods, what a question! Another nonsensical echo of my initiation vision. The black sea roiled with larger waves as if a great beast slowly wakened. "You want to see my power? Well, here it is!" I shouted. I wheeled around, spied a small chest with a twisted rope handle, and rushed to drag it across the deck. I was nearly panting with rage and frustration.

How *dare* Isis ask me where my power lay when she did nothing but watch as they took it all from me!

Did they truly take it all?

"Yes!" I raged. "Everything!" *Except this*, I thought. I stepped up on the grimy wooden chest and slipped off my sandals. I laughed at the gesture, as if it made any difference whether I kept my sandals on or off. I wondered how long it would take the black water to fill my lungs, for me to move into Osiris's realm. The ship rail felt damp and cold against the tops of my thighs.

I felt cold metal on my skin and drew my dagger out — Mother's beautiful dagger, the one Katep claimed she had tried to use on herself when she was captured. I had always believed that she had meant to kill her captor with it, not herself. But now I knew better. She had intended on leaving us even then.

The blade glittered in the moonlight. I would use Mother's dagger on myself before I jumped. In this one thing, I would succeed.

You are not your mother. . . .

"Stop it!" I howled. "Stop saying that! I know that! Must you shame me with the obvious?"

You have the power to choose something else.

The breath in my panting lungs rattled to a stop in bewilderment. What did she mean? I had spent my entire life trying to follow in Mother's footsteps, all to no avail. What did she mean, *"something else"*?

A treasonous thought wormed into my awareness: What would have happened had Mother chosen something else? What if she had chosen to *live* instead of abandoning us to our fates in Rome? What if we had not been left by both our parents to face *their* defeat alone?

Perhaps Mother would have been put to death in Rome. Perhaps we would have been killed along with her. But if so, we would have gone *together*, not set adrift alone in a sea of despair and hostility. She could have chosen to stay and protect us. She could have chosen to survive.

A wave of grief and loss and loneliness surged through me then, ripping at the roots of everything I had ever held sacred about

Mother — that she was a hero, that she had done the right thing, that there had been no other option for her. That she had made a noble decision.

That it was all right.

"You could have made a different choice, Mother," I whispered.

And the truth of that notion nearly brought me to my knees. How different everything would have been if Mother had chosen to live.

What do you choose, my queen? the Goddess whispered.

I moved back from the slippery edge of the ship, feeling my toes grasp for purchase as it rolled under me.

"I choose power," I whispered in wonder, remembering the words I had used in my initiation vision. I had thought, at the time, that I was choosing power over Egypt or over my enemy. Or that the Goddess was directing me to choose between men, between Marcellus and Juba. But that was not the kind of power she meant at all.

I stared up at the moon, higher and smaller as it arced over the night sky. Mother chose escape in the arms of Anubis. But I could choose something else. Even after all the pain, all the losses, all the grief, I could choose the power of *facing* my life, even as it veered in directions I never dreamed of nor wanted.

I laughed again then — not in a manic way, but with the fierce ache of knowing that this was a kind of power I had never before understood. Was this choice the "free will" the old rabbi from Alexandria had tried to explain to me?

I did not know. I knew only that, for the first time, I could make a clear choice to live *my* life and not my mother's. To face my future with dignity and strength no matter what had happened in the past or what might happen in the future, no matter what I wanted or thought I should have or deserved.

I stepped off the wooden chest, staring out into the rolling black sea. Without thinking, I reared back and hurled Mother's dagger into the sea with all the force I had left in me. The waves smoothed as if, in releasing the jeweled knife, I had finally slain the great black-coated beast that threatened to swallow me whole.

I tested the new thought once again: *I was not my mother.*

I could choose something different.

I could choose to live.

CHAPTER FORTY-EIGHT

"It is time to meet your betrothed," Zosima whispered in my ear.

I nodded. "Another minute," I said, though I'd been stalling for some time. I knew I would have to meet the king of Mauretania soon. But fear held me fast.

I sat on a cushioned vanity bench in my new chambers and looked at the tessellated tile on the floor, the paintings of stalking tigers and trumpeting elephants on the walls, the aromatic and immense blooms that filled alabaster and onyx vases in every corner of the room. This small but elegant villa, which the Mauretanians called their king's palace, was probably the height of luxury for the desert-dwelling chieftain.

The city of Iol, in Mauretania, where we had docked earlier, had surprised me as well. I had expected craggy beaches leading into sweltering deserts or wild jungles filled with beasts. But instead I found a thriving port city, rich with life and commerce, extending into vast hills dotted with green and gold fields of swaying grain. I remembered then that all of North Africa supplied wheat to Rome, not just Egypt. Palms thrust into a brilliant blue sky, waving in the crisp sea breeze, surrounded by lush bursts of blooming fruit trees and brilliantly flowering bushes. Small chattering monkeys leapt from tree to tree in a copse extending out over the water.

The port, though, was strangely quiet and empty. Roman soldiers outnumbered Mauretanians. I had groaned inwardly at what this meant: that Rome had only recently moved into the area and had probably strong-armed the local chieftain or king into "accepting" Rome's supremacy at sword point. I must have been a bargaining chip. The people were likely frightened, angry, and confused.

The king had sent an emissary to the port to meet us. The dark Mauretanian bowed and handed me a note and a small package. In perfect Greek, the note read,

It is with great sorrow that I hear of the loss of your beloved twin,
Alexandros. Perhaps this small gift will remind you of happier times.

But I could read no further. I set it aside. I did not for a moment believe that the Mauretanian king had written me a note in Greek. The desert nomad had probably never read a scroll in his life.

As our litter wound through the streets to the king's house, people stared at us with cautious curiosity. I heard mostly Punic, though I picked up smatterings of Greek, Latin, Aramaic, and even Hebrew.

And now, in this room, I was moments away from facing the life I had chosen to see through.

Zosima held up a bronze reflecting disk for me to inspect my appearance, and I caught my breath at how much my fierce expression and my malachite- and kohl-painted eyes looked like Mother's. I waved the disk away.

Tanafriti wound herself around my ankles, purring. Sebi sat tall, staring at me.

"Yes, yes," I muttered at him. "I should not make him wait any longer."

I knew my delay bordered on rude, but I needed to build up my fortitude. Despite my commitment to face my future, I was still frightened of what I would find. What if this chieftain was worse than a Roman paterfamilias and demanded full control over every aspect of my life? How would I maintain my own power if he tried to deny me autonomy?

I fingered the woven covering of the gift my future husband sent, running my fingers over the exquisite Mauretanian designs — chains of diamond shapes rendered in brilliant blues, reds, yellows, and greens. I removed the fabric.

A weathered scroll. *The Love Poems of Catullus.* In Latin. I unwound the old papyrus and my eyes lit on this:

Odi et amo. Quare id faciam, fortasse requiris?
Nescio, sed fieri sentio et excrucior.

I hate and I love. Why I do this, perhaps you ask?
I don't know: I only know that I feel it happening, and I am tortured.

I put the scroll down and watched it curl back into itself. Still, it was a good sign that he had sent a book. Perhaps he would not be averse to my plans for building a library worthy of the one that had been taken from us in Alexandria. I would fill it with the great works of Greek and Egyptian poets and scientists, as well as the beautiful writings of the Parthians, Chaldeans, Indians, and other great civilizations from around the world. If nothing more, *that* would be my legacy. I smiled with hope at the thought.

Outside my chamber, Zosima chattered excitedly to someone in Greek. I sighed. The king must have gotten tired of waiting for me and sent his Greek-speaking representative. I hoped my Punic would return quickly enough that we could dispense with the translator.

Taking a deep breath, I stood, lifted my chin, and stepped out of my chamber. In the same moment a handsome, familiar face looked up from sharing a laugh with my nurse. My stomach clenched.

Juba?

"What are you doing here?" I asked, shocked.

Juba furrowed his brow, his smile faltering. "What . . . what do you mean?" He tilted his head ever so slightly. "I wanted to see you. I got tired of waiting."

"But what are you doing here in Mauretania? Is Numidia allying with Mauretania — is that why you are here?"

Juba looked at Zosima with a wary, vaguely alarmed expression. With a quick look in my direction, she scuttled out of the room, closing the door behind her.

He faced me. "Cleopatra Selene. Are you all right?"

"I do not understand," I said, feeling slightly disoriented — much the way I had felt when I first stepped off the ship and wobbled on the dock as if we were still on the high seas. "Why are you here? Where is the king?"

"I am the king of Mauretania," he said.

"No you're not. You are king of *Numidia*! In your native homeland!"

Juba opened his mouth, then closed it. "Did you not receive my letters about what happened in Numidia?"

"Livia burned all my letters."

"Without reading them?"

I shrugged, not sure. "And about two months ago, we stopped receiving any correspondence at all. I assumed the war had blocked the roads."

He nodded. "Livia probably did not know then. Hardly a surprise; hardly anyone here in Mauretania knows either," he added with a rueful laugh.

"Knows what?"

"That Caesar moved me out of Numidia and into Mauretania, making me its first king. Based on the reception I have received — which is very little, I should add — it appears most of Mauretania does not know this news yet either."

I closed my eyes and shook my head. "But your *homeland* is Numidia. . . ."

"Let me explain," he said. "The native Numidian ruling class was happy to have me reclaim my legacy, but the Roman governor was, to put it delicately, incensed. So you can imagine my arrival in Numidia did not go over well. He incited his followers to rebel, and we almost had a small civil war. Caesar appeased him by moving me to Mauretania for the time being. This all happened only recently, and very quickly, to avoid a military confrontation."

"But Numidia is your homeland, your true legacy. . . ."

He smiled. "As soon as the governor either finishes his command or dies — whichever comes first — I will extend my kingdom to include Numidia." When I still didn't say anything, Juba shifted his weight. "I wanted to fight the Roman governor for Numidia, but Caesar wanted this compromise instead. I agreed to move to Mauretania on one condition."

"And that was?"

"That he release you and Alexandros to me."

The room tipped and swayed around me. I reached out to a curved ebony chair for balance. Alexandros. How thrilled he would have been to see Juba! To know that we were not just out of Rome and the shadow of Octavianus's hatred but with someone who had always cared for us.

I closed my eyes in grief for a moment, remembering how Alexandros had joked that leaving Rome made him feel like Persephone emerging from Hades. He had been right. But now I felt more like Orpheus, who looked back too early and lost Eurydice.

"I am so sorry about Alexandros," Juba said. "I will miss him greatly."

The silence stretched.

"Are . . . are you grieving over the loss of Marcellus too?" he asked quietly.

I almost laughed. I had not thought about him once since leaving Rome. I shook my head.

"You understand that Caesar never would have allowed a union with Marcellus, yes?"

I nodded, embarrassed at my misguided attempts at seduction. "But I still don't understand why he agreed to your terms," I said. "He *hates* me."

"Yes, but he also, despite himself, respects your determination and your will to rule. At least Livia always has. And this arrangement makes him look good, as he gets rid of you without a scandal at the same time that he pleases his eastern holdings. They will be happy to hear a princess of Egypt rules in Africa. It was a good — actually, a brilliant — political move."

I stared at Juba. Could this really be happening?

He squinted at me, looking a bit dismayed. "Did you get my gift?" he asked. He seemed suddenly shy, tentative.

I nodded. "Thank you," I said, worried that I sounded too formal. I tried to smile. "I would have expected Greek poetry from you, though, not Latin."

"You didn't realize, then?"

"Realize what?"

"It is the same scroll you left that day under the citron tree when you ran off. . . ."

Heat rushed up my cheeks. I had been reading Catullus? "The same one? You kept it all these years?"

He nodded, shrugging slightly, as if a little embarrassed.

My throat tightened at the memory of how much I had loved him, even then, even as a child. "You rejected me!" I teased as I tried to master my emotions. "You called me a gadfly!"

"You were barely thirteen! You took me by surprise. And I meant gadfly as a compliment — a gadfly who inspired me to reach beyond myself. Without you, I would still be hiding in the scroll stacks in Rome."

I marveled at the mysterious ways of fate and the gods. And how I had come so close to following Mother's footsteps to my death and missing this moment, missing this life.

"So," he said, coming closer. "Will you be my queen?"

By Roman law — and since this was now a Roman client kingdom — I had no choice, no say. If the paterfamilias ordered me to marry Juba, I had to, no matter how I felt or what I wanted.

But Juba was asking me to make a choice. To choose my fate, just as the Goddess had urged me, to make a choice to *live* and see my life through — alongside him. Again, I thought of the sweet old rabbi in Alexandria and his notions of free will.

For a moment, I could not speak. So I nodded.

A grin slowly spread across his face. As in the old days, my stomach fluttered at the sight of his beautiful, gleaming smile, and at the kindness, intelligence, and love that shone from his dark eyes.

"Yes," I finally breathed, moving toward him. "I choose this. I choose you."

THE END

CLEOPATRA SELENE AND JUBA II

Cleopatra Selene and Juba II ruled Mauretania and eventually parts of Numidia — today's Algeria and Morocco — together for more than thirty years. They developed the region into a shining hub of commerce and literature, complete with centers of learning and an impressive library.

We have no record of what their lives were like as rulers, only hints. Cleopatra Selene's image was minted on coins along with Juba's, suggesting that she ruled as an equal partner. Juba continued to make his mark as a scholar, penning multiple books on Latin history, Greek history, geography, painting, and theater. Pliny the Elder says he was a better scholar than a king, which also suggests that Cleopatra Selene handled the administration of their kingdom while Juba hit the books.

Cleopatra Selene and Juba had at least one child named Ptolemy Philadelphos, likely named in honor of her beloved little brother. Some scholars believe Cleopatra Selene also had two additional children, both girls — one named Cleopatra Selene II and another named after Livia Drusilla. We have no record of the lives of these daughters, most likely because ancient writers ignored the lives of women. However, it is possible that Cleopatra Selene's daughters survived to have children of their own, and that their descendants live somewhere in the coastal regions of northwestern Africa today.

Cleopatra Selene died in 6 CE. Juba ruled with their son, Ptolemy, until his own death in 23 CE.

Was theirs a love story? There is no way to know. I like to think so, for no other reason than Cleopatra Selene suffered enough losses in her life. There is some evidence, though, of Juba's devotion to her. He lived seventeen years after Cleopatra Selene's death. Some scholars believe Juba married again — to a woman named Glaphyra — in the interim years. Others are not so sure. But one thing is certain: When it came to deciding with whom he would spend eternity, Juba chose Cleopatra Selene. He had his body entombed beside hers, and you can visit their tomb near Cherchel, in Algeria. Like Cleopatra Selene's own parents — Antony and Cleopatra — they live on, in memory, together forever.

THE FACTS WITHIN THE FICTION

THE GENERAL HISTORY:

- The last queen of Egypt, Cleopatra VII, did indeed have four children: Ptolemy Caesar, known as Caesarion (Little Caesar), with Julius Caesar; and, with Marcus Antonius (Mark Antony), twins Alexandros Helios and Cleopatra Selene, and Ptolemy Philadelphos.

- Her eldest, Caesarion, was hunted down and murdered by Octavianus's men around the time of Cleopatra's death in 30 BCE. Although Plutarch claims he died after her suicide, other sources (Cassius Dio) are not as clear. In this novel, I placed Caesarion's death before hers. We don't know what prompted Cleopatra to commit suicide on that particular day, at that particular time — why not earlier, for example, right after Antonius's death? Creatively, it seemed plausible to me that the shock and grief of losing her firstborn would have served as the last straw, a sort of catalyst toward her final act.

- Although not included in the story in order to simplify the character list, Antonius's eldest son by a former Roman wife — Antyllus — was also murdered (beheaded) in Alexandria during the Roman invasion. Cleopatra's surviving children — Cleopatra Selene, Alexandros Helios, and Ptolemy Philadelphos — were taken to Rome and reared in Octavianus's compound.

- In this story, Cleopatra's children fear for their lives while under the guardianship of Octavianus. As paterfamilias, he had full legal control of all women and children under his guardianship. The paterfamilias could beat, sell into slavery, or even kill his charges without legal consequence. (To do so was looked down upon, of course, but one could still legally get away with it.)

- In 29 BCE, the children of Antonius and Cleopatra were marched in Octavianus's Triumph over Egypt. Most scholars believe the boys died sometime after the Triumph, for the two brothers are never mentioned in the ancient sources again.

- It was common practice for Roman emperors to rear the sons of foreign allies before sending them out to rule in their name. Juba was Octavianus's first appointed "client-king." The irony? The client-king model was exactly what Antonius was advocating in his alliance with Cleopatra. One scholar says, "Antony hoped to create a more stable political organization for [the East] than his predecessors had established by imposing direct Roman rule" (Jones, *Cleopatra*).

ABOUT CLEOPATRA VII, SELENE'S MOTHER

- Cleopatra VII became queen of Egypt at seventeen. At twenty, she was pushed out of Alexandria by her co-ruler/younger brother, whose handlers wanted power all to themselves. She then raised an army to fight for her crown. When Julius Caesar arrived in Egypt, she hid herself in a rug or bedroll to meet with him, outwitting her preteen brother and his handlers, and used her eventual alliance with Caesar to regain her throne.

- Plutarch reports that she spoke many languages, so that she could speak without interpreters to diplomats from Arabia, Judea, Nubia, Parthia, Syria, Medea, and many others. He also says she was the only one in her line of Ptolemaic rulers to learn Egyptian, the native tongue of her people. With such a facility for language, it is likely that she encouraged her children to speak multiple tongues.

- According to Plutarch, Cleopatra's beauty was "not incomparable," but the force of her personality, intelligence, and charm was undeniably powerful. He also says she had "a thousand ways to flatter," as well as a melodious voice.

- Cleopatra signed all her royal decrees with the Greek word *genestho*, which means, "make it so." A papyrus believed to have been signed by Cleopatra exists in the Ägyptisches Museum und Papyrussammlung in Berlin. In the document, she authorizes a tax break to the Roman who would later be in charge of some of Antonius's land forces during Actium.

- The Roman historian Cassius Dio says that Octavianus promised Cleopatra her kingdom, but only if she killed Antonius for him first. She, of course, did no such thing. Plutarch says Octavianus used "threats about the fate of her children" in negotiating with Cleopatra and that he used these threats like "a general uses siege engines" in battle.

- According to Plutarch, Cleopatra killed herself after tricking Octavianus and pretending she was going to Antonius's tomb to pray.

- Most modern scholars now acknowledge that Octavianus masterminded a thorough smear campaign against Cleopatra in order to create an excuse to declare war on Antonius. By almost all accounts — including histories recorded by early Arabs who learned to read hieroglyphic centuries before Westerners — Cleopatra was revered as an intelligent, serious, devoted ruler of her country. Contrary to the Western penchant for sexualizing Cleopatra, Arab historians described her as "chaste." After all, she had only two relationships her whole life — one with Julius Caesar and one with Marcus Antonius — both with the intention of preserving Egypt's independence.

OCTAVIANUS AND MARCUS ANTONIUS

- In 44 BCE, Julius Caesar posthumously adopted his nephew, Octavianus, in his will and named him heir. Many thought Marcus

Antonius should have been named Caesar's successor, thus creating the hostility between the two men.

- Octavianus was only eighteen at the time of Caesar's death. He immediately took on Caesar's name, but most historians refer to him as Octavian or Octavianus to avoid confusion. I used Octavianus to help differentiate him from his sister, Octavia.

- Antonius called Cleopatra to him in Antioch in 41 BCE and later returned to Egypt with her. In 40 BCE, while she was pregnant with the twins, he left her in Alexandria and went to Rome to marry Octavia and cement a peace treaty with Octavianus. He reunited with Cleopatra four years later and formally divorced Octavia in 32 BCE, which Octavianus used as an excuse to declare war on Cleopatra.

- Antonius did indeed bring little Iotape to Alexandros Helios for betrothal after a victory in modern-day Armenia. After conquering Egypt, Octavianus sent Iotape back to her homeland, and she was eventually married off to King Mithridates of Commagene.

- Antonius killed himself, according to Plutarch, in the manner described in this novel. I used creative license to insert Cleopatra Selene into the scene.

- Octavianus was renamed Augustus (the Revered One) in 27 BCE. Soon after, he renamed the month in which he defeated Antonius and Cleopatra (*Sextilis*) after himself (August). He died in 14 CE, when he was seventy-six years old — some say by the hand of his own wife, Livia, who may have served him poisoned figs. She lived until 29 CE.

- Cornelius Gallus — with whom I had Cleopatra Selene plan a coup — was indeed a low-ranking officer left in charge of Egypt by Octavianus. He did try to grab more power and prestige for himself and was later reported to have committed suicide after angering Octavianus.

JUBA

- Juba, according to ancient sources, was — like Cleopatra Selene — a prince of a defeated country (Numidia). He was the only surviving member of his conquered family. He was carried in Julius Caesar's Triumph as a baby, and because of his extreme youth, Plutarch says he was "the happiest captive ever captured." Most scholars agree that Juba likely grew up in the household of Octavia after Julius Caesar died.

- Juba's homeland, Numidia, became a Roman province in 46 BCE when Julius Caesar defeated his father's army. In this novel, I have Octavianus send Juba to rule in Numidia first, only to discover the Roman governor in Numidia gives armed resistance to the switch-over, which is why Octavianus moved him to Mauretania. There is no evidence it happened this way (but, of course, there's no evidence it *didn't* either!). Either way, Numidia continued to be ruled by a Roman governor, while Juba took over the kingdom of Mauretania. As a result, Juba is known to history as the king of Mauretania even though he started out as a prince of Numidia.

- One scholar writes, "It is possible that Juba was not the name given to [him] by his parents" (Roller, *The World of Juba II and Kleopatra Selene*). I used creative license to make Juba mean *king* in Punic. Punic is an extinct Semitic language.

- Juba wrote almost all his books in Greek. His topics included Roman archaeology, Latin, painting, history, and the great Carthaginian explorer, Hanno, as well as works on Arabia and Assyria. Once in Mauretania, Juba turned his intellectual focus to geography. He sent expeditions around the coast of Africa and wrote about one of his major discoveries: the Canary Islands. Plutarch wrote that Juba "became the most learned of all kings." He was also called Rex Literatissimus, which means "most literary king."

- After Cleopatra Selene's death in 6 CE, Juba ruled alongside their son Ptolemy until his own death nearly twenty years later. In 40 CE, the emperor Caligula killed Ptolemy in a fit of jealousy because Caligula thought Ptolemy's cloak was nicer than his own. Ptolemy of Mauretania, grandson of Cleopatra VII, was almost forty at the time of his death.

JULIA, AGRIPPA, AND TIBERIUS

- In 25 BCE, Agrippa came back to Rome from Spain to oversee the marriage of Marcellus and Julia, even though Julia was only fourteen. No one knows exactly why or what the urgency was, though some have conjectured that Octavianus's illness in Spain spurred him to solidify the line of succession. Marcellus died in 23 BCE from an unknown illness.

- After Marcellus's death, Octavianus forced his daughter, Julia, to marry Agrippa, who was older than Octavianus himself, for the sake of preserving succession. Years later, he made Julia divorce Agrippa and marry Tiberius in order to secure Tiberius as heir, even though Tiberius was her stepbrother.

- Octavianus later exiled Julia — his own daughter — for having numerous sexual affairs. The one that most horrified him was the passionate affair she carried on with another one of Antonius's sons not mentioned in this novel (again to reduce confusion and streamline the many characters in this story) — Iullus Antonius, who was also brought up in Octavia's compound.

- Tiberius, Livia's eldest son, ruled Rome as Octavianus's successor — the second emperor of Rome — until his death in 37 CE.

ACKNOWLEDGMENTS

First, I want to thank my husband, Bruce, and my kids, Matthew and Aliya, for putting up with my forgetfulness and distractedness during the long and intense process of writing this book. How could I ever have gotten through it without your laughter?

I also want to thank my friend and bookseller, Diane Capriola, who, when I told her I was thinking about writing Cleopatra Selene's story, grabbed me by the shoulders and said, "You *must* write it. Do you hear me? You have to." I am also grateful for my good friend Elizabeth O. Dulemba, who supported my efforts from the beginning, as did our dear departed friend, book illustrator Liz Conrad. I must also thank my fabulous, ever-patient, and always encouraging agent, Courtney Miller-Callahan.

I am deeply indebted to Carol Lee Lorenzo, leader of my writing group, for encouraging me not to give up when I discovered another novel on the same topic had been released. "Just write," she told me. "Tell *your* story, your way." And, of course, to my fellow writers in the group: Leslie Muir, Sandy Fry, Nancy Calix, Sheri Dillard, Karen Strong, and Kelly Williams; as well as the members of my Java Monkey writer group: Ricky Jacobs, Gail Goodwin, and Georgia Dzurica. I am also deeply grateful to Krista Greksouk for reviewing the Latin usage in the novel.

I also cannot forget my irrepressible and wonderful brother, Michael Alvear, who always believed in me no matter what I believed about myself.

Most of all, I want to thank my editor, Cheryl Klein, who, with endless gentle questions, teased out a far better, richer story from me than I thought I was capable of writing. I have been honored and humbled to receive guidance and direction from such a brilliant editor.

ABOUT THE AUTHOR

Vicky Alvear Shecter has been fascinated by the ancient world since she was ten, when photographs of classical sculptures like the Spear Bearer and the Venus de Milo led her to wonder about the cultures that created such transcendent beauty.

She has written two nonfiction books for young readers: *Alexander the Great Rocks the World*, a VOYA Honor Pick for Nonfiction, and *Cleopatra Rules! The Amazing Life of the Original Teen Queen*. This is her first novel.

Vicky lives in Atlanta with her husband and two children. Visit her at www.vickyalvearshecter.com.

This book was edited by Cheryl Klein and designed by Phil Falco. The text was set in Alisal, a typeface designed by Matthew Carter in 2001. The display type was set in Ehmcke, designed by F. H. Ehmcke in 1991. The book was printed and bound at R. R. Donnelley in Crawfordsville, Indiana. The production was supervised by Cheryl Weisman, and the manufacturing was supervised by Adam Cruz.